I0585323

TO TANGO WITH LOVE

IDA BRADY

Copyright © 2020 by Ida Brady
All rights reserved.

This book or any portion thereof may not be reproduced or used in any
form or by any electronic or mechanical means, including information
storage and retrieval systems, without the express written permission of
the author, except for the use of brief quotations in a book review.

This is a work of fiction. The events described are fictitious; any
similarities to actual events and persons are coincidental.

Cover design by Mila Book Covers
Formatting by Ebony McKenna
Editing by Ally Blake

www.idabrady.com

To Team Brida,
For all the love, support and chocolate.

To mum,
For your rocking chair.

CHAPTER ONE

*F*or a few hours every week, Mathilda Landrey could be anything but the boring, run-of-the-mill bookstore owner, who made thirty the new forty. Climbing the narrow staircase, she entered the dance studio and surrendered to her Friday night ritual. A rich, sensual melody reverberated around the long, rectangular space; violins stretched and sighed, calling like a Siren's song.

Tilda's shoulders loosened, the churning in her stomach subsided and she weaved her way around the circle of dancers. Slipping off her dark, square-framed glasses, she pawed through the black abyss that was her handbag. No sooner had her hand brushed the surface of her case, that she was jolted by a sharp elbow. The line of dance had somehow morphed from a circle into a rhombus. Tilda cried out as her one-week old glasses tore across the far side of the studio.

She scrambled to retrieve them and grimaced when

her head slammed into the dark-haired man crouched before her.

The pain was swift and sharp.

She tried to focus as two very familiar, very toned arms helped her to her feet. Tilda stepped back.

Alejandro held his head with one hand, her glasses in the other. Annoyance marred the smooth line of his brow.

At that moment, she would have killed to trade her boring, plain, white skin for the very appealing, bronzed gold before her. If only for the practical benefit of hiding her embarrassment.

"Sorry. I didn't see you." Which, if she thought about it, was stupid in itself. Alejandro Garcia was not a man to miss.

"Mathilda." Alé smiled.

His smooth Argentinian accent made her name sound sensual, seductive. She was sure she'd pitch her glasses across the room again, just to hear the concern that elongated those vowels. The man could make mould sound sexy. Exotic even.

She bit her lip. Exotic was not a word synonymous with Mathilda Landrey.

"You okay?"

"Yes. Fine, thanks."

She took her glasses from his outstretched hand and slipped them into her bag. Staring at the mirrored wall behind him, Tilda tried to catalogue the non-fiction section at The Book Nook, in her head. She was definitely *not* checking out the curve of his butt.

"Rise up on your axis, Elliot," Alé called to a balding man in his sixties. "*Muy bien.*"

Tilda tore her gaze away and studied the intermediate students who were grappling with a difficult move. The tango gods knew she needed to work on her own posture if she was going to make any progress. She tried to suck in her stomach, to draw back her shoulders.

"Thanks again for the save. I said that already. I mean it. I..."

Alé's eyes were warm with amusement.

"Nobody puts Baby's glasses in the corner, *si*?"

Her body tingled. "At least I didn't drop a watermelon."

Alé laughed.

It had sounded wittier in her head.

"I should let you get back to... I better get... shoed up." Tilda waggled her bag in front of him.

Thanks brain. Thanks very much. No wonder their conversations didn't last for more than a few minutes. She sounded like a cave troll, one who just discovered she could speak and make strange noises.

Tilda all but ran to the seated area. The rows of cushioned benches were already littered with shoe bags — some black, others a shimmering gold or cream. A few she noted, sporting the luxurious *Comme Il Faut* label.

She'd kill to have a pair of *Commes*. Tilda brushed aside the thought, along with a few of the glittering bags. The very cheap, black leather shoes she had bought online would do for now. Yes, they were scuffed after nearly five years of dancing, but the simple strap at the ankle and the demure triangle of leather that covered her toes did the job. Kind of.

The money she painstakingly saved to start renovations on the bookstore was worth it. The Book Nook was finally back open and doing business. That was a start. So what if she needed to see the bank about another loan? She would find out what the damage from her contractor was next week, then she would proceed, with utter caution and a whole lot of luck.

"*Hola, chica*!" Isabella's bright and buoyant tones carried across the humid studio.

"*Hola*, Izzy." Her friend pranced in front of her. "New outfit I see?" Tilda motioned to Isabella's black, baggy tango pants — the matching slits on either side revealed tanned, shapely legs. Tilda bit back a petty barb of jealousy.

"Hell yeah, honey! I'm going to The Red Lounge after class for a bit of sexy salsa and I intend to impress. Plus, we don't have performance group rehearsals until tomorrow afternoon, so I can sleep off the day."

"How's it coming along? You excited to finally try out your choreography?"

Isabella flexed her feet a few times before taking out her shoes. "You've no idea. Working with Alé has been a dream. We've got a great line up of dancers which makes it easier. You know, you're like the only one out of the Advanced Level class who hasn't joined the performance group."

"I like our lessons."

Isabella rolled her eyes.

"You know I love tango, Izzy, but performing is about as appealing as a root canal."

Joining Alé's Friday night class last year quietened any dissatisfaction that had lurked in the cottage since her grandmother's death. Alé's classes were so strenuous that she didn't have time to think about the mess she was in.

Tilda straightened, sitting up taller. Her aching back was a reminder that she needed to work on her balance in tonight's lesson. Not having the time to dance socially meant that her form was getting sloppy. She certainly didn't have time for a performance class on top of everything else.

"You've no idea what you're missing." Isabella tied back her dark curls and adjusted the strap of her bright red *Commes*.

Of course Isabella had been to Buenos Aires. Mecca of Tango.

Tilda looked down at her own sad-looking shoes and wondered whether she would ever manage to get out of the country and travel. To her mind, New Zealand didn't count; the three-and-a-half-hour trip hardly equated to a twenty-hour journey overseas.

Plus, travelling cost money. Something she sorely lacked in her life. A part of her — the one bogged down in debt and responsibility — wondered what would happen if she just closed the store, took out yet another loan and flew to Argentina?

What would happen if she lived life a little recklessly...?

Her stomach nose-dived. Plenty of people flew on planes every single day. Yet the very thought of travelling on an aircraft, to a place she would no doubt love, left her feeling queasy.

For a pair of Isabella's shoes, it may be worth it. She could shop away the days buying all the *Commes* in Buenos Aires and spend her nights dancing in the arms of skilled strangers...

Tilda gritted her teeth.

Was Isabella right? Was she missing out?

She stood, squaring her shoulders. Her parents were proof of what happened when you threw caution to the wind. When you lived life without responsibility. Or in their case, pretended like they didn't have any.

There was nothing wrong with living a quiet life.

A boring, safe, predictable life.

Isabella hooked her arm around Tilda's shoulders, steering them both to the floor. A few of the other advanced dancers were stretching and warming up.

"You should come out with us tonight. Let your hair down a little."

Tilda watched Janelle and Zach, the principal dancers in Alé's performance group, who were in a close embrace. They moved so seductively, oozing confidence with every step that it was hard for her to take her eyes off them. They were the perfect example of what performers needed to be — she was the exact opposite in every way.

Quiet, boring, predictable.

"Show offs," Isabella muttered. "Anyway, there'll be a ton of hot men out tonight and girl, I know you have the moves. Alé even said he'll come along for a drink." Isabella nudged Tilda in the ribs.

She had always wanted to be more outgoing, didn't she? To not overthink every little detail. To give in to the temptation...

On a surge of nervous adrenaline, Tilda turned to Isabella. "Sure!"

"Oh, c'mon Tilda, you always say — " Isabella froze.

Tilda's smile faltered. The fingers of dread slithered up her spine, shrouding her excitement. What had she done?

Isabella squealed and clapped her hands. "Yes? Oh, Tilda you are going to have such a *good* time! I'll find lots of *hombres* for you to dance with."

"I — I —"

"Next class, *por favor*!"

Isabella flounced off.

Tilda's heart raced. She could still back out of tonight. Feign a headache after class…fall down the stairs?

Tilda tried to focus on Alé's instructions. They began with flexion and extension exercises for travelling *ochos* to warm up the body. She lasted only thirty seconds before her mind wandered.

Maybe it wouldn't be so bad if Alé was there tonight. He was only going for a drink. In the year she had taken lessons with him, he had never socialised with his students. So why now? Curiosity piqued, Tilda decided she could go for one as well. She didn't *have* to dance. Right?

Whilst The Red Lounge wasn't anything like jumping on a plane to Argentina, it was a start. A small taste of adventure.

Tilda swung her leg back and forth like a pendulum. Keeping all the weight on her left foot, her body began to relax, finding its rhythm.

"Change weight, Mathilda," came the deep, smooth voice by her ear.

She gripped the barre. Mortified, she switched sides. She hadn't even registered that Alé was inches away from her. And smelt like heaven. Cedar and vetiver. Strength and sensuality.

"Isabella tells me you are joining us tonight. I look forward to it."

Her reply was garbled.

Attempting to find her Zen state again, Tilda begrudgingly admitted when she was in over her head.

There was not a damn thing she could do to stop it, either.

CHAPTER TWO

The bombastic sounds of the trumpet and percussion vibrated through the crowded dance floor. Lights dimmed; the dancers moved in one undulating roll. The heady beat set a punishing pace. Sexy. Sultry. Sensual.

Men and women — in various states of dress — were enjoying the live band, and each other. Yet Tilda sat, hidden in the crowd, wondering if she had lost her mind. She wished she had. That way she wouldn't feel annoyed at herself for being so easily persuaded.

The whirring fans did nothing to combat the scorching summer heat that sat heavy on the night air. She pressed her cocktail glass against her flushed cheek, desperate for relief. Allowing Isabella to herd her into her car, along with the other tango students, had been her first mistake. She was now at the mercy of her friend's party clock. And Isabella's watch never stopped.

Tilda waved away the devil in question who motioned

for her to dance. She pointed to her cocktail and shook her head.

She needed an escape plan.

She sipped her mojito. An impulse purchase. She rarely drank, but Isabella's bubbly, infectious nature was, well, catching. She figured that the burger and fries she chowed down before class would soak up a fair amount of the alcohol. And she had been nursing the same glass for an hour.

She rolled her eyes.

Mathilda Landrey here, poster child for responsible drinking.

It wasn't yet midnight, and if she left now, she could walk the five blocks back to her car on her own without serious risk of some Jack the Ripper enthusiast following her.

Tilda looked over at Isabella who gyrated ever so successfully to the salsa beat. The man with whom she had been flirting was matching her hip to hip. Tilda was torn between admiration and self-conscious embarrassment.

It was in this state, as she blatantly watched the sexual bump and grind of her friend and Mr. Chiselled Jaw, that Alé found her.

"Pretty sexy stuff, *no*?"

Tilda's head jerked to the right.

"Can I join you?"

No! She shook her head.

"Yes..." There was something wrong with her. "Sure." She patted the torn, black leather couch that had seen too many bottoms. She fought against the urge to pick at the remaining leather.

The minutes of silence ticked by. As did Tilda's nerve. "It's quite..." She gestured to the dancers. "Bumpy."

Bumpy? God brain, you suck.

Even as Alé laughed, Tilda prayed that the ground would swallow her whole. She needed to say something smart, or interesting. All she could do was gnaw on her straw and wonder what cologne it was that made Alé smell so *good*.

The times that he had asked her to help demonstrate a move in class, she had held her breath, from sheer nervous excitement and for fear she would sniff at him like a detection dog.

No doubt she smelled like an Elephant's armpit after the lesson they had. *Did Elephants even have armpits?*

"*Perdón?*"

Tilda nearly choked. "Nothing."

Alé's direct gaze was anything but cool. "Do you dance salsa?" He motioned to the couples on the floor.

"I took a few lessons before I moved to tango. Salsa was fun I guess." She shrugged, glancing across at all the bodies rhythmically swaying to the live band. "But tango..." Tilda's face came alive. "Tango was just something else. It made sense, ya know? Well, of course *you* know, you're a tango god...I mean, you've been doing it for a while now so you're really...good."

Alé's lips twitched. "*Sí*. I've been teaching for a while, dancing since I was a child." His amber eyes darted away. Those thick, dark lashes lowered, and a part of Tilda was jealous that she had to get her length from out of a plastic tube.

Tilda gnawed once more on her straw. "Do you ever miss home? Do you visit Buenos Aires often?"

"Never." Alé's jaw tightened.

"Never? Really? I just assumed you'd travel back and forth, like all the other tango teachers."

His shoulders jerked. "There's nothing for me in Buenos Aires. This is my home now."

Tilda bit her lip. His expression was closed. Unreadable. She managed to once again kill any conversation. She needed to make an exit. Five more minutes of awkward, stilted conversation should do it.

"Why haven't you joined our performance group?"

Tilda looked back out at the sea of swaying bodies. Her brows shot up. "I guess it's not for me."

"Why not? You've been dancing tango for five years."

Tilda shrugged, pleased he had remembered. She knew next to nothing about her tango teacher. The small talk they shared before class was always brief.

He was a mystery. Which was probably why his classes were packed with eager women. Not that she cared.

Alé was always professional. If anything, borderline aloof and distant. The fact that he agreed to come out tonight and socialise with the small group of Advanced Level students was out of character.

Tilda met his gaze. "Sure, it's been five years, but that doesn't mean anything. Tango is for me. For my enjoyment. Standing on a stage performing is my idea of hell."

It was a life her parents had pursued with reckless abandon. Not for her.

"That's a shame."

Tilda managed a garbled, "thank you." Praise from Alé was a narcotic. "That means a lot coming from you."

Heat crept up her cheeks, mirroring his own. She

always was a sympathy blusher. Could she get any more pathetic?

"It's the truth. You move fluidly. Your social dancing at *milongas* have built on those skills. You have potential, Mathilda," he murmured, his eyes never leaving her face.

There was something erotic about a direct gaze.

Tilda's mouth opened. *Shut up! For the love of all that is holy and sacred, shut up!*

"You should reconsider."

Tilda cleared her throat. "I think it's best to leave that to the Isabellas of the world." Just like the Energizer Bunny, Isabella never seemed to stop, let alone slow down. "I'll pass, thanks."

Alé's foot bounced up and down. He scanned the room, long fingers tapping an erratic beat against his knee. He glanced at Tilda then back at the crowd. Once. Twice. Then stood. "Let's see what you remember from those salsa lessons. *Si*?"

Tilda looked up, startled at his outstretched hand. "I thought you didn't dance socially."

Alé's eyes flashed. "I don't dance *tango* socially, this is true. But I'll make an exception for salsa. Just this once. Dance with me, Mathilda."

"But, I'm not —"

"*Por favor?*" Alé slipped the glass out of her jelly-like fingers and set it on the table.

At a loss for words, Tilda placed her hand in his, allowing him to lead her to the darkened dance floor. The light from the band illuminated the musicians but held most of the club in shadow. Had it not been for the dimly lit bar, Tilda would have lost her way in a matter of minutes.

She wanted to punch the spontaneous part of her personality that had gotten her in to this mess. She was like the heroine Jane Eyre; plain, self-conscious, boring. She would never be the beauty of the town like Blanche Ingram. Though she was certain Alé could play the part of Mr. Rochester...brooding, dark, detached.

What was wrong with her?

She was being asked to dance by her tango teacher. A professional. Taking classes with the man was one thing, but dancing with him socially, in a crowded club, to sexy salsa...was completely different.

Whilst tango had an erotic restraint to its 'A-frame' embrace, salsa was as uninhibited as a wild cat on heat.

Reckless. Fast. Primitive.

Not for the likes of her.

She cast her eyes around the room to the mass of scantily clad couples.

Her pulse scrambled. The ever so blatant display of bodies thrusting and swaying made her painfully self-conscious.

Alé drew her towards him and she wished she was dancing tango. Her face was on fire. Her body a jangle of nerves.

The beat slowed and the dance floor became an intimate roll and sway of bodies.

"Relax, Mathilda. Let go a little," Alé murmured, drawing her closer. The one-inch gap between them was good. Wasn't it?

Tilda moved her hips from side to side in a jerky, stilted motion. She was stiff and self-conscious, and the alluring, aromatic scent of the man before her, had her breathing like a fish out of water. Cocktail be damned. She could get drunk on his intoxicating smell.

Alé shook her hands. "You okay?"

Tilda lifted her chin. "Yes...it's just — I don't..." she licked her parched lips. And instantly regretted it.

Alé's eyes followed her tongue. Those amber depths reminded her of a jungle cat watching its prey. She pressed her lips together, waiting for her captor to take a bite.

"Salsa is very natural. Look around you." Alé gestured at the couples. Some were inseparable below the waist, others swayed in an open embrace, arms loosely around one another. "It's just rocking the hips in time to the music. A little leading here and there. But you're a very natural follower, Mathilda."

He placed his hands lightly on the outside of her hips, directing them to move like a pendulum. When her hips see-sawed in time to the beat, Alé smiled.

"See? Not so hard. I told you that you were a natural." He tilted her chin. She met approval in his gaze.

Alé moved in, placing her arms around his neck. Her breasts brushed against his shirt.

Tilda closed her eyes to the sensation.

She was on fire. Everything else became a blur except for the steady, sultry beat and the man whose arms rested lightly on her waist. All she knew was the rhythmic sway, sway, sway. She was surrounded by his scent, encompassed by his embrace.

Her eyes flew open. His embrace? When had he wrapped his arms around her waist? Her skirt had inched up her legs and settled mid-thigh. She straddled his jean-clad leg. Alé's hold on her was light, but the weight of his hands was sure on the small of her back.

Tilda closed her eyes once more and for the first time in her adult life, she let go. She blocked out the prodding thoughts, the fear, the anxiety — the realisation of what she was doing and with whom — all of it blurred and became background noise. It paled against the steady beat.

Her heaving chest reflected the music's increased tempo.

Tilda was jarred out of her reverie by an enthusiastic elbow digging into her ribs. Isabella's smiling face swam in to view; she was with a different partner this time, one at her height and twice as built.

"*Hola*, Alé! I'm so glad you got this girl on the dance floor. I see you two! Nice moves!" She winked, not pausing to stop even when the beat increased.

"That's what I tell her."

Within seconds Isabella had flounced away again.

The sultry pulse gave way to a faster tempo, the band challenged dancers to a frantic beat. More eager faces flooded the floor, whilst others watched in an outer circle.

Alé led her into half spins; retracting her close to his body only to fling her out again, all without bumping into the other energetic dancers. She giggled when Alé swapped roles and let her lead him into a twirl, smoothly shifting back to a head brush.

Alé teased and enticed her, inspiring Tilda to play with movement. She blissfully had no time to think and no time to apologise when their bodies collided, or when she tread on his toes accidentally.

Alé continued as if they had always danced this way. Never losing the rhythm, he swayed, stepped and weaved in time, encouraging Tilda to show off moves she hadn't realised she still remembered.

By the fifth salsa number, both Alé and Tilda were panting. She grinned in sweaty satisfaction; beads of moisture clung between her breasts. She signalled to him for a time out and they walked easily back through the thinning club.

"Only a few lessons, eh?" Alé raised one dark brow, passing her a glass of water.

"Well, perhaps more than a few. But a long time ago."

Tilda collapsed on the couch. She was tired, yet oddly energised. Her body hummed in satisfaction, but the long workday, tango lesson, and salsa dancing had left her struggling to smother a yawn.

She fished around the piles of cardigans and wraps for her bag. Taking out her phone, she gasped. It was 2.30 a.m.

"Everything okay?"

"Yes. I have to go. Early start."

"At the bookstore?"

"That's right." Tilda beamed, surprised that he remembered.

"I'll walk you to your car. I parked not far from here."

They walked the five blocks, talking easily of the band, music, and dancing in general. The warm night air, though balmy, was a reminder of the scorching days yet to come. By the time they reached her car, Tilda's limbs were heavy.

"I will have to come and see this store of yours sometime. Pick up that Lonely Planet Guide to New Zealand," Alé said, shoving his hands in his pockets.

"Sure thing. Maybe I'll interest you in one of the classics while you're at it. A romance even?"

"*Dale*."

Tilda shivered at the look in Alé's eyes. She ignored the quiver in her belly even when her brain echoed a warning.

Hunter. Prey.

She was certain she'd lose herself in those fiery depths if she wasn't careful.

"Good night, Mathilda." Alé's mouth grazed her cheek, then moved to the other, slowly, deliberately. He paused, their faces within an inch of each other.

Tilda's eyes widened. His mouth hovered above hers. She tilted her face closer to his without thinking. Quick as lightening his hands cupped her neck and she delighted in the delicious jolt that ran down her spine. Alé's lips brushed lightly across hers; once, twice, gentle as a breeze.

Tilda's pulse fluttered. The distance between their bodies was an agonising chasm, yet she stood completely still, afraid to break the spell.

His mouth teased, his tongue beckoned. Tilda was lost in the pleasure of the kiss. The pressure increased and a lick of fire simmered between them. Pulse thundering, she took him in, shivering despite the warmth of his touch.

Alé wrenched his mouth from hers, chest heaving.

Tilda's heart jack-hammered in her chest. She blinked, confused when his hands slipped from her neck.

A frown hardened his features and he stepped back.

Tilda willed herself to speak. But all she could do was stare at Alé's pained expression.

When he finally looked at her, his features were neutral. He shoved his hands in his pockets. "I... *Buenas noches*, Mathilda," he finally murmured.

Tilda leaned back against her car; eyes locked on Alé's retreating figure.

"Night," she whispered. Whilst the kiss made her pulse hum, Tilda was unable to move. What had just happened?

More to the point, what did it all mean?

CHAPTER THREE

*S*tupid. Stupid. Stupid. Alé cursed all the way to his car. He cursed when he started the engine, then again when he found himself back at the studio instead of at home. Taking it as a sign, he locked his car and climbed the stairs. Moonlight shone through the large rectangular windows, illuminating the empty space. The studio was proof of everything he had achieved since arriving in Australia. A reminder of the risks he had taken to open his business, of what he had still yet to accomplish in his career. Alé strode to the stereo system, searching for a song to match his mood. With a jerk of his fingers he turned it off again. No more tango. Not tonight. Climbing the second set of stairs at the end of the studio, Alé stepped into his haven. The large upstairs room afforded him the space to breathe when the past threatened to drag him under. It was sparsely furnished. A coffee table and sofa at the entrance, a bed in the far corner and his painting equipment at the back.

Exactly what he needed when his mind became overcrowded.Pacing across the worn and creaky floorboards, Alé raked a hand through his hair. He shouldn't have gone out tonight. He broke the first of many rules — don't socialise with students. He couldn't afford to let his guard down, to lose sight of the bigger picture. It was a moment of weakness. Using only the light of the moon as his guide, Alé uncovered the easel that waited patiently below the windowsill.Finding a blank sheet of canvas paper, he perched on the paint-splattered wooden stool. Pencil in hand, he released an unsteady breath and surrendered. His fingers flew over the white space, the rough lines of his sketch calming his blood with each stroke. He found solace in the basic connection of paper and pencil, to be able to transfer what captivated him on to the page.Images of Mathilda flashed through his mind like a reel of film. The joy in her eyes at the club, the gentle curve of her hips as they danced. The soft swell of her lips when...Alé looked out across the night sky and remembered the moment of temptation. He saw her face tilted up in invitation, felt the sensation of her mouth on his. He licked his lips. The taste of mint still lingered.

Dios Mio. Adrenaline pumped in his blood. He couldn't believe how stupid he had been. Unprofessional. Didn't he know better than to mix tango with pleasure? Hadn't he suffered enough for his sins? He never socialised with his students. No drinks after class. No messages after hours. Now this?Alé groaned. God help him, there was something about this woman. Something about her tonight that broke down every barrier. Alé's mouth twisted in a bitter smile. Who was he kidding? He let it happen because he wanted it to happen. His hand gripped the pencil; the small snap of the tip was as loud as a gunshot in the quiet dark. Blindly reaching for a new one, his hand soared across the page yet again. An urgency from deep in his gut compelled him to continue. It was always this way for him; the frenzied burst of energy, greedily clawing for release.It was only when he had finished sketching, when a dozen images of a heart shaped face with full lips stared back at him, that he lowered the pencil. He had never drawn her face before. Staring at the tiny sketches before him, Alé was baffled and fascinated. She enticed him in a way that made his body ache.He had no business being intrigued by Mathilda Landrey. Hell, by any woman. He made a vow long ago never to make that mistake again. Mathilda, for all her virtues, would be a big mistake. Weary and deflated, Alé walked over to the bed in the corner of the room and stretched out. Phantom pain lanced through his back. Like a spider spinning its web, the past weaved its thread around him once more.Lying alone, in the dead of night, Alé resolved to forget about the whole damn thing. Safer for the both of them to move on as if the kiss never happened. Right now, he had to focus on what was important. His career. This performance group could make or break his reputation; it was the only thing he had left. Without it, his studio would mean nothing. Every painful minute, every setback and humiliation he had endured over the years would have been in vain. He'd be damned if he let anything distract him.

CHAPTER FOUR

*T*he warmth of the early morning breeze beckoned keen breakfasters out of their beds and into town. Summer in Riversdale was bursting with activity. Even though the small suburb lay only seven kilometres from Melbourne's bustling Central Business District, it maintained its suburban charm due to the committed and long-standing residents who loved and cared for it as dearly as their own children.

The long strip of shops led customers from the town hall's large, yellow-brick tower on the hill, around the curved path of food stores and boutique shops, down to the end of the suburban boundary lines where the train tracks lay.

The Book Nook was just one of the stores that had been around since many of the locals could remember.

Tilda leisurely strolled past Betty's Cone and Cup, and crossed the road where George's Pizza sat, dormant and peaceful, until the Saturday afternoon rush.

She twirled the diamond studs at her ear out of habit,

just one of the many legacies left behind by her gran. Her smile faltered at the memory; the bittersweet ache had been an all-too familiar companion of late.

Tilda paused outside The Book Nook, keys in hand. Memories of her grandmother were as tangible as the displays in the shop front window. The once indomitable Ethel Landrey had presided over the bookstore with gusto and fervour, drawing in children and parents from far and wide. Everything sparkled under her supervision; the store had been friendly and inviting with a legion of loyal customers.

Now the weather-beaten wooden awnings and faded sign were sage reminders that The Book Nook needed work. Tilda's shoulders sagged. She had to bite the bullet and apply for another loan if she wanted it to thrive.

Tilda walked in, turning on the lights. Her eyes gravitated towards the dark, dilapidated upper level that ran along the right side of the store. What used to be the nook was now a dusty, abandoned space.

She turned her back on it and focused on the updated main area. Whilst it had taken all her meagre savings and then some to start the renovations, the ground floor of the store made her hum with pride.

The overhead lighting illuminated the floor-to-ceiling bookshelves. The polished wood gleamed. Cream walls, with hues of rose at the front register, added warmth to the large space. Thanks to Isabella's interior design expertise and persistent encouragement, the store tipped its hat to both old and new.

Tilda placed her bag on the counter, then turned to face the upper level. With a determined set of her heart-shaped face, she moved aside the rope partition and walked up the ramp to the first floor. The boards cried out in protest.

If it weren't for the two Palladian windows, one of which looked out towards the small children's park, the other affording a view of Main Road, the nook would have been ominous in comparison to the rest of the store. Tilda knew it wasn't a good look for business, but she couldn't afford to remain closed for renovations.

Alone at night, she sometimes couldn't help but wonder what her life would be like if her gran was still alive. Would she have travelled the world? Gone to those exotic places she poured over in Lonely Planet guides?

Her lungs seized. Travel involved risk. One she wasn't prepared to take.

An uncomfortable ache pressed against her heart. She wouldn't focus on the past. She chose this life. She owed it to her grandmother to keep the store running. She'd make it work. Just as gran always had.

Her little cameo appearance to the land of adventure last night, served to remind her that risk-taking had consequences.

Tilda turned her back on the memories and with a decisive step forward, fell through the floorboards. She cried out when her foot plunged into the splintered cavity below.

Rattled, Tilda pushed herself upright, crawling out of the broken floorboards. Pain lanced up her knees. Brushing the dust off her hands, she squinted against the dim light. She was no pest inspector, but what Tilda saw had her groaning in disbelief.

Ten minutes later, wrists aching, she began her work for the day, desperate for a distraction.

Which was easier than expected. Ever since waking up this morning, she couldn't stop thinking about the kiss with Alé. She grinned. Dancing with him was exhilarating. He had looked at her like she was... what? Desirable? Interesting?

Tilda caught her goofy grin in the reflection of her laptop screen. She must be out of her mind. Sure, Alé had kissed her. But then he frowned about it. And walked away.

Not exactly the reaction a woman wanted after being kissed by the guy she had a bit of a crush on for the past twelve months. Ever since she started taking his classes in fact. He was a man who made tango dancing an even more thrilling past time than she expected. A man who kissed like a demon and angel all in one. Her lips curved. Her body hummed.

Reality shoved aside her daydreams with a well-placed blow to the head.

What in the world was she going to say to him at the next class? More to the point, what would *he* say? The thought of that very humiliating exchange was enough to have her pacing. Playing out the awkward scene was too cringe-worthy to bear without another caffeine fix.

She'd simply forget about it, that's what she'd do.

The words of Jane Austen's Mrs. Croft danced around her mind: *we none of us expect to be in smooth water all our days*.

Tilda's lips pursed. She had a sneaking suspicion that Mrs. Croft had never been kissed by a smokin' hot Argentinian before.

An hour later, the familiar jangle of keys signalled the arrival of her right-hand man and ever-so-frank employee, Dexter.

"Coffee for the slave driver!" Dex sauntered through the store, with two take away cups in hand.

Tilda inhaled in appreciation, glad for the distraction. The hole in the floor had broken through her fantasies of Alé lounging around her house in nothing but his birthday suit.

Dex gave her the once over. His tall, skinny frame was encased in his usual button-down short sleeved shirt, with matching skinny jeans — today, dark blue.

"I thought I had a hard night. The vet said Teddy is getting steadily worse. Poor boy wouldn't stop whining at 3 a.m. because of the arthritis. And now this."

Tears shimmered in Dex's eyes. He recounted the updated prognosis from the vet. Poor Teddy, his beloved pit bull, had cancer. The outlook was grim.

"I'm so sorry Dex. Can I do anything at all?"

Dex sniffed. "You're gorgeous, but no. My sister said maybe a new puppy might cheer Teddy up, but it just seems so wrong."

"I get it. It'd feel like a replacement."

"Yes!"

"Bring him with you to the store if you need to, Dex. I don't mind having him here. And you know how much everyone in town loves Teddy."

"Not sure if the ol' boy feels the same, but thanks."

"Don't mention it. There's so much to do around here, a girl could use a friendly distraction. The delivery we've been waiting on is delayed, again. Alicia is late and I still can't find that box of merch out back."

Dex's grey eyes narrowed. "What's going on?"

"Nothing." Tilda reached for the coffee. Dex dodged it. "May the slave driver in question please have her coffee?"

Dex raised both cups. At just over six feet, he was adept at baiting her. But handy at reaching high shelves. "It may be un-God o'clock on a Saturday morning, Mathilda Landrey, but this boy is *not* blind." Dex stepped back. "You look a little dishevelled. What's going on?"

"I fell this morning." Tilda picked up the coffee Dex placed on the counter. "I'm fine, honestly...but there's something I want you to see."

Tilda drew him to the gaping hole on the first floor.

"You fell through there?"

"Mhmm. Not long ago. But —"

Dex had already bent down, his long frame doubled over. He drew out his keys, poked around underneath the loose boards. When he stood, his nose was wrinkled in distaste.

"Well, shit. I think we've a big problem."

The good mood she had woken up with only hours before, was now long gone, as was any thought of a certain Argentinian man and their steamy kiss.

CHAPTER FIVE

*I*t was with a heavy heart that Tilda picked up the phone the next day — with Dex's encouragement — to call the only man she could trust. It was after closing when he arrived.

Patrick O'Connell tipped back his baseball cap. His expression wasn't promising.

"Well?"

"Sorry to break it to you, Tilda, but I'm pretty sure you have termites."

His words were like well-aimed blows to the chest.

"Surely it isn't that bad? It won't have affected the whole store. *Right?*"

Patrick rubbed the day's growth of stubble at his chin. He jutted his square jaw. "It's bigger than just this store. It could be across the whole strip in town."

"Oh God. Don't say that." She groaned into her hands. "How will we know?"

"I ain't the expert, Tilda. But I'd say you need to get someone in here as soon as possible. The longer you leave it, the more damage. Worst case scenario, the whole town has got it, then you're all up shit creek and it's a council issue."

"And the best case?"

"That it's only in your store, and you can hopefully fumigate and get rid of the bastards."

"Whoopee."

"You'll probably have to close. We can still go through your plans for renovating this space in the meantime. Hey — don't look so down. It may not be as bad as you think." He squeezed her arm. "Not to shit on your parade, but this place is old. It needs work. Might be a blessing?"

Tilda pushed back her glasses. "Any chance you know a guy?"

"As a matter of fact, I do." He fished out his phone. "I'll give ya his number."

"Cost?"

"Can't say...you might be set back at least a couple of grand."

Tilda wanted to weep. She certainly didn't have a couple of grand to spare.

"Don't worry, Martin's great. He'll sort it out."

Patrick's reassurance fell on deaf ears.

It was times like these when she wished she lived the simple life in 19th Century England with no major responsibilities other than bagging a husband. Then again, as a pauper, she didn't fancy being forced to marry someone from the militia. Not that it hadn't worked out for meek, sweet, Anne Elliot. She nabbed herself the wealthy Captain Wentworth, didn't she?

Who was Tilda kidding? At thirty she'd have been deemed an old maid.

Suddenly, termites didn't seem so bad after all.

Young Frank Walker had been working at the bank since the end of the Second World War. He had begun as a junior cleaner at the Bank of Choice at fifteen and had big dreams of working as a teller and financial planner back when he was a child living through the shortages of the depression.

Young Frank was of course, Old Frank Walker's son, the founder of Riversdale Business society and the mayor of the district in his time. It was only natural that Young Frank had big aspirations. Despite Young Frank never having children of his own, and pushing his late eighties, people in town still called him the name his father bequeathed him.

It was a no-brainer that Tilda went to see him the next day, thankfully, on one of the two days he still worked. He had his own small office in the bank, out of respect for the sprightly man with a generous spirit. It was Bank of Choice's way of honouring a living legend.

Tilda sat on the edge of the plush blue chair and stared back at the man in question. Despite having lost his teeth many years before, Young Frank showed off his pearly dentures with a roguish smile.

"Thanks for seeing me on such short notice, Mr Walker."

"Ah now, Tilda. You'll make me feel old. It's Young Frank, if you please."

Tilda's mouth twitched.

His silver-white hair, whilst sparse, was neatly combed back, and the three-piece suit, resplendent with the time piece his father gave him sat snug against the slightly rounded waistcoat. He was a tall man, and despite his age, still had presence.

"I really just wanted to talk to you about the loan. I know I mentioned last time that I was looking to renovate again."

"Ah yes. The lovely bookstore on Main. How is it going then?"

Tilda bit her lip. She hated lying. But gossip tended to spread like an eagle's wings, far and wide, in this community.

"Things are good, but there's a lot of renovations that need to take place, and I require a loan for this next stage."

Faded blue eyes, set against a lined, but jovial face assessed her. "Not any trouble, I hope?"

Tilda's smile tightened. "No." She played with a loose thread in her skirt. "Just some preliminary work that needs to be done."

She didn't want to bring up how much was owing on the credit cards. He would find out about that eye-sore all too soon. If he hadn't already. "Then I'm looking to get a bigger loan for the renovations to the first floor — the nook."

"Ah yes. I recall when Ethel's own mother added the expansion. You still keep that split level then?"

Tilda cleared her throat. "Yes. Well, it's mostly dust and cobwebs right now, but I hope to renovate it as best I can."

"I see. Your great-grandmother had big ideas back then for the place. Caused a big stir if I recall accurately. She built the bones. Your gran, now, she was the heart. Ethel made it a sort of sanctuary for children to read, didn't she? The ah..."

"Story Time," Tilda replied around the lump in her throat.

She knew how important the store was — how much history it had in the Landrey family. How her own grandmother had bucked tradition and kept her maiden name even after marrying her grandfather, Edmund Stone.

"Yes, yes. Kids would come from far and wide to hear your gran read to them." He sat back in his chair, steepled his fingers together. "She had a beautiful voice, she did."

"That's right, sir. I hope to continue that tradition."

Young Frank blinked a few times and sat up. "I don't doubt that for a minute. We all miss her, your gran."

"So do I."

Young Frank's keen blue eyes held hers directly. After a moment he hummed. "Well. I'll set you up with your loan, once we make all the requisite checks. We need your other accounts with any other institutions — you most likely know the drill. I've a form here for you, which I'll print out."

Tilda shifted. "I'll ask if I'm not certain."

Young Frank grunted and passed her a pen. "You know how to draw then, young miss? I still have a picture Ethel had drawn for me, before you were born, that is."

Tilda's head whipped up. "I wasn't aware she gifted her drawings. How lovely."

Those blue eyes crinkled with humour. "Oh, I bet you

didn't. That was a long time ago. A very long time." He rifled through a drawer before he looked up, waiting for her answer. "Well?"

"Oh. No. I didn't inherit my grandmother's artistic skill."

"No more drawings at Story Time then?"

Tilda clicked the pen. "I haven't quite worked that out yet."

"I'm sure plenty of people would be happy to do some artwork for the store. Given all you do for the community."

"I hope so."

"Ah yes. You'll find life has a way of joining the pieces of the puzzle together. Sometimes when you least expect it."

As Tilda waited, she crossed her fingers and toes in hope that the octogenarian was right.

At this stage, she needed all the help she could get.

CHAPTER SIX

A week later, Tilda finally managed to get 'the bug man' to visit the store. She asked Patrick to be there for moral support, and to talk her through options once they knew the extent of the problem.

She hadn't wanted to worry George and Betty just yet. She needed to know exactly what she was dealing with before talking to the two most important people in her life. They were like family to her — pseudo grandparents since Ethel's passing — and she didn't want to worry them until she had all the facts. Besides, they had their own businesses to keep them preoccupied.

Martin bobbed his head and popped gum with the sharp 'clack clack' that had Tilda's nerves on edge. She'd been having nightmares that any day now, the bugs would burst through her beautiful floorboards with semi-automatics, Terminator-style, demanding their hostile takeover.

Martin's popping gum brought her back to the present.

"Nah ah ah." Martin placed his hands on his hips, scratched his dark, messy head under his dirt-stained cap, then shoved it back on. "You got 'mites a'right. A whole bunch 'o them."

"Is it bad?"

"See this?" Martin motioned her over. "When you see the wood start to crumble, that means it's tiiiiimberrrr." He made an explosion sound, whilst digging at the rotting wood with the back of a pen.

Tilda crossed her arms. She wanted to smack him and his nonchalant attitude.

Patrick squeezed her shoulder. "Is it worth fumigating?"

"It's beyond that, mate. Probably gone through her whole store. Might be better to just knock it all down."

Tilda's heart jackhammered. "Can't you just fix it?"

"Love, when you see it rotting like this, there ain't no 'just fixing' it. Termites probably ate through it all a long time ago. You're lucky it didn't give way earlier than this. It's all wood, right?"

Tilda looked at Patrick, face blank.

"I can ask my dad — he helped out with the initial renovations, so he'd know. Though I was certain the main level was concrete in structure."

Martin made an infuriating humming sound. "We'd need to tent the place then, blast it with chemicals and heat. But that half." He jerked his thumb to the upper level. "It's all gotta go, lady. We'll need to fumigate the whole area and toss the rotting boards. The framework, windows, whole structure's going down."

Tilda refrained from going all Bertha Mason on his arse. "When?"

"Gotta check. Preliminary observations maybe tomorrow. I'd suggest you get rid of these books in the meantime. It's stinky business, Miss. Don't wanna ruin them. I'd think about closing for at least five, probably seven days after. Maybe longer."

"What?!"

He snapped his gum. "These suckers survive an apocalypse. You don't wanna be here with all them chemicals flying around afterwards."

Tilda's voice was strained. "Right."

When he gave her an estimate of the cost, Tilda's eyes stung.

"Look it ain't so bad. Better ya catch it now than when ya roof falls on ya head."

"Think of this as a step towards preliminary renovations of the store. Just a bit earlier than planned," Patrick soothed.

Tilda wasn't certain that the loan she applied for would even cover it. She was in the deep end, and it had only just begun.

Once the gossip mill found out that the termite man had been to The Book Nook, Tilda had a steady stream of local business owners in and out of her store. She managed to allay their fears and give Martin some good business for the next fortnight, but it made her heart heavy to think she'd have to go back to Young Frank again so soon.

She turned to Patrick who had come by to assess the site.

"This is a big job isn't it?"

"Potentially. Yes. But you'd rather be thorough now than pay for it later. Tilda, we'll work this out."

"I need to speak to George and Betty." The phones were running hot with news of the bug invasion and she wouldn't be able to dodge their calls for much longer.

"Sure. We can meet at —"

Tilda jumped. A loud, very familiar voice carried through the store.

"...absolute disaster! Tilda! Where are you?"

Tilda smiled in apology, then winced when Isabella's voice grew even louder in volume. Patrick raised his eyebrows. She heard Dex's soothing voice pipe up before she could interject.

"It's a bloody mess and we *need* Tilda!"

Tilda turned at the clomping sound and rushed forward. "Oh my goodness! Izzy, what happened to you?"

"You have no idea!" Isabella ranted, hobbling up the ramp on crutches. "I broke my stupid ankle at rehearsals. I blame Anthony and his inability to execute a pretty standard lift. But you would know that if you had been around. You haven't been in class and it's such a mess and – oh." Isabella paused mid-tirade. She turned to Patrick. "Why hello there." She balanced a crutch under her arm to shake his hand.

"Hi." Patrick's smile was quick and full of appreciation.

"Patrick O'Connell, this is Isabella Diaz."

"It's a pleasure to meet you, Miss Diaz."

Tilda noticed Isabella's slow assessment of her contractor.

"Isabella is an interior designer," Tilda piped up.

"Patrick is my contractor. You remember his dad, don't you?"

Isabella ignored her. "Something tells me you're very thorough at your job, Mr. O'Connell." Isabella winked.

"Can't say I've had any complaints."

Tilda stepped around Patrick to her friend. "Should you be on your feet, Izzy?"

"Well I wouldn't mind being swept off my feet by a tall, handsome stranger." She smiled up at Patrick, then blinked. "But I need to talk to you first."

Patrick cleared his throat. "I'll grab some stuff from my van, start poking around here and jotting down some figures. We'll need to get rid of the rotten wood."

"Rotten wood?" Isabella's head whipped around.

"Sure. We shouldn't be too long, Patrick."

Tilda ushered her friend towards the back of the store to the break area they used for meals. "Tell me what has happened to your ankle, *slowly*." Tilda helped to Isabella sit down before closing the door behind them.

"Rotten wood?"

"It's nothing." Tilda flopped in the chair opposite. "Okay, so we may have termites."

Isabella scrunched up her nose. "Ew."

"I'm handling it. Don't worry about me. What in the world has happened to you? Are you okay?"

"He's hot."

Tilda threw her hands up in the air. "Are you going to focus?"

"I *am* focusing. On that very cute butt of his."

Tilda snapped her fingers despite the bubble of laughter tickling her throat. "For heaven's sake Isabella, you've a one-track mind."

"Is Patrick single?"

Tilda rolled her eyes and reached for the biscuit tin. She fished around, found a chocolate ripple and bit in. She'd get nothing until she had satisfied Isabella's curiosity.

"Well, is he?"Isabella asked.

"I don't know. Perhaps you could ask him that yourself?" Tilda walked to the small bar fridge and sighed at the empty bottle of milk.

"Maybe I will. I sure wouldn't mind sitting opposite him for a few hours on a Saturday night. Do you think he can dance?"

"You mean, can he dance Argentine Tango?" Tilda shook her head. "I doubt it. All I know is that he's early thirties, might be a few years older than us. No, he hasn't mentioned a girlfriend, but it's not what we usually talk about. What does it matter whether he can dance anyway? Surely that's not a prerequisite to date someone now, is it?"

Isabella shifted. "No. It's not. But it *is* a lovely bonus. Plus, you know what they say about those who can dance." She wriggled her eyebrows and made Tilda laugh for the first time in weeks.

"Ah huh. Now, stop getting distracted and spill."

"This performance is cursed. Did you know —"

Tilda snapped her fingers. "Focus, Izzy. I can't help if I don't know the problem. Facts."

"Okay. Last week, Janelle and Zach have this massive fight at rehearsal. Apparently, Zach had been cheating on her, and she found out a month ago, but gave him another chance. Well, we were on our fifteen-minute break when all of a sudden Janelle storms up the stairs, crying and screeching. She caught Zach flirting — with his whole-body kind of flirting — with Olivia and lost it."

"Ouch!"

"It gets worse. Zach and Olivia come upstairs, and Janelle slaps him in the face, then slaps *her* in the face and storms out."

"*Bold and the Beautiful* eat your heart out."

Isabella nodded, taking a seat again.

"It's spread real quick too. Don't know how any of them could front up to a *milonga* for a while at least. But it gets worse. Just this week, Alé tells us that Zach and Janelle aren't dancing, understandably. So poof, we lose our leads."

Tilda thought about the last time she saw Zach and Janelle. The evening of The Red Lounge two weeks ago.

"A lot has happened since I saw you last. Okay, so they're gone. Big deal. Surely you can get some of the other couples to lead? You could have taken her place, or Olivia?" Tilda's chest felt tight.

"No. Don't you understand? They're the best we had. And yes, we did think about having me dance with Alé and finding someone else for Anthony, but now that the second curse has happened, I can't dance. Everyone is dropping like flies which means we might have to call it off."

"It's early days. I'm sure you can get someone to fill in."

"Sure, we could get *someone*. But we don't want just someone... that's where you come in."

"Isabella," Tilda warned.

"Hear me out. It'll take a bit of time to get up to scratch, but I can help you. If I don't get someone, Alé is

41

going to make the call and cut it until next year. Plus, Anthony is a patient partner —"

"Do I know Anthony?"

"No, he's from Sydney, moves around a lot. Performed before with Bill's school in Paramatta. Anyway, he feels so bad about what happened to me that he is happy to do whatever we need to. He said he'll take some extra rehearsals to help you out."

Tilda's eyes narrowed. "Oh really? You've got this all arranged, have you?"

"Look, I *may* have jumped the gun on this, but I didn't want everyone to pull out."

"I'd like to help Izzy, I really would, but no. Performance tango is not for me."

Dancing in *milongas* — at social clubs — with friends was one thing. But being on stage was never her dream. It was what her parents lived for, took risks for; a jet-setting life filled with competitions and awards, never thinking about the consequences of their lifestyle.

Tilda at least understood what it meant to have responsibility. Right now, the bookstore and its success required all her energy. She wouldn't be distracted by anything else. She told Isabella as much.

"Oh please, Tilda. *Please*. Alé makes everyone feel like they can do it and he'll understand that you need a bit more time to catch up. It'll only be a couple of performances — I think there might be three that we booked, all low-key. And not too much of a time sink."

"Low key? Uh-huh."

"Tilda, c'mon! Don't you want to do something that is a bit thrilling? Something different? A bit out of your comfort zone?"

"No. I have enough thrills going on in my life to keep me occupied." And problems. She was beginning to fear that she'd never be able to afford, let alone have the strength to restore the store.

"Please?"

"No!" She softened her tone. "Look, I happen to like my comfort zone. It's a warm, happy place filled with order and great books - not to mention chocolate and wine. I'm sorry you couldn't be a part of the performance. I wish you weren't in this situation, but I haven't got a spare moment.

"Now that this place is bug infected, I have to clear out the stock, try to get the renovations underway and still keep this place afloat. Any time I have, I'll be spending here." She hated saying no to a friend, but she didn't think she'd manage. "Look, I'm sorry but I can't do it." Tilda stood, opening the door.

"Wait!" Isabella wobbled after her. "Slow down! I'm a cripple if you hadn't noticed."

"Ready to talk?" Tilda caught up with Patrick at the top of the ramp.

"I've punched in some numbers to ease your mind, but —"

"Tilda!"

"Ignore her," Tilda muttered. The troublemaker in question hovered behind her.

"I'm going nowhere until I get an answer."

"You got one, Izzy. You just didn't like it."

"I can be very persuasive."

Patrick grinned and cleared his throat. "Uhh, I can come in tomorrow if that's better? I've gotta head off to another site anyway."

"Don't ignore me, Mathilda. I can wait all day."

Tilda sighed. "Sure, tomorrow would be great. Thanks, Patrick." She waved him off then faced her friend.

"I know I've come on a little strong —"

"Nooo, really?"

"And you probably need some time to process things —"

"Izzy, no time in the world is going to change how I feel about this."

"I know. But give it some thought. Try to picture it." Tilda's back straightened. She saw the gleam in her friend's eyes. "Performance tango isn't just about being on stage. The glamour is just icing on the cake.

"Alé is running this purely on his reputation as a tango teacher so we know it'll be amazing. It's a chance for his advanced students to showcase their abilities to the community. To challenge themselves by learning a routine. It's about extending yourself as a dancer.

"It's not like you have to continue being a part of the performance group once this particular routine is over. You can commit to the three or four performances we have lined up and then be on your way. It's only a four-minute routine anyway."

Tilda arched a brow. "Izzy —"

"This means a lot to me. I've been waiting for my chance to put these ideas that have been bubbling in my head into practice. And Alé seems to be the only teacher who isn't so consumed by his own arrogance to let me try out my choreography. It's my chance."

If there was one thing that Tilda couldn't brush off, it was sincerity. She knew what it was like to lust after your dreams. She also knew how excited Isabella was about trying out her choreography.

Tilda's shoulders sagged. "Okay."

"Okay?"

"I'll think about it. Now go. Shoo. Scram."

Isabella squealed. "Thank you, thank you, thank you! It means the world to me!"

"I know it does."

"Okay, okay, I'm going. Thanks again!" Isabella's smile was a mile wide as she left the store.

Tilda leaned back against the counter and yawned.

"That was sure intense," Dex muttered, picking up his shoulder bag.

"To say the least. It seems I've got a lot to think about."

"Well, don't think too hard, sweetie. Like my nan always said, if in doubt, sleep on it. Not that I'm getting much of that these days." Dex yawned.

"Teddy?"

"I've moved him to my room. I just couldn't keep the old loaf out."

"Give him a pat from me."

Tilda shut down the computers. An uneasy sensation crept between her shoulder blades. She replayed her conversation with Isabella. Tilda knew that the performance was far from cursed, yet she couldn't shake off the tingling awareness that lingered on the back of her neck.

Curses came in threes. Whilst she wasn't superstitious, Tilda touched the wooden panel for good luck. Little did she know, Fate wasn't through with her just yet.

CHAPTER SEVEN

*T*he curse came in a form she had least expected. As the end of the following week approached, Tilda was itching to get her life back on track.

Even though she had been beyond busy, she made sure not to miss her volunteer work at Riversdale Primary School. It had been a small pleasure to listen to the first-year children reading, to see their eager faces light up when they pronounced a word accurately. It was a much-needed reminder of how important The Book Nook was to the community; a space for children to feel excited about books and reading. If she could just get through the bug problem and manage the renovations, she'd be up and running in no time.

Tilda sat across from Patrick amid the Friday lunch crowd at George's Pizza, under the shade of a large umbrella, to discuss those very plans.

She stretched her neck and fantasized about a long, hot soak in the bath, maybe even a quick massage over at Mind and Body. Her bank balance shuddered at the idea.

"I spoke to Martin. Fumigation is nearly complete. The top level was cleared of any bugs, not to mention the wood that accompanied it. You dodged a bullet with the main area."

"Finally, some luck my way."

"Now that it's all gutted, and we've got the gates up, we can really get stuck in. Those are the plans I sent you, with a few updates."

Tilda glanced through them on his tablet. But her mind wandered.

She was restless. She had been closed for over a week now and had to delay the release of the new Byron Skyes' fantasy novel. Not being open meant she was haemorrhaging money. Fast. She forced herself to concentrate on what Patrick was saying.

She glanced at the slice of George's pepperoni pizza that sat on her plate. Her stomach rolled. It had been her favourite since she was a teenager and yet she may as well have been smelling cardboard.

"Does that suit?"

Tilda blinked, refocused. "The designs look perfect Patrick. Exactly what I imagined."

Patrick grinned. "I thought you'd like that."

"But the cost is —"

"I know. Custom-made shelving and tables don't come cheap. Remember, we're literally building from the ground up again."

The pizza lodged in the back of her throat. She guzzled down water.

What would Anne Elliot do? Tilda bit back a snort.

Anne had her Lady Russell and her family money to save her, didn't she?

Tilda looked across the road to Betty's Cone and Cup. No doubt her grandmother's best friend would be working today. But it wasn't like she could ask Betty, or even George for help.

Yes, they were more like family than friends. George, Betty and Grandma Ethel were the triple threat growing up. Surrogate parents in so many ways. Tilda owed them so much for all their support. Which made her even more adamant not to burden them with her money problems.

She had to make it work on her own. Hadn't she learnt from a young age that life was unpredictable? Now that her gran was gone, she could only rely on herself.

"Tilda?" Patrick prompted.

"Yes. Sorry, I'm 'wool-gathering' as my gran used to say." She twirled the stud at her ear and contemplated the man across from her.

"I'll need to sort out my finances again. You should be able to start by next week if that suits your men?"

"It does. But I'll need money for the materials and the deposit up front."

Tilda bit her lip. "I can organise that."

"Great. In the meantime, I'll hunt around for cheaper craftsmen for the furniture you're after to ease the pain."

"Hey! Patrick!" George still had his apron on as he made his way out of the shop.

"Don't mention any money stuff to George or even Betty for that matter, okay?" She leaned forward.

Patrick raised his eyebrows but nodded, zipping his lips.

George's warm brown eyes were jovial. His silver hair was still full despite his age, and dark strands lingered at his temples. He called himself salt and pepper, essential in life, as in any meal.

Patrick stood, gathering his paperwork.

"I don't mean to interrupt." George motioned him back down.

"You weren't. We just finished. Great pizza as always, George." With a wave Patrick was gone.

George's grin was knowing.

"What?"

"I didn't say anything." He sat in Patrick's chair.

"But you have that look."

"Patrick, eh? He's a good guy. You've been spending a lot of time with him lately?"

Tilda rolled her eyes. "Oh c'mon, George. He's my contractor!"

"And a hunk."

Tilda sputtered. "Please, *please*, don't ever use that word while I'm drinking." She patted her mouth. "Actually, don't ever use that word. Period."

"What's wrong with a bit of flirting eh, Tilly? Would it kill you to ask him on a date? Live a little. Your gran wouldn't have wanted you working yourself to the bone. I know Betty would agree with me."

"George." She leaned forward, squeezing his hand. "I know you mean well, but believe me, I don't need to be going out on dates. Especially now. Especially with my contractor who —" she gave him a pointed look, "is interested in Isabella."

"Your dancer friend, Isabella?"

"Yes. Trust me, George, I have no time for a relationship, especially now. You will be the first to know if I do."

George tapped her hand in his. "I don't think so. You're secretive. You never date or talk about boys anymore. Tilly, you're like a grandbaby to me. When are we gonna see you settled with some bambinos, eh?"

Tilda's body stiffened. She tried to swallow but her throat was dry as parchment paper. She was vaguely aware that George had let go of her hand, but she wasn't paying attention to him anymore.

How could she when all the air had been sucked from her lungs? How could she when *he* was here?

Surely not, her brain cried out. She stared at the figure walking towards them. The man looked very much like the same Argentine who she hadn't seen in weeks. It couldn't be...

Tilda tried to look away, but her eyes drank him in, wanting to be sure. Wishful thinking. Right?

She looked back at George.

"What is it?" George turned in his seat just as Alé approached their table. "Friend of yours?"

Tilda pressed her lips together and mentally cursed as comprehension dawned. She had assumed Isabella's recent silence about the performance group had meant she'd finally given up asking. There was only one reason why Alejandro Garcia would be standing in front of her right now. Isabella had finally pulled out the big guns. She had threatened to in their last conversation – not that Tilda had believed her. She was going to kill Isabella.

Right after she stopped drooling.

George sprang up, all smiles, ushering Alé forward.

"I'm George, nice to meet you."

"Alejandro." He took George's outstretched hand and tucked his aviators in to his white t-shirt. Tilda reminded herself that she was a grown up. One who didn't ogle at sculpted men in t-shirts.

"I take it you're friends?" George looked between the two of them. Tilda hadn't moved an inch.

"I know Mathilda through tango."

George boomed. "Fantastic! Take a seat, buddy. She never lets us watch her dance. I bet she's as talented as her mother. She was a beautiful dancer, just like our Tilly. Her mother danced ballroom mostly, classically trained, but a real champion — won lots of titles before the —"

"Alé is my tango teacher." Tilda interrupted. Alé sat in the now vacant seat opposite her. "George is like family. Very chatty, but well-meaning family. He owns this pizza store. I've been coming here since I was a little kid. Really great food. I just had a slice with —" Tilda pressed her lips together. She was babbling again, and it was all his fault.

Alé's eyes were warm and focused solely on her. She wasn't prepared for this. Wasn't prepared for *him*.

The kiss they had shared danced in her mind. She hadn't rehearsed what she would say when she saw Alé again and now it was too late.

"A pleasure to meet you, George. You're right, Mathilda is a beautiful dancer. One who has a lot of skill. An inherited talent it seems." He spread his hands wide. "That is why I'm here. We haven't seen her at class. For a while now."

Tilda looked at him, then across the road.

"Our Tilda? Miss a lesson? Nah, that ain't right."

Tilda's face felt like it was burning; like she was

fifteen and got caught playing hooky. "I've been busy with the store."

It wasn't because she had no idea what to say to the man. Or that it was far easier to avoid the whole incident.

She could sense Alé's eyes on her face.

George cleared his throat. "Now that you're here, can I get you anything, Alé? Pizza? Cold drink?"

"A coke would be great. Thanks."

"Tilda?"

"Lemonade, please."

"I'll have Paulie bring it out. Nice to meet you." George shook his hand again. "Tilda." He kissed her on the head before leaving.

"No." Arms folded, Tilda spoke first. She was desperate for a fan, some ice, an Arctic breeze; anything to keep the heat from her face.

Alé's lips quirked. "Hello to you too, Mathilda."

"How did you know I was here?"

"I have my sources."

"Would they happen to be from an annoyingly persistent woman with dark curly hair and a bung foot?"

"A man never reveals his secrets."

Tilda nearly wept with gratitude when Paulie placed their drinks on the table. Biting her lip, she took the courage to meet his gaze. She was done for.

Alé was the first to look away.

It was torture to watch the woman in front of him take the straw in her mouth, to watch those lips move, plump and pursed, and not be tempted to taste them. Again.

It had been a moment of weakness. A moment of madness that had him acting on impulse that night. An impulse that had tormented him since she walked into his dance studio twelve months before.

It was a line he should never have crossed. Especially now that he would be working even closer with her. If only he could convince her.

His leg bounced up and down under the table. He had to convince her. The performance group was falling apart, which he couldn't let happen. It meant too much.

He had his reputation on the line; Alé had to prove he still had it as a dancer, but also as a teacher as well. *Dios*, he had screwed it up by giving in to a moment of weakness.

Passion. He knew all too well how dangerous it could be.

Alé studied her again, his fingers itching to paint her in colour. She had a vibrancy when she danced. An array of colours that made her a pleasure to watch. And a compulsion to paint. Not that he'd been able to resist.

Alé fought against the ridiculous urge to tuck the stray strands of that golden hair behind her delicate ears. He wisely kept his hands around the glass in front of him.

He hadn't seen her in over three weeks. It felt like months.

Heated images of her wearing nothing but those dark-rimmed glasses, a pair of heels and an inviting smile made his mouth dry. So much for that resolve.

Alé wondered just what her reaction would be if she knew how — despite his better judgement — he had thought about her. He'd been relieved when she hadn't shown up to class the first time, successfully hid his disappointment the second. But by the third class, he knew it was a problem.

Teaching private lessons, running his business and dealing with the fallout from the performance group had kept him occupied. For most of the day. But it was those late nights, when he lay in bed letting his mind wander, that it roamed to one blue-eyed, golden-haired bookstore owner. And that graceful gazelle-like body of hers.

Tilda fiddled with her earring. "I apologise. That was rude of me. Hello, Alé."

"I heard you didn't attend the Australia Day *milonga* last week."

"Oh. Yes. I've been busy with the store. I'm not sure how much your spy told you, but I'm in a messy situation right now."

"And hiding away from friends, *no?*"

Tilda looked down.

"Isabella told me about her conversation with you. And the bugs. I'm sorry to hear it has been difficult. She has been hounding you, *no?*"

"Isabella tried to convince me to fill in. I told her very directly that I wasn't interested in performing. But, for her sake, that I'd think about it. Clearly that's not good enough for my pesky friend.

"I'm going to be really busy over the next few months. On top of all those reasons I also have zero experience performing. So if you came here to pester me then you're wasting your time." Mathilda smiled, and Alé understood the polite but firm rejection for what it was. But that didn't mean he liked it.

"I didn't come to pester you to join the performance group."

She blinked. Shook her head. "How utterly presumptuous of me."

Alé moved to the seat next to her. "I wouldn't be so bold or direct as Isabella. I would appeal to your... what is it... softer side?"

Her lips pressed together.

Who knew he'd take such pleasure in teasing her?

"I would remind you to think of your poor dancers. Your friends. Isabella. Their hopes and dreams." He gestured. "Gone." Alé shook his head slowly, holding her gaze for longer than necessary.

He whispered now, moving closer, his knee brushing at her thigh. Taking her hand, he looked into wary blue eyes. "And if that didn't convince you, then I would remind you of just how exquisite you are as a dancer. It would offer so much to the performance to have you join us."

Who knew those eyes could turn a deeper shade of blue?

He released her hand. Watched in fascination as the pink tip of her tongue snaked out to moisten her lip.

"I prefer flattery to pestering." His grin was slow. "You've shown you're a fast learner, Mathilda. I would trust you can step up to the task." Lost against a will that was not his own, Alé's fingers stroked a tendril at the base of her neck, marvelling at the rich colour. He heard, rather than saw her breathing change. He shifted closer. His mouth hovered around the simple diamond stud at her ear.

"*That's* what I would say to you." The words almost

stuck in his throat. He didn't dare look at her until he had shifted back in his chair. He couldn't. Not with her scent surrounding him.

Mathilda blinked again, her chest rose and fell a few times before she spoke. "You sneak. That's just appealing to my vanity." She held his gaze now, hypnotising him. Yet the firm line of her mouth declared that she was no pushover.

Alé rubbed his chin. Tiny fingers of panic crept up his chest. He looked out across at the lunch crowd, some shuffling back to work, others tipping their face to enjoy the sun. Easy. Carefree. Relaxed. It called to him. But he wasn't there yet. There was a buzzing at the back of his head, in his body, that never let him relax.

He schooled his features. Calmed his racing pulse. He could convince her. He had to. This performance was...

Alé focused on her face. He couldn't think about the past. He may have left his professional career on the side of the road that fateful day, along with those dreams, but now he had a chance to make something of his life again.

He tapped his lips, studied the woman before him. "If you didn't want to be a part of it, then, I'd respect your wishes."

She didn't budge.

"Mathilda, the reason why I came here is not because of Isabella. She has her own reasons for wanting this show to be a success. I came here for me. It —" he threaded his hands together, cleared his throat. She was making him reveal more than he thought he could. More than he wanted. "I want you to be a part of this. It means a lot to me."

"Why?"

He noted the surprise in her raised eyebrow.

Alé shrugged. Her normally plump lower lip thinned out and he cursed himself for needing her. "It's complicated. Everyone has a past. Everyone has dreams. I need to run this performance tango class. I need to prove...I *need* this."

He heard the desperation in his own voice. He didn't care if he had to beg. He'd deal with his shame later.

Alé saw the instant her eyes softened.

She chewed on her lip. "So — hypothetically — if I did come along, what would that entail?"

Alé couldn't quite hide his triumphant smile. He sat up straighter. "If you were joining us, we would take it slow. I can change dates so we have more time. It would mean rehearsals every week, learning the routine. I can get you up to speed so you feel comfortable. Let me show you what you're missing."

She took a dainty sip of her lemonade. Then sighed.

"Okay...fine, I'll try it out."

Alé grinned.

"Don't get so excited. If I'm comfortable with it after a run through, then I'll join."

Alé rose before she changed her mind. "*Bueno*. Be at my studio at 10am tomorrow." He knew when it was time to make his exit.

After one last look, Alé left her sitting in the mid-afternoon sun, his heart in his throat. Tomorrow he'd get his answer.

One way or another.

CHAPTER EIGHT

*T*ilda looked at the tiny mountain of clothes at the foot of her bed and for a split second, wished she lived in the 19th century like one of her beloved book heroines. That way she wouldn't have to choose what to wear; she'd order her lady's maid to make the decision for her.

Not that she'd be able to afford one.

Before a fantasy of her in a corset being whisked away by a certain Argentinian could take hold, Tilda rifled through the pile and pulled out the first thing she could find.

A thong.

Hmm.

Summer's blistering heat, and her own time restraints eventually forced Tilda to settle on light-weight black cotton pants and a blue tank top. She fussed with her hair three times before tying the shoulder-length mess up in a short ponytail. She added a haircut to her mental to-do list.

After a quick dash to the store, with assurances from Dex that the re-stocking process was smooth sailing, Tilda climbed the stairs of the dance studio. Her belly quivered like a string ensemble, with much less finesse.

The sound of silence in the dance studio was unnerving. It dawned on her that she had never been there when it wasn't humming with eager voices or reverberating with the rhythmic swish of feet.

She called out, crossing the rectangular space, past the shiny dancefloor to the kitchen. She poked her head through the opened office door, adjacent.

"Alé? Isabella? Anyone here?"

"You came."

Tilda jumped. The rich, smooth voice she had come to know so well echoed across the room.

She turned, clutching her shoe bag. "You startled me. It's so quiet."

"I didn't hear you. I was upstairs."

"Oh, I didn't know there was an upstairs. I mean, of course I knew there was an actual upstairs, but I meant I didn't know there was a proper space up there..."

Alé waited, eyes smiling, until she finished. "I sometimes stay when I'm too tired to drive home. I'm glad you came."

"Right."

"Don't look so scared, Mathilda. It won't be difficult." He paused. "That's not the truth. It's hard, but you'll manage."

"Well with that ringing endorsement I better get my shoes on."

"Did you bring flats?"

Tilda turned and looked at him quizzically. "Err, no. Should I have?"

"When we rehearse, it's easier without heels. Go to Bright Life after class. It's a good investment. We only start wearing heels for the full rehearsal. But some *tangueras* prefer to work in heels — their blisters are marks of honour."

Tilda winced. "I'll buy those flats after class. It didn't click that I needed to get different shoes." Or that there would be extra costs involved.

Maybe she could find some second-hand ones, not that she had the time. She needed to head back to the store as soon as rehearsals were over.

"Next week will be soon enough. Today we mark the basics of what we've covered. To ease you in."

Tilda said goodbye to that much-needed haircut and calculated how much a pair of flats would cost. She slipped off her sandals and refused to give in to the panic that seemed to hover like a bad smell wherever she went these days.

She would find the time next week to get the damn shoes. Once she finished re-stocking the store this evening, The Book Nook would be open again for business. That meant she could begin renovations properly.

With her lip curled, she shoved on her ugly black heels and made a promise. If she ever travelled to Buenos Aires the first thing she'd do is buy a beautiful pair of tango shoes. Hell, she'd buy at least two from *Comme Il Faut*. And possibly a dozen from *GretaFlora*.

Which meant she'd have to buy a matching tango outfit.

Which meant she'd have to sell a kidney on the black market to afford it.

Which meant she'd die from some complication somewhere over the South Pacific.

Tilda shook her head and wandered over to where Alé stood, sifting through tango songs.

"Where are the others?"

Alé turned. "They're not coming."

"Excuse me?"

"I held off a group rehearsal until you are on your feet, so to speak." He grinned. "We are still waiting on confirmation of numbers after all this mess. I gave us a few hours today — alone, so that we could mark some of the basics. Isabella will help spot you when she arrives later."

"Right." Her palms grew damp. "Thanks, I suppose."

"*De nada*. Time to warm up."

Gotan Project's 'Epoca' flowed from the speakers. The sensual stroke of the violin rang across the studio, an enticement.

"Ready?" Alé asked, waiting for Tilda to move into his open arms.

Tilda focused on tightening her core, lifting up and finding her axis. She stepped forward. The weight of her body rested in the balls of her feet. She settled against Alé's firm chest, to form the traditional A-frame of an Argentine tango embrace — the *abrazo*.

Alé's earthy scent made the dance even more of a sensory experience.

She exhaled, placing her right hand in his open palm. As Alé's hand closed about her own, his right arm circled her waist, drawing her in. Her left arm draped across his back.

"Breathe, Mathilda," he whispered. "Relax your arm."

They stood, shifting weight from foot to foot; the pressure from his chest telling her everything she needed to know.

Beat by beat, by slow degrees, Tilda's arm relaxed. The tension began to fade. She rested her forehead against his temple and listened to the music, focusing on it rather than the sensation of his chest against her breasts.

"*Bueno.*"

Before Tilda could smile, Alé's chest drove up, his feet glided forward, leading Tilda to walk backwards, slowly, rhythmically in time to the beat.

Alé altered the length of his stride, marking short, almost on the spot steps, then shifting to long, sweeping strides.

He displaced her foot in a backwards, box-like step, a *saccada*. When he invited her to do the same, Tilda smiled in full. Dancing with Alé was daunting yet thrilling. He played with the direction of his lead, and never felt the need to dance large, grandiose moves like some teachers.

Alé teased her without uttering a word. The movement of his chest, the placement of his feet, told her a story that only she could decipher.

This. This was what enticed her to tango. She forgot her problems — the loan, the renovations, her own expectations — and simply existed. It was what made her come back time and again.

Her mind weaved its web of self-doubt, breaking her

out of the spell. Her breathing became shallow, straining in concentration to keep up with the skill of her leader.

Tilda was self-conscious and all too aware of the fact that she was dancing with an expert. Her right arm stiffened, her shoulders sagged, and she knew the rhythm was running further away from her. She stumbled over a simple *barrida*, a sweep of the foot.

Connection lost, they both staggered. To seal the deal, her scuffed black leather heel had found its way to Alé's little toe.

He cursed and pulled back.

"Oh my goodness! Alé, I'm so sorry! Are you hurt badly? Here, sit down. No, take off your shoe. Uhh. Do you have any ice? I can ice it and reduce the swelling if it's that bad? We don't have to continue if you —"

"Mathilda. Mathilda! I'm okay. I've had worse, from sharper heels. Give me a minute."

Tilda pressed her fingers against her lips, waiting for Alé to stand up properly.

He straightened, took one look at her face and laughed. "I'm fine." He reassured her, testing his foot. "Now. I think we are warmed up, *si*?"

Tilda nodded. "*Si*. And sorry. Again."

He brushed aside the apology with a casual hand. "Forgotten. Let's talk basics. The concept for this performance is based on the sensuality of tango. The moves are fluid. Teasing. Isabella will explain more, but we want the dance to be seen as a courtship. There will be stages in the performance that reflect the stages of love."

"That's very Isabella."

"It is. But this is tango, and tango is heartache. Love lost, love found. All the shades of it — sometimes all in one song. But we are still working on this. For now. The beat." Alé began clicking. "Tac, tac, tac, tac," he murmured as his fingers continued to mark a 4/4 rhythm. "This is the beat we work with. Very basic. Classic tango."

"Okay, so a classic, sensual tango. Pretty basic moves, right?"

Alé spared her a dry look. "There will be nothing 'basic' about it, we've chosen Osvaldo Pugliese's 'A Evaristo Carriego' — a beautiful piece, but not simple. We'll step through the moves and give you a feeling of the rhythm and the beat, then we worry about the music later. *Estás bien?*"

"Yep."

"We start the first few seconds apart. Think a lion stalking his prey. Or in this case, the beginning of attraction. A man seeing the woman, woman seeing the man for the first time. The spark."

Tilda shivered.

"We walk, slowly, sensually. Like you would when you see a man in a crowded room and you want his attention. Tease him."

Tilda walked, her steps jerky and self-conscious.

"Don't think about it. Here." He stood behind her. "Extend your leg, lean forward, hold your axis." His palms held either side of her waist. "Good. Now walk." His voice was deep in her ear. His body pressed against the length of her back. "Yes, perfect." His palm sat flush against her stomach. Heat radiated from his touch.

Alé shadowed her as she walked. "Extend the leg, follow with the body. Good, Mathilda."

Her waist tingled. The gentle pressure of his chest

behind her back and the soothing, smooth tone of his voice captivated her attention.

They travelled up and down the length of the room, the large floor to ceiling mirrors reflecting the intimacy of their movement.

Tilda continued even when he moved away. She turned to find Alé's eyes molten, pinning her in place.

She remembered how those tiger-bright eyes had looked at her in just that way. Right before he had kissed her.

He blinked, hesitated, then turned off the music.

"Was that okay?"

"Yes. We will add the turns later. But now, we step out the basics."

They practised the first minute of the routine. Alé wasn't joking when he said it was anything but simple. She stumbled over the last few steps, grimacing.

Performance tango meant that she wasn't guided by the lead's chest, which also meant she had to know the choreography in detail. She wouldn't be able to lag a second behind; it would throw out their rhythm, as well as the overall aesthetic. A slightly un-tango notion.

The bold, sassy show that was performance tango appealed to some. It frightened the hell out of her.

"Rise up, Mathilda. Hold your frame. No — not your breath, your axis." Alé poked at her stomach.

Tilda gritted her teeth, biting back a petulant retort. Her back ached from his strict instructions. It took all her concentration to focus.

"You're pushing your butt out."

Mathilda let go with a huff.

"Try again. Here, stand before me. Remember don't

sink your hips, keep your body on one plane, as if someone is moving your entire body side to side. Loosen your shoulders, relax."

Firm yet relaxed. Tight but loose. A dance of contradictions.

"You're doing really well, Mathilda. You've done *colgadas* before. You have to rise up and keep a firm core. Trust me. Let's move to open embrace. Now lean back. Slowly."

Alé sandwiched his feet around her left foot. Her right foot remained weightless.

Tilda held on to Alé's forearms, as he did hers in their open embrace. He guided her out, so that she was at a 45-degree angle from his torso, then eased her back to his chest. He repeated the motion over and over. Her stomach quivered. With every move, Alé reminded her to keep her axis.

"Good. *Bueno*, Mathilda. Think of a string at the top of your head, pulling you up."

Tilda couldn't think at all. Not when Alé's eyes roamed over her body, especially not when his hands touched her, correcting her sloppy technique.

In some far corner of her mind, she knew he was simply doing his job, but her body responded in a way that was far more elemental.

The bands of muscle at his arms were tense, his body strong and supportive. She caught his scent with the slightest of movement. It teased her in ways it shouldn't. The kiss had changed everything. It was as if her body gave her the permission to react to his touch, even when her brain screamed in warning.

Alé hadn't even mentioned the kiss. It was as if

nothing happened. But there was a look in his eyes that told her different. She wanted to bring it up, to clear the air, but didn't know how. The best she could do was try to ignore it. If it had meant anything at all, surely Alé would have mentioned it by now?

Tilda looked at him, desperate to maintain her focus. His amber eyes were watching her. His gaze roamed over her face, resting on her lips. A liquid heat travelled through her body.

"Breathe."

Tilda shook her head and Alé laughed, guiding her back to his chest once more.

"Relax." He released her arms. "Now you can breathe. That was spot on."

Tilda's lungs deflated. Pleasure sat triumphant on her heated cheeks. The temperature was climbing outside, and the fans did nothing to stop her feeling like she was a tender morsel of lamb inside a pressure cooker.

"Grab a drink. A quick break. By then Isabella will be here so we can go from the top. Maybe we'll try it with the music once you are comfortable. *Sì?*"

Tilda nodded.

By the end of their session, she didn't even blink when they made plans for her to attend the group rehearsal. She had ignored Isabella's triumphant grin when she promised to return.

Despite her aching feet, Tilda hummed through the hours of work back at the store.

It wasn't until late that evening that the thought struck her. In the span of a few hours, she had become a part of the performance group. She waited for the annoyance to come. It startled her when it didn't.

Tilda fell asleep later that night, still waiting.

Tilda found herself tearing up on Monday morning when Young Frank finalised her loan application. She hadn't meant to get so emotional, but The Book Nook was more than just a business. It was her family's legacy. This loan meant she had another chance at keeping that dream alive. Money would be tighter than ever, but Tilda was used to living on a budget. She would make it work. She had no other choice.

Young Frank's wrinkled, sun-spotted hand patted her own.

"I'm so sorry. I didn't mean to get upset." She offered him a watery smile. "Now the store is open again, there'll be revenue coming in. We do good business. Which my accounts show. I may have to scrimp here and there but I can make repayments."

Just. She thought. If everything remained perfect and she didn't see a dip in sales.

The scary fact was, she had no buffer. Nothing to save her if something went wrong. No grandmother to offer a safe place to fall. That terrified her more than she wanted to admit.

She wasn't a risk-taker. Yet here she sat, about to take the biggest one of all.

A fresh wave of emotion settled in the back of her throat. "Sorry. It's been a long weekend. We've been working trying to get the store open for today and I've been understaffed."

She had deliberately sent Dex home to be with Teddy

and get some rest. She knew what it was like to nurse a sick person – and dog or not - Teddy was Dex's family. He needed the support right now.

Young Frank offered her his handkerchief. "When you get to my age, you see some things aren't so important. And others are worth fighting for."

Tilda folded his handkerchief and passed it back. "Thank you, so much, Young Frank. You have no idea how much this means to me."

"Oh, I think I do, young lady." He paused. "Did I ever tell you that your grandmother and I were close friends?"

Tilda's head whipped up. She was certain they had this conversation before. But who was she to contradict a senior citizen?

"No, you didn't."

"She gave me a few of her paintings when we were young."

Tilda injected surprise in her voice. "Oh really? How lovely."

"We were, well," he mumbled, "kind of sweethearts of sorts when we were just in diapers."

Tilda's pen hovered over the form on the table. Now *this* was new. "I didn't know that, sir. I'm sure she appreciated your friendship."

"I'd like to tell myself that she did. Not sure your grandfather was so keen, however."

"I doubt he was."

"She loved him very much. I suppose she never recovered when he died. She deserved so much."

Tilda's throat closed over. There were so many people her grandmother had lost, so many she had left behind. It continued to surprise Tilda to hear of all the people who benefitted from Ethel Landrey's kindness.

Half an hour later, Tilda left the cool air-conditioned office and retraced her steps back to the store. Numbers and sales figures whirred through her mind.

Taking a deep breath, she straightened her shoulders and was overcome by the memory of Alé's capable hands guiding her, holding her while she learned the choreography. His words of encouragement at the end of their session comforted her now.

Maybe, just maybe, things wouldn't be so bad after all.

CHAPTER NINE

*T*ilda sat beside the other dancers that Friday night, waiting for their group lesson to begin. She gnawed at her lip; nerves and excitement wrestled for purchase in her gut. Alé had reassured her that she'd get extra time to rehearse with Anthony to catch up, but she still felt underprepared.

Her session with Alé felt like a lifetime ago. She had been so busy with the store that she wondered whether the practice she managed to squeeze in at home was enough.

Alé had encouraged everyone — if they were feeling the pressure — to halt their regular tango classes so that they could devote the time to the performance.

Everything was beginning to change.

"Hey Tilda," Elspeth whispered. "How are you feeling?"

"A little nervous. I've been trying to rehearse all week, but it feels a bit strange without a partner."

Elspeth's black ponytail bounced in agreement. "I

know what you mean. Ever since the whole bust up with Janelle and Zach all of our partners need to be changed."

"I just hope I can keep up."

"Relax." Elspeth patted her shoulder. "We're all pretty much in the same boat. Zach and Janelle were the only ones with performance history."

"Where's Izzy?"

"Not sure. Anthony is late too."

Tilda heard the tell-tale giggle drift up the stairs a few minutes later. Patrick carried Isabella in a fireman's lift over his shoulders.

"Put me down, muscle man," she squealed. Placing the crutches on the floor, Patrick waved goodbye and was out the door before Isabella could convince him to stay.

"I'll get that man to tango if it's the last thing I do," Izzy stated, fixing her wild curls.

"I see things are going well between the two of you?"

"Mhmm." Isabella grinned. "But you just wait until I'm on two feet again. That boy won't be able to run very far."

Alé motioned for a man and woman Tilda hadn't seen before to join them on the floor. With a nod from Isabella, he began.

"The fact that you're all here means you've made the commitment to be a part of this group. That means I need everyone rehearsing *mucho mas* every week at home.

"Even though we have had a — how would you call it — a rocky start, I'm convinced things can only get better." Alé shifted and gestured to his right. "Saying this, I want you to meet Marco and Diana. They've agreed to join the group and help round off numbers."

As everyone introduced one another Tilda bit her lip.

Marco was a thick, broad shouldered man, with heavy-looking feet. She prayed that she could still dance with Anthony.

Isabella waited until they were all silent. "Tonight we'll do a brief re-cap of the first section of the routine, but we do have to move on, so those of you who are still rusty, get up to scratch in your own time. Alé and I expect you to rehearse with your partner outside of class time. Especially for some of the lifts I've planned."

"More lifts?" Elspeth's eyes were round.

Isabella smiled. "Mhmm. But don't worry, Alé will walk it through with everyone. You'll be fine."

Tilda didn't think it was quite the right time to remind everyone of how Isabella had received her injury. Maybe it was a good thing Anthony wasn't here.

"But first, partners. We'll get them marking out the first minute before moving on?" Alé spoke to Isabella.

"Yep. We're all familiar with the start of the routine. Marco and Diana were working with us yesterday, so they're up to scratch. Marco has been a part of performance tango before so he's a pro. Right, Marco?"

Marco chuckled, running a hand over his closely shaved head. His blue eyes warmed, softening his bad-ass demeanour.

"I'll try, Isabella."

Isabella stood, balancing on the back of the chair. "Only the best. This is my first chance at showcasing my work, so I want it to be perfect. Okay, let's partner you up."

Tilda inched away from Marco. Everyone spread out into a straight line.

"So, Sara and Michael, we're splitting you up. Michael

you're now with Katarina. You both seemed to work well together when we stepped out the routine, and your heights match."

"Sara, that means you'll be with Phillip," Alé added, motioning for them to stand next to one another.

"Ben, you're now with Diana."

Tilda frowned. Anthony still hadn't arrived.

"Marco — you'll be paired up with Elspeth. You're both quite tall so that should work nicely. And Elspeth can help you play catch up on the routine."

Tilda's eyebrows shot up. This didn't make sense. She thought she was needed for this routine but now everyone had been matched up and paired off.

Isabella said, "and last but certainly not least, Tilda you're with —"

"Me."

Tilda's head whipped across to Alé. He smiled lightly, hands in pockets.

"What? What happened to Anthony?"

"Anthony had to fly up to Queensland for a consulting stint for two months. It's disappointing, but there was nothing he could do to change it."

Tilda shook her head. "No way." Partnering with Alé was *not* part of the deal.

Isabella hobbled across to the stereo for some music. "Everyone, warm up with your partner, Tilda can I speak to you over here, please? *Privately?*"

Her heart was beating out of time, to a song only she could hear.

The rest of the class paused in awkward silence. Alé caught their attention, instructing them to keep to the line of dance in their warm up.

She could sense his eyes following her across the room.

"What is all this about?" Tilda hissed.

"I don't know why you're making such a big fuss. We needed you to join the group and we needed another dancer."

"No. You don't." Tilda shook her head with such vehemence she was surprised it didn't fly off her shoulders. "What I just witnessed was a whole group of people evenly partnered off, with the new couple, Marco and Diana agreeing to join. Problem solved.

"Why does Alé have to dance anyway? I thought he was only doing the choreography with you and stepping out parts of it to help us out. Nowhere in this whole deal did you say that I would be partnering with him!"

"Why does it matter anyway? Plenty of people would kill to be partnered with Alé."

Tilda's jaw clenched. Isabella would need a crowbar and Patrick's muscly arms to get her answering that one.

Pairing with a fellow novice to help them out was one thing, but dancing with an expert on stage was another. It was embarrassing enough to stumble over Alé last week at rehearsals, their dancing levels clearly disparate. But to dance with him in a performance? It wouldn't work.

"Tilda, stop thinking disastrous thoughts and listen for a second. Please."

Tilda crossed her arms. "I'm listening."

"We didn't need Alé for the performance when we had Janelle and Zach because they could carry everyone else. But there are some parts of the routine that require lead dancers to make it work."

"That isn't me."

"Yes, it is. Or at least it will be. Trust me, if I had the ankle, I'd be the first to jump in and help, but I can't. That frustrates me more than you can imagine."

"I think I understand the frustration."

"Tilda, *please*. You promised."

Tilda opened her mouth to protest and paused.

"Did you know?"

"Know what?"

"Did you know that I would be paired with Alé when you made me promise?"

"No, I didn't."

At Tilda's raised eyebrow, Isabella laughed. "I honestly didn't. Anthony literally called at the eleventh hour and we had to make a decision. I know how well you dance, I saw it when you rehearsed with Alé last week. That's why I made you promise before you left. I didn't want you freaking out about some of the choreography I have planned. Don't look at me like that, Tilda. It makes sense that you dance with the best. Okay?"

Tilda groaned. "Fine. But if I come across choreography that I can't do or am not willing to kill myself in the process of doing, then you can't force me. Okay?"

Isabella rolled her eyes.

"Deal?"

"Fine. We'll work with that."

Izzy hobbled back to the group.

Tilda looked across at the couples dancing. Despite her annoyance, she could already see that they had been well paired.

"'No' seems to be the word of the month when it comes to you and me." Alé's voice lingered at her ear.

Tilda winced. "I'm sorry. I didn't mean for it to come out that way. I was just surprised is all."

Alé wrapped his arm around her waist and drew her towards him. "Relax," he whispered in her ear. "We can take it slow."

The vibration of his voice at her ear was just another reason why dancing with Alé was going to be a problem. Tilda closed her eyes. She could never get enough air when he held her.

"Easy for you to say."

Her brain conjured up images of all the ways they could 'take it slow.' Crisp white sheets, Alé's hands pinning her to the bed, his mouth...

"I think it would be best if we caught up on Sunday."

Tilda's back stiffened. "Caught up?"

"I thought you might feel a bit put off by dancing the lead role, so I told Isabella I'm happy to meet up with you on Sundays — or whenever suits you — to step through some of the parts we left out and get a bit of partner rehearsal time in."

Tilda was grateful that Alé could not see her expression.

"Yes, I think that would be necessary."

Tilda mentally castigated herself. For a split second she had thought that he was asking to see her. Like on a date. She brushed off the little stab of disappointment.

Tango was her safe haven. Her little slice of indulgence at the end of a long working week. Dating her dance teacher would only make things complicated. What she wanted — what she needed — was the exact opposite.

Hell, that kiss should have been warning enough. It

was safer for all parties involved if she stopped fanta-sising and kept it professional. Which was clearly the message he was sending.

She was glad of it. It meant they could pretend it never happened. Start fresh.

"You seem far away," Alé murmured.

Tilda's fingers itched to swat at her ear as a tingling sensation trickled down her lobes to caress her spine.

Ears were functional. For hearing. All other arousing purposes would hereby be...de-commissioned.

"No, no. I'm right here. Sunday is fine."

"*Bueno.*"

Changes. So many changes.

She could only hope her courage would hold.

CHAPTER TEN

To Tilda's mind, Sunday arrived with the speed of an executioner. She barely had time to recover from the onslaught of Friday's gruelling session, her body aching in places she didn't care to admit, before she was back at it again.

Despite all her self-talk, Tilda couldn't contain the zing of attraction when in Alé's presence.

She recalled how Roberto — her much older tango teacher who had guided her for the first four years — had told her that tango was a dance of the heart. Of passion, sensuality, betrayal, lust... *You'll lose your heart to this dance before long...* With an air of naivety, she had laughed it off.

Tilda wasn't so green to think that she was the only woman in the world who melted when those tawny eyes looked at her. But if she wasn't careful, her nerves would be ripped to shreds. And then she'd resort to chain-smoking, which would ruin her already less than perfect skin, and she'd wind up having to wear six inches of makeup and eye shadow the colour of rainbows to make up for it. So for purely aesthetic reasons she had to snap out it.

The empty studio brought her out of her reverie. It was deja-vu all over again.

"Alé?" She waited. No answer. "Alé?"

Tilda checked the usual hiding spots and paused when she heard the classical music trickling down the back stairs. She hesitated at first, her hand on the rail. She didn't want to disturb him. But on the other hand, she couldn't twiddle her thumbs waiting around the studio. She had a to-do list that mocked her back at the store.

Tilda climbed the chipped green staircase. She recognised Beethoven's Symphony no. 9 that vibrated behind the closed door.

As the violins reached a fever pitch, Tilda knocked.

She waited a few seconds and knocked again.

Tilda opened the door and paused over the threshold at the sight before her.

Alé's face was in profile, his body slightly turned away from hers. He perched on a stool in the middle of the room in front of an easel. The picture of a mother and child in what looked like a loving, candid moment was almost complete. A palette sat to his right on a small side table.

He was lost in the painting.

The stereo sat beneath the open windows. The volume was almost deafening inside the room.

Tilda drank him in; his profile was as every bit arresting as the rest of him. Strong jaw, regal nose and that obsidian black hair mussed and careless. He looked like a statue himself, all bronzed and golden.

His strokes with the brush were careful, but quick, his concentration focused, his back straight.

She couldn't help but wonder whether he would be this intense as a lover. The large bed in the far left-hand corner caught her attention. Didn't he say it was just a place to crash when he finished late? It didn't mean anything.

Tilda continued to examine the space. At the far end was a kitchenette. Plain white cupboards and drawers sat beneath a deep sink. There was a small, square table with a few chairs in the right-hand corner, covered in newspaper and half-empty jugs of water.

A tattered leather couch sat near the entrance.

Her eyes travelled back to the cream sheets. X-rated images flashed in her mind.

She glanced at Alé. Her heart leapt.

He sat, ever so patiently staring back at her. It was unnerving how he did that. Caught her off guard. She wondered now if it was the artist in him. The observer.

"Hi," she called out.

Alé stood, placed his brush on the palette and walked across to the stereo.

In the ensuing silence, all Tilda could focus on was the bed. And the fact that they were very much alone.

Alé studied Tilda's startled expression. She reminded him of a gazelle. Graceful, yes, but cagey. Alert. What was it that made her so jumpy? What went through her brain?

Even as his mind wondered, another part of him was caught up in temptation. Black tights covered up legs no woman should hide. The pink sports top clung to her in ways that had a man's imagination working overtime.

He was positively salivating. Which was dangerous. Very dangerous. There was a reason why he kept his distance.

Alé squared his shoulders. He had no business getting caught up with a woman like Mathilda. She wasn't the bed-and-back-away from type, and he sure as hell wasn't looking for a relationship. He made that decision long ago.

They were dance partners. Nothing more.

He shifted. So what if he had a moment of weakness? He had wanted to sample those lips. Just once.

Yet still she drew him in. She kept all that passion, all that desire locked up. She was so controlled that when she let down her guard — when he caught glimpses of her attraction to him — it made him want more.

How was a man to refuse such a tantalising combination? He had caved in that night, despite his better judgement.

But Alé had remained firm since in his resolve. He hadn't even touched her again, so he had nothing to worry about. *Madre de Dios.* Give him strength. Why was he even thinking about it? Especially when she was standing right there. Looking like that.

He picked up small towel and wiped his hands.

He was her teacher. There were boundaries to their relationship. He would make sure it stayed that way.

Plucking up the courage, Tilda drew herself up to her full

5'7" height and walked further into the room. She was drawn to the painting.

"Sorry to bother you. I didn't see you downstairs and I heard the music and followed it up. I didn't mean to intrude."

"Not a problem. I lost track of the time."

Alé moved to the sink to scrub off the remaining paint from his hands giving, Tilda a chance to study the painting.

"You paint here often then?"

Alé walked up beside her, cleaning his brushes with a cloth.

"Sometimes. I can paint freely and make a mess up here. Now that I have a bed, it's easier than going home some nights."

"I bet."

Alé agreed, moving over to the sink. She had no idea he had such a talent. Then again, they never really had a chance to chat about their lives up until now.

"You've an eye for detail," she called out. "What made you want to paint?"

Alé came back, drying off his hands. "My mother did it." He shrugged. "When I was little, I would draw, and my mother saw I had some talent there. When I wasn't dancing or trying to impress the girls, she'd sit me down and show me technique. 'Alé,' she would say, 'beauty is found in the detail.' When I was older, it became my private thing. Something personal where no one else was watching, but me."

Tilda could imagine being on the stage left no room for quieter pursuits. She understood how important it was to keep some things private. How some things were sacred. She was about to change the subject when Alé continued.

"As you can see, artwork is messy business, but something like this." He pointed to his current piece. "Needs that attention to detail."

"Do you have a preference? Watercolours? Oil?"

"I have painted in watercolours. But most times I prefer sketching with pencil and paper. It's easier to work that way, wherever you are in the world. This kind of work takes time."

"I'm so sorry for staring, but your work is stunning. You've managed to capture the intimacy of the moment between the mother and child and yet haven't made it seem too...cliché."

Alé scratched his chin, a lopsided grin forming.

"Thanks."

Tilda's eyes narrowed on the painting.

"What?"

She turned to him. "Do you work mostly in bold colours when you paint?"

"Not always."

"Do you feel comfortable sketching places as well as people?"

Alé raised a dark brow. "Why do I get the feeling that this is leading somewhere?"

"Oh, no reason." Tilda smiled innocently, her brain working overtime.

Alé crossed his arms over his chest. Tilda momentarily lost her train of thought at the flash of bicep.

"Mathilda?"

Tilda's gaze refocused on Alé's face and she smiled slowly.

"Well, I think that it is *mighty* unfair that I'm held up to such a rigorously high standard in being your dance partner. A fact which I did not know coming into this whole performance. A fact that, to be honest would have scared the living daylights out of me..."

"Your point?"

"I think because I'm doing the performance group a favour, that you perhaps need to do me a favour too."

Alé's eyes warmed. His grin turned wicked. "And what sort of favour do you have in mind, Mathilda?"

Tilda's cheeks bloomed at his insinuating look. The fact that she could easily think of a favour that would pleasure them both only deepened the crimson shade. "I want your hands."

Alé's eyes flashed.

Realising what she said, Tilda rushed on. "I mean, I want your hands in my store. For me. For The Book Nook."

He nodded, stepping slowly, deliberately towards her. "And what would my hands be doing for you in a nook, Mathilda?" He raised his long, tanned fingers, opened his palms in a gesture of affected innocence. She caught the gleam in his eye. She held back a nervous giggle.

"Well, what I meant was that I'll need someone to complete weekly drawings for the nook reading area. Once I've got it all built and running again, that is. My gran — she used to draw in chalk on the blackboard that we had in the store when I was little. For Story Time. She'd let me sometimes choose a scene from one of the stories that she read to the children, and she would draw it. The place needs that again."

"Ahh." Alé held his hand out for her to shake. "I'm happy with that offer. I will draw for you, Mathilda Landrey. Consider my hands, yours."

Consider my hands, yours.

Alé's words bounced around her brain over the next few days.

The man teased her and she had remained mute.

She shook her head. She wasn't that much of a block-head to not notice when a man spoke in innuendos. But it was the reason why he was doing so that left her perplexed.

Perhaps he just enjoyed taunting her? Some men did. Her pasty white skin betrayed her at every turn. It wasn't like he had acted on it. They were just words.

Tilda stacked the children's books that would feature in her new window display. She needed something to cheer her up in the wake of the bug saga, and she thought a new display would be just the trick.

Tilda cursed at her lack of concentration; her index finger welled with blood. She sat back on her heels and stemmed the flow with her mouth. Just for a second, she wondered what it would be like to be carefree and sexily sophisticated, or forthcoming like Isabella.

That woman had no fear.

Bold. That's what she needed to be. To take charge and be bold. And sexy. And flirty.

Tilda rolled her eyes. Who was she kidding? She was

the least likely person in the world to flirt. She was used to men making the move. Not that she had ever had men in droves. What a laugh.

She had inherited her gran's heart-shaped face; men saw her as sweet, even cute. Definitely not sexy.

What would have happened if she had said, 'yes, Alé, I want your hands over my body. On my breasts. Underneath my dress' ...she fanned her cheeks as graphic images dangled tantalisingly in her brain.

She needed advice.

She was happy to keep him in the friend basket and move on, but every time she did, he made her doubt resolve. Asking for advice meant that this was becoming a *thing*.

Her stomach lurched. No, she would stop thinking about his bits doing very naughty things to her bits and carry on.

Flirting was like breathing to Argentinian men. Hadn't Isabella told her countless stories about them?

No doubt Alé got a kick out of seeing the reaction from the plain, bookish and boring *gringo* like herself. Talking about Alé — thinking about the man — was not a wise course of action.

Yes, fantasising about him made early morning wake up calls with her builders slightly more bearable, but it wasn't healthy.

It was time to close the chapter on that steamy book and put it back on the shelf where it belonged.

It simply wasn't her love-story to tell.

Tilda could barely contain her excitement.

Normally rehearsals captivated all her attention, but all she could focus on was work. Not even the prospect of marking the steps in time to the music could distract her.

Tilda was practically vibrating with energy. The high arrived alongside the nearly completed building structure, which meant one half of the store wasn't subject to the summer heat and those pesky flies. It meant that they'd be able to have walls around the upper level and that the nook was one step closer to being properly built.

She'd used social media to her advantage, tweeting every bit of progress, eager not to lose customers. Despite Patrick's advice, she had restricted the builders from working whilst the store was open, which meant progress was slow. But she couldn't inconvenience shoppers like that.

Dex hadn't complained only because of all the half-dressed men loitering around. And the fact that they all loved Teddy. Tilda had arranged a little bed for the cantankerous Pitbull who seemed pleased at all the scraps of food the construction crew threw his way. And the little children loved him.

Tilda twirled her earring. Maybe, just maybe she'd make it work.

"... it's important that we focus on it."

Tilda forced herself to concentrate on the man before her. Which, given his appearance, wasn't all that difficult. Tall, dark and Argentinian. Yes please. Whilst half-naked builders had captivated her attention of late, Tilda still couldn't shrug off the jolt of lust that shot through her in Alé's presence. It was hard when she was pressed up against him for hours every week. But she gave herself credit for reducing the amount of naked fantasies she had been having lately. She was practically a saint.

Alé looked around the room. "The music we have is one of the most sensual in tango. As we said in the beginning, this performance will mimic a relationship."

Isabella continued. "It's about that messy, passionate network of human emotion. Those elements that make up attraction: lust, love and above all, the desire to reclaim love again, beyond hope. So our moves will reflect this. Alé, let's listen to the first fifteen seconds again."

"As you all know by now, we are working with the classic version of 'A Evaristo Carriego'. We have the file on our shared Dropbox folder. We also thought you might like to upload videos of us marking the routine. I know some of you have said you'd like to take footage of the sequences so you can watch them at home when you rehearse."

The tinkling of the piano filtered from the speakers. Everybody stilled. "Notice how the violin entices you at the beginning." Alé pointed out over the music. "It's around the thirty second mark that we begin with the partnered choreography."

The violins surged; it spoke of lust, violence and above all, the passion and restraint which epitomised tango dancing. The bandoneons entered brazenly, making their elastic and rich voices known. The music was poignant and engaging, something that called to the senses and arrested the mind.

No wonder she was smitten. Her eyes clashed with Alé's, held. The music slid beneath her clothes and caressed her skin as intimately as a lover; it sent her blood racing. She shivered in anticipation.

All this, in Tilda's mind, became a whirlpool of colours and movement. She saw the pointed feet, the straight back, the sharp strides.

"Beautiful, isn't it?" Alé spoke, once the last note had rung out. It was only then that he looked away.

Slowly, as if they had all been sedated, the dancers blinked, cast furtive side-glances to their peers and smiled. The music had the very magical ability to transport them all.

Once they were all focused, Alé continued. "Isabella and I have decided to revise the beginning of the routine. Rather than just interacting with your partner in the walk, we're going to have you search for one another, complete a move or *adorno*, then spin to the next partner, and so on. By the time we hit that thirty second mark, you'll be with your assigned partner."

"It's like a speed dating thing," Isabella chimed in. "Everyone is changing, unable to decide, but of course there won't be any talking. And we can go through the gestures and allocated moves to reflect that. I'll be writing up a copy of what the dance will be about so I can introduce it at your performance. But you don't have to worry about that stuff for the moment. Right now, we'll concentrate on getting this intro down pat."

Everyone nodded. Alé played the music.

"Okay, everyone spread out," Isabella called. "I'll talk you through what I'm thinking."

Tilda braced herself. She expected a foreboding, queasy sensation to follow, but was surprised at the sliver of exhilaration that had taken its place. She hugged the happy thought close to her, hoping that the difficulty of the routine wouldn't scare it all away.

Progress, as little as it may be, was still progress at the end of the day. Tilda was determined to focus on that and not the end product. She moved towards Alé, resolute in that aim, and curious to see what happened next.

CHAPTER ELEVEN

*B*y the middle of the week, with his curiosity as keen as a cat, Alé paid a visit to Mathilda's store. He expected to see most of it as bare as a construction site. Instead, it was appealing and inviting. Just how a bookstore should be.

He walked over to the front desk. Tilda's eyes rounded behind her black square-framed glasses. A man could get used to them.

"Alé. Hi. What brings you to the 'burbs?"

"I had an afternoon free. Wanted to see what I was in for."

Her blue eyes flashed with humour. "Don't listen to anything Dex has to say on the matter."

"Slave driver," Dex sang as he sauntered past.

Alé frowned.

"He's sulking because I've had to swap around shifts," she whispered. And he couldn't ogle the builders anymore.

"Understood."

"Sorry about all the mess, it's slowly resembling what I would call a room." She nodded to the space behind him.

"They work fast." Alé wandered over to the base of the nook.

"Luckily. I've tried to keep the hours to early mornings as much as possible. Some late afternoons to not interfere with customers."

Alé studied her. The slight smudges under her eyes contrasted her pale complexion.

"And it's taking its toll." He reached up and brushed her cheek.

Tilda froze.

He shoved his hands back in his pockets, cursing himself for her wary expression. She brushed her hand hastily over her face.

"How to damn with faint praise."

"I didn't mean you look bad. You're beautiful, Mathilda. I just noticed..."

She bit her lip. "I was joking, Alé."

He grunted. Idiot.

Better to keep things neutral.

"You have a great space." He motioned to the main level. The warm wood of the shelves, the clever placement of space and colour made the large area feel intimate. "It's a testament to your skill."

"I'd like to take all the credit, but I'm afraid I can't. My contractor, Patrick, has pretty much held my hand throughout this whole thing," she gushed. "Oh! Speak of the devil."

The front door jangled and Alé turned around. The

large, blonde, Norse God seemed to fill the room. Alé swallowed.

He was above average in height and build, but the man before him was like Thor.

Mathilda beamed a smile in Patrick's direction. "There's my saving grace!"

"Tilda." Patrick moved forward, gave her a peck on the cheek.

Alé took Patrick's proffered hand and exchanged pleasantries. All through gritted teeth. He forced his jaw to relax.

"I assume you've known Mathilda for long?" He tilted his head to look up at Thor and battled against his own frustration.

"Nah. Not really. May have met once or twice when my dad did up the joint. But we're bloody making up for it now, hey, Tilda?" He sent her a wink.

"Like an old married couple," Dex cut in. "Taking my break if that's okay dungeon keeper."

Tilda shooed him away. "More than okay my willing subject."

Tilda blushed when Patrick winked again.

Did the man have a twitch? Alé straightened up his 5'10" frame. It made him uncomfortable to see Tilda fawning over the 6'4" giant.

"I was just telling Mathilda that she has a great place here."

"That she has." Patrick slung a companionable arm around her.

Alé crossed his own.

"She's made it what it is, a rising success. Once we get

these floors down and polished, I reckon we can start the painting. We'll make it picture perfect. Just for you."

The air punched out of his gut at the way she beamed at him. Alé dug his shoes in to the floor stemming the urge to do something ridiculous like stake his claim. What the hell was wrong with him?

Tilda smacked her hand on her head. "Pictures! I forgot you wanted to talk about the pictures!" She looked back at him, then to her blond builder. "I asked Alé to draw for The Book Nook. He's amazingly talented."

"Great news! For a second there, I thought you'd be salsaing in the store." Patrick jiggled.

"It's tango," Alé replied.

"Alé, how about you head to the back room, just straight down the end there. I'll need five minutes with Patrick."

"We won't be long."

Alé walked to the back room. He tried to sit, then paced the floor.

So what if Mathilda was seeing Mr Fix-It? It wasn't any of his business. He repeated it like a mantra. With every step, he wore a small hole in the carpet. Alé couldn't shake the feeling that he'd seen the man before. Australia's Most Wanted?

But when fifteen minutes passed and Mathilda still hadn't come back, his temper took hold. When she finally made it in the room, her face flushed, Alé snapped.

She barely had time to close the door, before he had her shoved up against it, his mouth fierce and possessive over hers.

Alé's brain pleaded to him carefully, like a hostage negotiator, while his body burned with reckless need.

Her gasp was drowned by his tongue, demanding more. It didn't occur to him to stop. When she wound her hands around his neck, his body came alive. Alé crushed her against the door, delighting in the feeling of her body against his. His hands wanted to cup every curve, stroke every inch of that body. Alé gripped her hips instead.

Her mouth was every bit as demanding as his own; she stroked and teased, setting his blood on fire.

When she arched her back in a sensual, feline curve he wanted to rip away their clothes and take her up against the wall. If he didn't stop now, he wasn't sure he ever would.

Alé broke the kiss, vibrating with restraint. Looking down at Tilda's swollen lips, the almost purple hue of her eyes, he bit back an oath. For pulling away. For wanting more.

"Alé," she whispered, her chest rising tantalisingly close to his own. She giggled. "You've fogged up my glasses."

His mouth twitched.

In seconds they were in a fit of laughter. When he looked at her again, something danced across his chest. The jolt had him freezing in place. He looked away uncertain of the sensation.

"Mathilda. I shouldn't have — uhh —"

"Ravished me?"

"Sorry."

Fire kindled in her eyes. "For pity's sake, Alé. Don't apologise."

"S — right. So."

He watched as she rearranged her clothes, then shoved his hands in his pockets.

"You don't pash a woman in one breath and apologise in the other."

"Mathilda, I didn't — I'm not sorry for doing it, but I am sorry..."

Sorry, not sorry? He'd lost his mind.

"Alé —"

"I shouldn't have —"

"Stop."

He felt small and mean. And not a man at all. Why couldn't he just open his mouth and explain it properly?

"Mathilda..."

You make me want things I shouldn't. You're sexy and sweet and that combination is like fucking catnip.

"Mathilda, I —"

"I can't do this right now, Alé." She pressed her lips together. "I have to get back to work."

"Work. Right."

Those blue eyes were distant, her body stiff.

Alé shook his head but held his tongue. He had jumped her at work. Smooth Alé. Real smooth.

Before he could cause more problems, he left.

On the pavement, in the bright light of day, he knew one thing for sure: he was an idiot, and he had fucked things up.

Dios. Make that two.

Alé was in a bad mood. No, not just bad, foul.

It had happened again.

The nightmares were getting harder to shake. It hadn't been this bad for a long time. He had moved on, hadn't he? He was in control of his life.

A red-hot fear gripped his chest. Maybe he would never get over it.

Alé had woken up in the dead of the night — two in the morning to be exact — gasping and clawing at the bed sheets, desperate to escape. It took him ten minutes to register that he could, in fact move; that the dead weight of his legs was a type of mirage. But not one of hope.

The ache in his back, the persistent twinge, was enough to ground him in place and time. The searing pain all over his body, however, were remnants of the dream. Of his past.

'It's your body's phantom response, to put it in plain terms' his psychologist had told him. Argentina was as famous for its shrinks as it was for its tango. 'It is very normal for your mind to remember the trauma, and your body to believe it is true.'

The life he wanted to forget taunted him.

Alé took his time getting out of bed. With unsteady hands, he stripped the sweat-soaked sheets. The stuffy, cloying smell still lingered.

After staring at the ceiling for most of the night, he finally got up and paced. When that didn't work, he made himself a pot of coffee. He knew better than to go for the caffeine, but by daybreak he would do anything to forget. The drilling headache and nausea only served to remind him that his past was very much present.

No amount of denial, drawing or damned coffee would soothe him when it was this bad.

He hadn't seen it coming; ignored the warning signs. But then again, he never did learn.

Alé showered and walked to the train station in the early morning light. He knew better than anyone that he couldn't drive in his state. His aviators shielded him from the worst of the sunshine.

In an instant, the past and present collided. His hand clenched as the flash of bright high beams on a dark, rainy night, blinded his vision. The advance and retreat of the windscreen wipers marked a frantic beat in time with the pulsing pain in his head. He gasped, gripping the park bench, willing the horror film on loop in his head to end.

At times, he saw his life through an unfocused lens, as if it was someone else's memories that plagued him at night. But then the familiar wave of loss would engulf him, the pain would pinch at his nerves until he claimed the bitterness and longing for what it was; his own.

Alé blindly reached inside his shoulder bag for the protein bar and aspirin he had snatched off the kitchen table. He was grateful for the small miracle. Even as his stomach pitched at the smell, he took a tentative bite then swallowed two small pills. He shook his head to rid himself of the memories; the pounding pain ricocheted from side to side.

He just wanted to forget. But he knew better than most that life didn't give you what you wanted. It very rarely gave you what you had planned for either.

Forty-five minutes later, Alé approached the gate of

the studio and stopped short. The lock that normally was attached to the gate had been cut in two.

Stepping over broken glass, he forced his jaw to unclench. The drumming in his head was nothing compared to the simmer of anger in his gut.

Alé climbed the stairs, tentatively, eyes alert. He groaned when he noticed the missing stereo and sound system. The back room had been trashed — needlessly wrecked — cleaning equipment broken, coffee beans strewn on the floor, soggy toilet paper thrown everywhere.

He walked upstairs to his private studio. His shoes ground against shards of broken glass; the windows were smashed, the stench of broken beer bottles clung to the walls.

He swore a ripe litany of invectives. The painting he had been working on was strewn across the floor, ripped to pieces and defiled. Most of the pictures he had sketched were torn in the same fashion.

Alé's hands clenched and released. He tried to rein in his temper. The stolen equipment was a pain in the ass, but replaceable. The windows a mess, but repairable. What he wasn't going to get back was his painting.

It was one of the times when his hand had a mind of its own, when he painted without thinking.

He blinked back the red-hot anger that threatened to blind him completely. He wanted to rage. Instead, he fished his phone out of his pocket and rang the police.

Three hours later, the tattered pieces of his artwork - the ones he couldn't salvage — lay in the trash heap downstairs, along with the shards of glass. Temporary bags covered the upstairs windows, stuck together with masking tape until the window replacement crew sorted the job. Everything looked almost back to normal, except for the sharp smell of disinfectant, and the lack of equipment.

He was relieved that they hadn't smashed the mirrors, even if they did use his expensive paint and markers to tag its once shiny surface. The police had taken photos, believing it to be a local youth gang who had used similar tags in a textile factory last week. They were hoping CCTV footage could tell them more.

Alé sat on the floor and opened his laptop.

His head pounded. His schedule showed a hectic day of private lessons and all he wanted to do was crawl back to bed. Alé closed his eyes, wary of the dark emotions that hovered at the brink of his mind. No matter how far he ran, those ghosts never seemed far behind.

Ten minutes later he heard the clomp of feet on the stairs. Bracing himself, Alé stood.

With his past hanging like a monkey on his back, Alé squared his shoulders. He'd carry the weight of it for as long as he could. He had no other option.

Alé took long, greedy gulps from his water bottle, and wondered if there was a target sign stamped on his back. His last student had left, a particularly arrogant young dancer who insisted that Alé change *his* technique of all things.

He squeezed the bridge of his nose. He expected the performance group to arrive any minute.

Too late to cancel. Not that he ever would.

Stabbing fear pierced through his fatigue. He couldn't let this performance fail. He needed to prove to everyone that he was capable of success.

Weary after a long day, he succumbed to the memories, to a time when his life was different.

He lived for the adrenaline of competitions; the choreography, sore muscles and endless rounds of rehearsals. He had been training for that championship title and working three jobs to live his dream.

In a split second, it had ended.

Out of hands, out of his control.

He was lucky to be alive, let alone dance. Stupid to still bleed over a boy's dream.

He may have missed his chance at winning the *Mundial de Tango*, but he was damned if he was going to let this performance be anything but perfection.

Isabella's loud, boisterous laugh snapped him back to the present.

"*Hola*, Alé!"

He winced and helped her up the stairs.

"What's eating you?"

"Nothing."

"Alé, don't bullshit me. What's going on?"

Isabella glanced past him. Her eyes grew round in disbelief. The graffiti tags and broken windows were ugly reminders of what had happened.

"We had a break in last night. A youth gang stole the stereo and the equipment. It's a fucking mess. I've had back to back privates all day, and if I ever have to speak to the police or an insurance agent again..." he bit his clenched fist in gesture.

Her brown eyes softened. "Alejandro. I'm so sorry.

You should have called. We could have cancelled rehearsals."

"We're behind already, Isabella. Time is not on our side."

"Can I help?"

Alé shook his head, and grimaced. "Do you have aspirin?"

Isabella's eyes brightened. "I do. But this bag is like a cave. Give me a few minutes?" She hobbled over to the padded benches.

Voices travelled up the stairs. Alé glimpsed a flash of blonde hair and turned away.

It was like someone had punched him in the gut. Seeing her there, in the flesh, brought to light just how important the painting was to him. The loss of it, the savage tearing of its image, became all too real.

Alé couldn't handle this possessive need to protect her. Not when the past sat beside him, smug and critical.

Before anyone spoke to him, he grabbed two aspirin from Isabella and stalked over to the small kitchenette. He just needed a minute to breathe.

Whatever it was that drove him to paint Mathilda's heart-shaped face needed to be squashed. He wasn't going to think about her that way. *Dios*, the last time he saw her, he'd had his tongue down her throat. Kissing her in the bookstore proved that he couldn't trust himself around her.

He would focus solely on the performance. They didn't need any more complications.He turned at the sound of footsteps. Before he found the words, Mathilda spoke.

"Alé. Hi. Look, Izzy told us what happened. I'm so sorry." Mathilda soothed, squeezing his arm.

He took a side-step and nodded. "Yeah, thanks."

"Are you okay? Do you need anything?"

Alé folded his arms across his chest. "No. I'm fine. Really. Go back to warming up. We'll start soon," he responded, inching closer to the door.

"Isabella started already. We're warming up in partners. If you don't want to, I totally understand. Maybe we can meet up during the week to organise a rehearsal, just us?"

He shook his head.

"Alé, c'mon. Talk to me. It's good to get this stuff off your chest. Especially after what you must have gone through. Friends talk to one another."

"We're not friends, Mathilda. You're here to dance. To learn the routine. I'm not a child, I don't need to talk. Drop it, *si*?"

Alé felt the words grate against his tongue. He bit back the apology.

Mathilda stepped away. "Okay... I won't bother you then. I just — I guess I thought — I'll leave you alone."

Alé watched her leave. He ignored the sensation in his chest and joined the rehearsal. Isabella directed the group, keeping his input, thankfully, to a minimum.

When he gathered a stiff-backed Mathilda in his arms to practice, he kept his mind blank and any feelings buried deep. He all but ground his teeth together to silence the jumbled, incoherent thoughts that bounced around his brain.

When they finished rehearsals early, Mathilda left without so much as a goodbye. He welcomed the stinging sensation around his heart as punishment. It was better this way.

After listening to Isabella lecture him on his attitude, he mopped up the floor of the studio, then crawled upstairs to bed.

Alé needed sleep like an addict did their fix. Last night's nightmare still lingered in the dark corners of his mind. His body ached in response, but he no longer had the energy to fight it.

When his eyes grew heavy, he whispered a quiet word of thanks that the day was finally over.

There was little relief in his mind when he did.

CHAPTER TWELVE

The woman sat back against the leather seat of the luxury hire car and slipped her black Gucci glasses down the length of her nose. Eyes that burned with derision and disdain greedily absorbed the landscape before her. The street was paved with eager young bodies shouting and laughing. Melbourne's summer heat distorted everything it touched.

The woman flinched when the large metal vehicle obstructed her view. A tram rattled past; a funeral pyre packed with sweaty, foul-smelling bodies. She flicked away her disgust with a slender wrist; manicured nails flashed blood red against the hot glass. It was beneath her to be here. But as curious as her feline counterparts, she came anyway. If just to stare at the tall brick building that sat unobtrusively along the mismatched shop fronts.

It was only when the blonde woman ran out of the building, leaving the gate half open that she sat up straighter. She would have dismissed it, if she hadn't seen her there before. But she made it her job to be observant.

Piqued by this additional piece of information, her eyes glinted, and her body relaxed against the firm leather at her back.

She signalled to the driver to follow the car. Time to get to work and dig a little deeper.

Things were going exactly how she planned. There was no reason why that shouldn't continue.

She'd make sure of it.

Like all best laid plans, Tilda's went slightly awry.

She awoke Saturday morning, at first feeling ashamed, then slightly forlorn. The desire to sit in bed with a tub of Connoisseur ice-cream and a stack of trashy magazines was too tempting. The longer she remained in bed, the more appealing the idea became.

Determined not to wallow, she forced herself to get up and take a shower. She had barely begun to lather her hair when annoyance struck. By the time she dressed and made her first cup of coffee, she had worked her way up to truly pissed off. The hurt and confusion of the night before had transformed into a simmering anger, so much so that she didn't even wince when the first sip of coffee scalded her tongue. She embraced it.

Tilda had gone to the store to open for the day, leaving Dex in charge with Alicia. Both had sensed her mood and stayed clear. She'd have to pick them up something sweet when she returned in apology. She was never snappy with her staff. Which made her even angrier at Alé.

Her plan to go in and quit the performance group had

taken on a new hue. She would not only quit, she'd give him a piece of her mind. He had no right to speak to her that way and she'd make sure he damn well knew it. She reminded herself of this, repeating it several times on the driver over. She was furious by the time she arrived.

Tilda yanked at the noisy gate, the words jumping around in her brain, refusing to form coherent, expressive sentences. Her nerves bubbled to the surface. She had this. Words were her friend. He, apparently, was not.

She faltered when she reached the landing.

She hadn't expected Alé to be standing in the middle of the studio, mopping the floors. Her bold determination stalled. The words lodged in the back of her throat, clinging to her tongue. She had thought he'd be in the back office at least, or even upstairs.

Then he looked up.

Tilda wanted to ignore the dark circles under his eyes, the slump of his usually impeccable posture. She brushed aside the pained expression on his face and didn't even notice the stubble that marked his jaw.

She was certain she'd be happy that he didn't sleep well. Smug, even. She just needed to get rid of all that pity in her system. Any minute now. She'd totally —

He really did look dishevelled though.

Scaredy cat.

Tilda tilted her chin and gripped her handbag. She had wanted to start with a preamble. A zingy, memorable line that made him burn. But as well-read as she was, her tongue would not comply. So she got straight to the point.

"I quit."

Alé stopped mopping. He didn't move. His eyes never

strayed from her face. She repeated it, with greater force. Nothing. Tilda shrugged and turned to leave.

"Wait!" he rasped. His voice was gravelly and as discordant as his appearance.

Tilda faced him. "What?"

"Why are you quitting?" Alé placed the mop against the wall.

"I don't want to be a part of this performance group anymore." She injected venom in her words. "Actually no, let's be honest about it. I don't want to be dancing opposite you."

Alé rubbed his chin. Tilda ignored the fact that the stubble on his jaw only made him appear more dangerous, and compelling as hell. She was starting to understand what Cathy must have seen in Heathcliff.

"We should start from the beginning."

"No, Alé. We shouldn't. I've made up my mind. I don't want to be dancing with someone so rude. And I get that you had a lot to deal with last night, but I was trying to help you. I overstepped my boundaries. You made that abundantly clear."

"Mathilda —""Don't 'Mathilda' me!" Especially not in that sexy Spanish way that drives me a little crazy. Fool. "I'm in this group as a favour. And whilst it pains me to have to go back on my word, I don't appreciate working with someone who thinks they can speak to me that way. You run from hot to cold and I don't know what to make of it." She paced now. Anger simmered. "One minute I think we're friends, the next thing you tell me we aren't. One minute you're kissing me, the next second it's like that never happened and —"

"It was a mistake." Alé blurted, before she could continue.

Tilda's head whipped around to his and she stopped pacing. "A mistake?" Her mouth was painfully dry, her chest erratically fast. "That's what you're going to tell me?"

"The first time, we were both drinking —"

"Spare me." Tilda put her hands out, riding on the adrenaline. For a woman who hated confrontation, she was embracing the feeling of indignation far too well. "You kissed me and then didn't even have the balls to talk to me about it. Then you kiss me *again*, and apologise for it? Who does that? Don't kiss me in the first place if you don't mean it!" Her voice echoed across the studio, vibrating with anger. "You just pretended like none of it ever happened."

"I apologise."

Tilda growled.

"I take full responsibility for that."

The calmer and more rational he was, the angrier she became.

"What am I? A chore? To take responsibility of? I don't play games. In fact, I'm a pretty straightforward kind of girl. Do you get a kick out of kissing everyone you know? How many other students do you mess around with? Says a lot about you, doesn't it?" Derision lashed out in the open space between them. She wanted to wound him for making her hope for something more. That made her a fool.

Tilda's chest heaved with her barely restrained passion. It hadn't gone to plan. She didn't intend to even bring up the kiss, but it had been jumbled along with all the other words in her brain. It had been simmering away, beneath all her nonchalance.

"You know that's not true. Yes, I kissed you. I regret it, and should have said something after it, but we — I," he amended when she glared at him furiously. "You want the truth? I did it because I wanted to. We were in a moment. Like dancing. It doesn't have to mean anything."

Mathilda tried to channel the storm that swirled through her body. She cleared her throat.

"So the kiss was some weird aberration? You kiss me once, because you wanted to. You kissed me twice but that was a mistake. If that's the case, I don't want you kissing me again. I don't play games. Understand?"

"*Si. Claro.*"

Tilda paced back and forth. "Putting that aside, last night you behaved badly. Regardless of whether you think we're friends, or just acquaintances who exchange saliva every now and then, you don't treat me that way."

Alé winced. "I deserved that. Mathilda —"

"No, you listen to me, Alé. I get that we have had a working relationship, you're my dance teacher and I'm the student. But when we started working together on this performance, when you *asked* me to be a part of this, I believed — no I knew — that we were becoming more than just acquaintances."

Alé's shoulders hunched over.

Tilda stopped pacing. Her eye had caught sight of the ripped painting. She was overcome by a sense of familiarity. Ignoring Alé's protests she crouched down beside the papers, rifling through the images.

Some were small, barely the size of her hand,

sketched in pencil. Others were bigger, painted in colour. Understanding bloomed. Every single drawing, painting or sketch, were images of her.

"Mathilda, *por favor.*" Alé crouched down beside her, his eyes pleading. His voice raw.

She studied the different angles of her face; the colour of her eyes, the curve of her lip but —

"It's me. They're all of me."

He rubbed the back of his neck.

Tilda sat on her haunches, marvelling at the woman that stared back at her.

In resignation, Alé settled before her.

"You've taken some artistic license, Alé. You've made me look... well, beautiful." She could hear the awe in her voice. "I — I don't get it. Why?"

Alé drew a long-suffering sigh. "I don't control what I paint."

He looked at her now, and every nerve-ending tingled."Your face," he whispered. "I wanted to paint it. You've a very expressive mouth, Mathilda."

"And the colour of your eyes? Bright as the sky. But sometimes, like now, it changes — darkens." His eyes searched hers, unwavering. "I wanted to capture that. As a gift for taking on the performance. I wanted to give it to you in a few months, but..." he gestured helplessly.

"But they destroyed it." Tilda's shoulders sagged. The anger had shifted into something else. Something she couldn't quite place. But it wasn't unpleasant.

"It doesn't excuse how I spoke to you yesterday. I was angry and hurt. And out of line. I shouldn't have said those things."

"I thought it was just about the studio."

"No... not just the studio."

"Just goes to show you that I'm right. *Friend*."

Alé laughed. "And stubborn. I'm not used to being friends with my students."

Tilda's eyes narrowed. "Or just having friends? Someone to talk to?"

Alé's look said she was spot on.

"I'm going to forgive you for being so rude. But you've got to let your friends help you out. Now —" she held up her hands, "if you really don't want to be friends, then that's fine. But I won't be a part of this performance group if I'm not treated with respect. Is that clear?"

Alé felt exposed. Vulnerable. Two things he hated more than anything.

The panic he felt when she had first walked in had started to subside.

Maybe he could do friendship. They could be...buddies. Who was he kidding? He was already checking his ideas for the performance with her... she was a friend whether he liked it or not.

Mathilda was a woman who deserved his respect — hell, she already had it.

Here was this fierce woman, sitting before him, making him confront everything he thought he could brush aside. He respected her for it. Completely. Even if it made him want to run.

He didn't have to lose Mathilda just because he was attracted to her.

He wasn't eighteen and wide-eyed anymore. *Dios mío*, give him strength.

This attraction for her would pass. He had danced with many beautiful women. Mathilda would be no different.

"You're right," he said eventually. "Of course I want to be friends, and I think we should start fresh."

He fought not to squirm.

"Don't look at me that way. I mean it, Mathilda. I apologise for everything. I should have spoken to you about the kiss — kisses — but I —"

"Took the coward's way out?"

He rolled his tongue in his mouth. Swallowed his pride. He deserved that. "*Si*. I won't kiss you again. You have my word. We start fresh?"

"Apology accepted. Sorry for yelling at you."

Alé shrugged one shoulder. "Eh, I deserved it. You still want to dance with your *culo* friend?"

Mathilda's lips twitched. "Maybe not right now, but eventually. I won't leave the group. Although..."

"Spit it out."

"If you ever decide to paint another picture of me, I can't say I wouldn't mind."

"I'll see what I can do."

"But not before you start those sketches for the book nook, okay?"

"Right, boss." He saluted.

This time she laughed, shaking her head.

"Friends?" Alé held out his hand.

Mathilda looked down at his open palm and carefully placed hers in his grip.

"Friends," she agreed.

Alé ignored the bolt of electricity that seemed to pulsate from her slender hand to his groin.

He gave her his word that he wouldn't kiss her again. That they were friends.

His word was as good as gold. He'd keep his promise. Even if it killed him.

CHAPTER THIRTEEN

*I*n accordance with their truce, Alé decided it was time that he returned to The Book Nook.

Once the claim from the insurance company was processed, and the studio back in working order, Alé was keen to start the sketches for her store.

Through all the repairs, he thought of Mathilda, of their deal. The trouble was, now that they agreed to this friendship, all he could think about was the kiss.

It was better this way. He couldn't get tangled up romantically with anyone. Especially not Mathilda. He reminded himself of that as he entered the bookstore. What caught his eye was the brand-new upper level.

Patrick, for all his initial feelings towards the man, had ensured that the floors shone with polish. They had accented the Palladian windows by using a soft lilac on the walls and had added in a small staircase to complement the ramp.

A new banister ran along the upper section to

complete the look. It wouldn't be long before it was ready for customers.

Alé wandered the empty space, studying the design, then turned back to the main level to find Mathilda.

Eager children huddled in corners and amongst the shelves. Faces flushed, brows sweaty, they chatted loudly over their books.

It was more than just a bookstore. It offered something more than just a place to find the next adventure or fantasy, or even romance. It was family.

Mathilda offered that to the community. Because of it, the place had come alive.

A small cherub-faced two-year-old toddled up to him, offering him a book.

"Gosh, I'm terribly sorry," said the mother, who appeared to be no older than a schoolgirl herself.

Alé grinned. "No problem."

"Book! Book! Read 'Illy book!"

"Okay Jilly-bean, let's go read your storybook. Leave this gentleman alone."

Alé waved back at the little girl. He watched the mother guide her child to one of the low stools. The little girl dived into her lap and sat contentedly.

He could see — once furnished — how the upper level would enhance the comfortable atmosphere she created.

He was about to find Mathilda when the need to capture the sweet image of the mother and child took over.

He opened his folio and began sketching. He marvelled at the white-gold of the child's hair, one that would no doubt melt into her mother's honey-gold hue by the time she became a teenager.

When the mother pointed out interesting parts of the story, the child would babble excitedly. Alé's hand whipped across his sketchpad. The myriad of expressions compelled him to capture each in its entirety. The woman, whilst young, had the tired look of a parent who still didn't manage to conquer sleeping patterns.

When the little girl curled up even closer to her, and her big brown eyes began to droop, Alé knew he found the moment. All he could see were the lines and shades of his pencil, the glow between mother and child. It made him miss his *barrio* for a micro-second. No. Not his hometown. His family.

His hand worked feverishly to reflect the scene before him, before it was lost, before anyone disturbed its magic.

Alé focused on the details; the child's long lashes, the round curve of her cheek, the hands of mother and child entwined. The tenderness at which the woman smiled down at her daughter had his own mouth curving.

Alé was so wrapped up in the sketch, that he didn't pay attention to the yearning in his chest, or the joy that accompanied it.

Tilda was helping Mrs. Carrington find 'The Idiot's Guide to Social Media' when she spotted him leaning against the pillar, sketching.

Ignoring the jolt of pleasure, she followed his line of sight. The young mother and sleeping child captivated his attention. His hand flew across the page. She stopped herself from approaching and forced herself back to the front counter.

It was nice to see some of the local primary school kids whom she read to come inside and browse. Even if they didn't exactly purchase anything.

She brushed aside the lead weight in her gut. So what if they had a slow start to sales this month? It didn't mean anything. It would pick up again. She had the loan from the bank which she was able to repay - just. She had counted on being done with most of the basic construction by now, but she could manage for the time being. It wasn't an issue. Yet.

With rehearsals preoccupying her time, she hadn't quite gotten around to organising a date for the launch. She needed the store complete before she did. She had to drum up business, even though she knew customers didn't like coming in when it was still under construction.

Her gaze flew back to her friend. That's strictly what they were now. Sure, it was healthy and normal to find Alé attractive. She wasn't blind after all. But she had cut short any silly fantasies that had somehow managed to take hold prior to their truce.

All was great! All was fine! All was —

"What *are* you staring at?" Dex whispered conspiratorially in her ear. He slung his arm around her shoulders. "Oh, I *see*," he drawled, before she could open her mouth. "Well honey, who wouldn't?"

Tilda rolled her eyes and served a customer.

She heard an effusive squeal and looked up. Alé had shown the young mother his sketch. She had one hand against her chest, the other holding her now sleeping toddler.

She waved off the customer and focused on the pile of books on the counter. She was on dangerous ground.

Alé made it very clear that kissing her was an aberration. She had a healthy dose of bruised pride because of it, but it would pass. Elizabeth Bennet had been through worse. Not that she was comparing Alé to her fictional husband, Mr. Darcy. Tilda bit her lip.

It's not like Darcy stuck his tongue down Eliza's throat a couple of times and flounced off like it meant next to nothing. That was more of a Wickham move.

Tilda shook her head. She *had* to stop giving way to fantasies. It wasn't normal. At her age, it was borderline sad.

The whole thing was a timely reminder that she liked her life as it was; she was in control of it and had no desire to change that. She had somehow let herself lose sight of that along the way.

They were just beginning to establish their friendship. Tilda wouldn't jeopardise that for the world.

No matter how much Alé made her yearn.

"You look confused," Alé commented ten minutes later.

After saying goodbye to the mother and child, he found Mathilda behind the counter, staring at a range of new release children's books. She gnawed at her lip — a detail he would ignore — and looked at the splayed books with despair.

"I used to be able to pick out what book would feature as the book of the week when gran was around just like that," she said, with a snap of her fingers. "As

I've gotten older, it's getting harder and harder to decide."

"That's why I'm here. Sorry about earlier. I got distracted."

"Yes, I noticed. Hard to stop when the inspiration takes hold, huh?"

"Exactly."

He felt the inspiration at this minute to capture her perched in the sunlight, a slight frown creasing her brow, her lip pouting in annoyance.

Those lips of hers would be the death of him.

Alé shifted his focus back to the books. "Maybe brainstorm some ideas with some of the kids in the store? Hey, what about the community calendar? There might be some festivals coming up that might influence which book you display?"

"That's a fantastic idea, Alé! Absolutely perfect." Mathilda's face lit up.

"What's absolutely perfect?" Dex walked to the counter. "Y'all wouldn't be talking about me, would you?" He smiled sweetly.

Mathilda repeated the idea.

"That does sound great."

"I have my moments."

"Oh I bet you do, sugar," Dex hummed.

Alé laughed, finding Dex's candid quips amusing more than anything else. He was Mathilda's 'right-hand man' and from what he had seen, great at connecting with customers.

At Mathilda's pointed look, Dex got out the tablet. "Let me see what I can find."

A minute later he was smiling in satisfaction. "Well,

whaddya know folks. It's International Friendship Month! How perfect is that?" Dex grinned.

Alé's mouth twitched. He tried not to laugh at the irony.

Perfect indeed.

In honour of International Friendship Month, Alé volunteered to help Mathilda with her social media campaign to drum up more business. He had done it all before when he opened the studio, so it made sense that he offered his advice.

They had already decided on the image — more a collage of characters — that he had used in his sketch for her website. He had altered it slightly for the Instagram and Twitter audience to keep it fresh.

When Mathilda had mentioned sales weren't great because of the renovation, he suggested she run pamphlets with a few of his sketches included to draw in more customers.

So what if that meant he spent the next week working late to get the pictures just right? Or that he offered to take the design to the local printer he used for his own business? It was all in the name of friendship.

He had added a little owl with a miniature book at the bottom of The Book Nook lettering, a logo he thought might suit the store. When those big blue eyes had beamed with excitement, he knew he had made the right choice.

When she rocked up on Friday night for rehearsals,

fatigue written all over her body, he naturally offered to help her deliver the pamphlets on the weekend.

This friendship business was easy. He hadn't thought about touching her once today. Or the way her lips had him wanting to devour every inch of her. Or the way her tongue...

Alé knocked on Mathilda's front door, trying desperately to ignore the back spasms that had plagued him all week. Even the strength training at the gym didn't alleviate his pain. A timely reminder for his overheated brain. He had too much to lose to give in to temptation.

"Hi! Sorry, been a mad morning." Mathilda opened the door, bright and sunny in an orange summer dress. He didn't notice the way it clung to her breasts or brushed against her thighs.

Dios, those legs...

"Come on in while I get some sunscreen on. Can't be too careful with this pasty skin."

Alé gestured to the simply furnished, but colourful lounge room. "Take your time. I'll wait in here." It would give him a chance to cool his over-heated brain.

He wandered the small space taking in its detail. Anything to re-direct his thoughts.

Polished floorboards, rich and dark contrasted with the sunny pale yellow of the room. The large L shaped sofa in the corner had a patterned throw on it, whilst a table of dark oak sat across from the small open fireplace, now bathed in sunlight.

Just like the store, Mathilda's home was one of comfort.

Alé smiled at the picture on the mantel piece. He assumed that the bubbly little blonde girl was Mathilda, sitting on her grandmother's lap. She had a toothless grin and was pointing to something in the book.

It was a picture he wanted to capture. The merry eyes of her grandmother and the abandoned, carefree happiness of the little girl, safe in her world.

"That was me and gran when I was four. I lost my tooth only the day before and I was very impressed with myself."

Alé shifted when she stood next to him, her sunscreen and perfume teasingly floral and beachy. He focused on the picture.

"You both look really happy. I can feel it."

"We were." She frowned. "But that was a very long time ago."

"I didn't mean to —"

"No, no, it's fine. You didn't. It's been a while since we lost her, but sometimes grief hits you hard. Steals your breath away, you know?"

"Yeah, actually. I do." Alé looked back at the photo and noticed another one behind it. On impulse he picked it up. A sunny one-year-old baby was in the arms of two glowing parents. A first birthday cake in front of them.

"My parents." The expression on her face made him curse. He wished he hadn't picked it up. Her sky-blue eyes were distant, her mouth formed a thin line.

"I should stop."

"Don't be silly. It's a good memory, even if I can't recall it. Or them much... they died in a plane accident when I was just coming upon my sixth birthday. They were coming back from a ballroom dancing competition — they were fierce competitors — I wasn't old enough to really understand what it all meant. Then I went to live with my grandmother." Her voice wobbled.

Alé drew her to him. He held her, wanting to take the pain. He pulled back and tilted her chin. "*Estas bien?*"

Mathilda's smile faltered. "Sorry. Yes, I am. What a terrible way to start the day." She shook her head and wiped at her eyes.

"It's not terrible at all. Look outside." He turned her around. "The sun is shining, the birds are singing, and we are going out to be paper pushers!" He said in mock enthusiasm.

It surprised a laugh out of her.

"Slave labour, you mean. And you don't even get a wage."

Alé clutched his heart as if wounded. "I'll find some way to get you back."

"More rehearsals I'm sure." She turned and picked up the bag of pamphlets.

Alé caught a flash of thigh.

Images of Mathilda, legs wrapped around him, begging for him to pleasure her, came to mind.

Following her out of the house, he wondered at her reaction if he told her the kind of repayment he had in mind.

He didn't dare find out.

Hours later, Alé and Tilda sat outside Betty's Cone and Cup eating their double waffle cones. On the house, Betty insisted when she caught sight of their red faces.

"What's the rainbow like?" Alé asked. "That's a lot of colours."

Tilda looked at him aghast. "You've never had rainbow ice-cream before?"

He looked at her like she was an alien species. "No, is it an Aussie thing?"

"It's a childhood thing. Here —" she thrust her cone at him. "Swap."

Alé took one tentative lick then grinned. "This is mine now."

Tilda was happily enjoying her cone and didn't see the warning glint in his eyes.

"Swap again?"

She turned towards him and straight into a face full of rainbow flavoured ice cream.

In shocked retaliation she brandished her cone like a sword, marking his face with cookies and cream, laughing demonically.

For a few seconds no one moved. Alé lunged towards her. Tilda sprang up from the curb, squealing. They laughed hysterically chasing each other up and down the sidewalk, covered in ice cream. Curious residents and children looked on in amusement or disapproval, depending on the age.

Breathless and slightly winded, they called a truce back outside Betty's Cone and Cup, only to be met with Betty's stern disapproval. She stood over their collapsed forms.

"Ice-cream is meant to be eaten, not worn." Her warning did nothing to appease their laughter.

She threw her hands up and left, only to return moments later with George and a bucket in tow.

Before Alé and Tilda could react, the chilly water doused them both.

"Who's laughing now, ey?" George guffawed.

They could only sputter in shock.

With the white flag raised, they walked home an hour later, still damp.

Alé's stomach was aching. He couldn't remember the last time he had laughed so hard. "I had a lot of fun today."

"Me too. I forgot how sneaky and underhanded George and Betty can be sometimes."

"Thick as thieves." He smiled across at her, eyes warm with affection.

"When my gran was alive, the three of them were inseparable."

"What was she like? Your grandmother?"

"She was amazing. My everything, really. I have only faint memories of my parents. My mother's perfume, my father's laugh. But they became strangers to me when I was growing up. I know that sounds terrible, but I didn't know any better."

"Not terrible. They were gone. She was there."

"Yes. I never thought of it like that before. I just felt guilt that maybe I hadn't loved them properly, but you're right. Anyway, my gran raised me in that really fearless way of hers. She was never afraid of a challenge. No matter how difficult it was to lose her husband, then her only child. Even when her health started to take a turn for the worse, she would never wallow."

Alé squeezed her hand.

"She always said, you get dust on cheek if you lie down too long, Tilly. I used to cry so many things as a child. My grandmother would remind me that tears were important but crying over aspects of life that you couldn't change was a waste of energy."

"Wise woman."

"Very. I looked up to her so much, everyone in the community did. Wherever we went, I was Ethel's granddaughter. It made me proud. But also afraid. Big shoes to fill and all that."

"And responsibility that came with it, *no*?"

Mathilda shrugged. "I guess so. I never saw it that way. Not really. I would have done anything to make her proud. She encouraged me when I wanted to stay inside my turtle shell. I really want to prove that I can do this on my own, to make it work. I want to make her proud."

"If George and Betty have anything to say about it, your gran would be 'mighty proud,'" he said, putting on a broad Australian accent.

Mathilda's laugh was so light-hearted that Alé had to stop himself from holding her close.

"Thanks, Alé. I appreciate it."

"Hey? What are friends for, right?"

Alé walked through the front door of his apartment later that evening. It took him less than thirty seconds to accept that he was restless. It took half that to unlock his phone and find Mathilda's number. He had an overwhelming urge to call her and ask if she wanted to finish their fun day with dinner and a movie.

What the hell?

He couldn't call her. They'd spent an amazing day

together. As friends. Calling her now would be a stupid move. Especially when he wanted nothing more than to fill his hands and mouth with that hot-as-hell body of hers.

Dios Mio.

It was all his fault.

He had opened Pandora's box in the first place, and here he was, when things were cruising along, trying to screw it up again.

Idiot.

So what if he'd noticed her that way? He was a red-blooded male after all, wasn't he? She was a beautiful woman. Many of his old friends back in Buenos Aires wouldn't have thought twice before kissing her again.

But it wasn't simple like that. Some part of Alé — the annoying and smug part — told him that kissing her again would change everything. He had made a promise to her. He would keep it.

He paced back and forth in the hall, calculating the time difference in Buenos Aires. He cursed. It was the last place on earth he wanted to feel connected to right now.

He needed to get out of the house.

He'd go for a drive, cool his head, maybe even go to the beach. It was still warm. Anything to get him moving again. Anything to stop him thinking about her.

Alé's hands hovered over his car keys. Better to walk it off when he was this distracted.

Some fresh air would be exactly what he needed to clear his head... and any other part of his over-heated anatomy.

CHAPTER FOURTEEN

*A*lé glared at his computer screen.

Camila Morales and her partner, Alberto Lopez were in a stage-esque pose. She had her back to the camera, one that was barely covered by the thin red straps of what could — technically — be called a dress. Her long, shapely leg draped across his torso, while his hand splayed across her exposed thigh.

Camila's upper body twisted slightly so that she looked over her shoulder, face set in a sultry pose; her trademark Tango-cool expression. The image screamed sex and lust.

Gritting his teeth against the nausea, Alé closed his eyes. The image still lingered as if etched on his retinas. Mocking him. Infuriating him.

He forced his eyes open to stare at the image of his ex-girlfriend. He had hoped he'd never have to see her again.

He studied the picture. Camila almost appeared

elegant. Almost. There was something artificial about her face now. He supposed it matched her personality.

Alberto was encased in black; his suit unbuttoned so her hand rested against his bare chest. His face, almost in profile, looked down at her.

Blazoned across the image were their names, beneath it a biography of their dancing careers.

Alé read hers and laughed bitterly. The line mocked him.

With a difficult start to her career, Camila Morales found fame after coming runner up in the 'El Mundial de Tango' finals of 2006. Her career took off when she met and danced with Alberto Lopez, of 'Dance to Win' fame. "If I hadn't found Albie, who knows where I would be? Connection is everything, and this is why I want to teach others the art of the embrace."

Alé snorted and shoved away from the laptop. The connection? The embrace? The only thing Camila cared about was flashy moves. She went to classes on *adornos*, learning pretty footwork that she'd mimic from the greats, but never learned to lead. She only cared about what her dancing looked like in the mirror. By the time of the accident, any attempt at choreography that wasn't 'show tango' was dismissed.

Her desire to dance only certain routines, for the benefit of the judges, left him creatively empty and emotionally exhausted. Camila had always been greedy for success. It didn't matter who she hurt along the way, as long as she got what she wanted.

Alé's mouth twisted in disdain. It hadn't taken very long for her to hurt him in the deepest way possible. When he was at his worst, his weakest, she danced right over him, intent on making herself a star.

He wasn't sure what hurt the most. The fact that she abandoned him as his girlfriend or as his dance partner. It didn't take long for her to find someone else to perform with — someone whole.

But he had learned to walk again, and eventually, to dance. His mouth twisted. Sure, he had lost many 'friends' along the way. Nobody wanted to nurse a cripple. One who had nothing to offer them but his pain.

He had been blinded. By her, his own ambition.

Eat. Teach. Train.

He gave up that life long ago. Hell, it was more than a decade since his accident. He wouldn't allow the past to swallow him whole like a viper. He had moved on.

Focusing on the glowing screen, Alé scrolled through the email, clicking on the link.

PRE-NEW ZEALAND TANGO FESTIVAL MINI SHOWCASE the banner screamed. He stopped at the picture of Camilla with Alberto. *Our lucky New Zealanders get the chance to participate in a two-day pre-festival workshop with Camila Morales and Alberto Lopez - El Mundial de Tango runners up from Argentina. They will be available for private lessons throughout the duration of the tango festival for those unable to attend workshops.*

Whilst New Zealand was another country away, it was too close for comfort where Camila was concerned. The tango community was ridiculously small.

The last time he saw her was before Mundial. 2006. Alé shook his head; some things just never change.

He was man enough to admit that at times the dream he had failed to achieve still plagued him. But when he thought about his old life in Buenos Aires, it was like he was watching a film; like it had happened to someone else. That he was someone else. Almost.

Alé had made a concerted effort after the accident to make a positive change in his life. He did. Despite what doctors had told him, he was his own boss again. Alé decided he would deal with the situation — if there would be a situation — when the time came. For now, he would focus on what mattered. His work.

A blonde-haired, blue eyed goddess swam in to focus. Alé's shoulders lowered. Heat replaced the icy frost that had settled on his chest. His body began to thaw.

He needed to paint.

More than anything at that moment, Alé needed to lose himself in the face of a woman he had no business wanting. He reminded himself that he was his own boss.

He'd do as he damn well pleased.

CHAPTER FIFTEEN

*S*ince his accident, Alé had come to accept many things about himself that he didn't like and probably couldn't change. Beneath the jagged silvery scars, he was a stubborn, demanding and often moody man; and those were some of his finer qualities.

Accepting that he was the world's biggest idiot was still a bitter pill to swallow.

He had suggested to the performance group that they all go out for a night of social tango dancing. What compelled him, he couldn't say, but he knew it had been a long time since he wanted to go to a *milonga*.

Instead of questioning it, he dusted off his sharp single-breasted blue suit, unearthed his finest tango shoes and left the house before he could change his mind.

Standing outside the abandoned church, Alé realised with some surprise that he was nervous. It had been a stupid idea to come tonight, but he wouldn't walk away now. The rhythmic pulse of Di Sarli reverberated through the abandoned church and rang out into the night air. Alé felt the knots loosen in his gut.

The cicada's' shrilling echo contrasted to the lure of the *bandoneon*, the sobbing violin. There was an essential part of him that would always be drawn to the dark, sensual enticement of that world, but he knew now there were limits.

He had tried to give up dancing. For a short time, he did; the very sound of a *bandoneon* or violin would set his teeth on edge. Which was why he left Buenos Aires as soon as he had been able to walk again. Out of physical therapy and on to a plane.

Those years he spent travelling around the world, teaching Spanish and working odd jobs was exactly what he had needed to feel whole again. All he had wanted was a meal in his belly and shelter over his head. And to never dance again.

But it had been in Ireland — of all places — in a small local pub off the coast of the Atlantic sea that he felt something shift inside him.

Watching an assorted bunch of girls and boys dancing an impromptu jig in celebration and lament of their loved one's death had been odd at first. It wasn't until the barman had explained their tradition that Alé understood that heartache and joy could sit side by side.

It had taken a stranger in a far-off land to tell him something he had always known. Life, like tango, was more than just pursuing one's passion. It was about living with those bittersweet emotions, of pain and loss and joy all woven together and still taking that next step forward.

At that moment he knew he couldn't run away from his feelings, or his livelihood. At that moment he understood what he wanted to do with his life. It hadn't taken him long after that to begin again.

As the past melted into the inky night, Alé stepped through the crescent shaped door. He wouldn't ever be able to leave tango again. It was in his blood, *that* he knew for certain.

He embraced this new-found sense of freedom in coming out tonight. He would be with his performance group, see his friends, and enjoy himself.

The past be damned.

Tonight was for tango.

Mathilda's senses were on red alert. Try as she might, she couldn't stop the jolt of attraction that lightning bolted through her when Alé walked in. He was dressed in a bold blue suit and crisp white shirt. It only accentuated the gold of his Argentinian skin.

Before he had even made it up to their table, Alé had been swamped by *milongueros*. He was a respected teacher in the community, and his fellow teachers never pressured him to attend *milongas*, even if they did speculate about his past behind his back.

Tilda saw Henri, the organiser of the *milonga* greet him. Henri was a big, tall man — imposing to many women who started dancing socially; he had hands the size of a butcher, and the stature of a mini giant. He grabbed Alé in a bear hug, and his booming laughter carried over the music. Tilda had danced with him on occasion. Henri made an effort to dance with all the women who attended his *milongas* as a courtesy.

The memory lingered on her body. Her mouth curved

in good humour. His hands had dwarfed her own and she had been so fearful that he would half drag, half stomp his way through the *tanda* with her.

Yet he had been surprisingly gentle. Strong and very skilled, but by no means crowding or aggressive in his hold. For a large man, he had a very comforting embrace. Granted, she found it disconcerting when she couldn't rest her temple against his, or look out over his shoulder, but after an awkward minute of the first piece in the *tanda*, she felt surprisingly at ease.

The hall, whilst moderately sized, was filling up fast. Members of their performance group trickled in. Tilda waved them over.

Even though it was an old venue, it had been well-tended by Henri and his group of tango volunteers. It was always a challenge to be able to find a space that had good floors and a nice atmosphere to match. Dancers flocked like bees to honey when he ran his monthly *milongas*.

"*Hola milongeuras*, you all look beautiful," Alé called out as he approached. "*Milongueros*." He nodded to some of the men.

"It's a real buzz tonight, isn't it?" Sara looked around at the growing crowd.

Alé sat across from Tilda. "*Si*. I'm glad we were able to reserve a table. Henri was a hard man to convince. It's easier in Argentina. The door bitch at *El Beso* tells you where to go! Here it's more relaxed."

"*Hola seniorita!*" Tilda heard the familiar voice behind her.

"Izzy, hey!" Tilda pulled out a chair. "What in the world are you doing here though? You're still not able to dance." Tilda gestured to the massive moon boot that encased her dainty leg. Isabella had tied a colourful silk scarf around it to match her yellow dress.

Isabella waved a careless hand. "I'd rather be sitting in a *milonga* than wallowing in my bed at home. Anyway, it means I get to talk to you."

"Not so fast, Isabella." Alé cut in, moving around the table. "I hear a *milonga* calling and I think it has Mathilda's name on it." He raised a dark eyebrow and tilted his head to the dance floor in a blatant *cabeceo*. "*Bailar conmigo?*"

Tilda's eyes rounded in surprise. She didn't think Alé would ask her to dance, especially not a *milonga*. First dances were usually reserved for partners, or close friends. Dancing a *milonga* set was risky. It was a quicker form of tango, that ranged from manageable to manic in degrees, depending on the music.

Whilst Tilda enjoyed dancing it, she was always so conscious of the fact that she wasn't as good a *milonga* dancer as she would have liked. She was much more comfortable dancing tango or vals.

She took Alé's outstretched hand. "I'm warning you that I suck at dancing *milonga*."

"That's a lie, Mathilda Landrey. No one sucks when it's Canaro. Follow the beat, let it be your guide."

Tilda shook her head. "You, my friend are deluded."

They walked hand in hand to the large dance floor. She settled into his embrace and felt, rather than saw the eager eyes assessing them. After all, it wasn't every day that Alé frequented *milongas*. His presence no doubt left tango tongues wagging.

"Let's give them something to talk about, *no?*"

Alé's arm circled around her back and held her close. The jaunty rhythm of Canaro's '*Criolla*' rang through the bottom of the church hall.

Alé danced the main beat, leading Tilda in a melodious quick-stepped walk. Her breath caught in her throat.

"Take your time," he soothed, cutting off her hasty apology when she faltered.

She stretched up, elongated her spine and relaxed her shoulders. He led her in small, petite steps, as indicated by the music. Roberto Maida's smooth, dulcet tones rang out, the violins moved up and down its playful scale and Tilda couldn't help but smile.

He lowered them both, by degrees down into a well-executed butt wiggle that had their table laughing.

Alé's voice rang low, accompanying Roberto Maida.

Her knowledge of Spanish was rudimentary at best, and she could only make out snatches of the words "heart" and "milonga".

The next song followed in quick succession. It seemed it was a Canaro *tanda* and the DJ, Dario was true to form, playing a song faster than the one previous.

Tilda wanted to murder him when the violins jovially bounced across the hall in their exuberance. Alé laughed at the look on her face.

"*Vamos,* tango girl."

He propelled her backwards in a series of *cunidas* followed by *seguidillas*, the movement so fast she didn't have time to think. Before she knew it, the song had finished; they were breathless and smiling.

When Canaro's '*La Milonga de Buenos Aires*' played as

the last in the *tanda*, Tilda nearly walked off the dance floor.

She laughed when Alé tightened his hold. He shifted his weight from left to right, his feet setting the rhythm.

Her heart thudded, not only from exertion, but the luxurious feeling of his body nestled closely to hers. He was warm, strong, and so appealingly male, that she didn't want him to let go. Tilda was painfully aware of her breasts crushed against his chest, how the sensation made her mouth dry.

The violins flew once more in jaunty celebration. It heralded the sweeter sound of Ernesto Fama and his spit fire barrage of lyrics.

Tilda closed her eyes and let her feet fly. The other couples whirled around the *ronda* in fevered appreciation of the music, many desperate to keep in time to the rhythm. She once or twice included a rushed *adorno*, a playful trill with her foot; she knew with Alé leading her that she was able to execute anything.

She felt his heart thudding in syncopation with her own.

Her whole body was alive, music throbbed in her veins; on a laugh, she let herself go.

Alé guided her back across the floor once the *tanda* had finished.

"What were you singing — to the first song in the tanda — Canaro's '*Criolla*'?"

"Ah." He smiled. "It roughly translates to something like romance with a man can be...uhh..."

"Difficult?"

"Si — *complicado*. Tricky." Alé stopped at their table.

"Oh."

"But," he added, pulling out her chair, his eyes locked on hers. "The feeling will vanish when they dance, *corazon a corazon* — heart to heart — to a *milonga*."

Tilda swallowed. The liquid fire that seemed to ignite her senses when she danced with him had been hard to resist. Alé's tawny eyes caressed her face. She told herself not to read into any of it.

Alé cleared his throat and gestured to the vacant chair. She sat, on shaky legs.

"It's one of my favourite lines of the piece. Tango is passion, as it should be, Mathilda."

"Mmm."

He inclined his head. "*Muchas gracias* for the dance."

"Of course," she mumbled, reaching for the glass of water on the table.

She looked across at Isabella's raised eyebrow and small smile. Fire burned her cheeks, but before she could fumble around in her bag for a fan, she was approached by another gentleman, his *cabeceo* a silent invitation to dance the next *tanda*.

Tilda nodded her head in acceptance, grateful for a chance to escape Isabella's very pointed look.

She took the older man's hand, but her senses were still besieged by Alé's touch.

An hour and a half later, Alé sat down with a contented sigh. He fished a small face towel out of his bag, wiping his forehead, slightly damp with sweat. It was largely his fault. He had danced with many lovely *tangueras*, ranging from novice to advanced, not to mention all the women in his performance group. When the twinge in his back began to pester him, he begrudgingly conceded defeat.

His eyes sought out a familiar blonde head in a striking blue dress amongst the crowd. It hadn't escaped his attention that Mathilda barely had a chance to sit down this evening as well. He had intended to grab her for another dance, but ol' Charlie had beaten him to it. As the man had been close to 80, Alé hadn't protested. Verbally.

She now twirled with a man in a *vals*, a man he noted, who looked no older than a boy. His gut clenched. The last time he gave in to his instincts he had Tilda pressed up against a door, his tongue in her mouth.

He greedily devoured the sight before him. In particular, the way her dress fit snugly around her butt. He reached for his water. Alé's eyes travelled down those slender legs, and he had to stop himself from wincing at her shoes. Those stems of hers needed six inches to show off that lean muscle and dainty ankle. Her ugly black heels weren't fit for such a *milonguera*. Despite them, she moved with such presence and joy. Did she know that of herself?

His eyes narrowed when the boy's hands slid to her lower back. Watch it, buddy. The boy grimaced a moment later. Tilda's leg *gancho'd* a little off aim, kicking between his opened legs. Alé smiled, knowing that as she didn't apologise, she was very much aware of the boy's wandering hands.

Dancing with her socially was a pleasure, and watching her dance was even more arresting. Her footwork was careful, at times elegant. He hadn't felt this way about dancing with someone since —

Alé sat up. He refused to go there. It was enough that he was coming to a *milonga*, he didn't need his ugly memories sitting at the same damn table too. This was different. Mathilda was... something else.

So what if he noticed her tonight? No one could blame him for it. It was natural to be caught up by a beautiful woman. His lips thinned. And problematic.

He would ignore the sizzle. Ignore the sheer lust that had his body burning. It had been that way for him the very first moment she had walked in the studio. She looked hungry for knowledge and eager to learn. Her tango was already exceptionally good, so he had moved her up to the advanced class after a few weeks of intermediate, despite her protests.

She wrapped her leg in another *gancho* and Alé had to look away at the flash of thigh.

"Uncomfortable already, Alé?" Isabella taunted. She sat down next to him at the empty table, a plate of fruit balanced in her hand.

"Not at all Isabella, just settling in actually."

"Mmm, I bet. Enjoying the view?"

He dragged his gaze away.

"Very good dancers here tonight," he agreed, taking a sip and setting his cup down carefully.

"Especially a particular blonde in a blue dress, wouldn't you say?"

"I don't know what you mean."

Isabella scoffed. "Oh, come on, Alé. Any idiot who has eyes can see you can't seem to take yours off your dance partner tonight. Not that I blame you. All that gorgeous porcelain skin, stunning features. You'd be dead not to notice."

Alé breathed in deeply. "Your point being?"

"Why don't you make a move, stupid?"

"Mathilda and I are friends. That's all. I can appreciate that she is a beautiful woman without having to pounce on her."

"Who said anything about pounce? I'm just talking about dating. Ya know. That thing that people do. With people that they like?"

Alé spared her a dry look. "As I said, Mathilda and I are friends. No more."

"Alé, when was the last time you liked a woman?"

"I like plenty of women. I liked you before you became annoying."

"Ah huh. When was the last time you liked a woman enough to go out on a date with them?"

"I took your advice with that friend of yours, Melissa."

"That was ages ago. And you made it very clear she was in the 'friend zone.'"

"*Dios mío*, Isabella, what is this? The Spanish Inquisition?"

"Worse. Your dating life."

Alé sighed and sat back in his seat. He stopped his eyes from wandering to the dance floor. The fact that he struggled to do so fired his temper.

"What do you know about my dating life? I'm taking it slow. What's wrong with that?"

"Normally it wouldn't be an issue. But you're slower than a tortoise."

"So?" He hated the defensive tone in his voice.

"So? Alé, you are a young, hot, successful man. You should be in a relationship."

He waved off the suggestion. "I don't have time for a relationship." She was worse than his mother.

"Bullshit. You make time."

Alé crossed his arms.

"Look, all I'm saying is be a bit more open. If not with Tilda, then maybe someone else. I have this friend... she's gorgeous."

"Isabella." His tone was warning enough.

"I'll give you her number. Just go out on a date. What could it hurt?"

"Will it get you off my back?"

"Yes! You know what they say, practice makes perfect."

"What?"

"Just promise that you'll call her, okay? Shake on it?"

Alé took Isabella's hand, ignoring her triumphant grin.

People went on dates all the time, right? This was no big deal. It meant nothing.

His eyes wandered back across the dance floor, to the mesmerising woman in blue silk.

He told himself it was for the best; that it was time to dip his toe in the water again. It'd be no big deal.

So why the hell did he feel like he was drowning?

CHAPTER SIXTEEN

*T*ilda checked her phone. For the tenth time that morning. She scowled when the door opened and tried to focus on her work. "Well hello to you too, sour puss." Dex set her coffee down on the table.

"I'm not a sour puss."

"Well you could have fooled me. You're annoyed. No... that's not it." He narrowed his eyes. "Restless."

"You, dear Dex, have been reading too many crime novels."

"Mhmm. Spill then. Why did you look annoyed when I just walked in, oh boss of mine?"

Tilda huffed, miffed that he could read her so well. "It's nothing. Just planning the day ahead."

"Uh-huh." He sipped his coffee, waiting.

"It's just that he didn't give a time! Who doesn't give a time these days? I'm busy..."

"He?"

"Alé."

146

"Ohhhh." He drew out the vowel with a knowing look.

"Don't 'ohhh' me. And what's that supposed to mean anyway?" She motioned to the sly look on his face.

"Oh, just the sexy Argentinian is bugging you, that's all. Getting under your skin, dare I say."

"For pity's sake Dex, does your mind ever get out of the gutter?"

"Rarely. But when it does it's only to get under the covers. Eight hundred thread count, satin if I can manage it." He wriggled his eyebrows.

Tilda shook her head and laughed. Dex always knew how to cheer her up. She was more than grateful that she could talk to him. Even if he did irritate her sometimes.

"All I'm saying is, that man is easy on the eye."

"And all I'm saying is, I prefer to know specific times, so I can figure out my schedule for the day."

"Planning, shmanning. Just go with the flow. And go put on some lipstick. Would it kill you to tart yourself up?"

"Be gone." Tilda banished him to the storeroom so she could focus on her social media updates. By the time the store opened, she had finalised her orders and reviewed a few more books for Story Time.

One set of bookshelves would be going up today — fingers crossed — and she still needed to pay Patrick before the rest of the work could be completed.

He'd been lenient of late, but she didn't know how long that would last. So what if she'd been late on her loan repayment? She managed to get by this fortnight. Tilda gnawed on her lip, she'd find some way to pay Patrick. If the social media strategy worked, she'd be getting more business in, which meant more money. She just had to pray it would be enough.

Tilda was busy serving Dotty, their local florist when Alé walked through the door an hour later.

"Morning Alé!" Dex waved him over to the counter, nudging Tilda.

"*Buenos dias*." He smiled, waving the bag. "I brought some pastry. Brain food."

"You are a God," Dex cheered. "I could do with something carby."

"I was talking to Mathilda." Alé smiled apologetically.

"What's hers is mine, my good man." Dex handed Dotty her receipt. "I'll wheedle it out of this one eventually."

"Good morning, young man. And who may you be?"

Alé put down the food. "I'm Alé, Mathilda's friend."

"Friend?" Dotty winked at him. "A fine man like you, and a beautiful woman like her?" She let go of his hand only to wave hers about. The colourful bangles at her wrist danced down one wrinkled arm. Dotty didn't allow age to diminish her presence. At 'perpetually sixty' Dotty still wore vivid swathes of colour to match her bold make-up and jewellery. Black wasn't a colour in her opinion and shouldn't be worn.

"Dotty," Tilda explained. "He's my tango teacher. He's also the man who sketched those images from our pamphlets — the ones you've been admiring. Alé, this is Dotty Freedman, she's our florist across the road."

Dotty's eyes lit up. "Oooh. Tango. Just the thing needed for our community centre. I've been telling them that dance is the best way to keep young and active. And alive. Do you have a card?" Her bangles clashed in protest. "Never you mind. I'll get my helpers to ask Google, hey?" She winked. "Well, now. The whole town has been talking about Tilda's pamphlets. I could use something similar for the store. You come by and visit the shop when you get a chance, you hear?"

Alé saluted her. "I will."

"Do. I have plans for you, young man."

Alé laughed. "Yes, Mrs. Freedman."

"Dotty, please." She turned to Tilda. "And you, Miss, you need to stop volunteering more hours at the school, ya hear? You've got enough on your plate. Plus, it robs us older folk out of a job. And before you know it, we'd be dropping like flies. And you!" She looked at Dex. "Come over the flower shop and I'll fatten you up. Got myself the new Tim Tam flavour."

Dex shuddered. "I'll pass, thanks all the same, Mrs. Freedman."

"Suit yourself!"

Dotty turned to Tilda who had come out from behind the counter. "You best keep an eye on your man, Tilda. I've a weakness for Latin dancers."

Tilda opened the door for her, suppressing a grin."Dotty, Alé isn't —"

"Hmpf." She batted away Tilda's mumbled protests and walked away, a kaleidoscope of shades and hues, bangles dancing.

Tilda turned back to the counter.

"That was...interesting," Alé proffered.

Dex rolled his eyes. "That's Dotty Freedman for you, mad as they come. But a sharp old bitty to boot."

"Shall we head out back?" Tilda asked, leading Alé

towards the break room. Her body tingled, remembering their kiss. She left the door open.

Alé ripped the pastry bag; a blueberry and custard tart had been cut in half. "I asked them to divide it for us. I've a wicked sweet tooth."

"That makes two of us." She sampled a corner of pastry and closed her eyes in pleasure. She opened them to find Alé watching her, paused in mid-bite.

"What?" She asked around another mouthful.

"That good, huh?"

Tilda blinked. She hadn't realised she'd made a sound.

"It's been a while."

"Sounds like I need to feed you pastry more often."

Heat rushed through her. What the hell did a woman say to that?

They ate their pastry in silence for a few minutes. She reminded herself that friends were allowed to tease one another. But flirting with Alé wasn't why they were meeting today. Tilda opened the box at her feet.

"So I started searching for some kids books we could use in Story Time."

Alé brushed his fingers and carefully opened the books she placed on the table.

"This is for the website?"

"And for the launch. Once the renovations are complete then I'll be holding an official opening of the nook, so it'd be good to have some books we can hype up in the lead up to it. I'd also like to put your paintings of some characters on the walls too."

Alé nodded. "I can use a few of the characters I've sketched for Instagram already and maybe a few from whatever we find today."

"Sounds good."

It didn't take them long before the ideas began to flow. They had a short list of books and before she knew it, they were choosing characters and landscapes for the paintings. Alé was on board with her plans for advertising and marketing. His experience starting from scratch in his own business had her mind buzzing with possibilities.

"I can come in next week to show you the rough sketches. Monday okay?"

Tilda scrolled through her phone, nodding. "Yep. And we have our one on one rehearsal Sunday, yeah? I was hobbling around last week I'll have you know."

His grin was lethal. "No pain, no gain. How did you go after the *milonga* the other day?"

"I have a proud blister to show for it. But it was fantastic."

"Always a good sign. Wait 'til you go to Buenos Aires, your feet would fall off you'd get so many dances."

"I don't think my bank balance would approve." Or her anxiety over the plane trip. The pastry sat like a lead weight in her stomach just at the thought.

"It'd be worth it."

"One day," she replied. "I don't really speak Spanish all that well, so I don't know how I'd cope in a foreign country."

"How have you coped before?"

"Pardon?"

"When you've travelled. What did you do then?"

Tilda shook her head. "I haven't travelled anywhere else."

"Really?"

"Not apart from New Zealand, and that doesn't count as 'foreign' to me."

"Why not?"

"Well, my gran was sick for starters —"

"*Perdón*, I meant, why not afterwards? After she passed on."

Tilda looked away. "I dunno. I guess, I didn't have anyone to travel with, and didn't know where to start." She hated to admit that the thought terrified her. She knew logically what happened to her parents was an accident. It didn't stop her feeling sick at the thought of flying.

"You've mentioned it a few times, I was under the impression you had travelled before. Mathilda, if you have the opportunity, you should take it. Don't let fear hold you back. Travel can be the best experience you have. An adventure. I know it was for me."

Tilda bristled. She lowered her shoulders knowing she wanted to bite back. "Each to their own. I appreciate the advice — "

"But I should mind my own business, *sí*?"

"Something like that."

Alé's alarm beeped on his phone. "Lucky for you, that's my cue. I have a private lesson with an eager wedding couple."

"Sounds like fun." Tilda walked with him back through the store.

"Not if you're the groom with two left feet."

"Ouch."

Outside, summer was finally bowing down to autumn. Tilda welcomed the breeze on her overheated cheeks.

"Mathilda." He turned to her. "You really have done a

fantastic job with the store. You should be proud. It takes a lot of hard work to do this on your own."

"Thanks, Alé."

"I look forward to the launch."

"Whenever that will be. It feels like this renovation will never end."

"Have patience. I'll see you at rehearsals, *si*?"

"Slave driver." She smiled, then stilled when he gave her a quick peck on the cheek.

He smelt like heaven. As usual.

Tilda waved goodbye and walked back to the store.

She wandered over to the nook and assessed the space. Patrick and his men did an amazing job; it was exactly how she pictured it, warm and inviting, with enough natural light to make the space glow. Not long to go before it was ready for business. She just needed everything to go to plan until then.

Tilda tapped her foot on the floorboards for good luck. She had a feeling she would need it.

The woman watching the bookshop through the window of her car smiled. The twisted, pained expression distorted the neat line of red that sat on artificially enhanced lips.

Her slender hands clenched even as she told herself that she didn't care. The scene before her was pathetic. But useful.

She had been smart to take her time. See? She could be patient. It wasn't so difficult. Especially now that she had a new plan. A much better one.

Those idiots hadn't caused as much damage as she had hoped. But no matter, she knew what she wanted. And no one stopped her from getting what she wanted. Life had taught her to take what others wouldn't give. She wouldn't end up some loser scrambling to make it big.

She wouldn't let anything, or anyone stand in her way.She was the best. Would be the best again. But that meant increasing the pressure.

Watching the blonde through the window, she weaved the threads of her new plan.

She answered her phone, voice as sweet as honey. The taste in her mouth was as bitter as lead.

CHAPTER SEVENTEEN

a small crowd had gathered on the pavement in front of The Book Nook. Tilda glanced at her phone; it was way too early for customers. When she spotted George and Betty in the crowd a tremor ran through her body.

Crossing the street, broken glass scraped in protest under her black work flats. Stepping carefully, she looked past local business owners to find a massive hole in her shop window.

"Tilda, honey," Betty began. She shook her head.

"Tilly!" George called after her.

Ignoring their concern, Tilda stepped through the smashed front door, glass and splinters covering the floor. The sight before her made her stomach heave.

The main section of the store was in chaos. Bookshelves were splintered and upturned. Graffiti tags stained the walls, books were defiled and strewn at random. She spotted the police officer who stood at the entrance of the nook. Bile rose up the back of her throat.

"Miss Landrey," he began. She pushed past him and stared at the wreckage before her. Tears burned her eyes.

"No, no, no..." She pressed her lips together afraid that she would scream, or worse, be sick.

"Miss Landrey, I'd like to speak to you privately, if I may?"

She looked at the officer, unable to comprehend. All she could hear was the roaring of blood in her ears. Tilda walked slowly up the ramp to the nook. The beautiful custom-made shelves that had just been fitted were now smashed to pieces. Graffiti covered the floors. Windows were broken.

Everything had been ruined.

"No!"

Confusion clouded her mind. She was painfully aware of every ripped book cover, every splintered segment of wood.

Every broken dream.

When George's arms wrapped around her, Tilda's grief rained down in a torrent of tears.

It was enough to drown them both.

Tilda sat at the police station, with Betty and George on either side, propping her upright. It was as if she had no control of her body — like her bones had become liquid — not that she really noticed. She found it difficult to concentrate. Her mind was filled with shards of glass and broken wood.

Sergeant Banks, the police officer who was at the scene, sat opposite her.

"Only a few more questions then you can go. I know this may seem like a stupid question, but do you know of anyone who has a grudge against you, Miss Landrey?"

Tilda looked up out of swollen eyes. Her voice was thick and raw. "No." She swallowed, mouth dry. "I don't know anyone."

"Are you sure about that? Disgruntled employee? Annoyed customer?"

She shook her head. "No."

"Everyone loves Tilda, officer," Betty added. "Riversdale is not the kind of town that this happens in."

He grunted. "Do you have any store cameras we can review?"

Tilda shook her head, sick to her stomach.

"Like Betty said." George squeezed her shoulder. "We don't really get crime in these parts. Everyone is close in this community."

"I'm just going through procedure here, sir."

He turned to Tilda. "Can you tell me your movements from when you closed up last night, until this morning?"

"She was having dinner with us!" George boomed. "What are you implying?"

"Easy, George."

"Miss Landrey?"

Her mouth was thick as cotton. "Like George said, I went to his Pizza place with Betty, just along Main street. We had a meal together. Left around ten, then George closed. Who would do this? We were just renovating the store." Her stomach was in knots.

"Usually that attracts hooligans. There are a few tag marks we noticed from the graffiti. It's most likely that a youth group. Sometimes blow-ins venture out from their usual haunts. They may have noticed the workmen moving to and fro, and they decided to go for it. There were empty spirit bottles around the back of the store, and some found in the local park."

Tilda just shook her head.

"Could I have a word alone with Miss Landrey please?" Tilda waved off George's protests. The sooner she was able to get in contact with Patrick and start the clean up the better. She was wasting her time here.

"We'll be outside love." Betty offered a small smile of encouragement when they left. Tilda's shoulders slumped.

Sergeant Banks directed piercing green eyes at her. It was just now that Tilda noticed his bearded face, the lines deep around a thin mouth and full nose.

"Was any money stolen? Valuables taken?"

"Like I said earlier, nothing other than the few laptops and tablets we had there. I just don't understand why they would do something like this."

"It very well could be a youth gang, with those tag marks. But... Tilda, I know this is a delicate question, but I want to ask whether you have insurance."

Tilda blinked. "Insurance? What has that got to..." She trailed off, her eyes rounding in surprise.

"We can find out through our own means, but I wanted to hear it from you."

"You think that I..." She couldn't bring herself to say it. She vibrated with anger.

"I had a look at your financial records. You've taken out a hefty loan. You've a lot of debt, Miss Landrey. Enough to reap rewards from insurance if something like this were to happen."

Tilda's body shook. She pressed her hands together. "I may be struggling a bit, but why would I do something like this? The store was nearly finished. We were so close..."

"And it cost you a fair bit to get it done."

She looked at him square in the eye. "It's not possible that I organised for my store to get broken into for the insurance."

"And why is that?"

"Because I stopped paying insurance for it the moment renovations started," she whispered. Despair sitting heavy on her brow. When he didn't ask questions, she continued. "I couldn't afford to pay it, and thought that once the renovations were finished, then the store would be earning more money..."

"And you could afford it again."

She bit her lip. "That's right. You can double check if you don't believe me."

"I'm surprised your agency allowed it. We'll certainly do that, Miss Landrey."

"Sure."

"If you could leave some contact details for us at the desk, then you can go."

"Can I go back to the store?"

"Yes. We'll let you know if we find who is responsible."

She walked out on unsteady legs. The buzzing in her head made it hard to focus.

"What did they want?" George asked.

"Just checking I wasn't committing insurance fraud."

"What?"

"George, it's fine."

Betty ushered them out of the station.

"Like hell it is!"

"Calm down, silly man." Betty shook her head. "They'll contact your insurance and they'll see there's no foul play. Don't you worry about a thing, Tilly. They'll handle it. You'll be covered for all the damages, and once that clears, you can get back on track to renovating in no time. Hmm?"

Tilda looked away. She couldn't tell them the truth. She couldn't bear to see them disappointed in her.

She had to handle this on her own. She would figure it out. Somehow.

CHAPTER EIGHTEEN

*T*ilda woke the next morning, her overwrought brain buzzing with fragmented thoughts and distorted images. The bitter taste of defeat coated the back of her mouth. All she could think was that she had failed her gran.

Shaking off the heavy weight in her limbs, she went through the motions of her morning routine. Fortified by a large coffee on the way to work, she reminded herself that her gran didn't raise a quitter. It was only blind hope that had her lifting her chin high, despite the extent of the damage. Not to mention the state of her finances.

She couldn't afford for this to have happened. She hadn't a cent to spare.

The sight of the boarded-up windows stabbed at her resilience. Seeing it that way, when she had been so close to having it completed stung more than ever.

Patrick waved her over.

"You okay?"

Tilda shrugged. "I go from angry to sad every few minutes. I'm exhausted."

Patrick patted her shoulder. "I'm so sorry, Tilda. I know it looks bad, but we'll get this sorted. You'll have your store back to new. I promise."

Tilda's eyes burned. She blinked back the tears. "Thanks, Patrick. I appreciate all your help."

"Don't look so down. Sure, it's bad for now, but your insurance will cover it. You'll be back on your feet in no time."

Guilt jabbed at her conscience.

With the help of Patrick, Dex, and a few lovely volunteers from council, they began to move about the main store, clearing up the debris.

Dex had placed a hand-written sign up on the door closing the store until further notice. Even though her heart trembled, she told herself it would only be a temporary measure.

Tilda's heart ached if she thought about it too long.

She posted the news on social media, alerting customers to come forward with information, but reassuring them that they would be open again soon. She prayed that it wouldn't be a lie.

When Alé arrived she very nearly crumbled again. She didn't analyse the fact that she wanted only him by her side. All she knew was that she wanted him there.

"Are you okay?" He looked around at the broken shelves; the shards of glass had been swept up, but piles of books were still strewn across the floor. They were going through what they could salvage.

"Not really. But I will be."

He wrapped his arms around her and for a split

second, Tilda believed that she'd get through it. That everything would be okay now that he was here.

Alé stepped back and rolled up his sleeves. "What can I do to help?"

Not able to face going to the bank on Friday, Tilda called Young Frank.

"I heard about the store. Are you alright, dear?"

"Yes, thank you. It's kind of why I'm calling."

"We've been trying to contact you regarding your late repayments. We'll need to discuss the terms of your loan if you're unable to manage it."

Tilda's heart thundered. "No, it's fine. Just a few glitches." She bit the bullet. "I wanted to ask if it's possible to apply for another loan? Even a personal one? If I want them to fix everything in the store, I'll need to borrow a bit more."

Young Frank was silent for so long, Tilda was afraid he had hung up on her.

"Are you sure about this?"

"Yes...I am."

"I'm actually not certain if that's possible. Surely your insurance would be covering it? Look, I've another call coming through, let me crunch the numbers and get back to you, m'dear." He cleared his throat. "I'll see what I can do for Ethel's girl."

"Thank you so much. You have no idea how much this means to me."

"Oh, I have a clue. I'll be in touch."

Tilda kept her fingers crossed. She desperately needed

the loan. She'd never be able to repair all the damage and restore The Book Nook without it.

Later that evening she collapsed on her living room couch, muscles aching. The last image she saw before her eyes closed was a picture of Ethel on the mantelpiece.

It was with a heavy heart that she found comfort in sleep.

CHAPTER NINETEEN

*T*ilda stewed. For days she stalked around the store like a bear woken up too early from hibernation. Dex had deigned to point out why she may be in a bad mood and nearly lost his coffee all over his new shoes.

She knew she was beyond annoyed at Alé, but she had every right to be. Friends were supposed to tell each other when good things happened to them. Like when they got a promotion or was currently dating a super-model who gave Jessica Rabbit a run for her cartoon money. For heaven's sake.

Tilda stared at the numbers of her bank balance and saw shapes and blurred lines. It was a relief that Young Frank managed to secure the new loan, but also petrify-ing. She had so much riding on getting the store up and running again that she had barely time to make rehearsals.

It irked her that dancing with Alé had been the only

thing that seemed to quiet her mind of late. When she wasn't at the store, she was at rehearsals.

She couldn't afford to pay her employees for any extra hours — despite their protests that she needed help — so it had been up to her to carry the slack.

Now if she could just concentrate, she'd be able to figure out a way through the mess she was in.

Standing up from the small office adjoining the back-room, Tilda shut down her computer with a snap. She had to sort out her finances, but every time she looked at her spreadsheet, she saw a buxom red head wrapped around Alé at the studio.

She needed to vent. Quickly. Before she made an even bigger mess of the situation.

Fifteen minutes later, with a large chocolate milkshake in front of her, Tilda sat outside on the wrought iron table that lined the pavement of Betty's Cone and Cup. The air was cool, but the biting wind did nothing to tamper her anger.

She didn't need to say much when she marched to the front counter. Betty could see that she was radiating anger and had ushered her deftly outside and into the weak Autumn sun.

Betty sat, eyes patient, hands crossed, waiting for Tilda to begin. It was times like these, that Tilda yearned for her gran.

"You didn't need to take your time away from work to babysit me."

"Hush now, Tilly. Tell me what's on your mind. You're positively brimming with agitation."

Tilda shifted again, only to prove Betty's point.

"I just thought we were friends!" She blurted out, midway through her inner narrative. Betty narrowed her eyes. "I mean, we said we were friends. He helped me out when he saw the store was damaged and he's been so wonderful with the artwork. I assumed that this meant we were friends."

"Did something happen with Alejandro, my dear?"

"No. Yes. Not really." Tilda sighed. "I just — I'm so mad at him!"

"You're going to have to explain this a bit more. Out loud."

"I saw him giving a tango lesson to this *amazon* of a woman." She gesticulated. "I mean, I walk in and she's all boa constrictor over him. He casually mentions they've been dating. For weeks now! Did he tell me anything about her? Of course not!

"She's this gorgeous looking red head, by the way. You'd think he'd tell me about her before I had to bump into her big busty boobs. But of course, I find out by accident. Had I arrived at our rehearsal a bit later, I'd be none the wiser!"

"So you're upset that Alé didn't tell you about dating this lady —"

"Tiffany. Yes! It's not like I wanted details of his relationship or anything, but I didn't even know that she was in the picture. Then, he has the audacity to tell me that he thought I'd be upset about him dating her, which is why he didn't tell me. I mean, how arrogant is that. To think that I'd be mooning over him so much that I'd give a damn."

Betty raised her eyebrows.

"And that's it? There's no truth to that statement? You wouldn't be upset that he's dating another woman, would you?"

A trickle of discomfort slid down her spine.

"No." She hunched her shoulders.

"Really?"

"No."

Betty sighed. "Mathilda darling, it's perfectly normal to be jealous. Alé, whom you've grown close with, has begun a relationship —" Tilda snorted indelicately. "So he's started dating Tiffany, the young lady whom you say is very attractive. So of course you might feel a bit jealous. It doesn't take away from anything that you are."

Tilda pouted. "I don't *want* to be jealous. Alé and I are just *friends*. We made this very clear with one another. I shouldn't be surprised that a gorgeously attractive man like him is seeing someone else. I keep thinking about our kiss, and sometimes the way he looks at me... I dunno. I guess, a very small part of me may be jealous. I shouldn't be. But I am. There. Are you happy now?"

"The question my dear is, are you?"

"I was. I am. I'm just so stressed out." She pressed her hands to her eyes. Temper tears welled. "I've a hundred and one things to organise at the store. The site is a mess. We need to re-open so we can make some money. Now Patrick said his men are contracted on another site and it could take up to another month to get the work completed."

Betty leaned forward. "Is the store in some kind of trouble?"

Tilda looked Betty in the eye, willing away her tears. It took all her strength to swallow the truth. She couldn't — wouldn't weigh Betty down with her problems. She'd find a way to make it work.

She needed to pay Patrick for materials, re-order stock, pay her staff... the list went on. She was barely able to make repayments; with no money coming in and no buffer to take the pressure off, Tilda was up most nights desperately trying to find a solution.

"No trouble. Other than the obvious. I'm just anxious about getting it done. I don't feel comfortable being in debt."

"But the store is okay, isn't it?"

Tilda looked away. "Mhmm." She looked back at Betty. "The new loan is covering it, I just need to bring in the customers again, get my stock back up."

"Is there anything we can do?"

"No. You've done more than enough."

Betty's stare was penetrating. "If you say so. But I don't want you worrying for nothing. You're looking worse for wear. I can tell when you're pushing yourself."

Tilda shrugged. "I didn't sleep well last night." Or every night for the past few weeks. "Thanks for the chat, I should get back."

"What about the Alé situation?"

"I don't know. I was starting to feel good about where Alé and I were heading, but I'm not so sure anymore."

"Why should anything change that?"

"He's dating someone else, Betty."

"So what?"

Tilda frowned. "But you —"

"Didn't you just say you were happy with where it was heading?"

"Yes."

"And are you enjoying your friendship with him?"

"Yes."

"What has him seeing another woman got to do with it?"

"Well —"

"It doesn't," Betty responded firmly. "Listen here, and listen well, young lady. Don't you ever, ever let another woman get in the way of a friendship. You hear me? So what if he didn't tell you? He didn't. For whatever reason the man had, don't take it as an affront on you. Accept the man's friendship for what it is, accept him for who he is, and carry on, Tilda. It might not be the type of friendship you're used to, but friends understand and accommodate. That's part of your relationship. Isn't it?"

She nodded, feeling like a child.

"Good," Betty replied, looking out across the road. "Don't let anything come between it."

Tilda looked over her shoulder following Betty's line of sight. George was ushering in a young mother and child for the lunchtime rush. His voice boomed, almost carrying across the street.

"Betty —"

"Now finish your drink and go back to work. No point wallowing over things you can't change," she implored, shutting down the subject before it even had the chance to get started.

CHAPTER TWENTY

"Today is the day everyone." Isabella clapped her hands gleefully. "Today is the day we face the trickiest part of the routine. The ending!"

There was a mixture of whoops and groans.

"We've come a long way since we started," Alé continued. "But I warn you that we are going hard. Now is the time where you need to put more effort. Not practising at home on your own is not good enough. Not practising with your partner is not good enough. We've secured our first gig at Henri's *milonga* for their anniversary. It's going to be a big occasion. Lots of people, lots of pressure: we are one of only two performances. It's a big deal."

Isabella nudged Alé. "Don't forget we said we'll arrange a practice run in the hall if we can. Oh! Costumes. We'll have to sort that out too."

"Any questions?" Alé asked.

Elspeth raised her hand. "Is it too late to back out?"

Everyone laughed.

"Warm up time."

. . .

"Tac. Tac. Tac." Alé clapped, marking the rhythm. "That's the beat, but we're dancing with the *bandoneons*, so you need to focus. This is the 3.20 mark up to the 3.40 mark of the music. That's where all the technical details will come. The last five seconds is for the split leg turn and flourish."

He played the music again and again. Then broke it down so they could begin.

They were all sweating. Even with the cool breeze coming through the windows, they still struggled with the frenetic pace. The last fifteen seconds in particular.

It was the intricacy of the footwork, the weaving *adornos* coupled with changes in direction that had them tripping over their own feet.

"There's the drawn-out step and extension of the arm and leg at 3.30. Good Diana and Ben. Then a race to the finish as the *bandoneons* pick up speed down the scale. *Si*. The final few steps need to be precise, Mathilda," he called out when she nearly tumbled. "Aaaand the twirl and flourish."

They marked it out once more without the music. They worked on their footing and posture. Still it took time and effort. When they rehearsed with the music, it was a hot mess. The timing was off, their footwork basic and Tilda was sure her posture would give the hunchback of Notre Dame a run for his money.

"Ladies, you have to have it polished!" Isabella coached.

Tilda cursed her feet.

"Try to not turn your leg out as you brush the floor,

Tilda." Isabella moved to her. "It's more a turning of the foot, rather than the knee. You don't want to get an injury. You need to be brushing the inside of the foot, tracing the floor almost with your toes."

Tilda tried it and grimaced.

"Here." Alé lined up the women in a row. "Let me show you." He bent down to Tilda's feet and gently turned her foot on an angle, whereby her big toe rested on the floorboards. "Like this, everyone. Now practise writing an 'S' shape on the floor."

Everyone tried. Everyone failed.

"No knees, just your feet."

Tilda shoved her hair back in her ponytail and tried again and again.

"Yes! Perfect Mathilda!" Alé called out. "Good work!"

Tilda shook out her leg. "It feels stiff."

"That's 'coz you're trying too hard," Isabella said. "Trust me, with practice you will be able to make it as fluid as it needs to be. The music will be buzzing so fast that you'll fly through it."

The pace was hectic enough without adding in the trills and fancy footwork. Tilda was relieved when the others struggled as well.

"Remember it's sexy!" Isabella called over the music. "You all look like you have a backache!"

"Ow!" Michael exclaimed as Katarina stomped on his foot accidentally. "That hurt like a motherf-"

"Break!" Alé called. "We can try it to music again after you've had a rest. The more you work at it the easier it will get. Trust me."

. . .

"Whilst we're all sitting down, it might be a good time for us to talk costumes," Isabella said, motioning for everyone to huddle together. "Alé and I agree that we want to keep the routine sleek, to make it sexy with not only costumes, but our connections as we dance. The routine is meant to mimic that sexual zing you feel at the start of a relationship."

Alé nodded. "The music lends itself to this idea, so that's why it's so fast paced in the end, it's the crescendo." He looked at Tilda. "The peak of desire."

Her mind migrated to south of decent. Sweat trickled down her back. She was certain that even if Alé said, 'foot fungus' her body would react instantly. There was something seriously wrong with her.

"Alé and I are thinking a black and red colour scheme. Ladies you'll be in dresses, preferably with a split. I have a friend who can alter clothes if need be. I'm thinking thin, spaghetti straps or even halter necks. We want this to look sharp."

"So black dresses and red shoes?" Sara clarified.

"Oooh hot!" Phillip nudged her.

"This is where it's up to you. We want a balance and uniformity in the look. So long as you match as a couple, we can have varying styles across the group. We want to be striking for all the right reasons."

"For the men, classic black pants with either a red or black shirt," Alé explained. "And potentially a Fedora hat with a red material around the base of it — I'm talking tango in the forties style. Maybe a red pocket square? Make it cool, sexy. *Si*?"

The guys assented.

"Alrighty. Break time over." Isabella clapped her

hands. At their collective groans, she conceded. "One more run through, I promise. I want to video it so you can have a copy when you're rehearsing at home."

The routine still needed a lot more practice, but the break seemed to have worked; they ended up rehearsing for an extra thirty minutes and had made considerable progress.

Tilda pressed the cool bottle of water to her cheek. She was worn out but satisfied with her progress so far.

"Great work everyone!" Alé clapped. "You've earned the rest. But I want to see even more progress by the next group rehearsal."

Tilda examined her aching feet. She had to order new tango shoes for this routine, and definitely needed to go shopping for a new dress. Not that she could afford either of those items. She could only hope that one of the second-hand stores in the city might have what she was after.

Isabella hobbled over. "Don't look so upset. You and I are going on a shopping trip."

"We are?"

"*Si*. You, my darling are going to leave it all to me. We'll find you a sexy hot dress and pretty little shoes to wear. Just wait."

Tilda laughed. "Why do I have a bad feeling about this?"

Isabella waved an impatient hand. "You joke now, *seniorita*. You wait and see." Isabella gave her an air kiss. "I'll call you. Gotta go!"

Tilda said her goodbyes and was about to leave when Alé called her back.

"Can I have a quick word?""Sure."

Tilda walked back to him slowly. They hadn't spoken since her blow-up with him about Tiffany. It had been two weeks of maintaining a polite distance. She was following Betty's advice and feeling sanctimonious about the whole damn thing.

"What's up?"

The studio felt smaller now that they were alone and Tilda wished she had something to do with her hands.

"Two things. First, I am sorry I didn't tell you about Tiffany."

"No, Alé. It's your business who you date. I was tired and angry. So it's me who should apologise. It's been a stressful few weeks and I've a lot to do."

"Can I help?"

"Not unless you're able to swing a hammer as well as you draw?"

Alé grimaced. "Not as good. But I can paint walls if you like. Have you hired anyone for that?"

"No but —"

"Then I'm your man."

Tilda frowned. "Alé —"

"*Por favor* Mathilda. I paint pictures, how hard can it be to paint walls? I did the studio here myself. I know how expensive it is to hire people. Consider it a gift, *si*?"

She frowned. "Alright. Thank you, I suppose."

"But I do want something in return."

Tilda's eyes narrowed. "Oh?" She should have known there was something coming.

"More rehearsals. I know you're busy but we're losing momentum with the performance. We need to rehearse more."

Tilda didn't know when she'd find the time. Perhaps in her sleep?

After consulting their schedules, and tentatively adding in another evening of rehearsal, Tilda turned to leave.

"I'll let you know about Wednesday night." She called over her shoulder.

"Wait. I've something for you."

Alé came out of his office a second later with a wrapped, square-shaped box. He motioned for her to sit next to him on the benches, his face all but radiating excitement.

Tilda looked at the box.

"Open it."

Her fingers gently peeled back the wrapping. The label on the box made her gasp. She looked up at him unable to think properly.

"Alé... you didn't!"

Hands trembling, she lifted the lid.

Then simply stared.

Sitting inside mountains of tissue paper were a pair of exquisite black and red *Comme Il Fauts*. "I -" she shook her head. "You — you bought me tango shoes?" She sputtered. "But — but, why?"

Alé shrugged. "Because you needed them."

Her eyes narrowed. "Hold on, this isn't like a pity present for what happened the other day, is it? Like, sorry I didn't tell you about my girlfriend, here's some shoes to shut you up?"

"*Dios Mio*, Mathilda. Who do you think I am? The mafia? I know you're busy with the store, and money is tight. This is incentive for you to practice more, *si*?" He nudged her, grinning.

Tilda blinked back tears.

"You deserve beautiful shoes. I've told you, you're a beautiful dancer. And you should burn those other ones. Ugly witch shoes."

The warmth bloomed on her cheeks. "You say the loveliest things sometimes."

Alé laughed. She looked back down at the box in her hands. "This means so much, Alé. Thank you!" She threw her arms around him.

"*De nada*."

Tilda shook her head. "You have to let me —"

"If you say pay me back, I *will* confiscate them."

Tilda hugged him again, then examined the open toe shoes in awe. The black leather was so shiny she couldn't resist bringing it to her nose and inhaling. She laughed ruefully. It was the best smell in the whole world.

She stroked the thin, straight line of the red heel, accentuated with a dainty, red ankle strap. The golden sole had her sighing in reverence.

After another few minutes of ogling, she placed them back in the box.

"What are you doing?"

Tilda paused. "What?"

"You can't go home without giving them a test dance, can you? Dance with me, Mathilda. One more time before you leave?"

All complaints of her aching feet long forgotten; Tilda accepted.

Alé crouched before her, resting her foot on his knee. His fingers brushed against her ankle as he buckled the slim strap. It fit like Cinderella's glass slipper. And that's exactly how it felt. Like some kind of fairy tale. She pressed a hand against her stomach.

"It fits."

Alé looked up at her and grinned. "I took the liberty of sneaking a look at your shoe size after one rehearsal."

"Devilish."

"Let's give them a test run, eh?"

Tilda rose, took one tentative step and nearly slipped. They were high. Over three inches and wicked as sin. It made her previous pair look like baby shoes.

"You may need to scuff them a little," Alé said, catching her. "Or put a little water under them to make them stick. It's the way with all new shoes. They'll be a bit slippery, but by the performance they'll be perfect."

She couldn't imagine practising let alone performing in them but forced herself to enjoy the moment. The next four minutes would be for pleasure only.

A sensual tango rang through the speakers. Tilda couldn't place it immediately. She didn't care.

"May I have this dance?" Alé asked bowing slightly.

Tilda took his hand.

When he drew her to him, everything ceased to exist.

As Alé's arm held her close, her right hand found his, and they stood, shifting weight from one foot to the other.

Then they moved.

Tilda felt like she was floating. Alé started slowly, increasing his pace alongside the music.

Her pulse began to scramble when he changed direction, leading her into the standard *media luna*, before changing again. Tilda played with her footwork, experimenting with her *adornos*. She brushed her feet against his, her own playful humour reflected in his fiery gaze.

Alé held her close even as the final note rang out. His head rested on her temple, his arm strong around her waist.

It was this combination of drowning and floating that had her anchored to him. Dancing with Alé was all-encompassing.

Tilda couldn't wipe the grin off her face. This was what made tango dancers slaves to passion.

Her legs were shaking slightly from the height of the new shoes. She only had to tip her head slightly and her mouth would be on his.

She licked her lips. Parched.

He was dating someone else. They were just friends. And kissing him would be a bad move.

Tilda stepped back. "Thanks for the dance, Alé. And the shoes."

He cleared his throat. "*De nada*, Mathilda."

"I better actually leave this time."

Alé's smile was tight. "I think that's a good idea."

CHAPTER TWENTY-ONE

*A*s autumn's golden leaves littered the pavement and the wind followed commuters in to work, Tilda began to re-build the store. It had been two months since they had been vandalised, and whilst she had finally re-opened her doors again, she had yet to see much in the way of sales.

What momentum she had built up over summer had dwindled along with the vestiges of heat; the cold had set in and her sales had been the worst she'd ever seen.

She was behind on repayments. She knew that. But she had to have some kind of plan in place. Her dream was morphing into a warped nightmare. Every time she had tried to contact Young Frank, she couldn't get through. It only increased her anxiety.

With more expenditure than income, she was finding herself sinking, fast.

Tilda shook her head at the site before her. No wonder people didn't come to the store. She didn't have the luxury as she did before of limiting their working times to not annoy customers. Her life was a mess.

She had reduced Todd and Alicia's shifts so that she could juggle renovation costs, upkeep with the store and mortgage repayments. Of which it seemed she didn't have the funds to pay, now that she was haemorrhaging money. She had already locked in an interest only loan repayment but that still wasn't helping.

The bone-rattling fear that she couldn't sustain this business jolted her awake in the middle of the night. Worry gnawed at her insides. She could barely stomach anything anymore.

Tilda called Young Frank yet again. The automated service droned on in the same vein: the number was no longer in service.

A woman from the bank, a Sylvia Preston, had called a few times now, but Tilda just wanted to speak to Young Frank. She didn't want to explain matters to another adviser.

Between tango rehearsals and crazy-hour renovations she wasn't quite managing to keep up. She had ignored the letters that had started coming in, hoping and praying she'd find a solution. She knew Young Frank would give her more time. His compassion had been her saving grace throughout the whole process.

With her stomach in knots, Tilda made a decision. She knew exactly what to do.

CHAPTER TWENTY-TWO

"*I*'m sorry, Frank doesn't work here anymore."

Tilda stared at the woman in front of her, but all she could hear was the blood roaring in her ears.

Sylvia Preston. Her beige name badge all but blinded her. Tilda blinked.

"What do you mean Young Frank doesn't work here?"

Sylvia placed her hands on the desk between them. Tilda noted how they gleamed. Blood red.

"Frank has been offered a retirement plan. He chose to accept it."

Tilda's eyes narrowed.

"You see, Miss, we are reshuffling staff. Making quite a few changes. As such, I am taking over his accounts."

"So he isn't here at all then?"

"No." Her brown hair was pulled back in a severe bun. "Is there something I can help you with?"

Tilda ignored the itch between her shoulder blades. "Actually, there was. I've been asked to contact the bank, and received some letters..."

"May I have your name please?"

"Mathilda Landrey." She sat forward.

"Ahh." The woman sat back. Her mouth curved in what appeared to be a smile. It made Tilda want to retch.

"Aren't you going to key it into the computer?"

"We don't need to, Miss Landrey."

"Excuse me?"

"We've been trying to contact you. You've missed quite a few repayments. We take that very seriously. We're in the process of taking legal action."

"Wait. I spoke to Young Frank when I went to interest only loans, he said he'd take care of it."

"As you see, Miss Landrey, Frank doesn't work here anymore. You moved to interest only payments —"

"Yes, to cover the costs, but I —"

"And you've used your store as collateral for the second payment."

Her stomach heaved. "That's correct," she added carefully. "It was my grandmother's store. Look, I've been paying it fortnightly. But I think if I try to pay interest on a monthly basis it'll help. Frank knows me. He knows about the break in. He's been handling this." Desperation crept into her voice. She didn't care.

"You really shouldn't have been allowed to borrow this much, Miss Landrey."

Beads of sweat dampened Tilda's blouse.

The woman made a discouraging sound in the back of her throat. "It seems that Frank has overestimated the store's contribution abilities. And allowed you to borrow more than you're able. How, I have no idea."

Pure fear pinned her down. It took all her will to speak. "It's been slow. As I said, I've had a few issues. We had to close, then we had a break in. It's taken us longer to get back on our feet."

"We're sorry to hear that. But it doesn't change facts. You owe us money and we have been more than patient in getting it. I'm sorry to say that we have no choice but to start legal proceedings."

Tilda wanted to pull out her hair. She gripped her hands together instead. "What does that mean?"

"We need to sell your business."

"Please!" Tilda implored. "Don't do this. I need more time. Give me more time."

The woman looked at the computer screen. "You have until the close of business on Friday, to settle your affairs. Unless you come up with a miracle, Miss Landrey, I'm afraid it's too late."

Arguments, protests, words of reason ricocheted in her mind. Her throat closed over them.

The woman continued to talk through the process, but it was as if she was under water; everything was distorted. Tilda left the bank in disbelief.

On the busy street, the realisation of what had just happened burned through her. The chilly wind was warm in contrast to the deep frost that settled in her bones. She failed her grandmother. She'd lost the store. And she'd never be the same again.

❦

It was with the saddest of hearts and bruised pride that Tilda returned to The Book Nook. It took her until the following day before she could tell anyone what happened.

Patrick was the first. When he arrived early in the morning for renovations, Tilda had opened her mouth and the truth had flown out like a confession.

She admitted that she didn't have insurance, that the store needed to be sold to pay the loan, that his men needed to leave immediately. All his offers to talk, to help, fell on deaf ears.

She was hollow inside. Dazed and confused, but insistent.

What broke her heart was having to sit down with Dex, Alicia and Todd and tell them they no longer had a job. She didn't think it was fair to string them along. She couldn't even afford to pay them anyway. They protested. Rallied against her insistent dismissal, but she begged them to leave.

What hurt was knowing that Dex's dog Teddy had taken a turn for the worse. She knew firsthand how pricey medical bills could be; instead of giving Dex comfort during this time, she had made him unemployed. It didn't bear thinking about.

By the end of the week, she received the letter from the bank detailing their intention to repossess, with a barrage of missed calls from Betty and George, including one or two from Alé.

She looked down at the clinical directive in her hands and tried to think of a way through. She couldn't see past the fog in her mind. The metallic taste in her mouth was nothing compared to the gut-wrenching guilt and agony over what she was losing. She failed her family. Her grandmother's legacy. Her great-grandmother's dream.

With unseeing eyes, Tilda scribbled a note and posted it on the door.

Closed for business.

The shame brought fresh tears to her eyes. With a glance over everything she loved, everything her grandmother had given to her, she turned off the lights. While other shop owners were busy starting the day, Tilda was all-too aware of her own predicament; she didn't want it to end like this.

She fitted the bolt, locked the door for one final time and turned away, straight into Alé's arms.

Tilda gasped.

"Mathilda?" Alé steadied her with his hands. "Didn't you hear me? What's happened?"

The dam broke; like a torrential flood, she sobbed uncontrollably. Alé held her tight, his body a warm haven, the only one she had left.

"It's okay. Let it out."

She clung to him. Let all her fears, disappointments and guilt pour out in his arms.

"Is there somewhere we can go? To your place?"

Tilda nodded. It wasn't like she had anywhere else to be.

The first thing she noticed when he pulled up to her house was George's car.

"We heard the news." Betty raced up to Alé's red hatchback. "Are you okay?"

"Alé, good to see you." George patted him on the back. "Thanks for bringing Tilda home. We were worried sick when we couldn't reach you, Tilly."

"Come inside dear, I'll make you a cuppa and we can talk."

Alé hovered.

Tilda reached out, held on to his hand. Through the fog, she could see the cloud over his eyes. The frown etched between his brow.

"I'd like it if you stayed. If you could?"

His shoulders relaxed, and she knew she was right to ask it of him. He nodded.

He sat beside her at the kitchen table, while George and Betty fussed with tea and biscuits. She wanted a coffee but knew it would burn like acid down her empty stomach.

Betty handed her a cup of tea.

"What happened?" Alé held her hand.

Tilda knew that news would travel faster than cable in the community. The whole town would know by Monday, if not already. She deserved their censure. She didn't think she could handle their pity.

"I can't make repayments on the loan. The bank is selling The Book Nook."

"That's not right. They can't just take your store. It takes months before they get to that point." Alé sat forward.

Tilda merely raised her eyebrows. She explained everything.

George shook his head. "Why didn't you say anything? We had no idea you were using the store to help pay for renovations."

"How could I George?" She stood, paced. "After everything you have given me? I needed to do this on my own. No one has that kind of money lying around anyway."

"Yes, but you should have spoken to us about it

regardless, Tilda." Betty motioned for her to sit. "That's what family does."

"It's embarrassing. I'm a grown woman, yet I can't seem to even function on my own. Do you know how that feels? I'll never be able to buy that store back from the bank. My credit history will be ruined."

She wished she could start over. But life wasn't a fairy tale story. There would be no knight to save her in the end.

Tilda looked across at the concerned faces before her and shrugged. There was nothing more she could do but accept what had happened.

She had tried in those last few days to change their minds. She sought advice from every lawyer she could find. But she was unable to stop proceedings.

"Look, it's no use. Trust me, I've tried to find a way. We all just have to accept the truth. The Book Nook is closed for business. It's over."

CHAPTER TWENTY-THREE

*A*lé's number one priority over the following weeks was Mathilda's wellbeing. He knew what it was like to lose everything; to stare into the future and see only the failures of the past. He also knew how difficult it was to overcome such pain. He'd be damned if he let her face it alone.

Because of it, he was with her when she had to visit her lawyer, to take down details and ask questions, to make sure she was aware of the process. But mainly he was there to hold her afterwards, when reality struck through the fog like a lightning bolt, jolting her out of her trance.

Lucky for all, it would take some time. It was a small, saving grace that would give her a reprieve, a chance to find herself through the loss — if only temporarily.

He stopped by every few days to make sure she ate, worried about her frail appearance. But with each visit he noticed small changes, positive ones, that made him admire her strength even more.

That Thursday evening, she answered the door in her dressing gown. He noted she had washed her hair. It was the sweet, fresh scent that he had begun to know so well that alerted him to the fact. Apples and vanilla. The combination did something strange to his gut.

The dark smudges beneath her eyes brought him back to the moment, reminding him of her insomnia. He hated the haunted, lost way about her these days. He wanted to do everything in his power to make her happy.

"I brought us some wine and takeaway."

Mathilda's smile was more like a grimace. "You don't need to babysit me, Alé."

"I'm offended." He walked past her and into the lounge. "And I'm here on strict non-babysitting business."

Mathilda followed him. "I've already been given enough casseroles and food to last until the end of winter. It's like everyone thinks I'm dead."

"Not quite."

She sat on the couch and opened a few containers. Hunger was a good sign. Another improvement. Dumplings sat plump and heavy in the plastic takeaway container.

"I hope you're in the mood for Chinese food."

"I'll eat anything. It all tastes like cardboard anyway. Look, Alé." She turned to him as he sat down with two wine glasses. "You don't need to be doing this. I get that I've been out of it, but no amount of takeaway will make me feel better about what I've done."

Alé held her hands. "You're allowed to wallow. You've been through hell, Mathilda. But you'll get through it. I know this, because I've come to know you.

You're the most determined, strong-willed, *stubborn* woman who, beneath all that self-pity, will bounce back again. It's in your stock, your blood. That is how the Landrey women are made. And if I had the pleasure of knowing your grandmother, I'm sure she wouldn't disagree."

"Being the stubborn breed that we are —"

Alé silenced her with a raised eyebrow. He'd happily spar with her than the ghost of the woman who had taken her place in recent weeks. *This* was Mathilda. *This* was his —

Nope. Not going there.

Alé released her hand and opened the wine. "Plus, I'll be the first to say I told you so when you bounce back. Now do me a favour. Shut up and eat."

Mathilda rolled her eyes. "You really are bossy."

"That's what friends do, *si?*"

"Yes, but I'm sure you have other things to worry about. Dates with certain red-heads to be on?"

Alé flicked his wrist. "If I had places to be, I'd be there." He swallowed. Total honesty he had promised her. Even though something jittery bounced inside him, quicker than a *milonga tanda*. "Plus... Tiffany and I are no longer seeing one another. It was just —"

"A fling?"

Alé's look was dry. "Something I thought I wanted, but realised I didn't."

Mathilda nodded. "What made you think that?"

He shrugged. "This and that. Isabella set us up, thinking I needed to get out there more."

"Isabella will do that. Did she want more? Tiffany?"

Alé poured a glass of the cool, buttery chardonnay. "I

don't think so. She's a beautiful woman, but after a few dates I realised it wasn't what I wanted. She wasn't —"

Mathilda's eyes were steady on his face. He looked away first, heart hammering against his chest.

"Well, thanks for letting me know." Mathilda reached for the proffered glass.

"Friends, eh?" Alé forced his mouth upwards. Hoped that the smile was casual.

They ate in silence, neither of them feeling the need to fill the space with useless talk. It comforted him to just sit beside her, to share a meal, to know she was okay.

"Tell me, how are you really feeling?"

Mathilda put her plate down. "I'm honestly sick of people asking, so I guess the numbness has worn off. Depression is now officially in pole position."

Alé assessed her. "I know what it's like to lose what you love, Mathilda."

She looked at him. "I've heard that a lot these past few weeks."

Alé placed his plate on the coffee table. Every instinct inside screamed at him to run, hide, protect himself. She needed to know she wasn't alone. His stomach lurched in protest.

"I was in a car accident, years ago, back in Buenos Aires." Alé fought to keep his voice steady and winced when phantom pain shot down his back. "I found it hard to cope. The injuries caused me a lot of problems. I was depressed for a very long time. My point is, I understand. The scars inside are not easy to see, they take more time to heal."

"I'm so sorry, Alé. Were you badly hurt?"

"My body still struggles sometimes, but I work

through it. I have to." A weight seemed to lift from his chest. It was an odd sensation. "I didn't tell you for pity, or to make you feel bad. This isn't about me. I wanted you to know that you're not alone in how you feel. I understand what it means to lose what you love. That's what I'm trying to say. I lost my dream... but I'm here for you. If you want me."

"Thanks. It helps having you here. I just feel really lost."

"Look, it's difficult to start over again. It was a lot of hard work, and some magic to get where I am today. But you can work through this. You're a strong woman, Mathilda."

Her eyes shifted to the mantelpiece. When she looked back at him, he could see the guilt on her face.

"I've let her down, Alé. Nothing I can do will bring the store back." She dashed away a tear.

He moved closer. "You've had it rough, Mathilda. First termites, then a break-in. But you kept your head high and did everything you could to make it work. That takes courage."

"I don't feel that way." She stood, pacing the room.

Alé rubbed his jaw, contemplating. "Maybe this is too soon, but I had a conversation with Mrs. Freedman."

"Dotty Freedman? The florist in Riversdale?"

"*Si*. She spoke to me about creating pamphlets for her flower shop. But she also asked if I could give tango lessons in Riversdale. She's been trying to get the older people together for community events and she thought tango would be a great idea."

A ghost of a smile passed on Mathilda's face. "And?"

"It's a crazy time for me right now. I have workshops

in Sydney booked and rehearsals take up time, so I could use a helping hand. A partner in crime." Alé shoved his hands in his pockets.

Mathilda frowned. "Hold on, are you asking me to teach tango? With you?"

"I'm asking you to consider it. You're a natural, Mathilda. I see how you guide others, how you understand more than just the steps." He held up a hand. "The classes would be in Riversdale as many people can't do stairs at my studio. You'd know the people you teach, and it would be a part-time thing, until you get back on your feet."

"My instinct is to say hell no."

Alé grinned. "I know this. Just think about it. I wouldn't ask if I didn't think you could do it."

Mathilda looked at the pictures on the mantelpiece. "My mother and father were great dancers. Did I ever tell you that?"

Alé nodded, standing beside her. "Ballroom?"

"Yes... they loved what they did. I don't remember much, but I recall how they would dance around the kitchen table, laughing and carrying on. I didn't understand it when their plane crashed, and my gran told me they had died. I suppose I was too young.

"But it was different from when I lost my gran. I was much older for starters, and she was my world. Now I feel like I've lost her all over again." Her voice cracked. "I miss her, Alé."

He placed a hand on her shoulder and squeezed. "She was a big part of your life."

"I love that store. So much. I didn't understand it 'til last week, not truly, how much I loved it. Yes, it was my gran's passion, my great-grandmother's dream, but I realise how much of her I thought I still had, by just being there." She turned to him.

"Give yourself time to grieve."

"It doesn't change anything."

"For others maybe not, but for you, it is everything."

Alé held her, soothed and murmured words of encouragement until her shoulders relaxed, and the tears subsided.

It broke his heart to see her like this. It shook him even more to recognise the fact that he wanted to protect her from all the pain. For as long as he could.

"Are you sure about this?" Alé asked.

"I'm going to go crazy wallowing and I won't let the group down by being behind in rehearsals." Tilda stirred her coffee, cradling the phone to her shoulder. "I'll come to the next rehearsals. Sunday, right?"

"No!"

Tilda's hand stilled on the spoon. "What do you mean, no?"

"We can't."

"Why not?" Tilda gripped the phone in her hand. Sure, it had been a month since Alé's pep talk, but surely things hadn't changed so drastically since then?

"I can't make it."

"Why?"

"I just can't. But we'll do one during the week okay? Mid-week. I'll tell the others you're ready to join us again. What are your plans today?"

Tilda frowned and sipped her scalding coffee. Something was up. "I might go visit George. I haven't been back to town since... anyway, I think I should suck it up and go in." She was sick at the very thought but hated that she had come to rely on others bringing her food supplies. In fact, she couldn't recall the last time she went to the local grocer.

"No!"

"What? Alé, what is wrong with you?"

"Don't go there."

"Why not?"

"Give yourself more time, Mathilda. I don't think you're ready yet."

"Is that so, Dr. Phil? Just a few weeks ago you were telling me I needed to grieve in my own way."

"I lied. You need to take it slow." There was a voice in the background. "And Isabella wants to come over."

"What? Now?"

"*Si. Por favor,* Mathilda. Take it easy."

Tilda studied the phone after Alé's hurried goodbye. Shaking her head, she took her morning brew to the bathroom. She hadn't initially realised how much she had needed to grieve until Alé had pointed it out. It was still painful to think about going to the store, let alone to town.

Yet as each week passed, she was coming to terms with the idea that the store wasn't hers anymore. Even if it made her tear up at the thought, she was beginning to accept the situation for what it was. She had no other choice.

With every passing day, Alé's suggestion to teach beginner's tango with him in Riversdale started to take on greater appeal. She had been so eager to dismiss dancing as a child, afraid that it somehow was to blame for her parents' death. But when that curiosity grew stronger as a young adult, she had leapt at the chance to give it a go.

Tilda missed The Book Nook more than ever. But she was beginning to realise how much pressure she had put on herself to make it a success. She had been so eager to do her grandmother proud that she hadn't stopped to figure out if it had been her dream too.

Guilt coursed through her. She shouldn't be excited at the idea of teaching tango with Alé — of daydreaming about what that might look like. But she was.

Suddenly she was eager for Isabella's company. She needed to talk this through with her friend. She stepped into the shower and welcomed the scalding hot water on her skin.

Tilda had no doubt that Isabella would keep her mind distracted — clearly Alé's intention in sending her over. It was like no one wanted to leave her alone for too long these days. Tilda's lips twisted.

And didn't that speak volumes?

CHAPTER TWENTY-FOUR

*I*sabella's visit had been exactly what she needed. After her friend had left, Tilda had looked online for short courses in dance. There was a whole world out there for teaching she could participate in, she just hadn't given herself the chance. Unfortunately, they all cost money.

So it was out of necessity that she applied for the casual job as secretary at Riversdale Primary School. The fact that she had been volunteering there for years, helping the first-year students with their reading, was a tick in her favour. She reminded herself that it was okay to enjoy working there as well.

She couldn't shake the feeling that she should have worked harder to save The Book Nook. The pangs of guilt would strike at odd times, usually when she was caught up in a moment, enjoying herself. It was as if a part of her was still missing.

Despite everything, she kept busy. With work, rehearsals and friends in and out of her home, she had started to think about the future. In doing so, she accepted Alé's offer. It left her a little breathless to think she would be teaching alongside him.

She had just begun to lay out ingredients for a hearty pumpkin, leek and potato soup, when the doorbell rang.

She immediately regretted answering it. The biting winter wind slapped at her cheeks and penetrated through her oversized woollen jumper. Her toes curled in her fluffy bunny slippers.

George, Betty and Alé stood on her porch with grins on their faces.

Betty eyed her tracksuit bottoms as if they were the devil. "Get dressed dear."

"Hello to you too. I was just about to make some soup, so come on in." Tilda plucked at the sizable hole in her jumper. She hadn't expected company.

"No time. We're taking you out, so get dressed."

Tilda groaned. *Jane Eyre* sat patiently on the couch, begging her to read the worn pages just one more time.

"I don't wanna go out."

"Shoo!"

"Something nice!" George called out. "And hurry!"

Tilda walked out a few minutes later in a clean hoodie. Betty took her arm and marched her back to the bedroom.

"*Nice*, darling. *Nice*. It hasn't been that long since you understood that concept. No sweatpants."

Tilda's outstretched tongue said it all. When she finally slumped in the car, in her robin-egg button down coat, and her warm merino sweater underneath, she was in a full-blown sulk. Alé sat beside her, a sunny smile on his face.

"She's got that hangry look."

Tilda rolled said eyes and slumped back. "That's what you get for hijacking me when I was in burrow mode. It's freezing out and yes, I am hungry." Tilda glared at the tie Alé pulled out of his jacket pocket. She jerked her head back when he tried to wrap it around her eyes. "This some kind of kink?"

George guffawed over Betty's sharp interjection.

"Behave, Mathilda." Alé's low drawl moved the heat from her cheeks all the way through her body.

"Seriously! Are you three abducting me now?"

He grinned. "I'm blind folding you. Don't ask questions."

Tilda shrugged her shoulders and allowed Alé to cover her eyes. By the time they manoeuvred her out of the car Tilda's curiosity set in. "Where are we?"

"Patience, Mathilda." Alé breathed in her ear. Heat trickled down her spine. Her senses were on fire. Alé's clean, masculine scent lingered in her nose. His touch burned hot on her cool skin.

Tilda licked her lips and stepped over a threshold. Alé's scent had faded, replaced by a familiar smell that made her blood run cold.

"Alé, where are we?"

"1, 2, 3. Ta daaa!" Betty and George sang as Alé carefully untied the knot.

Tilda blinked. "Is this some kind of sick joke?" Her whole body trembled.

"This, my dear," Betty began, "is the new and improved The Book Nook."

"Why did you bring me here? To rub it in my face?" Tilda's heart pummelled in her chest. "That's just cruel."

"Your store, dummy." George grabbed her shoulders. "It's your store again."

"What?" Tilda's body vibrated with tension. "I don't understand."

"We couldn't let you just lose this place, Tilly dear." Betty guided her up the ramp of the nook. "So, we got together. The town, our community." She looked at Alé. "And settled the debt."

"You what?!"

"It was Alé's idea," George continued. "Don't look so surprised, Tilda. We couldn't let you lose this place."

She sputtered. "But — how? It was so much money." Her eyes were wide with shock.

"Consider it paid. We raised enough money to save the store. The school chipped in, the council too. Which is how we managed to persuade the bank. I wasn't going to tell you this but, Young Frank pitched in too. He didn't want you to know, but I thought you'd like to hear how much you're loved by this community. Frank is being moved to an assisted care facility — dementia is getting worse — he didn't want me to tell you that either."

Tilda was touched beyond words and guilty to have received such good fortune. She was sure she didn't deserve it.

Alé stood in front of her now. "I can see what you're thinking. Let all that guilt go. You deserve to have your dreams, Mathilda. You've worked hard for this place and we didn't want you to lose it. Neither did the community."

Tilda burst into tears, vaguely aware of the three pairs of arms that circled around her.

"I don't — I can't... but how did the bank agree?"

"Your Argentine friend here can be very persuasive."

Alé shrugged. "We had the money. The petition and weight of the council helped. The local representative for parliament didn't hurt — that was Betty's connections."

"Rodney owed me a favour." She winked. "Everyone knows how important this place is to you. To our community. It's time we all had it back."

She looked at her three saviours. "I can't believe this... thank you! So much! How can I repay you?"

"You don't need to. Just run this store like you always wanted to Tilda," George added.

Betty nudged her. "Well, are you going to take a look or not?"

Tilda wiped at her eyes and did just that.

It was exactly how she had pictured it in her head. Exactly what she wanted. The thin winter light filtered through the Palladian windows.

She brushed her fingertips along the custom-made tables, the bookshelves. Bean bags of every colour were strewn in corners. She wandered down the aisle of shelves to the open space of the nook and noticed the blank space on the wall.

She turned to Alé. "What's this?"

"I told the boys to hold off putting in the blackboard just yet. I thought you might have wanted to do it yourself. For your gran."

Tilda's heart burst with joy. She launched herself in his arms, her mouth fusing to his. She poured all her thanks, all her gratitude into the kiss.

Alé's mouth shifted on hers, his arms came about her, holding her close. Every inch of her body came alive.

She broke the kiss, aware of Alé's hands on her hips. The pressure increased; his mouth inched closer.

George and Betty cleared their throats. "When you're done... admiring our handiwork, we have lunch reservations." George cut in.

Alé winked and stepped back.

Heat flooded her cheeks. "I can't thank you enough, Alé."

"I think you just did."

Tilda walked back down the ramp, heart lighter than it had been in months. Her eyes lit up. "I have to thank Patrick and —"

"They'll be waiting for us at the pub."

Tilda grinned. "Well then, what are we waiting for?"

CHAPTER TWENTY-FIVE

*D*espite her slight hangover, Tilda couldn't stop smiling.

She stood in the nook the next day and watched Patrick and Alé drill in the blackboard. It felt like she was in a dream.

"One more thing." Patrick pulled out a plaque. "It was his idea." He jerked his head in Alé's direction. "For your nan."

Tilda's eyes stung. "It's beautiful." She read the inscription. 'In loving memory of Ethel Landrey, may her warmth, creativity and legacy live on, forever.'"

"Thank you. So much." She hugged Alé, then Patrick. "I'm indebted to you all. I can't believe George did so much of the renovations as well. At his age especially."

"He insisted. It's done now. And one thing you certainly aren't in, is debt. Now the fun begins."

Tilda had the honour of drilling the plaque to the wall; of seeing it shine.

"Time to get the launch organised." Alé squeezed her shoulder.

His hand seemed to burn a hole through her thick sweater. The kiss — her impulsive, reckless desire — had shifted something between them. Or at least it felt that way every time he looked at her.

She had broken the no-kiss clause. And in doing so, seemed to unleash sensual fireworks between them.

Problem was, she didn't know what the hell she should do about it.

In the fortnight since she had been given back the store, Tilda had drummed up enough interest in the new launch of The Book Nook, given notice at Riversdale Primary and settled all her legal obligations.

On principal, she visited the aged care facility to thank Young Frank in person. He had been more than generous in his support, even though he blamed himself for her finances. She had left with the promise to write to him with updates about the store. She hoped to visit as often as she could too.

Even though the police had contacted her, informing her of their inability to find those who trashed the store, they were confident it was the same youth gang that had targeted the dance studio. No charges or arrests had been made as they were unable to locate said gang.

Tilda thought it an odd similarity but focused on the fact that she had The Book Nook back up and running. She should be over the moon. Yet a creeping sense of unease pervaded her joy.

In between updating social media, restocking the store and preparing for the launch, she didn't have time to feel guilty. But she just couldn't shake the feeling. It was in this anxious state that Alé found her, shoulders slumped over her laptop in the back room.

"What's wrong?"

"Nothing." She tried to focus on the website.

Alé sat down opposite, gently pushing her laptop screen down. "Tell me."

"Now you sound like Dex."

"Mathilda." The warning in his voice made her pout.

"I'm one hundred percent grateful for everyone's help in making this store mine again..."

"But?"

"I can't help but feel like I don't deserve this."

Alé took her shoulders, then tilted her chin. His amber eyes flashed in temper. "Don't ever say that, Mathilda. If it wasn't for your persistence, your courage, your dream to make this place a home again, you'd never be where you are."

"Yes, but that's exactly my point! I didn't make it happen. I didn't do it on my own." She stood, pacing.

Alé leaned against the table. "Did your gran?"

"Huh?"

"When she started this place. When she set up the store, did she do it on her own?"

"I don't know. I was a kid."

Alé's eyes narrowed. "I'm sure George and Betty told you the story. I've heard it a few times over the past month.

Tilda rolled her eyes. "Okay, so the community may have helped build it."

"And they donated time — and money — while she cooked and provided for their families. Helped their children with their reading."

Tilda stopped pacing, crossed her arms. "My gran still did the painting and put up wallpaper. She still swung a hammer and balanced cheques."

"Ha!" Alé pulled her towards him. "You admit it. She had help, and yes, she worked to set it up, but she didn't begrudge others or herself when she needed help. You've worked so hard — alone — to do it all. So what if you got help?

"You give yourself so generously to this community. I didn't know about half the people you've supported, in time and money, until I went around asking for donations. You tell no one this. Yet you put so much pressure on those shoulders and expect to be able to do it alone. Stubborn woman." He squeezed her hands. "Just because you were given help, that doesn't make this any less of a success... you have to start learning to be proud of yourself, *si*?"

Tilda's breath shuddered out. As did her sense of failure.

"You're bossy."

"And right."

She rolled her eyes, enjoying the pressure of his hands around hers.

"Feel better?"

"Sort of." The dread she had felt before his arrival was now replaced by butterflies in her stomach. "Or at least, I will be."

"*Bueno*." He slung his arm around her shoulder. "Now stop being a baby and let's get back to work."

CHAPTER TWENTY-SIX

"*D*aisy the Duck searched for Freddy the Frog. But just when she thought all was lost, just when she believed she would never see her bestest friend in the whole of Lallyville again, Daisy heard a noise —"

Tilda paused for dramatic effect.

She watched as the sea of little faces looked up at her expectantly. Some sat forward — eager and captivated — others had kneeled in anticipation. She bit back a smile that threatened to break the spell of Story Time.

"Rrriiiibit," Tilda croaked loudly, making some of the little children gasp. "'Freddy!' Daisy cried out. 'I'm so happy that I found you again. You had us all worried sick!'

'Apologies, my dear Daisy,' Freddy replied. 'I went out picking flowers to make you a daisy chain.'

With that, Freddy the Frog, gave daisy her gift, placing it around her long neck.

'Freddy, oh Freddy! Thank you!' exclaimed the little

duck, 'I'll wear it always,' she said. 'In honour of our friendship.'"

Tilda held the page up and slowly showed the children the image of the frog gifting the duck her chain.

"'From that day forward, Daisy and Freddy were always together. If Freddy went to the river, Daisy followed. They read stories, played games in the park and loved each other more than anyone else in Lallyville. Daisy and Freddy were friends for life. They had each other. And that's all that mattered. The End.'"

Tilda showed them the last page of the picture storybook of Daisy and Freddy toddling off together through the park in the sunshine.

An eruption of sound broke the spell; the children clapped and spoke all at once. Their excitement about the story was infectious. Tilda held up her hand and waited for them to settle down.

She glanced across at Alé, standing at the back of the crowd. The new flyers they delivered in haste had evidently worked. The store was filled with eager young children, their parents and older individuals who remembered her gran's Story Time just as fondly as Tilda did.

She smiled at him remembering what he said when they chose the story.

'It's a great little book, Mathilda. It celebrates the differences. The duck and frog - still friends even though they overcome a few hurdles. Opposites attract, no?'

Tilda had wondered if they did, indeed attract.

She focused on the children. She couldn't let herself be distracted by a certain someone today of all days.

"I'd like to thank you all for listening so attentively to 'When Daisy met Freddy' and for being a part of The

Book Nook's first Story Time. We have a bit of time for a few questions if you would like, before we have some morning tea. We then have activities with our guest speaker and local author of the hilarious series, 'I Don't Wanna', by Michael Faraday."

There was a whoop from a bunch of seven-year-old boys who were huddled together, clutching the latest copy in the series.

A few hands went up from some of the younger children in the group.

"Can we meet Daisy and Freddy?" A wide-eyed, dark haired, little boy of three asked. He gripped a plush bear close to his chest.

"I'm afraid we won't be able to, but you can always grab a copy of the book to have a read when you like," Tilda supplied, trying not to smile.

"It's not real, dummy!" An older boy replied with all the wisdom of the world.

"Boys, please," their mother admonished from behind them.

Tilda tried to answer all the questions and promised them a chance for more after the break.

"One last question before morning tea."

"Did you draw that picture?" A little girl in pigtails asked, pointing to the chalk board behind her.

Tilda turned to look at the image that Alé had drawn. It was a large replica of Daisy and Freddy, at the point when Daisy was wearing her chain. He had used coloured chalk to contrast the green of the frog with the white of the duck. In the background was the lush park, pond and tree-lined path behind them with an inviting sun showering the two in a golden hue.

"I'm afraid I'm not that talented, but we do have our artist here today if you would like to ask him any questions later. Alejandro Garcia is at the back." She gestured, and he waved to kids.

A barrage of children called out, wanting to show him their drawings too and asking if they could draw on the chalk board.

"I think it's time for a snack, and if you want to ask Alé anything about his drawing or even browse the store, then feel free. We have a discount on children's books today only.

"But before we go, I'd like to say a massive thank you to everyone in the community who has helped make today's launch possible. I know my gran would have loved to see it." Tilda's voice wobbled.

She adjusted her dark framed glasses. Blinking rapidly, she thanked those close to her heart individually, knowing she was beyond indebted to them for their generosity.

When the children rose in thunderous applause, Tilda was touched beyond belief.

Various members of the community came up to Tilda during the break to offer their congratulations. It buoyed her more than she had expected.

It was half an hour later before she managed to make her way across to where Betty and George were introducing Alé to a range of people.

As she approached, George grabbed her in a bear hug and boomed his congratulations.

Betty's smile was warm. She whispered, "your gran would have been so proud, my dear."

Tilda blinked back tears.

"Thanks so much for coming along. I couldn't have done this without you."

"Don't mention a thing, darling girl."

"Don't be silly, baby doll!" cajoled George. "We wouldn't have missed this for the world."

Tilda looked over at Alé, stuck in a conversation with Dotty Freedman. Alé eventually joined them.

"Congratulations, Mathilda. It's a big success." He leaned in close, quickly placing a kiss on both cheeks. The current of electricity that shot through her was immediate.

He'd been there for her every step of the way. She had come to rely on his advice. She found it hard to think about what life was like before Alé. It was more than just the humming in her blood that had her yearning for more.

"Thanks, Alé. I'd say your drawing has been a pretty big success."

"You can bet he had all of them little ones eager to ask him if he knew Daisy and Freddy personally." George chuckled.

"It's been a fantastic opening, Mathilda. The place is full. People are buying books. It's a smash."

"He's not wrong there, Tilly." George bobbed his head in agreement.

"Now there's no excuses."

Tilda frowned at Alé. "Pardon?"

"Dotty cornered me just before. She's got a group together already, eager students wanting to learn tango."

"The crazy woman has ten people who want to dance. Ten!" George sputtered. "She's been drumming up support like an army leader."

Betty hid her grin. "Now, George, don't be like that."

George made grumbling noises. "If it weren't for this woman standing next to me, I would have said forget it! But you know I can't say no to a pretty face, can I now?" He one-arm hugged Betty who went slightly pink.

Alé winked.

"I should probably grab a bite to eat before introducing our author." Tilda's stomach was louder than the crowd.

"We'll continue our rounds." Betty and George gave her kisses and made their way through the crowd.

She turned to Alé. "Thanks again for coming along."

"Trying to get rid of me so quick?"

"I — oh." She swallowed. "I just mean — if you..."

"I'm teasing you, Mathilda."

"I know." She bit her lip. His eyes lingered on her mouth, his gaze setting her alight. Tilda swallowed as liquid heat coated her body.

Big mistake.

Alé couldn't look away. The pulse at the base of her throat throbbed. He didn't care that there were people about. He wanted to grab her and taste the soft, lush sweetness she had to offer.

He leaned towards her. The small strangled sound at the back of her throat was more invitation than dismissal. Her eyes widened.

Alé clenched his fists against the overwhelming

desire to graze his teeth along the slender column of her neck, to taste her. She always smelt intoxicating to him. Floral yet sultry. Sweet and sexy. The combination left him with a prickling sensation at the back of his neck.

She still wore those hot little glasses; dark and square, contrasting against her pale skin, now flushed. But there was a light in her eyes now, an energy that enticed him. No wonder she was driving him a little crazy. What man could resist?

Images of her naked and willing flashed through his mind. He wanted to be the one to give her pleasure, to see her writhe in satisfaction, and beg him for more.

The need was so strong that he took a step back.

Mathilda looked back with wide eyes. He ran a hand through his hair and tried to stop his thoughts from wandering down a sinful path. "I don't have anywhere else to be, but here, Mathilda."

She nodded, wet her lips again and offered a small smile.

"I'll see you later."

She turned to leave, and he couldn't resist grabbing her arm. "Hey, *felicitationes*! You should be proud."

She smiled. "Thanks, Alé. For everything."

Mathilda stepped through the crowd leaving Alé with a heavy sensation in his chest.

It disturbed him that he couldn't place it, couldn't name it.

The fact that he was already looking forward to seeing her bothered him. Sure, they had grown even closer over the past six months. It was a natural progression in their friendship.

He watched her as she mingled, the way she beamed at the crowd when introducing the author session.

Warmth bloomed in his chest. He released a shaky breath. That's exactly what it was — he cared for her. Like any normal person would about another friend. He could handle that. He had promised her his friendship, he'd kept his word.

But a lot had changed since then. Something had shifted inside him. She had kissed him and unleashed a need that he fought so hard to keep tethered.

Did she want more? He would have sworn on his manhood that the look in her eyes said she did.

What terrified him was that the look in his eyes said the same thing too.

CHAPTER TWENTY-SEVEN

*A*lé walked into The Book Nook that Monday morning, eager for a distraction. The images that had jolted him awake in the middle of the night still lingered. He knew the reason for it and could only hope he had been mistaken.

It may have been a decade or more since he had seen Camila in the flesh, but he would have sworn he caught a glimpse of her at the Riversdale Fair.

The whole weekend had been filled with celebration; stalls were packed with eager children lining up for hot pastries, hot chocolates and even hotter stuffed peppers.

Riversdale had transformed itself into an amusement strip of games and good food. Alé had naturally spent the day with Mathilda, sampling food and talking to locals about their plans to teach tango in the community. They had taken the time to talk about their ideas for the lessons. He had been impressed by her vision, knowing that she understood not only the aesthetics of tango, but what was needed to break it down for beginners.

But as dusk had fallen, he caught a glimpse of dark hair, of a red painted mouth slashed upwards in that tell-tale smirk. Though her eyes had been covered by shades, Alé could have sworn he had seen Camila.

Like the phantom that she was, no sooner had he caught a glimpse, that she had disappeared. He had known she was in the country. He had expected to hear about her tour from other teachers and students. But he didn't like the fact that she was lurking around. Why would she come to Riversdale, of all places? It hadn't made sense.

Because it seemed ludicrous, he had shrugged off the sighting as a product of his over-active imagination. But he had been caught in the maze of his past, bound by nightmares later that evening.

Beneath it all, was the niggling fear that the performance would never work. That he'd never be as good as he once was.

Shoving the thoughts aside, he continued through the store. He'd make it work. They'd make it a success.

He had to believe it.

Alé paused mid-stride. He had wanted a distraction and boy did he get it. All the air in his lungs deflated.

Mathilda stood less than a meter away in a dark figure-hugging skirt and white blouse.

His greedy gaze travelled lower; sensible black ballet flats had him lingering on her slender ankles which he couldn't help but want to see in six-inch heels.

A very civilised part of him was disturbed by the primitive urge he had to bite, just at the curve of her neck. He clenched his hands. Lust shot through him. He had to get a grip, or he was going to embarrass himself.

"I was just admiring your new domain," he called out.

Mathilda's eyes warmed then clouded over. "What's wrong?"

Alé silently cursed. It was unnerving how she was able to read him. "Restless night."

She nodded, even though he could tell she didn't believe him. "Looks like you need a coffee. Care for a drink while we talk business?"

"Sounds perfect."

He needed to keep his hands occupied even if his mind was filled with doubt. While Mathilda's life was back on track, his was hanging together by a thin thread.

He couldn't lose momentum now. It was his one chance to prove himself. His last chance to make it right.

His life depended on it.

CHAPTER TWENTY-EIGHT

*T*ilda had never been great with numbers. She had much preferred books to balancing figures, but she was determined to get the hang of the new software Dex recommended so she could manage all those figures with greater efficiency. Her mind was lost in the program when she answered her phone.

"Hello darling, I'm sorry to call you at work, but I've some news."

"Betty, hi! News?" Tilda chirped. "Hey, do you use BalancePro? Trying to figure out this bloody program. Why don't you come across to the store and we can chat?"

"No, dear, I can't. Mathilda darling, I don't think you quite understand. It's — well — I've got some bad news."

Tilda's hand hovered over the keyboard. The air hung heavy with Betty's weary, leaden tone. Tilda gripped her phone. She had felt the same unspeakable dread when her grandmother had sat her down, at six years old, to tell her that her parents died in a plane accident.

"Betty? What is it? What's going on?"

"George is in the hospital."

Tilda's hand shook. Adrenaline barrelled through her with the speed of a bullet train.

"But... I spoke to him a few days ago. Is he okay?"

"He had a heart attack. But I don't want you to worry, the doctors have operated on him. He's in the best care." Her voice pitched, heavy with fear.

Tilda's mind whirled. All she could hear was George. Heart attack. Hospital. The words echoed in her ears and closed up her throat.

"What happened?" she whispered.

"Oh. I was — it was —" Betty's sobs pierced through the phone. Tilda shivered.

"It doesn't matter. Just tell me where you are and I'll come over."

She noted the details of the hospital before hanging up. Tilda willed her legs to stand, yet she could only stare into space. She needed to get to the hospital. To see George. Still she sat. It was as if she was bound to the chair.

"So I wanted to know if —" Dex came in and crouched down. "Tilda, what's wrong?"

"I have to leave." She jumped up, picking up her phone and racing towards her bag. Dex ran after her.

"Tilda! Wait! What the hell is going on?" he grabbed her by the shoulders. "I'm not letting you leave until you tell me what's happening. Was it Alé? You look like you've seen a ghost."

"Alé? What? No, George is in the hospital."

His hands bit in to her arms.

"Ouch! I don't know the details, but Betty just called

to say he had a heart attack. I —" she breathed out shakily, holding back tears. If she cried now, she'd be a mess by the time she got to the hospital. She needed to stay strong. For Betty. For George.

Dear God, please, please, let him be alright.

"It's okay." Dex relaxed his grip and held her close. "I totally understand. You go. Don't worry about anything here. We'll sort it all out."

"I — oh, I'll need a bus. I don't have my car."

"I'm calling Maree, Dotty's assistant." Dex shooed her out the door. "She'll take you there."

Tilda's throat closed over. "Dex, you've no idea how much this means to me."

"Go, before you make me cry. Give our love to George and Betty."

Tilda nodded and waved, racing across to Dotty's Floristry, hoping that she'd get a lift as soon as humanly possible.

CHAPTER TWENTY-NINE

*T*ilda navigated the starchy white corridors of St. Mary's Hospital with her heart in her throat. She spotted Betty, shoulders slumped, sitting on the hard, plastic chairs, and felt dread settle low in her gut.

"Betty?"

She looked up, then burst into tears.

Tilda sat beside her, holding her tight. She looked down at an errant bit of foil on the floor, blinking away her own tears.

"Are you okay?"

"I am. I will be. Thank you for coming, it's nice to see a familiar face. I had been trying to get through to George's brother all morning and I couldn't."

"Don't worry, I've got Dex on to it, so he'll let his family know."

Betty nodded. "I can't seem to concentrate on more than one thing at a time. It frightened me the way he just crumpled."

"It's okay. You helped him. It's all that you could have done. He's getting the best care possible."

Betty sniffled.

"What's happened?"

"The doctors — a young man — Dr. Matheson, came by not ten minutes ago to say... oh Tilda, he slipped into a coma."

A coma. Tilda's eyes stung. "Have you been home?"

Betty shook her head. "I couldn't leave him."

"What happened with his surgery?"

She needed to keep talking. Being unable to do anything would drive her insane.

"They operated on him and said they found some blocked arteries. That was what caused the heart attack. It was successful, but they don't know how well he is until he wakes up." Betty gripped her arms. "Oh Tilly. I'm so glad you're here."

"I'm not going anywhere. So, you were with him when he had the heart attack?"

Betty turned slightly pink. "Oh. Yes, I was."

Tilda's brows drew slowly upwards. "And?"

"I went over to George's for dinner. He sometimes asks me to share a meal with him, and I did. He cooked a wonderful carbonara — my favourite. We spent the evening talking, he brought out the pack of cards and we played a little. He was his usual charming self. Lots of laughter. There was no sign of anything being wrong." She twisted the tissue in her hand. "If I had only —"

"It's okay. He'll recover soon. You'll see." She soothed and patted until Betty settled again. "Have you had something to eat?"

Betty shook her head.

"You should get some food. Go home, grab a shower. Sleep a little."

Betty shook her head. "I can't leave him alone."

Tilda's throat closed over. Betty and George were a team. They always had been. Even if they never said they were a couple, in Tilda's mind, they were a unit. Partners.

What had they been waiting for all these years?

What was the point to life if you never took a chance? Tilda swallowed, throat tight. It was as if something shifted inside her mind. A clarity that had been missing before.

Tilda squeezed Betty's shoulder. "You won't be leaving him alone. I'm here. I promise I'll watch out for him. I'll call you if anything changes."

It took an hour to convince Betty to go home. Tilda put her in a cab herself and sat in the hospital.

She never felt more alone in her life.

Tilda jerked out of her dazed state when nurses wheeled George into his room an hour later.

She stood immobile as his usually animated face was now grey and expressionless. There was a drip in his arm, he was connected to monitors.

"Can we help you, ma'am?" One of the nurses asked politely.

"I'm here with George. He's family," she added, fearful of being cast out of the room.

"Are you with the elderly lady who was with him?"

Tilda blinked. "Yes, I am. I sent her home for a bit of a rest and I'm sitting in with him." She gave them a few minutes of arranging him on the bed in the ICU. "Is he okay? Is he still in a coma?"

A gentle-faced man with sandy blonde hair turned to her. "You'll need to wait for the doctor. In the meantime, I would suggest that you hang tight."

Tilda nodded. "Am I allowed to stay in here, with him?"

The blonde-haired nurse patted her shoulder. "Of course you can. If you need anything, or something changes in his condition, press this button here." He pointed to a red call button.

Tilda took it all in and thanked them. She stared down at George and indulged in a few tears. Then quickly brushed them aside.

Tilda examined the man who had been a father, grandfather and uncle, all rolled in to one.

She couldn't remember a time when George wasn't in her life. He taught her how to kick a ball properly, to ride a bike without training wheels. He always seemed to be her rock.

It was what made the image before her so very shocking. She sat down on the chair and held his hand. She found it disturbingly cool.

Tilda shook her head, taking in his lined face and slightly yellow pallor. He was in a place where she couldn't reach him. She squeezed his hand, called his name. It came out as a squeak. She tried again.

"Hey Georgie-boy." She smiled, wanting to keep him company, wanting to give him the comfort that he had always, unreservedly given to her. She hoped he could hear her. "What a crazy day isn't it?"

She bit her lip. "I don't know what to do. You'd think with all my experience caring for gran that I would."

She knew her gran's situation was different. Her sickness had been prolonged. George's ill-health was even more shocking because it was so sudden.

"I wish there was something I could do to make it all okay. I know that you'll pull through this George. You've got to. Everyone is counting on you, you hear me? Damn it, George." Her voice hitched, the sound wretched through her clenched teeth. "You can't leave us. You can't leave me."

She wanted him to jump out of the bed, a cheeky expression on his face, having tricked them all. That was the George she expected.

"Betty was here. She's worried about you. Wouldn't leave your side. I had to practically shove her out the door. Stubborn. You're alike in that way. You need to wake up and tell her she's the most important thing in your life. I know she is.

"Do you remember the time when I accidentally broke gran's swan? I was practising the soccer moves you had shown me and chopped the head clear off the bird." She laughed, wiping at her tears. She began talking and found that she couldn't stop. There was so much she wanted to say to him. So much she wanted to share.

Tilda wondered what that was like — to have such a bond of friendship that nothing could break it. A bond of friendship that was so strong that it lasted beyond the changes of time, even past death itself.

Alé's face swam in to view. She shook her head to clear it.

She had been so focused on the past, on those whom

she had lost, that she had begun to take those still living for granted. If she wasn't careful, she'd end up on her own deathbed and find out that she never took chances.

That she never truly lived.

"You have to wake up, George. I love you, you hear me? You have to wake up." She begged, resting her head against his arm, praying for a miracle.

CHAPTER THIRTY

*T*ilda winced. The headache at her temples was sharp and unrelenting. She had sat so still, had been so vigilant since the doctor left, that she was now stiff all over.

She had called Betty to reassure her. Not that Dr. Matheson had said anything new.

There were no head injuries from the fall, and he hadn't regained consciousness since his heart attack. According to the doctor, comas were a way of allowing the body to repair itself. There was no indication of when — or if — he would wake up.

Tilda stretched. Shutting the door behind her, she walked across to the nurse's station to leave her number in case anything changed. She needed a tea to soothe her jittery stomach.

Tilda turned. Her heart trembled.

Alé stood in the middle of the corridor, his hand raised in greeting. She walked towards him, wanting nothing more than to be comforted by his touch.

She threw her arms around his neck, burying her head in his chest. He was warm and solid. Safe. And he was here. Hot tears fell hard and fast, her body wracked with sobs; Alé tightened his hold.

She couldn't bear the thought of losing him. She didn't want to be like Betty and George, hiding their feelings, settling for a friendship but never being satisfied that it was enough.

In his arms she felt that everything would be okay. If only for a few minutes. Tilda reluctantly pulled away.

Alé guided her to the chairs in the little waiting area. It was thankfully empty. "Sit while I go get you something to drink. Coffee? Tea? Water?"

Her mouth felt thick, like it had been stuffed with cotton wool.

"Tea. Please. I was just about to go and get it myself actually."

"Consider it good timing. I'll be back in a few minutes."

Tilda sat on the hard, plastic seat, rubbing her hands over her face. For so long she was accustomed to facing problems on her own. Now she didn't have to.

Her heart soared. Depending on Alé felt natural. Right. She didn't want to fight that anymore.

Alé came back with a small stash of food. He handed her the steaming tea and placed a sandwich, banana bread, and a chocolate bar on the seat beside her.

Tilda smiled.

"So how did you know I was here? How did you find out about George?"

"Dex told me. Mathilda, I'm so sorry."

"Thanks."

She cast a glance back at George's room.

"Did you want to go back in?"

Tilda apologised. "Yes. Sorry, I don't want to leave him alone for long. I know that sounds silly, but I want to be there, in case."

"Of course. *Vamos.*"

"Oh. Don't you have to go back to work?"

Alé waved that suggestion away. "Isabella is taking the class this evening."

As Tilda began to protest, he held up a hand.

"It's done. This is more important. Plus, hospitals are cold places to be alone. Trust me I know." He picked up the items and placed them in the bag. "Well?"

Tilda paused before they went in. "I know you're really busy, but having you here means a lot to me. I just wanted you to know how much I appreciate it."

Alé took her shoulders and squeezed. "This is when you need your friends and family around you the most. No more talk of leaving. If —" he added as she opened her mouth, "I want to leave, then I will say so. *Claro?*"

"*Claro.*" Tilda opened the door to George's room bracing herself for the long wait ahead. It was a huge relief to know she wouldn't be waiting alone.

Later that evening, Betty arrived back at the hospital with an overnight bag and a determined glint in her eye. She had shooed George's cousins, and eventually, Alé and Tilda, out of his room, demanding that the staff need only make up a small cot for one. She was staying overnight and everyone else had overstayed their visiting hours.

Tilda had no choice but to agree. She knew reasonably that there was nothing she could do to change the situation, but her anxious mind was afraid that something bad would happen if she wasn't there. She sat in Alé's car, staring out of the window, conjuring up terrible scenarios.

It wasn't until he pulled up in her driveway that she stirred.

She frowned when he got out of the car with her.

"What are you doing?"

"I'm coming in with you. That's what I'm doing."

"Why?"

"Because you need something to eat. I know you won't bother making something for yourself, so I'm going to do it for you."

"But —"

"No buts." He gestured to the shopping bag in his hand.

"When did you get that?"

"On our trip over here? Remember?"

Tilda blinked. She vaguely recalled Alé saying he needed to stop for a few minutes, but she couldn't remember any details. It was like her mind had blacked out. She was in a thick fog.

"Sure. Yes, okay. Come in. I apologise for the mess. I wasn't expecting company."

Alé hoped the warm, cheery interior of her home would bring her some comfort.

They walked through the lounge, past a sitting room where the bookshelves lined the walls, and into the kitchen.

He manoeuvred her to sit on the dining room chair at the far side of the kitchen, whilst he made her another cup of tea. He took groceries out of the bag, cast a quick glance at her and noticed her eyes were beginning to droop. Five minutes later when the kettle screamed, Mathilda was fast asleep, her body splayed in an awkward position.

Alé placed the teapot back on the stove.

She mumbled in protest when he carried her down the corridor to a room that was half open. A bra was strewn across the bottom of the bed, so he assumed the room was hers.

Alé ignored the lacy white contraption and lay her down on the bed. She sighed when he placed the patch-work blanket across her body. He couldn't resist smoothing back her sunny hair. His gently unwound the ponytail, revelling in the feeling of her silky strands through his fingers.

Alé's gut clenched. The scent of apples and vanilla surrounded him. He breathed in deeply and placed the elastic on her bedside table.

She was stubborn and endearing. Tough in ways she couldn't possibly understand. And yet, it was her warmth and open nature, that generosity of spirit that made people gravitate towards her. Made *him* feel good being around her. It was what had him wanting more.

Alé's hand shook as he stroked the curve of her cheek. He fought against the very real temptation to curl up beside her. Turning on her bedside lamp, he stepped back. He'd never get around to cooking if he gave in to impulse now. Leaving the bedroom door slightly ajar, Alé walked back to the kitchen.

He had a feast to prepare.

Tilda woke nearly three hours later, mouth dry and mind disoriented.

Images of George, grey and lifeless crowded her mind. She sprang out of bed curious at the sounds emanating from the kitchen.

She padded out, barefoot, to find Alé tossing a salad in her grandmother's old apron. She shoved her hair out of her eyes, absently wondering when it had come loose.

Tilda's mouth twitched. The frilly apron clashed wonderfully with the masculine man in it. Despite his attire he still managed to look ridiculously appealing.

"How did you sleep?"

"Too well."

She looked around in awe at the table filled with food; cold cuts of meat with olives and bread, steaks, and pastry parcels. "Is that —" she pointed.

"*Empanadas*. Beef. I thought you might need a feast after today."

Tilda shook her head. She noted the opened flour by the sink.

"You hand made the pastry?" she goggled, walking towards the golden and gleaming brown parcels. They were still steaming hot.

"*Si*. My mother's recipe."

Tilda looked around expecting to see a stack of dishes to tidy. At least that's what happened when she cooked.

"I had time to wash up before you woke. Nobody wants to deal with dishes at midnight."

Tilda shook her head. Then burst into tears.

Alé wrapped one arm around her even as he chuckled softly. "I can't say I've ever had that reaction to my domestic skills before." He led her to the dining table. "It's been a crazy day. You need to eat something and get a good night's sleep." He kissed the top of her head.

Tilda wiped her tears. "I'm not used to crying so much. So often."

Alé shrugged. "Emotion is expected. No big deal, eh? Sit. Relax."

Tilda pointed to the green dip. "What is that?"

She picked it up and smelt it. Garlic, spices and an earthy scent assaulted her senses.

"*Chimichurri*. An Argentinian speciality. You have it with meat. It's great when we have an *asado*."

At Tilda's raised brows, Alé explained. "It's a barbeque. Loads of meat, cooked for hours with amazing flavour. As you don't have a barbeque, I had to settle for the frying pan."

"Everything smells fantastic."

"Eat." He gestured.

Tilda picked up an *empanada*. She bit into it and was immediately bombarded by an array of flavours; the chilli and beef complimented the raisins and olives. She hadn't tasted anything like it. She told him as much when she polished off the first and reached for a second.

Alé laughed. "Good?"

Tilda assented around a mouthful of food.

"I like a woman with a good appetite. Try the *chimichurri* with the steak too."

Thirty minutes later, Tilda leaned back in her chair. "Oh my goodness. I'm so full." She patted her stomach. "Alé, that was the best Argentinian food ever. Not that I have anything to compare it to mind you. I'll have to get you cooking more often."

"I'm glad you enjoyed it."

"I'll wash," she said, rising.

"No, let me," Alé protested.

Tilda swatted him back down and cleaned up the few dishes whilst he talked to her about his current painting. He divided leftovers into containers, then dried the dishes.

They moved to the lounge room with tea and chocolate biscuits.

"If you ever visit Buenos Aires, you have to try an *Alfajore*," Alé recommended.

"What's that?"

"Pure heaven." He described the biscuit, with its chocolate and *dulce de leche* combination.

Tilda didn't even think twice when Alé snuggled closer. She curled her feet up on the couch and leaned into his shoulder. The combination of a full belly and Alé's presence had her utterly relaxed, despite the stressful day.

She studied his profile, mentally tracing the line of nose, the angle of his jaw. She wanted to bury her hands in all that messy dark hair, to lose herself in him for a few hours. Her stomach quivered.

She hadn't a clue what the time was and didn't even care. Tilda couldn't imagine anyone else she wanted beside her right now.

"It means a lot that you were with me today."

"Anything for a friend."

She bit her lip, her throat still raw from crying.

She couldn't help but think of George and Betty; anyone could see that they meant more to each other than either of them let on.

Was a friendship enough when it came to Alé? She was so focused on protecting herself, on not wanting to get hurt, that Tilda was beginning to wonder if she had made a mistake.

"Stop worrying," he whispered, rubbing her knee. She started at his touch.

"I'm trying not to. It's just hospitals always bring out this fear in me."

Alé nodded, mouth tight. "I understand. They aren't the best places when you're vulnerable. Too bright. Too noisy. Or in some wards, not noisy enough."

"Of course... your accident. Tell me what happened all those years ago, Alé. Tell me everything."

Alé looked at the woman beside him, in whose eyes held no judgement, only concern. The warmth of Tilda's small hand on his, the comfort of being beside someone who he wanted to connect with, eased the vice around Alé's chest.

He swallowed the scalding tea. "It's not an easy story."

While the past seemed to be everywhere he turned these days, he found himself opening his mouth and giving voice to a ghost he knew would always dance beside him.

Tilda sat very still, eyes wide.

"The accident happened because the other driver was high out of his mind. I would have seen him crossing over the wrong side of the road if I had been paying more attention, but my mind was elsewhere." He recalled, gripping the side of his mug.

"It was dark, slippery wet. The other man was speeding on top of being drugged up." Alé gestured. "I slammed into a pole. And spent nearly a year in hospital. He got out with just a broken collar bone. A few other people were injured but I was..." He shook his head. "I can still see that flash of light. Those headlights." The darkness.

Mathilda squeezed his knee.

"I couldn't walk. I had therapy for many years just to do simple movements."

She covered her mouth. Shook her head.

"I still get headaches. My back isn't as strong. Physiotherapy helps with the pain, but it flares up when I push my body too hard. I take painkillers on the bad days. But even with all these reminders, I know I'm lucky. They said I'd never walk again."

Mathilda shook her head. "How awful to be given such a definite diagnosis."

"That's doctors. It was like a death sentence. I had some feeling in my back and legs. But they didn't think that was enough. After they told me that, I hit a low point. I was barely out of my teens and suddenly all my dreams of tango championships had vanished."

Alé brushed away a tear from her face. "Why are you crying?"

"I'm sad for the young boy and those dreams. It couldn't have been easy, Alé."

"It nearly killed me. Up here." He tapped his head. "I was in a dark place for a long time."

"What changed?"

"One day I realised I had two choices. Accept their sentencing or make my own. It was a hard lesson. A bitter one. But over the years I learned to walk. Finally, to dance. Before my thirtieth birthday I left Buenos Aires, travelled for a few years and landed in Australia wanting a new life." He shifted, feeling oddly relieved.

"I'm sure it wasn't as easy as you make it sound."

"No. But I had more than one reason to want to leave Buenos Aires..."

The peal of the bell made them both jump. Mathilda frowned. "This can't be good news."

Alé trailed behind her hoping she was wrong.

"Dex! What in the world are you doing here? Oh!" Mathilda cooed. "Who is this gorgeous little guy?"

"Well hello to you too."

Dex came in with a small, shivering bundle in his arms.

"I couldn't sleep coz of this little gal, so I thought take a walk and see if your lights were on."

"New puppy?" Alé stroked the head of the small, black Labrador.

"She is. I caved into my sister's suggestion and bought little Lola to keep Teddy company through all his treatments, poor boy. The vet says he isn't doing as well as they'd like, so Lola here provides him with plenty to live for." Dex scratched her ears. "She's been a great distraction for the both of us to be honest. Though my shoes and pillows are paying the price."

Alé had seen Teddy at the bookstore every now and

then. The grumpy arthritic dog was popular with the small children even though he grumbled at all the attention.

Dex and Lola sniffed the air. The little puppy yipped, squirming to get down.

"What is that gorgeous smell, Tilda?"

"Alé cooked an Argentinian feast."

Dex raised an eyebrow. "Cooked, did you? Well, well, well, I'm impressed."

"There's plenty of leftovers if you're hungry."

Mathilda nodded. "Help yourself."

Dex placed the puppy on the floor before wandering to the kitchen.

"It's been a long day." Alé turned to Mathilda. "I'll go." He headed for the door.

"You don't have to leave." Mathilda followed. "I enjoyed our evening, despite the circumstances. You're easy to talk to."

Alé could have sworn Mathilda's eyes seemed to deepen in colour. In the quiet depth of night, with faint noises from the kitchen to keep them company, Alé felt the ripple in the air.

Mathilda's body swayed closer. Every inch of him wanted to stay, to see where the night took them. He swallowed hard around the lump in his throat.

"*Gracias, non*. I'll give you a chance to rest."

Mathilda nodded slowly, eyes never leaving his face. "Thanks again for today."

"It was my pleasure." Alé closed the distance between them. His mouth brushed against her lips, once; a soft, comforting kiss. He shifted, kissing her left cheek. Then her right. The faint day's growth scraped against her soft skin. "In Argentina. Both cheeks."

"That was three."

He grinned. "Text me, *sí?*"

"I will."

Alé opened the door and left quickly, before he could convince himself otherwise.

CHAPTER THIRTY-ONE

*T*ilda juggled work, hospital visits and tango rehearsals, trying to maintain a positive attitude despite the fear in her heart.

A week had gone by and still there was no sign of George coming out of his coma. Betty had arranged for her 'Betty Brigade' to run the Cone and Cup, so she could stay with George.

Every time Tilda looked at her schedule she wanted to run and hide. Especially when she thought about the performance. The one-hour session she managed to squeeze in mid-week proved she was far from ready to step on the stage.

She didn't have an outfit, still couldn't quite master turns and was failing to keep in time to the change in tempo.

Even through her frustration, she had to smile. The Book Nook was booming. The launch had been the burst of energy the store had needed. Which was great for business, but not so good for relaxation. Not that she could complain. She had been given a second chance and was lucky to say the least.

Tilda rolled her shoulders. The niggling feeling was back again, making it hard for her to unwind even when she was exhausted. She put her increasing dissatisfaction down to George's coma.

She was nearly finished work for the day when her phone rang.

"Tilda, *chica*! Any news about George, honey?"

"Izzy, hi. No news yet."

"He'll get through this. Did I tell you about this friend of mine whose aunty came back from the dead?"

Tilda's lips twitched. Isabella never failed to amuse.

"Not that I am saying George is, you know...because he isn't. Anyway," she continued speedily. "She was undergoing surgery — gall stones or something, when her heart just stopped, bam, she's out. They can't revive her. Five minutes later, I'm not joking, Tilda, she wakes up. Heart starts beating again and everything. Doctors couldn't explain it."

"Is this supposed to make me feel better? If so, you kind of suck at it."

"What I'm saying is, if my friend's aunt can come back from the dead then George is gonna pull through just fine. You wait and see."

"I appreciate you looking out for me."

"You're lying. But that's okay. I've been praying too, so that always helps. My mamma used to say, if you got no other option, then pray — it's quick fix for a bit of peace of mind."

"I'd end up in a nunnery if I did that at this point."

Isabella laughed. "They're overrated. Awful outfits.

What you need is a bit of a distraction. You've been going a million miles an hour and you haven't stopped to take some time out for yourself. Get a spa treatment. A massage. Alejandro told me that you fell asleep at the dinner table last week."

Tilda's back straightened. "He did?"

"Mhmm. And that he cooked you a meal as well," Isabella pointedly remarked.

"He did."

She could all but hear her friend rolling her eyes.

"Let's just say that any man who is cooking for a woman — any Argentine man — well, it means something."

"You're out of your mind. You know that, don't you?" Tilda played with her split ends. She couldn't remember the last time she was at the hairdressers. Let alone a spa. "He made *empanadas,* Izzy, it's not —"

"What? From scratch?"

"Ah-huh." Tilda jerked the phone away from her ear as Isabella yipped.

"I told you so! No man cooks for you from scratch without it meaning something. Wake up!"

Tilda didn't think it wise to mention the kiss. Or the fact that she had dreamt about him naked. Doing very non-friend like things to her body.

"You're seeing things that aren't there. Alé and I are friends. That's what friends do by the way. They care." She squirmed. Why did that sound like an excuse?

"Not hot, sexy, single friends. You know what they do? They stick their tongues down one another's throats and make beautiful babies. He's single. You're single."

"So what?"

"That means he's available for sweaty, do me with your clothes on you're so hot, sex."

Tilda laughed. "You're mental."

"I know for a fact that he wasn't into Tiffany. A guy doesn't throw away sex with a willing woman, and believe me, she was more than willing, unless he is sweet on someone else. And you know who that is? I'll give you a clue. Her name rhymes with builder!"

"Wait. Hold on. How did you know they didn't have sex?"

"Durr. Tiffany told me! That's when she knew he really wasn't that interested."

Tilda's cheeks glowed. "That doesn't mean anything." Images of Alé's hands on her body, his mouth on her breasts flooded her system.

"Tilda?"

She cleared her throat. "Yes... sorry, tickle in the back of my throat."

"See? You're not taking care of yourself. Like I was saying earlier, you need a break. You're not working tomorrow — let's go shopping!"

"I'm going to see George at the hospital and give Betty a bit of a reprieve."

"Well after that — for a bit. Tilda, you need to take a break!"

"I'll see."

"I know what that means."

"Look, I promise I'll go shopping with you soon, okay? We've the performance creeping up on us. I'll get a dress."

"Promise?"

"My word."

245

Isabella sighed. "Alright. I'll hold you to that. But please get some rest okay?"

"I will."

"And Tilda — don't cancel out the Alé thing. You'd be great together."

"I'll speak to you later." She hung up before Isabella could add any more suggestions.

While she wasn't ready to admit anything to Isabella, Tilda couldn't stop the flutter of hope in her chest whenever she thought about him.

Something was happening between them. Something they hadn't defined or given voice to. But she felt the sensation building, with every time he touched or looked at her, with every phone call they shared.

Magic. That's what it felt like whenever she saw him. A tingling sensation that had her grinning like a loon. And dreaming not so PG fantasies.

She hugged the feeling to her chest and locked up for the evening. Her phone rang as she stepped out on the pavement.

Tilda grinned. It was Alé.

Tilda made coffee that Sunday morning on autopilot. Her eyes drooped, her back ached. She was beyond tired. She had dreamt in numbers again — a sure sign she was stressed. Every time she did, she would wake up trying to work out elusive mathematical equations.

Rationally, she knew that loving someone came with risk, but she didn't think she could handle losing George right now.

Dr. Matheson wasn't thrilled about the fact that he was still in a coma and she didn't know if she was strong enough to handle another loss. It was now three weeks since he had been admitted. Not a hopeful sign. She saw it in Dr. Matheson's eyes. She resented the discussions that began to centre around long-term plans and George's 'wishes'. Did he want to have his organs donated? How long would the family be willing to leave him in this state?

When her gran had died, it had taken months of zombie-esque wallowing and mourning before she was able to function. She gritted her teeth at the stabbing sensation in her chest. She had vowed she wouldn't put herself through another heartache. Life was best experienced without the loss that came when one loved so deeply, right?

Tilda rubbed at her face. She found it harder with every passing week to believe that. Not when things with Alé were going so well. She was learning so much about him, about herself in getting to know him. But every time she felt giddy, a wave of guilt would course through her.

How could she feel any kind of happiness, when it was very likely that George wouldn't pull through? The sinking feeling in her stomach didn't dissipate. Every time she visited the hospital, with every passing week, her optimism wavered just that little bit more.

Whatever she thought was happening between her and Alé, she had to deal with life as it stood. At this point in time, her thoughts and prayers had to be focused on George and supporting Betty if things got worse.

Tilda buttered her toast and squared her shoulders.

She would handle whatever came her way. It's not like she had any other options.

With a resolved heart and mind, Tilda showered and dressed for the day. She had just opened her front door, when her phone rang. It was Betty, incoherent, in tears.

"Tilda, darling. It's George!" she cried. "Come to the hospital quick!"

Tilda's heart thumped. Betty's voice became white noise.

The moment she dreaded had finally arrived.

Tilda ran down the halls of the hospital. Her heart was beating an erratic rhythm. She forced herself to walk on unsteady legs down the familiar corridor. Betty was seated outside George's room, crying. Alé had his arm around her. Bile burned the back of her throat.

"Mathilda!" Alé called out to her.

It couldn't be true. She couldn't have lost him. "Wait!"

Tilda shoved the door of George's hospital room open, hands shaking.

A group of doctors were standing around him, talking all at once. Tilda hovered at the door. Dr. Matheson shifted.

"Tilly?" George rasped, turning his head. "Tilly, my girl," he said, motioning her closer.

Tilda buried her face against his neck, hot tears of joy and relief pooled on his hospital gown.

"I'm so glad you're awake. I'm so happy you're okay."

George patted her head and chuckled weakly.

"Try not to drown me, will ya, kid?"

They let her fuss over him before Dr. Matheson cleared his throat.

"We were just in the middle of our check-up."

"Oh." Tilda sniffed. "Yes, of course, I understand. How long will it take? Can we come back in?"

"Yes. We'll be running a few tests, but you'll get to see him. Not for long mind you. He'll need some rest."

"Rest?" George huffed, "I've been asleep all this time — what more rest do you think I need?"

Dr. Matheson's lips twitched.

Tilda patted George's arm. "Awake and already causing trouble."

Tilda walked back out, adrenaline wreaking havoc with her body. She was still jittery.

Alé wrapped his arms around her, rubbing her back.

"I thought —" she shook her head. "I thought that because you were crying —" Tilda took a closer look at Betty. Happy tears.

"He's going to be fine, Tilda. Just fine."

"Oh! I guess I didn't think to ask!"

Betty laughed in relief, batting her hand away. "You hung up before I could explain."

"What happened?"

"I was with him this morning, and Alé had come to visit, to make sure I was okay."

She shouldn't have been surprised that he would have volunteered more of his time. It was a part of his character that she was starting to understand. A part that she had come to count on. He was unlike any other man she knew.

"Alé and I were talking in his room, and all of a

sudden we hear George say, 'left me for a younger man, have you?'"

Tilda's laughter rang through the corridor. "That's George, alright."

"Scared the living daylights out of us. We called in the doctors and that's when I rang you."

"I'm so relieved! It's so good to have him back." Tilda sat down on the hard, plastic chair and thanked Fate for their good fortune. She only hoped it would last.

The following evening, Tilda was determined to relax. She had a busy day at work followed by a great visit with George at the hospital but was still wired.

She had taken Isabella's advice and after a sumptuous dessert with wine, she donned a face mask and soaked in the bathtub until the water turned cold.

Tilda slipped on her silk nightdress and robe, lathering her arms and legs in a vanilla scented shea butter Isabella had sworn by. The pampering had been just the trick.

She was about to indulge in another glass of wine when the doorbell rang. Tightening her blush pink sash, she opened the door, to find Alé on the porch.

Pleasure saturated her senses. She couldn't help but grin.

"Hey you."

"Hey yourself. Mind if I come in? I can't stay long."

"Sure." She noticed the cab idling at the curb. "Going somewhere?"

Tilda closed the door behind her. The night air was close to freezing.

"Actually, yes. I didn't mention it at the hospital, as I didn't think it the time and place, but I'm off to Sydney for a week. Running some workshops and filling in for a teacher who needs some help at the Latin festival."

"Oh. Right... you never mentioned it."

"Slipped my mind with everything that was happening."

"Okay. Well..."

"I didn't want to leave without saying goodbye. Without seeing you."

A tide of pleasure swept away her disappointment. "I'm glad you did."

"Sorry to get you out of bed."

Tilda swallowed. She fiddled with the collar of her gown. Alé was staring at her in a way that made her feel utterly feminine and all too exposed. Liquid heat pooled between her thighs.

"I wasn't..."

Alé leaned in and held her.

His clothes were cool against her heated skin. She shivered, cursing herself for not keeping her bra on.

She felt indecent... and utterly aroused.

"Mathilda." He drew back, arms still holding her. "I —"

"Tell me," she whispered, heart thudding.

"I'd rather show you," he murmured, voice low.

She tilted her head a fraction of an inch. A clear invitation.

There was nothing soft and gentle about the kiss. His mouth was demanding. His lips burned.

Tilda whimpered with need when his arms tightened around her.

Alé's tongue traced her lips; his teeth followed, teasing her mouth open, demanding a response.

Tilda matched his ardour and pressed her body against his, desperate for more.

His hands skimmed up, past her nipples — peaked in desire — and framed her face. He led her backwards, trapping her body against the wall.

Tilda arched against him. Her tongue stroked until she heard him groan.

"Alé," she moaned, when his mouth found her neck. "Alé..." she had no words. She didn't need them.

"Look at me." His voice was low, rough. "Open your eyes." She did as he asked, lost in those whiskey depths. "I want you to remember my kiss when you fall asleep tonight. God help me, but I couldn't resist." He kissed her softly this time, eyes never wavering from her own, hands stroking her face.

He finally pulled away.

The loss of contact made her shiver.

"I'll see you in a week. Call me."

She watched him walk back to the cab, grateful for the winter breeze that followed.

CHAPTER THIRTY-TWO

*I*t wasn't hard for Tilda to keep herself busy over the following week. Whilst she replayed the kiss a million times since Alé had left, she didn't get much spare time to wallow in his absence. She had a to-do list as long as her arm, rehearsals to attend and a store that was busier than ever.

Story Time — one of the things she had loved being a part of as a child, was in hot demand. She had kids crammed in the nook eager to listen to the new Story of the Month. Which meant more work, more displays, and more time spent on social media drumming up attention. Which was fine, if she hadn't had a million other things on her plate.

The police had phoned as a courtesy to let her know they were still investigating the vandalism of the store. Not that she expected any answers after all this time.

By the end of the week, George was finally released from the hospital. Tilda made sure to visit him with supplies when he did. She balanced a heavy casserole pot and Tupperware containers, letting herself in to George's home.

She called out, voice echoing down the hallway.

"Hey, hey Tilly! Out here!"

Tilda made her way through the spacious home to the back porch where George was sitting, a newspaper unfolded on his lap.

Tilda bent to give him a kiss. "Brought you some stew."

George looked over his glasses at her, before taking them off. "And working yourself ragged I see."

Tilda sat beside him on the plush wicker chairs. "No. I'm fine, thank you very much."

George grunted, then patted her hand. "Thank you for the stew Tilly, but you don't need to be minding me."

"That's what family does, isn't it?"

George laughed and tweaked her cheek. "Got me there, girlie."

"So, how's life in the slow lane?" She motioned to the newspaper and the tea.

George grumbled. "Pain in the arse!"

"Betty got you on the herbal tea."

"That woman is driving me nuts," he said with a smile. "No Pizza. No coffee. No cheese. No bloody fun."

Tilda threw him an arch look.

"Don't be giving me sass, young lady. God knows I get enough of it from her."

"She cares about you, George. We all do."

He waved a lined hand around. "I know. I know. The whole thing is a pain in the arse. But a wake-up call, ya know?"

Tilda squeezed his hand. "I can only imagine."

"I know it's all cliched crap, but Tilda, it was a kick in the pants. I've never been to the hospital in my life, save when I was born!" He shook his head slowly. "It was a wake-up call for sure. I needed it too. I always prided myself on being strong as an ox. What's pride when you're close to death's door?" He brushed a hand against her cheek. "Now I get to see those who I love again. So I'll put up with herbal crap for it."

"We're glad to have you back."

"Feeling's mutual. But what good is it if you don't admit your true feelings. To tell the love of your life that you adore them."

"Hold up. Are you telling me that —"

"She's been the love of my life for decades, Tilly. I finally told Betty that I love her, that I was crazy for never acting on it — wasting all those years — for what?" He waved a hand around. "But this isn't about regrets. It's about life. And that means celebrating when the woman you love returns your affections."

Tilda couldn't contain her joy. She hugged him tight, tears dampening her lashes. Finally.

"It's about bloody time, George. I'm so happy for you both!"

"We're pretty over the moon ourselves. I know I'm luckier than most." His jovial face turned serious. "My point is, don't wait for something like this to tell the ones you love how you feel. You start to understand what's important in life. Catch my drift?"

Tilda wiped at her tears even as the prickling sensation crept down her back.

George scratched his cheek, overgrown with stubble. "You know me, Tilly, I'm a straight shooter. And I don't like to meddle in other people's business, especially not yours. But what about love?"

"What about it?"

"That's what I mean! You're a smart, beautiful woman. You have a fella who looks at you like —"

"Hold on. I don't have a fella."

"Your Argentine friend, Alé?"

"We're just friends." Tilda blushed, thinking of the kiss. She could hear the lack of sincerity in her own voice. She winced.

"Bullshit. I know the 'just friends' cards. Heck, I invented it. But that gets old real quick - especially at my age. Tilda — if you have feelings for him, you need to let him know. Don't get to my age and live with regrets."

Tilda couldn't protest. She knew her excuses were just that. She was telling everyone around her a lie that she didn't quite believe herself.

It struck her then, like a blow to the head. Maybe it was not seeing him for a week that did it, perhaps it was George's coercion, but Tilda wondered what would happen when rehearsals were over. Would she still see Alé so frequently? Would they still be spending time together? It made her ache to think of it. She cared about him, wanted him. But they never acknowledged that desire. Until the other night.

Tilda squeezed his arm. "Alé and I are happy as we are. I don't want you worrying about me, okay? Focus on getting better. Speaking of which, I'm going to go heat up some casserole. You sit back and relax. It's your turn to be pampered."

"Tilly —"

She ignored his protests on her way to the kitchen. Leaning on the counter, her hands shook.

A sense of urgency ran through her. Gulping in air, Tilda stared at the stove as fear bound her heart.

She craved more than just Alé's company. She wanted him. All of him. Those dreams she had been having ever since he left were making her yearn for more. She thought about the night he left for Sydney. The not-so-tender kiss at her front door. She trembled when she recalled the way his tongue had played with her mouth, the way his hands had brushed over her breasts.

If he hadn't had a plane to catch, she wasn't sure she would have been strong enough to resist him.

But what if whatever they were building towards lost its steam once the performance was over? What if she never had the chance to give in to her desire?

She had run away from intense passions for so long that she had successfully convinced herself that it was the road to ruin. Until Alé.

She was beginning to understand what it might feel like to never share such a passion. He was the only man who made her crave for more.

The only man who had the power to break her heart.

CHAPTER THIRTY-THREE

*T*ilda sucked at turns.

A small part of her wished that Isabella had come along to her rehearsal session with Alé, just so she could get a break from his punishing pace. But she thought they may have needed privacy after the way they left things.

She shouldn't have bothered. In his usual Alé fashion, he hadn't said a word about the kiss. He acted like nothing at all happened, treating her with a polite distance that set her temper alight.

He barely looked at her. When he did, it was only to call her out on her poor technique. Which only pissed her off even more.

Tilda gritted her teeth, attempting the deceptively simple manoeuvre over and over.

The routine required a double turn, which meant she frequently ended up on her ass.

"Look, let's leave it for now." Alé no doubt could see the steam rising from her face. "We can just practice with one revolution. But you need to do drills at home. If you're in the kitchen making tea, practice. At the book-shop, practice. Keep your balance and focus on one spot when you turn. Don't overdo it."

"I *am* trying to relax, but it doesn't work! Then I try harder and I just end up all over the place."

"The performance is here, Mathilda. We have dress rehearsals next week — this can't keep happening."

"I said I'm trying." She hated how his criticism stung. She hated feeling raw and vulnerable. More than anything, she hated his reserved attitude towards her. She had expected more, yearned for more than just a polite friendship.

Something had shifted in her this past week. She thought it had for him too.

Fool. She shouldn't have been surprised. This was what it was like between them. It was the pattern of their relationship. Pretend like nothing happened. Pretend she didn't have feelings.

Pretend. Pretend. Pretend.

"This performance means a lot to everyone. We're all working hard. We're all struggling. You can't give up, Mathilda. I won't let you. Now work through it."

Tilda clenched her fists. She knew she was sloppy. She didn't want to be reminded of it right now.

Not when he wound her up so tight.

With temper tears threatening to spill over, Tilda threw her hands up in the air. "Maybe I just can't do it, Alé. Have you ever thought of that? I'm not some super-star who has perfect balance and neat turns," she gestured. "I'm not you. So how about you just give me a break?"

"Give you a break? I've done nothing *but* give you a break. Reality is, Mathilda, we're performing. We have a range of venues booked and you need to nail it. I told you it would be tough. We have a show to put on, so toughen up. I know you can do it."

"Oh really? Because you really know me *so* well, don't you Alé?" Sarcasm won the day.

"Where is this coming from?"

To her horror, tears blurred her vision. "Can't we just accept that I'm not good enough and move on?"

Alé's eyes narrowed. It was like a tiger stalking its prey. "This self-pity bullshit isn't you, Mathilda. What would your grandmother say? It's weak quitter talk."

It struck a nerve. Tilda hissed, "what the hell would you know? I'm giving it everything I have -

"Bullshit."

Her mouth dropped. "Excuse me?"

"You heard me, Mathilda." He leaned forward, "Bull. Shit."

She glared at him, chest heaving. Afraid of what she might say, Tilda stormed over to her bag. She bent down to undo the strap of her beautiful *Commes*, but her shaking hands couldn't seem to manage the simple task. A shadow fell over her.

"You say you're pushing yourself. You say you aren't good enough, but as soon as something is too scary, you run. Face up to your fear for once in your life and take a leap."

"For once in my life?" Tilda scoffed. "You arrogant bastard! What happened to all that encouragement? 'Oh, Tilda, you're so great! Oh, Tilda, you're so brave!'"

He mimicked her in falsetto. "Oh, Mathilda," his voice dipped low, "you're being a pain in the ass."

She picked up her bag, face flushed. "You think you know me? Oh, that's right, Alejandro Garcia, the great world champion who learned to walk again."

She didn't see him flinch. Not through her red, hazy vision. "How dare you stand there and lecture me? News flash, buddy, if I don't want to do something, then I won't." She winced at the petulance in her voice. What was wrong with her? She faltered, hating herself for attacking him when a part of her knew she went too far. Knew she was lashing out.

But she didn't want to hear his criticisms. She didn't want to deal with 'Alé, the tango teacher' right now. Instead, she wanted, 'Alé, the fiery Argentinian.'

To have him look at her the way he did when he kissed her.

She craved to be the type of woman that drove him a little wild. The type of woman he couldn't keep his hands off. Reality was, she needed him to take the leap. To declare his feelings so that she wouldn't have to.

Alé glared at her. "I'm no champion. But I appreciate what it is to work hard for things that aren't easy." Temper had him biting out his words. "It's you who presumes things about me, Mathilda. I'm far from perfect, but at least I'm not a coward."

Tilda jerked back. It was like a slap in the face.

"You surround yourself with everything that is safe, peaceful, predictable. For what? *Madre de Dios*. Push yourself, Mathilda!

"Do you know how much this performance means to me? How much time and effort I've put into it? It's *my* life. *My* reputation on the line. I would have thought you — of all people — know what it's like to have dreams. But you can't see past your own self-pity."

Tilda scoffed. "You sure can dish out the advice, but you don't like taking it, do you? It's so easy for you to say that. So easy for you in your privileged position to cast judgement on me. But I liked my life, thank you very much. I liked it just fine before people like you decided you knew what was best for me. You don't know me."

"I know you enough to see you hold on to the safe option to protect yourself, when a part of you is screaming to break free."

"You're such a hypocrite! You're the real coward. You keep every woman around you at a distance. You kissed me, then shrugged it off, kissed me then apologised. Kissed me then pissed off to Sydney! You say we're friends, but you don't let me in. Look at what happened with Tiffany. You couldn't even date the woman for heaven's sake!"

"What's Tiffany got to do with this?"

"She was a bloody Victoria's Secret model and you pushed her away."

Alé blinked. "She was?"

"No, you idiot! But that's my point." The sound that emanated from her throat was one of pure frustration. "She was gorgeous and you didn't give her the time of day. You have a wall up. You're happy for things to be light and fluffy but you don't let anyone in."

Alé muttered something in Spanish.

"Don't you curse at me."

"It wasn't at you, princess. It was at the Good Lord for ever giving me such a woman!" His eyes were burning.

"You have me all worked out now, is that it? What do you want from me? What do you expect? Except for my blood and first born. Eh?"

"I don't expect anything from you!" Her breath hitched. She knew it was a lie. It's what drove her crazy the most. Tilda wanted more. Much more than he seemed willing or able to give her. More than her fearful heart would risk taking.

She trembled. Perhaps she really was a coward.

"Really, Mathilda?"

She barely moved. She would not give way to tears now. She would not fall apart in his arms. Not anymore.

"This isn't about me, is it?"

"Funny that — it never bloody is! But that's how it's always been with you. You run hot and cold. As soon as someone threatens that barrier of yours, you take a step back. Hell, we may as well be strangers. It's not like we have to see each other very much after this is over anyway."

"Damn it, Mathilda." Alé grabbed her shoulders. "We're nothing like strangers. You forget, I know you, and you know me, in the most elemental way possible," he whispered, his face inching closer to hers, his voice dangerously low, accentuating his accent.

"I - I don't know what you mean." Her chin lifted.

"I know how your body comes alive when you're in my embrace."

"Arrogant son of -"

"That may be the case, God knows I've heard it before. But I can feel it. When we dance, Mathilda, you come alive. You become someone you keep hidden. It's time you accept that part of who you are. Can't you see what we've shared? Can't you see your potential?"

In a lightening move, Alé had his arm around her waist, he jerked her body forward, so that her breasts were crushed against his chest. He threw her bag across the room.

The music echoed their passion. The violins clashed, the bandoneons soared. It spoke of anger and heartache, love and loss.

"No? You don't know what I mean?"

Tilda shook her head, body vibrating. A part of her was thrilled by the way he looked at her, even when her heart ached for more.

Her body betrayed her, hyper-aware of the hard planes of his body. She wanted this passion. Wanted his desire.

Alé changed his grip, so they were in a standard *abrazo*. Tilda couldn't breathe. She didn't want to.

"What are you doing?"

"Teaching you, Mathilda. Showing you what we have shared. What *I* have shared with *you*."

Angry, tawny eyes clashed with wary blue.

It was an invitation as much as a challenge.

The electric current travelled through them; from the connection of their hands to the pressure of his chest against her breasts. Tilda breathed in and everything in that moment erupted.

Alé's long, demanding strides relentlessly forced her to follow his lead.

They moved fluidly, vibrant in their anger. He led her in to a *gancho*, her leg whipped between his, then back out.

Alé taunted her. "Are you afraid, Mathilda?"

"Never." She searched for the venom but could only cringe at her breathless response. There was a wild, reckless part of her clawing to get out ever since that first kiss.

"Are you afraid of this?" He anchored her against him. "This is what we share. Are you afraid of what it makes you feel?" He slid his leg between hers.

Tilda responded by draping her own up the side of his body, brushing her thigh against his hip.

"I'm not afraid." Hell, she'd never been more alive.

The dance had become an erotic game of cat and mouse. Catch and release.

Teasing him with her *adornos,* Tilda kept her face close to his, their lips a whisper away.

On a guttural cry, Alé executed the final lift from their performance. Tilda's body hovered above his. She arched, held position. She felt light as silk when he swung her low to the ground, never breaking form.

Slowly, with a restraint that signalled of more than just his strength, Alé drew her back up to face him.

The music continued. It took only a beat before Alé's mouth devoured hers in a kiss that branded as much as it beckoned. The hard length of him pressed at her thigh. His hands took their fill, inflaming the need that throbbed between her legs. Long fingers searched, caressed and ignited every nerve-ending. Still she couldn't get enough.

Alé dragged her down to the floor, mouth frenzied, matching the fervent stabbing of the strings. His teeth found her neck and she arched up against him.

Tilda sobbed when his teeth greedily devoured her

breasts. She wanted to rip off her bra, to feel his mouth on her skin. She wrapped her legs around his waist. Her hips gyrated against him in a dance they both recognised. One they both wanted.

His tongue was scalding, a brand against her neck, her ear, her lips. He nibbled at her mouth, traced the plump curve with his tongue, demanding access. He was like a man starved. It thrilled her right to her core.

Alé's hand brushed over straining breasts, caressed the curve of her belly, teased down her thigh. She was drowning. All rational thought sunk alongside her anger.

She bowed up when he cupped her. She was wet and warm through her cotton pants. He stroked relentlessly, his mouth teasing her nipple through her shirt.

Tilda wrapped both hands around his neck, savouring the muscle, the strength, the sheer delight of his weight, heavy on top of her.

He tugged down her pants, then gripped her hip. Hard.

Her blood roared. It was a few seconds before she registered that his hand didn't move.

Alé rested his head against her shoulder, his body vibrating above her. He was thick and hard against her hip, his muscles corded bands of rope.

Alé reared back, groaning.

She could see the storm of emotion swirling in his eyes. He hovered over her again, took her mouth once more, then pulled back completely.

"Not like this." His voice was rough as gravel. He kissed her temple.

Tilda's body throbbed. She couldn't understand it.

Couldn't think properly with all the blood pulsing through her.

The metal grate slammed and footsteps trailed up the staircase.

Alé jerked his head up and cursed, covering Tilda's body with his own.

Isabella's eyes popped wide, her mouth gaping open and shut like a fish on dry land.

Alé dusted the talc powder from the floor off his pants and drew Tilda up with him. "Your timing is, as always Isabella, *muy bien*."

Isabella's wicked laugh carried through the studio. "That's my cue to leave."

Alé and Tilda spared a furtive glance at one another, before he turned off the music.

"Isabella. A minute *por favor*."

Tilda ignored her friend's knowing grin and retrieved her shoe bag, straightening her clothes. She needed to get out of here. Fast.

"I was going anyway." Tilda walked towards the stairs.

"Mathilda – wait, I'll see you out."

She half-turned and shook her head. She couldn't make eye contact with him now. She couldn't even think straight.

"I'll see you tomorrow," Isabella called out to her retreating figure. "We have some serious shopping to do."

Tilda waved an absent goodbye and left without looking back.

She was certain that's not all they'd be doing.

CHAPTER THIRTY-FOUR

*W*ild images of Alé naked, doing the horizontal tango had plagued Tilda all night. It was no wonder she was restless. He seemed to ignite something within her that both thrilled and terrified her. She prided herself on being calm and reasonable. Careful. It scared her to lose control like that.

Despite their argument, she was still unclear what he felt for her — if anything at all.

It had been brewing. She could see that now. It had been bubbling away — all that anger, all that lust — only to manifest itself right when she was at her most vulnerable.

The main problem was, she never knew quite where she stood with Alé. Just when she thought they were progressing towards something, one or both of them would take a step back.

Tilda heard the quick 'beep beep' of Isabella's Mazda MX-5. Shaking off the feeling, Tilda locked up. The sporty car was idling by the curb, the top was down and Isabella sat behind the wheel looking glamorous even in the cold. It was a public holiday and Isabella finally managed to coerce Tilda to go shopping. Not that it required much needling; she needed an outfit for the performance otherwise she'd be dancing naked. Which wouldn't help matters one bit.

"So where are you whisking me off to today for our shopping extravaganza?"

Isabella pulled out of the curb and around the corner with a screech of tires. Tilda had to stop herself from squealing and clung to the arm rest instead.

"We're going to Glendale. I figure the biggest and most exclusive shopping mall should be exactly what you need to find a hot little dress. And it's open on a public holiday."

"I see the physio is working wonders on that lead foot of yours." Isabella tilted her sunglasses to the tip of her nose, arching one dark brow. "Honey, you better believe these aches and pains aren't stopping me. I don't ever want to wear a moonboot again."

"It's been ages since you've had it removed."

Isabella shuddered. "And I've been traumatised ever since."

Tilda shook her head. She tried to relax even when her friend turned corners with all the gusto of a formula one racer.

Despite her restlessness, the gusty wind rejuvenated her sleep-deprived mind. She couldn't help but tilt her head back and enjoy the sensation. The light danced behind her closed eyelids; she relaxed into spots of colours and patterns.

If she was going to go shopping with Isabella, she may as well give herself up to the adventure.

A half an hour later, Tilda found herself towed around by Isabella, who knew some of the people in the stores on a first name basis. She dragged her in to a flashy looking boutique store.

"Isabella! So good to see you again!" A perfectly groomed blonde woman in her fifties approached.

"I brought my friend Tilda here to try on some of the clothes." Isabella gestured to the racks of colourful outfits.

Within minutes Tilda was ushered towards a changing area with piles of clothes.

"Izzy, wait. These can't all be for me to try on, can they? I only need one tango dress."

Isabella waved off her protests. "No, silly. They're for the both of us. We're just having a bit of fun. Try on some clothes. See if there are any you like. Live a little for God's sake, Tilda!"

Apparently, that would be her motto for the long weekend.

A few hours and few more purchases later, they still hadn't found Tilda's dress.

"Relax, Tilda," Isabella soothed. "I know exactly where we need to go for your outfit."

"You've said that all morning and it's nearly lunch time. Need food. Will beg."

"Okay. Come with me." Isabella motioned, leading her through the shopping mall to a storefront that showcased a stunningly beautiful ruby red dress. "That is your performance outfit."

Tilda looked up at it, admiring the rich, shimmery silk. The dress had a diagonal split to mid-thigh with folds of lace resting enticingly down the edge of the skirt. The bodice was fitted, the straps thin, and the dress was cut so low and the back that Tilda was afraid it would be indecent.

It was daring. Sexy. A dress that made her self-conscious even without trying it on.

"It's perfect, isn't it?" Isabella nudged her.

"It is...but I don't think I should be wearing it."

"Why not?"

"It's a bit conspicuous."

"Exactly."

Tilda rolled her eyes. "How many of the other dancers are wearing something like this?"

"Leave that to me." She shook her arm. "Stop worrying! This dress is perfect. The moment I saw it, I knew it would be the exact outfit for you."

"Mmm."

"Try it on! I guarantee you, when you do, you won't want to take it off."

Isabella was right.

The moment Tilda put it on, she loved it. The dress clung to her body and screamed seduction. It took her fifteen minutes of humming and hawing before deciding to throw caution to the wind and buy it. If she was going to perform a sexy tango, then she had to dress the part as well.

It was only when they were at lunch, sipping champagne and munching on fries that Isabella gave her a pointed look. Tilda wondered why it had taken so long for her friend to bring up the incident.

"So... you and Alé, huh?"

"Mhmm." Tilda sipped her bubbly and didn't bother to feign lack of understanding.

"It seemed pretty hot and heavy when I walked in. Just *friends*? Care to enlighten me?"

"I don't really know what to say."

"How about that you and Alé were getting naked when I interrupted."

Tilda bit her lip. "It's not something that - we just -" she huffed. "It just happened. We were arguing — he was being arrogant and I was getting frustrated with him. I said some unkind things, which I regret...but I think we both just snapped."

"And?"

"And what?"

"Did you say anything to him today? Call or text? Did he call you?"

Tilda laughed. "Hell no. If I'm going by Alé's track record, I'd say he's going to chalk that up to another mistake and pull away. Again. It's not as easy as just leaping in."

"Forget about easy. What do you want?"

Tilda looked past her. She wanted it all. But time and again, Alé proved to her that he wasn't ready for more. Tilda couldn't say, with absolute certainty, that she knew how Alé felt. Or that he wanted more than just sex.

"Look, I see something there that you both can't. It isn't just the tango connection. Or the sexual chemistry. It's more than that."

"Isabella, I get where you're coming from. But I can't

risk losing him and his friendship on a whim. Do I want him? You'd be blind not to. But I can't go there with him. I just can't."

"He cares about you, Tilda. I know he does."

Tilda shrugged. "I care about him. But I'm not going to get in to all the reasons why this can't work. He means too much to do that."

Isabella squeezed her hand. "Suit yourself then. But don't say I didn't warn you. Honey and bees, Tilda. Honey and bees."

After a long day of shopping and a sumptuous lunch, Tilda and Isabella headed out of the busy shopping mall, slightly giddy from their spending spree.

With the champagne bubbling through her system, Tilda paused at the exit of the centre. Without a word, she marched up to the salon.

"Uhh...what are you doing?" Isabella turned back.

"I'm getting my hair cut."

"You're - what?"

"My hair cut." Tilda replied, making a chopping motion with her hands. "You know, cut. Off. Chopped."

Isabella opened her mouth and then closed it again. "I know it's probably the champagne talking, but I think that's a fantastic idea."

Tilda grinned. "So do I."

A pixie-like woman with colourful hair bound past. "Won't be a minute, love."

The place was relatively big for a shopping centre salon. The surfaces sleek and shiny, the air punctuated by sprays and creams of every variety.

Tilda knew she needed an outlet. Her desire for change had been gnawing on her heels and racing up her spine even since she had shared that kiss with Alé all those months ago.

Their last dance reinforced how intense their passion was, how dangerous it could be.

This unsettled feeling with her life wasn't something Tilda could ignore. She may not be able to control what happened with Alé, or even his feelings for her, but she was able to decide what changes she wanted to make. Right at this moment, she wanted her hair cut.

"Hi! I'm Delia. Welcome to Sleek. What can I do for you?"

"I want it cut off." Tilda motioned to her hair.

The woman looked at her, eyes round in surprise. "Hey now, I like a decisive woman. Sit over here honey and we'll sort you out."

Tilda piled shopping bags on Isabella's lap and sat in front of the mirror. As the woman guided her to the basin and began washing her thick locks, Tilda's mouth twitched. She felt the tremor in her stomach. Nerves were there, that was normal. But she also couldn't wait for her transformation.

"Now what exactly are you after?" Delia guided her to a plush black leather chair and buttoned the styling cape around her neck.

"I want a sleek, sexy look — not boy short, but up to or just past my chin."

"Like this?" Delia found a magazine of hairstyles where there was a woman who had long bangs covering one eye, and hair that framed her face, finishing at chin level.

"Do you think it's okay that it'll be shorter at the back?" Tilda asked, feeling slightly uncertain again.

"Darling, with those cheek bones, you could pull off a buzz cut and still rock it. You'll look smoking hot, and super sexy — if that's the look you're going for."

A small smile played at the edge of her mouth. A thrill shot through her. Whatever had happened the other day with Alé, whatever it was that had been building inside of her was just another reason why she needed to start taking charge of her life. The change she craved was up to her.

She wanted something different. Something adventurous in her life. Isn't that why she joined the performance group?

Tilda thought about her conversation with Isabella at lunch. Sure, she didn't want to jeopardise her relationship with Alé, but hadn't she also come to realise that nothing was gained without risk? She would never live life to the full unless she took that step herself.

Tilda smiled up at the woman standing behind her, waiting expectantly. "Do it."

CHAPTER THIRTY-FIVE

*A*lé tried the door of The Book Nook, surprised that it was unlocked. It was close to 7 p.m. and the streets were dark. He would have thought Tilda would be extra vigilant after all that happened. The very idea that Mathilda could be hurt made him physically sick.

He rubbed the back of his neck. He was tired. He had had to fly back again to Sydney to run his musicality workshops, which helped drum up word of mouth about the performance, but it meant he had missed the last crucial week of group rehearsals.

The last time he had seen her had been that day at the studio. They had spoken a few times on the phone, but that was it.

It felt like an age.

He needed to see her, to make sure there was no awkwardness before tomorrow's performance. He didn't want to wait until their final rehearsals tomorrow to do it. Alé wanted to be sure they were okay.

He latched the door closed, making certain no one would wander in off the street. He'd remind her to lock up when she worked late. Not that she would take his direction willingly. Especially after their last argument.

Alé didn't know what he would say, if he could say anything at all. The only thing he knew was that his life was so very different than it had been only six months before. He didn't think that Isabella would have broken her ankle and he would have lost his leads. He didn't think that he would be showcasing his sketches at The Book Nook or looking forward to spending his time with its owner.

His world had shifted. He was beginning to realise he didn't want to go back to the way things had been. Before Mathilda. It frightened the hell out of him.

Alé looked across to the nook. A few mounted wall lamps illuminated the space. Soft music carried across to the front of the store from her laptop. He didn't hear any voices. She was alone. When Mathilda stepped out from behind a bookshelf, Alé froze.

She had cut her hair in to a sleek chin length bob, her bangs sitting diagonally across one eye, resting over her black framed glasses. He swallowed. She was wearing a white blouse and black skirt. As he approached, he noticed the small black heels. He bit back a groan of appreciation. She was a woman out of every man's fantasy. Alé's blood stirred just looking at her. When she walked across to the next set of shelves Alé called her name. She squeaked. Then slowly turned. Her blue eyes locked on his.

"Alé, what —" she took off her glasses.

"Don't." He walked to her. "Leave them on," he

growled. It was the feline smile that whipped across her face, the invitation in her eyes that had his resolve snapping. He pulled her towards him.

"I should wear these more often," she purred.

The kiss was akin to striking a match. The fire that blazed between them became an inferno within seconds. His mouth demanded utter abandonment. His hands, supplication. Tilda gave him what he asked for and more.

Alé's hands stroked, his senses feasted. She moaned when his tongue beckoned, duelling with her own. The sound was as heady as any drug. He wanted to give her pleasure; he almost shook with his need.

Alé ran his fingers through her hair, like blonde silk. He abandoned her mouth and explored the soft curve of her neck. Like an addict in need of a hit, he groaned. He wanted her with a desperation that had shattered his defences. But did she?

His hands gripped her waist. He needed to know she wanted this as much as he did.

"Mathilda, *mujer hermosa*. Is this what you want? Tell me. Do you want me?"

Her blue eyes captured his, they spoke of desire, a longing that made him weak. But he needed to hear her say it. Her words still burned him. He wouldn't selfishly take what she didn't freely give.

"*Si*, Alejandro. I want you." It was more than enough. He devoured her mouth; his hands squeezed the delicious curve of her butt. She quivered.

Dios mío. He knew, but never could imagine such exquisite pleasure. It was painful to feel her against him, to feel himself hard and ready and yearning, but with so much between them.

The fact that she met his frenzy with her own fervour, only made it hotter. It ignited every burning need inside. He promised himself he wouldn't make the same mistakes. That he wouldn't get close. He knew it would be his undoing. He knew it could break him. But he didn't care.

He nibbled her neck, tracing the smooth column of her throat, up to her delicate ears. Alé scraped his teeth along the round lobes, delighting in the way her arms clutched the back of his shirt.

She pleaded again, her breath coming in quick gasps, her body jerking against his. He held her when her knees began to buckle.

This was what it was like to feast after a famine. This was what it meant to have succour.

Alé walked her back against the shelves.

Hadn't he fantasised about this scenario? He groaned when his body jutted in expectation.

Alé filled his hands with Mathilda's breasts and thanked the heavens for womankind. Soft and lush. Nipples straining for his attention. He unbuttoned her shirt, shoved aside the scrap of lace and released one round, heavy breast. His fingers quickly found the pink-tipped peaks, already hard and waiting. She gasped as he teased her. Then arched, wanting more.

"Mathilda." He choked out, looking down at her, cheeks flushed, lips swollen and pink. "I've dreamt about this. This exact moment."

"Oh." She licked her lips, eyes almost violet.

"About taking you like this, up against the shelves, your legs wrapped around me while I pound into you. You've no idea what it's doing to me right now. What you're doing to me."

Her fingers shook as she slowly unbuttoned his shirt.

"Well why don't you just do it." She teased, drawing his face to hers, branding him with a kiss that had his body pinning her against the shelves.

Tilda's nails raked down his back. Her fingers stilled abruptly over the scars on his back. She looked down at his bare chest. Faint shimmering scars marked his abdomen too. He fought against the embarrassment, the instinct to cover them up. She bent her head, tongue snaking out to lick his chest, to trace one of the silver lines.

Alé trembled. She commanded his body, just as she did him.

She stretched up, biting his neck. His hips bucked, and he pressed her harder against the shelves.

Tilda arched back, crying out as his tongue licked and sucked, bit and nibbled.

"I don't — I can't...Alé, please," she begged. Her hips gyrated restlessly; her body strained for more.

He shifted lower.

"Let me pleasure you my — Mathilda." The words tripped over his tongue and landed at the back of his throat. He shoved it aside and focused on the goddess before him. He wanted to please her. Wanted to hear her moans, feel her body tremble, just as it did now. He wanted to give her everything.

"I can't — just —"

"You will stand it, Mathilda. Let me show you."

He ran his hands up her skirt and approved of the black lace stockings that ended mid-thigh.

"You're killing me. You know this, right?"

His finger slid aside the matching black triangle of lace. He kneeled before her, stroking her gently until she writhed. He teased her again and again, enjoying the damp heat. He kissed the silky skin of her hip. Far more intoxicating than any perfume. When he slipped one finger inside, she gasped his name.

She was tight. Like an iron glove around his fingers. And so hot. The combination drove him nearly to the edge. He gritted his teeth and kept his fingers gentle, rocking in and out of her wet folds.

She fisted his hair in her hands and begged him, sobbing his name.

Alé never felt more alive. Only when he was satisfied that she was ready, did he stand on shaking legs.

Tilda half ripped at the buckle of his jeans. She bit and sucked his neck, snaking her hands down to his butt. He hissed and ground himself against her in reply. Finding the zip, she shoved his pants down.

Alé covered the hard, already weeping length of himself.

He was shaking with a need stronger than any dance they had shared.

In one move, he had her skirt up again, his pants around his ankles. Her hands were free to grip his arms, straining through his unbuttoned shirt.

Mathilda wrapped her legs around him and before she could say his name, he thrust into her.

They both stilled. He waited, for what felt like an eternity until she rocked her hips. His thick, hard length buried deep inside her.

Feeling her wet and warm, he pulled out, only to

enter her again in one fluid motion that had them both crying out in pleasure.

Alé's body was slick with sweat. He strained to control himself. He was nearly crazed with arousal.

If this was a sin, he would happily be punished for it.

Alé teased them both, moving in and out of her wet core. She was dripping and willing. And all his.

Her legs wrapped tighter around his waist; his hands gripped her butt.

Every nerve ending urged him to pick up the pace.

"Don't stop Alé," she panted. "Don't you dare stop." She writhed and moaned, hips straining against him. She shuddered, tightening around him, once, twice. "Alé — oh God — I —"

"Come for me, *amor*. *Dios Mio*. Come for me, Mathilda."

She cried out, writhing against him. She squeezed him like a vice. She came. Hard.

That was the moment when Alé's control shattered. He drank in her moans, knew only the pleasure of her wet, shaking centre. Her soft, full breasts strained against his chest, the smooth silk of her thighs urged him on.

But it was the molten, pulsing heat that throbbed around his hard cock that sent him over the edge. The pressure built until his control shattered. He came, with her name on his lips.

Alé slumped against her, muscles straining. He gingerly lowered them to the floor, resting his back against the shelves, now scattered with books. Carefully, he held her in his lap.

Mathilda lay against his chest, limp and glowing. Their laboured breathing was the only sound in the room.

"Wow." Alé was the first to speak.

"Mmm."

"Still friends?"

His heart soared when she laughed. "Perhaps with benefits?" She raised one eyebrow, smile wicked.

Alé grinned, but her words struck a chord within him. They were so much more than that. She meant more to him than that. But there were no words for what just happened.

"I'm -"

"If you say you're sorry I'm going to brain you with my heels." Tilda looked up at him, brushing away a dark lock of hair.

"I wasn't too rough, was I?"

She shook her head. "Did I give you any indication it was?"

Alé studied her flushed face, the marks of his unshaven jaw evidenced across her swollen lips and neck. Those eyes of hers were happy and warm. She looked like a woman who had been thoroughly taken, but there was no evidence of any displeasure. "No but, I —"

"Then hush."

Alé blinked.

"Let's just enjoy the moment." She settled against him.

Alé held her close. He couldn't move even if he wanted to.

. . .

Tilda allowed every inch of her body to relax against Alé's naked chest. He was warm and hard and very male. She loved every bit of it.

The awareness that she very well had feelings for him had butterflies dancing across her chest. She didn't want to spoil the moment with words or 'what ifs'.

She didn't want to over-analyse what they had just shared. She hugged the warm feeling inside of her. Kept it close. Just for herself. She wouldn't worry about it. She knew that was her go-to response and she just wanted a chance to enjoy being with him.

After all, not many women could say they had wild monkey sex up against a bookshelf, could they?

She wriggled against him, shivering. He wrapped his arms around her, fingers brushing against her breasts. He stirred beneath her.

"Well, well, well. Look who's up for round two." Tilda raised her eyebrows. Her smile indulgent.

Alé caressed her cheek. She had to blink away the tears at the gesture.

His hand lowered to her breast, and she gladly succumbed to the sensation. Tilda straddled him, teased and tantalised his tongue with her mouth.

She swatted his hands aside and covered him herself this time, enjoying the sense of power she had over them both.

Tilda rose, then lowered herself down slowly, taking him inch by inch. Not once did she break eye contact. Alé shuddered. Her smile was the epitome of female satisfaction.

"Mathilda...you're...there are no words," he managed on a strangled groan.

"Then don't speak." She moved her hips slowly, taking them both on a journey that climbed higher and higher to heights unknown.

When she came, fingers stroking her slick, pink folds, Alé's eyes went blind.

His body stiffened; he joined her in the abyss, moments later.

CHAPTER THIRTY-SIX

*A*lé paced back and forth. He was nervous as hell but couldn't do anything to calm himself down.

Last night had changed everything. He had wanted to talk to Mathilda before the performance.

But how could he explain his feelings? Drawn to her at every turn. Like a teenager in need. Always on fire. No, there was no explanation.

They were performing in a matter of hours. It didn't leave much time for a last-minute rehearsal, let alone an in-depth discussion. Damn it, that's why he went to see her last night. To talk. He laughed. Look how that ended.

He was even less certain about their relationship. The last time he had seen her, she had been semi-naked and riding him until he couldn't see straight. They hadn't even spoken about their previous argument. And that bothered him.

How the hell did he move from that to...to what? What exactly were they now? Everything was tangled. Complicated. He ran his hand through his already worried hair. He didn't care for the feeling. The problem was that he didn't know where to go from here. He paced back and forth in the backstage area of Henri's *milonga*.

He should be focusing on the performance. It was one of the most important nights of his career. Yet he was distracted by a woman. He told himself never to get involved again, didn't he? He knew the consequences of it. But boy, what a woman...he smiled at the memory of last night.

Focus, man. Get a grip. Alé breathed in deep. In his mind he stepped through the routine and positions. His body knew the steps, but he needed to feel it, to own it. To prove he was no longer broken.

They had space enough to practice backstage without being disturbed and could go out to the *milonga* when they felt ready. It had started a half hour ago, but many people were already flooding in. His first performance in a long time. It would prove his worth as a teacher and dancer. His career. His hands shook.

The wooden door opened. He didn't have to worry much about thinking. Ever again.

Mathilda walked — no, sashayed in, looking like every man's wet dream.

He knew just how soft that skin was under her dress, and it took all his self-control not to walk over there and take her in his arms.

She had styled her hair in a messy, funky look. Blonde strands covered her right eye and fell across sharp cheek bones. Her mouth — *dios mío* — was painted the same electric red as her revealing dress. Every scrap of the material clung to her body, cupping her breasts, skimming her slender waist, clinging to her hips.

Mine.

The sheer force of his need made him shake. He wanted to cool the lust that had reared its hungry head.

Still, he couldn't look away. He knew what it tasted like to kiss her. Could almost feel the soft curves of her body beneath his palms. Everything about her tonight screamed sex. And all Alé wanted to do was bury himself inside her.

Tilda spotted him and smiled, slowly. His body jerked like an eager stallion.

Mine. The word echoed and reverberated around his brain until he couldn't stand it. Alé walked towards her, clearing his throat. He opened his mouth. No sound came out.

"Hello Alé," Mathilda's voice was low, seductive. At least that's what it sounded like to him. "Ready for tonight?" She placed her bags down on the leather couch.

He tried again.

"Mathilda. You're breathtaking."

"Thank you." She looked up at him, brows raised. The smell of her perfume surrounded him. Beckoned to him. Its floral, sweet scent contrasted with her sex-kitten look. The echo of the bandoneon rang out, charging the air with an undercurrent of sex and longing.

"Your hair looks...wow."

Slender fingers brushed through the sharp ends; a flash of blood-red nails completed her vixen look.

"Thanks." Her eyes clashed with his before moving away. "Did you want to go through a dry run?"

It was as if everything she said was on a time delay. On a far-off planet.

"Alé?"

He licked his lips and nodded.

"I'll go put on my shoes then." She turned. It seemed the view from the back was just as dangerous as the one from the front. He didn't know how he would manage to concentrate. Let alone perform.

"No!" Alé shook his head. He didn't think his body could handle her in those sexy shoes. Not right now at least. "Let's just step it out in flats for the moment and we can work on the next one with heels."

Her mouth twisted. Her face was expressionless. "Okay, sure. I'll put my flats on then."

Alé offered up a silent prayer of thanks.

He wanted to reassure her but couldn't find the words. He wanted to kiss but was afraid of what it all meant. He was breaking every rule he had put in place to protect himself. Rules that helped him get to where he was today.

But in staying true to them, he seemed to be messing up whatever it was that was happening with Mathilda.

He wasn't sure what to say about the other night. He wasn't even sure how to bring it up. Now wasn't the time to talk about it. But they needed to. Soon.

The hum of activity from the *milonga* filtered through backstage. The air was heavy with nervous excitement. Tilda had stepped out a few times through the side door to get some fresh air. The cold bit into her bare arms. She focused on her breathing and refused to bow down to terror.

This was the reason why she never did performances. It wasn't anything like dancing socially. Here all eyes gazed upon her and she didn't think she would be able to walk, let alone dance.

Tilda had seen Betty and George sitting at one of the tables. Their presence eased her nerves a fraction. George's colour was back, and he seemed in good spirits. He was out and about again, albeit grumpy that he couldn't drink the wine.

It was a good feeling to have family there to support her. Especially when her two favourite people seemed to be moving their relationship a big step forward. George's possessive arm around Betty's shoulder tonight said it all.

She rubbed at her bare arms and tried to focus on the routine. Images of last night flooded her brain. Sex with Alé had shaken her in more ways than one. It opened everything within her. But being intimate with him only made her even more nervous. Yes, she had wanted to appear confident walking in with her freshly blow-dried hair, careful makeup and that revealing dress, but one look from Alé and she was an uncertain mess.

A part of her hated not knowing where they stood. Last night had thrown everything off kilter. She was worried and liberated all at once. This new-found sense of sexual freedom felt good. The after effects still lingered on her aching hips. Why should she care about anything else?

A little voice reminded her that Alé hadn't even mentioned what had happened, not that it was the time or place. In fact, he hadn't said much to her at all. Tilda shook her shoulders. Hadn't she learnt that that was Alé's style? To keep silent and pretend it was all okay? Well, Tilda could do that too. Hadn't she decided that it was finally time she let go?

"You're up in five minutes." the DJ had poked his head in. "Good luck everyone."

All fear momentarily gave way as Alé branded her with one look. A tingling sensation caressed her breasts, shot down to her tummy and settled at her core. She couldn't seem to control the need.

"Tilda - shoes on!" Isabella called out.

She jerked and raced over to her bag, fumbling with the clasp of her shoes. Her hands shook.

"Let me," Alé murmured, kneeling before her.

"Thanks." She looked down at him as he placed her foot on his bended knee. Once he finished, he grabbed her hands in his and kissed the tips of her fingers.

"Don't worry, you'll be fantastic out there. You're an amazing dancer. You've got this, Mathilda."

Her heart turned over. Confidence coursed through her. She stood beside him, chin raised.

"Let's do this then."

"That's my girl," he laughed, leading her out.

Tilda ignored Isabella's Cheshire cat grin.

She had a crowd waiting and a tango to perform.

They took their place under beaming lights to a room filled with tango dancers. From fresh and wide-eyed beginners, to seasoned and humble veterans, up to the arrogant and disdainful masters; it seemed all of Australia was present to watch the performance. Tilda ignored the sea of faces and focused on Alé.

Isabella's voice carried over the microphone explaining the concept of their dance, and Tilda held her position. She turned her leg out, extending her right foot.

Tilda lifted her chin and let Alé's words sink in. The way he looked at her, his words of encouragement, made her believe she was every bit the strong woman he made her out to be. For so long she had waited to feel this way about herself. And it was Alé of all people who helped her see it.

She rested her left hand on her hip, with her left knee bent slightly. She never felt more alive.

At the tinkling of the piano, her feet glided before her in a walk that spoke of sex and confidence — despite the fact that her heart was beating erratically. She vibrated so much she was surprised she didn't just bounce off the dance floor.

At the charge of the music, where the rich metallic sounds of the *bandoneon* met the searing call of the violin, Tilda spun towards Alé. He held her, and they strode forth in a basic walk, which he cut by displacing her foot.

The music advanced in a stabbing, stirring rhythm, as did the performance. The *gancho* was lightning fast as Tilda's leg sliced between Alé's open frame. She looked into those knowing, tawny eyes, and enjoyed the way his heated gaze claimed her. In this dance, at this moment, the communication between them was more than just a performance.

Tilda displaced his foot and kept her eyes locked on his, unable to draw away. He winked at her — a flicker of movement and she grinned. It was playful, teasing.

She followed the ribbons of joy as it wound around her heart. The hours of practice and self-doubt didn't matter. Her body responded to Alé's touch, as if hypnotised. The passion of the night before only increased the power of their connection; it showed in the touch of his hands, the caress of her feet. She stumbled slightly on the double spin, but he held her, and she recovered quickly.

The stretch and sigh of the *bandoneon*, the upward bow of the violin, the echoing of the piano gave their dance meaning.

Tilda stayed on her axis, and he positioned her in to a *calesita*, her right leg extended out in elaboration and embellishment then wrapped around the back of Alé's body, showing off the slim leg no longer covered in silk. Images of her hip hooked around him in a different dance entirely teased her. She wanted to repeat last night's performance.

She caressed his foot, stepping over it, in to a one revolution spin, her hand stroking his face. She swallowed, overwhelmed by him, the dance, her feelings.

The violins begged to be heard, and encouraged the dancers to elongate their steps, to slow down at the *lapiz* then stride back again.

The music picked up speed and the buzzing *bandoneon* whistled in its frantic pace. Tilda held her breath. The fast-paced sound of the great instrument was bee-like in movement, playfully buzzing up and down the scale, urging Tilda's feet to move in quick small steps. Heat radiated between them, an energy that had nothing to do with tango.

He half lifted her in a travelling *planeo*, where her right leg curved around his body. He set them up for the lift, then trailed her down against his body to the floor, sending sparks of desire through them both. She extended her leg, back arched, looking up at him as the final note rang through the church hall.

They waited a beat. Applause erupted like thunder.

Wolf whistles and cheers echoed around the hall, some standing in ovation at the performance.

Chests rising and falling, they straightened. Tilda's smile was a mile wide as they bowed to the audience. On slightly adrenaline-fuelled, yet shaky legs, Tilda walked backstage.

She was giddy, breathless and ecstatic all in one. Her heart couldn't beat any faster. Then Alé planted a long, possessive kiss on her lips, in front of everyone. And she was proven wrong. Tilda blinked. Before she knew it, she was caught up in bear hugs and kisses from the other dancers in the group.

She all but beamed. She felt alive and carefree. She had taken a leap, had been coerced out of her comfort zone, and found herself in a world that was rich and vibrant, tantalising and exciting. She had stepped into a life that she hadn't known she wanted. Stepped into experiences that she had longed for only in books.

She'd never go back to the way things had been. She couldn't. Tilda accepted that wasn't the same person who had begun this journey. She didn't think she ever would be again.

CHAPTER THIRTY-SEVEN

*T*ilda was flushed by the time they joined everyone for supper out in the hall. Relief flooded her system. Yes, she had muddled up the double turn, but she didn't care. She had enjoyed herself. It had been easy to ignore the crowd once she started dancing. The way Alé looked at her was a big enough distraction. Everything else seemed to fade away. She should have known tonight would be no different.

A small part of her was beginning to understand why people performed.

Elspeth turned to her and squealed, "I can't believe we did it!"

"Me either." Tilda grinned, giddy.

"Good work everyone." Michael slapped shoulders, whilst his partner Katarina poured out champagne.

"Time for a group photo!" Henri boomed.

Alé's arm snaked around her waist, he leaned in close to her ear.

"How about a nightcap back at my place? After the *milonga*?"

Tilda didn't dare look at him. "I would...if I knew where you lived."

His grip on her hip tightened.

"I'll message you," he growled, before stalking away.

Tilda was wired. It was as if there were a thousand bolts of electricity that coursed through her veins. Yet all the currents seemed to be heading south.

Then and there, Tilda decided that Heathcliff had nothing on Alejandro Garcia. Her life was better than any book of fiction. She couldn't wait for the *milonga* to end.

Tilda knocked on Alé's door as nervous and excited as she had been hours earlier. Except this wasn't a performance. And there certainly wouldn't be anyone watching.

Alé's front door whooshed open. Alé's mouth curved slowly and Tilda's heart danced.

He looked delicious as sin and twice as dangerous.

Tilda wouldn't let that stabbing fear of losing the man before her interrupt her pleasure tonight. She reminded herself that she was taking life by the reins now, that she would just ride on over those fears.

Tilda walked through to a large sitting area to her left. It was a masculine room, greys and whites, with splashes of colour from the paintings on the wall. There wasn't much in the way of furnishings, but it was neat and tidy. Minimal.

"Would you care for a drink?"

Tilda whirled around to see him standing next to a dark mahogany cabinet. She noticed his glass sitting on the sideboard, amber liquid at its base.

"What are you drinking?"

"Whiskey."

Tilda wrinkled her nose in distaste. "I think I'll pass."

"Thought so. I have some vodka, or rum, if you prefer?"

"Rum sounds great."

"Mojito?"

"Sure, why not. I'd say we earned a bit of a celebratory drink."

"I'll be right back." Alé brushed his hand against her arm. "Make yourself at home."

Tilda sank into the couch. Then sprang back up again.

"One mojito."

"Thanks." Tilda sipped quickly. She needed to calm down quick or she was going to make a fool of herself. It wasn't like they hadn't had sex before. She knew exactly where this was headed.

Alé sat beside her, casually caressing her knee. He made small talk, but all she could focus on was the delicious pattern of his fingers on her overheated skin. She placed her drink on the table.

"I think we've done way too much talking already." Tilda crawled on to his lap and straddled his hips. She needed to act, to move, to stop any thoughts invading her mind. Alé's hands immediately cupped her butt.

"Mathilda, before we —"

"Alé. You don't need to say anything. The other night

was incredible. And if that's anything to go by, tonight will be too."

"But this...you know that it's just sex, right?"

Tilda swallowed ignoring the ache in her chest. She concentrated on the lust in his eyes instead. The lust she put there. She didn't want to think. Didn't want to be responsible. She was sick of worrying. She needed him. Wanted him. That would be enough.

Before she lost her bravado, she gyrated her hips.

"It's not just sex, Alé. Its fucking incredible sex."

Alé's laughter was hollow.

Tilda reared back. "What is it?"

His face was in profile, turned away from her. The light, playful mood had disappeared.

"What did I say?"

Alé's eyes were guarded when he looked at her. His jaw, tense.

"Nothing. Nothing at all, Mathilda. Like you said, we don't need to say a word."

She frowned. Then lost herself in his kiss. It was only when his body relaxed beneath her, that she let go.

She would take this. She would have him. Without reservations, without question. She owed it to herself to finally give in to this hedonistic pleasure. She didn't want to care about what the bronzed man with the talented hands would or would not give. This, whatever it was, was all for her.

Tilda rubbed herself suggestively against him, laughed wickedly when she felt him hard as iron beneath her. Alé's hands wandered up her legs. He paused when he reached the smooth, satin material at the apex of her thighs.

"I thought you'd like these," she whispered against his ear before taking a bite.

One long, tanned finger flicked against the silk red panties she had worn especially for tonight. She had bought them knowing she would end up in his bed.

"*Si*, I do like them. But I think." He continued, his hand travelling up, over her dress to circle her nipple. "I'd enjoy it if you were naked. With nothing between us."

Tilda's laugh was wicked. "I'll see what I can do."

Alé carried Tilda to his bedroom, despite her protests. She wanted it hard and fast, so that she didn't have any time to think about what it all meant.

Tilda scrambled to rip off his shirt. After the adrenaline of the performance, Tilda didn't want to take her time. But Alé's bright eyes bore down and into her — through her, and she felt her fervour dissipating. Only to be replaced by a slow burn.

"Alé," she whispered, her hand brushed against his cheek. In a move that nearly undid her, Alé kissed her palm; softly, slowly, moving up to the inside of her wrist, then over to her neck. "Alé," she murmured again, her heart filling, trembling, tumbling despite her best efforts to convince herself that it meant nothing. Her throat closed over.

"Let me make love to you, Mathilda. Let me dance like this with you. Naked. In my bed."

He undressed her first, placing kisses along her collarbone, nibbling at her skin, as if she was a delectable sweet, instead of flesh and blood. His touch was featherlight, brushing over her breasts, teasing her nipples, igniting a fire within her that she never thought would cease burning.

A deep part of her knew that it would somehow always be this way with him. No matter what. He would ignite that fire in her. Always.

He knew her, saw her in a way no one else did. Being with him soothed that restlessness in her heart, in her soul.

Yet her body hummed in need. His hands and mouth sampled her, his teeth extending her longing, until she begged for release.

Her hands discarded his shirt and pants, her fingers found him warm and hard, and she smiled in wicked abandon.

"Slowly, Mathilda. We have all night."

His fingers circled her soft folds, rubbing the delicate nerve endings until she was sobbing his name. Those long, tanned fingers of his disappeared inside her. She was a tightly wound coil ready to snap.

She licked her lips and moved her hands up and down his shaft. His left hand gripped the bed covers, muscles straining. Her hands raced faster over the thick length of him. She relished in the trembling man above her, the way she was able to reduce him to his baser self, as he did her.

Tilda teased and taunted him. She captured the white pearls forming at his tip with her fingers. She wanted to taste him. To feel the hard length of him inside her mouth.

"Mathilda," he groaned, burying his head in the base of her neck. His hips thrust forward in jerky movements that spoke of his ever-decreasing control.

Alé suddenly reared back, gripped her hands in his

and pinned her to the bed. She laughed when he panted above her.

"Little witch."

"What are you going to do, Alejandro? Punish me?"

His eyes seemed to glow. "I just might. Later."

Her mouth curved in satisfaction.

Hands pinned, Alé bent his head and feasted on her breasts, suckling and biting until she writhed and bucked. She was wetter than she thought possible and in desperate need. Wrapping her hips around his waist, she opened for him.

The heat that beckoned, the heavy, musky scent of her was enough to have his control snapping. She could see it on his face.

He sheathed himself hastily. Before she could breathe, he thrust inside of her. Her legs tightened around him; they each found their own pleasure.

Then he moved. Slowly, achingly; that they both trembled with restraint. Tilda closed her eyes, blood pounding. She wanted the powerful release only he could give her. The erotic pleasure of his body devouring hers.

"Look at me," he whispered.

Tilda whimpered.

"Mathilda, I want to watch you come."

The gravelly request, the plea for connection had her hands cupping his face, her eyes opening. She captured his mouth with hers and surrendered to him.

Tilda couldn't look away from his hypnotising gaze. Not when his eyes spoke of more than just lust. His branding kiss, that smouldering look — the intensity of his touch — made her feel like he could see into the heart of her.

"Mathilda. I need you...*dios mío*...Mine. You're all mine," he growled.

His words broke her. On a wave that threatened to drown them both, Tilda rose up, crested and shattered around him, her mouth called his name in surrender, until she felt his release, heard his twin cry. All the time her eyes were locked on his in what felt like more than a meeting of bodies. More than a need fulfilled.

With his eyes tiger bright, Alé kissed her. He gathered her beside him, planting soft kisses at her temple. Then drew the blankets over them both.

Tilda shivered. Something bloomed within her. She was afraid she'd never be the same again.

Daylight crept in to Alé's bedroom, outlining the angles of his face in the early morning light.

This was more than just sex.

She turned as carefully as possible, not wanting to wake him. His hand had managed to sneak around her waist during the night, she had woken up to find herself pinned under the weight of him.

Tilda shifted to her side, leaving Alé's hand at her hip, relishing in his touch, even though he was deep in sleep. She resisted the urge to sweep away the dark strands at his temple. He looked very much at peace.

A smile danced at the corners of her mouth. Who knew that the slow, tortuously tender way he took her could be just as devastating as fast and furious? Who knew that he had so many hidden angles, that she was still attempting to understand? All depending on whether he let her in.

Tilda bit her lip, gnawed at it as she continued to drink in the man who lay beside her. A man who was capable of so much feeling, yet kept it locked away. She knew she didn't have all of him. Knew that she wasn't nearly close to it, but she decided on sharing his bed knowing it all the same.

In the bright light of day, Tilda wasn't so sure she was okay with that. Every action had consequences.

She examined his face, trailing a finger down his cheek. Her hand trembled, along with her heart.

She couldn't be here when her emotions were so raw. When she felt so exposed. Tilda had ignored all those barriers she had placed around her, and she didn't think she could go on pretending.

She turned away gently lifting Alé's hand from her belly. Tilda squealed when he pulled her back, flush against his chest. Her b curved against his morning erection.

"I didn't mean to wake you," she whispered.

Alé kissed the back of her neck. "No, you were sneaking out of my bed. No woman ever sneaks out of my bed this early in the morning. Plus, I was already awake." He thrust himself against her butt. Groaned appreciatively.

"Alé." Tilda tried to face him, but his hand kept her in place. "I should leave." His mouth continued its torturous journey. When he nibbled on her ear lobe, Tilda's body turned to jelly, even though her heart was heavy.

"I think." He nipped at her shoulder. "You should get rid of this 'should' word from your vocabulary." His accent seemed to have thickened in the morning light.

His rolling r's reminded her of how adept he was with his tongue.

"Oh really?"

"Mhmm...and stay in bed with me. All. Day."

Tilda turned. "All day?"

Alé nodded.

"But you know we've got another performance this evening."

"So? That's then. This is now...stay?"

Tilda looked at him, sincere and sexy. Her heart turned in a slow rolling somersault. She drank in his dishevelled bed hair, the faint stubble on his cheek and that sincere, open expression on his face. All resolve melted away like wax to a candle.

Her mind screamed at her to leave, to run, to protect herself. But her heart yearned to be with him, to spend all the time she could in his company. To cherish what he gave her, even though it hurt, even though it wasn't enough.

"I'll stay."

"*Bueno*." He pulled her down towards him, grin wolfish. "Because I'm hungry."

Tilda's laugh was muffled by his kiss.

She'd live in the moment. For now. The time for hard decisions could wait.

That's what she told herself as she sank back into his open arms. Even though she knew it was the road to ruin.

CHAPTER THIRTY-EIGHT

"*T*he most important thing for the lead is to make sure you are on your own axis and are not doing this." Alé pressed down on Tilda's shoulders. She yelped at the pressure. "As you can see, it isn't pleasant for the follower, and can actually cause serious damage. Sorry, Mathilda."

Tilda straightened. Now was not the time to think about the week of hedonist pleasure she had shared with him. Or the way his touch drove her a little insane.

She looked at their students. They had finally managed to organise the tango lessons for the senior citizens in Riversdale, and to Tilda's surprise, sixteen eager individuals had turned up.

She didn't know if it was years in watching and learning, or Alé's unwavering confidence in her, but once Tilda began the lesson, she felt like she was at home.

She enjoyed teaching tango with Alé. It felt natural and right to guide others, offer her support, to help them find joy in a dance that had given her so much. Doing this was so different than running The Book Nook. The store was a family legacy. Tango — and now teaching — was an individual pursuit. She wasn't tied by a sense of obligation. Only by her self-imposed restrictions. She brushed aside the guilt. She had her feet planted firmly in both worlds — exactly how she liked it.

"What you want to do is rise up from your core, as if there is a string that runs through your body and comes out at the top of your head. Like so." Alé demonstrated. "You need to lock in your core. Tighten those abs I know all you leaders have — George, I'm looking at you. And lengthen that spine." Alé pointed at him. He adjusted the postures of the other leads, dolloping praise.

It was Alé's gentle guidance, his unwavering faith in his students that made teaching with him a pleasure. His unwavering faith in her, that made her feel —

"Mathilda?"

Tilda blinked, hastily snapping back to the present. "Yes. Followers...the same concept applies to you. But this time, not so stiff. Eventually." She continued, keeping her upper half straight, but swivelling her hips so that she twisted left to right. "You want to be able to disassociate like this, so your top half stays locked in, but your bottom half is free to move."

"Shall we get them walking, Mathilda?"

The image of Alé in the shower last night, taking her against the tiled wall left her throat dry. Her cheeks were on fire. "Yes?"

Alé's frown was fleeting.

"I'll put on some music and you can practice walking in the line of dance. When you're hitting those *milongas* you'll be ready to go." Alé pressed play. "In a circle please.

Ready, and 1, 2, 3, 4." He clapped the beat, setting the pace. "Extend the leg, Dotty, then put the weight of your body down." Alé guided her. "Good."

Tilda sighed. She had desperately tried to keep her distance, but the past week had been hard. They had a string of performances together, not to mention the work they put in to planning this lesson. In the evenings, she couldn't resist his kisses or the insatiable need that clawed inside her.

But with every waking morning, she was finding it harder to keep it casual.

"Excellent work everyone," Alé called out turning down the music. "Let's now review the basic eight steps. Leaders with me, followers with Mathilda."

Tilda moved down the hall. Alé ran a hand down her arm as she passed, winking.

She stiffened, then relaxed, throwing a quick smile over her shoulder. Keep it light. Not too serious.

Tilda was grateful that the hall had doubled as an old dance studio, so the mirrors, whilst it had seen better days, were still in use.

"Followers, you can watch yourselves in the mirror, or watch me. Ready?" She half turned to face them guiding them through the steps. "Okay then, feet together. Palms up, as if you are connecting with an invisible leader. Now, with me. *Salida*," she said taking a small step to the right. She rotated her upper body as she placed her weight on her right foot.

Some women started to wobble, so Tilda began again. "*Salida,* disassociate, and extend the left leg back. Excellent." She watched the others behind her in the mirror, stepping through the basic eight.

"Mathilda, how are the followers?" Alé squeezed her shoulder causing her to jump in fright. She was wound up tighter than the figure eight.

She offered an apologetic smile when he frowned. "I was in the zone. Sorry. My followers, however, are doing wonderfully well, and ready to partner up I think."

"I can see that." He nodded, his eyes assessing her. "You've a fine teacher, ladies." He added before herding the group back together.

"I'll be dancing with the most beautiful lady in here, Alejandro." George boomed and took Betty's hand.

She giggled delicately and swatted his shoulder. "Such a card you are."

"I don't doubt it, George. I'm hoping to steal the lady for a dance later, with your permission." He winked at Betty. "And hers of course."

"I'd be glad to," Betty replied.

George kissed her hand and bent low. "My lady."

Tilda sighed at the exchange. It was ridiculously sweet that they had found romance, after all this time. Two people in the world she loved, being in love was just too much happiness. She rubbed the ache in her chest.

Tilda tried to focus on the couples dancing but couldn't. She felt a rushing feeling, as if she had stuck her head outside a speeding vehicle. Something was building. But what? It wasn't until she looked at Alé, as the light of the winter sun streamed through the windows, that the sensation reached its peak. He turned his head and offered her a slow, sweet smile.

Her world shattered.

An invisible force slammed into her, with all the momentum of a head on collision. Yet her body felt alive.

Her fingers tingled; her chest warmed. A steady tango rhythm pulsed at her neck.

Alé caught up with her on her way outside. "Are you okay?"

"Yes, just need a bit of water and some air. Didn't eat breakfast this morning."

"You're flushed." He brushed his hand across her cheek.

"Overheated." She looked away, eyes filling.

Alé's gaze was penetrating. She could tell he didn't believe her, but he had no choice but to let her go.

Outside, she pressed her back against the cool brick building and trembled. Her heart knocked against her ribs. Adrenaline sped through her system.

She was in love with Alé.

Unequivocally. Undeniably. Unashamedly in love with Alejandro Garcia.

She was joyous and sickened all at once.

So this was what romantic love felt like. She thought she had loved her other boyfriends, but it was nothing in comparison to this. Everything else was grey. But this, this was a kaleidoscope of colour.

This was definitely not part of the plan.

How could she have allowed it to happen?

The bigger question was, what - if anything - was she going to do about it?

CHAPTER THIRTY-NINE

"*Y*ou love him." George was direct, his eyes piercing. He stated it as if it were a well-known fact.

"I beg your pardon?"

Tilda wrapped the blanket across her shoulders. She'd normally be wrapped up in Alé's bed on a Friday evening, but after the success of their performances, and the YouTube clips that had accompanied it, he was in hot demand. This time in Adelaide.

In need of company, she had visited George, not wanting to be alone with her thoughts. They sat on his porch, drinking tea, waiting for dusk to succumb to darkness.

It had only been ten days, but she missed him. The rational side of her brain reminded her that this was a good thing. That having some space to figure out what she was going to do with her feelings was important.

Even though their performances had slowed down, they spent all their spare time together, collaborating at the bookstore, teaching beginner classes, or lazing about in bed. The months, and their new relationship had flown by.

"I said, you love Alé. You heard me."

Tilda gulped down more tea then sputtered.

George gave her a thump on the back. "Don't be wasting that gunk, or Betty will kill me. Green tea. Takes like grass if you ask me. But that's the price I gotta pay for love, eh?"

Tilda tentatively swallowed another mouthful.

"Anyway, like I said. You're in love with him."

"No, I'm not." Oh yes, she was. But admitting it to George meant she would have to do something about it.

"Tilly, I got eyes. I could see it last week in class. Well, Betty could see it and she told me and then I could see it, but we know our girl. And you seem smitten with this man."

Tilda opened her mouth.

"And don't even pretend you don't know who I am talking about, kid."

Tilda groaned and set down her cup.

"What's going on in that head of yours, eh? Why do you look suddenly like you've seen a pizza without cheese?"

"If you've noticed, then what about Alé? It must be written all over my face." She buried her head in her hands. The mortification was enough to leave a permanent flush on her cheeks.

"If he's a man, or anything like me, he probably doesn't know yet." Tilda's laugh was muffled. "But seriously, Tilly, what's the big deal if he does know?"

Tilda whipped her hands away and stared at him in shock. "You've got to be kidding me, right?"

"Does this look like the face of a man who would lie?"

"Geooorge. You are not helping!"

"What's this man not helping with my dear?" Betty's voice carried through to the porch.

Tilda jumped. "You scared the hell out of me!"

"Don't curse. Sorry dear, our crochet ended early this evening."

George grumbled, answering her. "I told Tilly that it wouldn't be a big deal if Alé knew she loved him."

Betty shook her head, taking a seat beside Tilda. "Sometimes you've as much tact as a bull, George."

"Whaa?"

"Of course Tilda wouldn't want him to know, especially if she doesn't know how he feels in return. Right?"

Tilda nodded. Had she been painfully obvious? This was a disaster. She said as much to them.

"It's not a disaster. It's simply what happens when we love. And that's okay." Betty gave her a one arm cuddle.

"Who cares if he knows?"

Tilda's eyes felt like they were going to pop out of her head.

"Don't look at me like that," George said to them both. "Love is a precious gift. You know it is. And if felt, is something you should be screaming from the mountains so everyone knows, especially to the person whom you love. Regardless of whether they feel the same way about you."

"But George —"

"I should know." He looked at Betty who smiled.

"Oh George." Tilda squeezed his hand.

"It took for me to be laid out on a hospital table, having my heart cut open and bleeding, for me to realise just how much I had to lose. The man upstairs," he said looking up and pointing to the inky sky. "He gave me a second chance. Probably conditional on the fact that I didn't blow it again. Ya hear what I'm saying kid?"

"But I'm terrified of him not feeling the same, of losing his friendship. Losing him." They hadn't even defined what they were, what the 'thing' was between them.

Betty cut in. "We know you keep your relationships at a distance. Why they don't seem to work out after a certain time."

Tilda crossed her arms.

She patted her shoulder. "We've stood back and watched and waited. But Alejandro is different. We can see how much he means to you. We want you to experience a fulfilling relationship — that includes being loved. Isn't it time my dear?"

George cleared his throat. "I know it's been hard since Ethel passed. You keep your heart locked away. It's like you need a million Prince Charmings cutting down the brick wall to —"

"A thorny bush."

"Whatever. This is different. How long can you keep this up before you want more?"

"But —"

Betty cut Tilda a sharp look. "No buts. Don't back away from something that's so wonderful because of fear. Think about what loving Alé entails, and what that means to you. Where your relationship is headed. The answer will come."

That night, head full of questions, Tilda lay on her side of the bed, and sifted through their advice.

She allowed herself to fantasise about a life with Alé, a proper relationship based on love, and trust and respect. It was a thought that warmed her as she drifted off to sleep. A fantasy that she hadn't let herself crave since losing her parents a long time ago.

CHAPTER FORTY

*A*lé was suffocating. The weight of everything and nothing pressed down on him all at once. All he could hear was the blood roaring in his ears, and all he could see was darkness. The metallic smell burned his nostrils and scored the back of his throat.

He grabbed his legs. He couldn't feel anything. His heart hammered again and again, a persistent knocking. The black dog demanded entry. Alé's fists clenched and his throat closed over. Not again. He would not let it happen again. *Por favor.*

He jerked up off the couch and in to the present.

Rubbing his hand over his face, he sat back against the cushions and cursed. He had fallen asleep waiting for Mathilda. He had taken one of the last flights back from Adelaide, and now his head was pounding.

Mathilda was the last person he wanted to see right now, but she had said she'd come by after Dex's birthday and he had been too weak to resist.

Weak. That's exactly how he felt. And sick to his

stomach. He should have known that he'd see Camila eventually. The fact that he hadn't been paying attention to the program, to the fact that her and her new partner were teaching workshops at the same Winter Festival in Adelaide proved that he was more distracted than he should have been.

He had been thinking about Mathilda when he spotted her standing across the hall, with that tell-tale smirk on her face. Alé couldn't even find the words. When she had looked him over, pity pouring out of her dark eyes, it took him back to his accident. Back to all those feelings that he thought he had dealt with. Or at least shoved aside.

He had ignored her. Carried on like it didn't matter to him. Pretended he was fine. Yet lying in his hotel room, he had no peace; it was as if his skin had been turned inside out. He was raw. Exposed. Vulnerable.

Seeing her reminded him of everything he had lost. Everything he could have been.

He was deluded to think he had dealt with the pain. Deluded to think he could break away from it and live a normal life.

Alé braced his arms on his knees. Yet here he was again. Mixing tango and pleasure. Caught up in something he couldn't define.

He should have learned that lesson long ago. A bitter laugh burned at his throat. The fact that he had another nightmare was proof that he was out of control.

He stood up and poured himself a drink. His hands shook. What happened to his resolve? What happened to his promises? He had gone way too deep with Mathilda. She made him feel —

He gulped back the whiskey, poured another. This wasn't going to work. He was losing more and more control, becoming vulnerable again. Vulnerability meant weakness.

He vowed he'd never be weak again.

Madre de dios. Mathilda made him want things he couldn't give. He was simply incapable of doing this. That is something that she would just have to accept.

"Alé?" Mathilda's voice carried through the corridor. He had left the door open for her. That was his mistake. "Hey! Welcome back. How was Adelaide?"

He turned and saw her smile falter.

"What's wrong? What's happened?"

She walked over to him, apples and vanilla teasing his senses. Despite the late hour, she looked fresh and lovely. He wanted to bury himself in her and just forget. He gripped his glass even tighter and sat down instead.

"Nothing."

Mathilda looked at his drink.

"Don't judge me, okay? I've had a shit two weeks."

She shook her head. "I wasn't. Are you alright? Did something happen?"

"No — nothing happened, okay? I came home, fell asleep and woke up."

"I mean in Adelaide." Her voice was cool.

Alé jerked his shoulders. He didn't want to get into this now. "Had a bad dream. I'm fine."

She frowned and sat beside him. "Another of your nightmares?"

Alé gulped the whiskey, nearly choked on the liquid. The fact that she had witnessed that — before he had left — made him sick to his stomach. He had shrugged it off at the time, distracted them both with sex, but it had left him exposed.

He nodded, rising from the couch. "I need some air. Don't wait around."

"Alé — wait!"

He picked up his jacket and keys and left before she could stop him.

Tilda sighed, pacing the lounge room. It was 3 a.m. and Alé had yet to return. It was clear that whatever had been bothering him had been bad. Bad enough that she stayed.

Part of her said to just leave, to not get involved. But it was too late. His pain was now hers. She couldn't just shrug it off.

All through Dex's party she had wished Alé was beside her. Seeing Dex with his new partner, so in love, and so openly a couple, had reminded her of what she wanted from Alé. What she needed to tell him.

She couldn't keep pretending that what they shared was nothing. She couldn't keep pretending that she wasn't in love with him. He needed to know how she felt. Maybe, just maybe if he did, he wouldn't be so afraid to open up to her.

To know that she loved and supported him no matter what might move their relationship down the path she had hoped it would naturally take.

Her stomach clenched in nervous anticipation. She could only hope that he felt the same way. It was one of the reasons why she had wanted to see him this evening. She couldn't keep up the pretence. Even though she wasn't sure of his feelings, it was getting harder with every passing day to continue as they had been.

Her heart bled for him and for the distance he maintained. The distance he insisted on, really. She had expected him to drop those barriers over time. Told herself that he would let her in. She may be sleeping with him, but it didn't mean he trusted her with his heart.

An hour later, after two cups of coffee and a text message to Alé, Tilda worried that something had happened.

At close to 6 a.m. he returned.

Tilda rushed to the front door, mind foggy with fatigue.

"Are you okay?"

"I'm fine," Alé took off his jacket.

"Your hands are freezing. Let me make you a coffee."

"I said, I'm fine, Mathilda." He poured himself another whiskey.

"You're far from it." His back was hunched, defensive. "I think you should talk about it. There's no shame in —"

"I said, I'm fine. Drop it."

Anger sparked liked a tinderbox. "No. I will not 'drop it' okay? How about that for an answer?" She marched up to him. "You've got to start opening up to me. I don't think you seem to understand just how destructive you are when you get like this."

"Get like what?"

"Closed off, defensive. You won't let me in."

"*Mierda*, Mathilda. I need space! I don't need to talk. And you hovering isn't going to change that!"

Tilda shook her head. "Do you think bottling everything up is any better?"

"Works like a charm." He ground out, draining his glass.

"Oh, that's real mature, Alejandro."

"What can I say? That's me. Take it or leave it, sweetheart."

Tilda took a step back. Biting back her anger, she swallowed her accusations. She wanted to soothe not ignite his temper.

"Alé," she said gently. "I get that you're probably feeling a range of emotions right now, and you don't want me to butt in."

"You'd know, would you?"

"I —"

"You'd know what it's like to live with the ghosts that won't go away? To find yourself face to face with your past after all these years, and feel just as useless, just as weak, as if it had happened yesterday?"

"What are you talking about?"

"I saw Camila. I saw her and —"

"Who is Camila? None of this makes sense."

His mouth clamped shut.

Tilda's heart thumped. "Alé, I can't help you if you don't let me in."

"I don't need your help, Mathilda. I don't need anyone's help. I've managed on my own for years now."

"And look where that's gotten you. Staring down the bottle of whiskey, not dealing with the truth."

"The truth? I can't seem to feel normal again. To get rid of the nightmares that paralyse my body. Or the fear that

I'm stuck in the past, numb, unable to move. My muscles are weak, my mind is weak. I can't stop the pain, I can't get rid of the reminders of what my life would have been.

"So I deal with it in the only way I know how, Mathilda. If that isn't good enough for you..." his shoulder jerked.

"Alé." Tilda moved to him. "Oh, Alé."

"Don't —" he stepped back. "*Don't* look at me like *that* —"

"Like what?"

"I don't want your pity. Poor Alé, poor cripple. You don't think I see it?"

"It's not pity —"

"Don't bullshit me!"

"It's not bloody pity, you idiot, it's love!" Tilda pressed her lips together, her eyes wide.

Alé looked at her in horror. "*Perdon?*"

Her stomach lurched. She wanted the first time she told him to be a gentle, sweet declaration of love, not some knee jerk retaliation. "I didn't want to tell you this way, but you're so *stubborn*, and George —"

"George?"

"He knew." She smiled ruefully. "He convinced me that I should tell you, and I wanted to say it but...I was afraid. I love you, Alé. I want to help you through this. Let me love you, let me help you."

Alé winced. He shook his head. "They convinced you?"

Tilda frowned. "Well, I didn't really want to see it but, Betty —"

"Betty too?"

Tilda shivered. It wasn't coming out right. "I didn't
—"

"How convenient for you all. To decide what I
needed. To decide what you felt for me."

"It's not like that, Alé. I love you. I want to help you."

"No. It doesn't work like that in the real world,
Mathilda. Grow up."

Tilda swallowed, heart racing. "I can get you professional help if you don't want to talk."

Alé laughed. The sound cut through her, bitter and
hollow. "Sweetheart, I've had all the help there is. But
there's no magic fix. Your pity won't 'save' me. Wake up.
You don't love me."

"Excuse me?"

"You're confused. Letting older people convince you
of something that isn't there."

"What the hell are you talking about?"

"You. Don't. Love. Me. You are just confusing passion
and lust with love. Trust me, I know what that's like. I've
been there before." Alé's body shook. His eyes were
distant. Haunted. "You see them all loved up and you
think oh, that must be us. And the music, it gets into
your soul." He slapped an open palm to his stomach.
"The lyrics make you yearn for that passion, that connection so you convince yourself *that* is love. But it doesn't
exist. It's just a word. It doesn't make people stay. It
doesn't change anything." He looked at her now. "Wake
up, Mathilda. Dancing together, sleeping together,
doesn't make us a couple."

Tilda took a step back. Her voice hitched. "How dare
you!"

"How dare I?" Alé stepped closer. "Because I know all

this." He gestured between them. "Is a show. It's all a show."

"You arrogant arsehole! How dare you tell me how I feel?"

Tilda bit back the tears. She suspected he may not feel the same, but his words ripped through her like a sledgehammer, leaving her broken and bleeding.

"You're deluded. There is nothing, was nothing, and will be nothing between us, Mathilda. Get that straight. Love only leads to suffering. I'm doing you a favour."

Her voice wobbled. "Love is a gift. It —"

Alé's cold laughter — his derision — silenced her.

"Love? Love is a smokescreen. You can give your heart to someone, give your trust to them and still find yourself alone at the end of the day. Love? It's all pretend."

"You don't mean this, Alé."

"Hey, take it or leave it. Believe what you want. People in love always do."

"So what? What does that mean?" She rubbed her shoulders against the cold.

Alé threw his hands up. "I told you where I stand. The performances are over. So is this one. I don't need your help or support. We clearly have different views and I don't think there's any point continuing with this charade. Do you?"

His voice was so cold. So final. Tilda shivered, sure that for as long as she lived, she'd never forget the feeling. Never forget the detached look in his eyes. It was as if she was talking to a stranger. Not Alé. Not the man who had believed in her, supported and cared for her.

She thought he'd be able to confide in her, that she

could help him through his pain. She was wrong. So very wrong about him. About their relationship. It would never work out with someone who thought so very little of her. Of love.

As if in a trance, Tilda walked to the front door. She had given herself to someone who would never, ever be what she needed.

Dazed, she stumbled. Alé was hunched on the leather armchair, whiskey glass re-filled and dangling from his fingertips. She had assumed that he was capable of more. Believed it deep in her soul that he would be the type of man she could depend on.

Tilda paused. She stepped back to the entrance of the lounge room. Her voice was thick and heavy with emotion.

"Love is a gift, Alejandro." She swallowed, refusing to cry. "I only — I hope that one day you'll accept that. It was never pity, but compassion. Despite what you think, I do love you. I'm sorry you can't see that."

She thought she saw his head move, a small almost imperceptible shift towards her. She waited a beat, bracing against the pain, the palpable anguish that swirled around her. She couldn't even be sure he had heard her.

Tilda walked out of Alé's life as the quiet dawn made its presence known to the world. She marvelled that no one could hear the sound of her heart breaking.

CHAPTER FORTY-ONE

*S*he was drowning. For weeks, Tilda couldn't get her head above water. The pain was always present.

She had tried to focus on work, on the booming sales of The Book Nook, on supporting Dex through Teddy's treatment, but nothing gave her comfort or relief.

One look from Dex had her taking the following weekend off work. She drove up to Mount Sunshine. A place where her gran used to take her when she was little, and consequently where her gran was buried. Even as she poured her heart out to the rolling green mountains, she wasn't comforted.

Tilda longed for more space. For freedom from her anguish.

When George and Betty had visited her, thanks to Dex's big mouth, she had told them an abridged version of the story. Enough for them to know, without worrying too much. She begged them not to speak to Alé. To keep their distance, even though their natural instinct was to fix it.

This was why she had kept herself so guarded over the years. This was why she couldn't bear to open her heart. The loss was too great, too overwhelming. It left her hollow-eyed, numb. A phantom of the woman she had once been.

Yet, ironically so, life went on.

By the third week, Tilda was going out of her mind. It was when she walked past the local travel agent and spotted flights for Buenos Aires that she found the solution.

She didn't just need to leave Riversdale. She needed to leave the country.

Panic kept her feet firmly on the ground. Since her parents' accident she couldn't bring herself to be on a plane. It had kept her safe and ultimately, stuck in the same damn place.

Tilda swallowed past the pressure in her throat. So what if something happened to her? She had already experienced the worst. It wasn't like she really had anything to lose anymore. She'd been through it all.

Even as her conscience pinged, she decided she would give Dex a chance to manage the store while she was gone. He was beyond capable and he had been doing it for the past three weeks anyway.

She ground her teeth together and made a decision that was selfish and spontaneous.

It was about time she did.

CHAPTER FORTY-TWO

"*Buenos dias*, Alejandro. *Estas bien?*"

Alé froze. His hand hovered inches away from the pause button. The intensity of the violin reverberated through the empty dance studio. A part of him knew that this would happen ever since he saw her in Adelaide.

He turned slowly.

Camila Morales stood at the opposite end of the studio. She was exquisitely made up, impeccably dressed. His mouth curled in disdain.

Her dark hair was bundled in a youthful ponytail. But her face had aged beneath all that make up and surgery. He could see that now. Her dark eyes assessed him. Depth-less. Like everything else about her.

"*Perdon*, I should speak in English," she mocked, her accent clear and ever-dripping with derision. "I forgot you are like, a, what is it called? A kangaroo." She made twitching noises. "Like the zoo pet."

"What the hell are you doing here, Camila? Don't you have anywhere better to be?"

Camila clucked her tongue, a note of disapproval. "Alejandro Garcia, is that any way to say hello? You were so quick to ignore me in Adelaide. So I thought I'd visit. For old times' sake."

Alé shifted. He remembered how Camila had left him in that hospital bed. Even after he pleaded with her to stay, to help him through it. But what they shared wasn't anything more than a dance partnership. She wouldn't have left him otherwise. He'd never forget how she'd looked at him then.

Pity. Not love.

His body stilled. The jumbled mess in his mind — of past and present — was clearing. His last meeting with Mathilda plagued him still. He was beginning to realise something.

Camila sauntered towards him, her long, luxurious body sashaying across the studio. She exuded confidence in open-toe stilettos. Always on show.

Alé shook his head. How had he compared what he shared with Mathilda, to...to this? His gut clenched.

"I came only to see your new, *little* dance studio." She smirked.

He gripped her wrist when it trailed down his shirt. She let go, and executed a series of perfect *giros*, circling him, drawing an imaginary box with each turn. She danced around him now, taunting him, just like she did all those years before. And he had been too stupid to see it.

Alé gripped both her wrists this time. What was he doing? How could he be baited in to dancing with her? Of all people?

"I think it's time you left."

"You've made quite a life for yourself, Alejandro." She replied, wrenching her arms out of his hold. She inspected the studio. "So very different to where you were in Buenos Aires, *non*?"

"Enough with the games." Alé stormed up to her. "Enough! You don't come near me or my studio again, *claro*? I have nothing to say to you."

"Is that any way to treat an old friend?"

"Friend!" Alé's temper reared its sharp teeth. "You betrayed me! For fame and fortune. You know where I was? I was stuck in a fucking hospital..." he bit his tongue, cursed when he tasted blood. He wouldn't give her the satisfaction of knowing how much she took from him. How much she made him bleed inside. How much, apparently, it still hurt. He hated that the most.

Alé had never confronted her once he had been discharged from the hospital; not even when he learned to walk again. He had convinced himself she wasn't worth his hatred. But look at him now. Over a decade later and still bitter. Still plagued by nightmares.

It needed to stop. He finally needed to face it, head on. Mathilda had been right.

"Oh, *Alejandro*. Always so dramatic. Don't you want to know how I found you?" She smiled seductively at him.

"I don't care."

"Oh? But I think you do. You forget how well I know you. You and me, we're not so different. Don't you want more...than this?" she waved her hand derisively. "You could have been great."

"Spare me, Camila."

"Camila? So formal... We were once very good together." She inched closer to him. "Don't you want to see if we could be again?"

Understanding dawned in Alé's eyes, he knew now what she was after. Camila Morales only ever wanted what would benefit herself. It was a trait that had her dancing around the world, true, but one that left her empty inside and always greedy for more.

"What happened to the great Alberto?" Alé asked, a small smile played at his mouth. The initial blow of seeing her in his studio was starting to recede. Especially now that he knew why she was here. How he had wished, in those early days of recovery that she would come back, begging, to him again. Now, he found it pitiful.

"Nothing *mi amor*. But I saw your little performance. Recorded by your adoring fans. You are YouTube famous." She laughed. "Not bad for a washed up *milonguero*. But I can offer you more...I can offer you greatness."

And it would be drinking out of a poisoned chalice. He had sampled from that cup once, when he had stars in his eyes, and a hunger for the title, almost as strong as hers.

"Sick of Alberto already, Camila? Or is he just not up to your standards?"

She shrugged a toned shoulder, examined her nails. "He is more than adequate. We are, I agree, amazing. But." She looked up at him. "I am willing to exchange him for you."

It was then that it came to him. Any bitterness he had once felt at losing out on his dream hadn't been about the title or the fame.

It had been about him. His belief in himself. That he was more than just an object of pity in some fame-hungry tango dancer's eyes. That he was more than just a shell of a man, broken by bad luck and a failed relationship.

He was someone worthy of love. Worthy of everything he had convinced himself wasn't worth fighting for.

He had run away from his past. Held on to the bitterness. It's what gave him the drive to move on, to open his business, to find tango and success on his terms. But that festering wound needed to heal.

How had he not seen the way Mathilda had given him that support? With every kind word, every sweet look, she had built up his sense of self-worth as a man.

Breaking those habits, opening up to her, admitting how he felt, didn't make him weak. He trembled. Joy — unbridled happiness that he never believed he deserved — broke free.

It was then that Alé admitted to himself that the past was no longer important. Yes, it had moulded him, but his relationship with Mathilda was what filled that empty shell. It was her love for him that had helped him grow. He had everything he wanted in her and had stupidly thrown it away.

It was time that he changed all that.

Camila clicked her fingers.

"Had I known you were able to dance so well again, Alejandro, I would have found you sooner. But you always were a man of secrets."

Alé crossed his arms. Hadn't Mathilda told him the same thing? Hearing it from Camila's mouth, as if it were something to be proud of, made his chest hurt. He didn't

331

want to be that person. He was starting to see, that perhaps he had been.

Alé assessed her with fresh eyes. She looked confident, but she lacked sincerity. Compassion.

His heart pounded. It could have been him. In staring at the self-centred and unfeeling person before him, he recognised some of those traits in himself. Defensive. Cold. The metallic taste in his mouth was more fear than anything else.

He derided Camila for her soulless nature, yet he hadn't behaved any better. Hadn't he rejected Mathilda with careless and hurtful words that he knew would drive her away?

The bitterness and anger that he drank like poison all these years started to fade. He looked at the stranger before him. Relief was a cool balm on his fiery soul. He had no desire to accept Camila's offer. No residual hatred for what she had done. He thought he had been trapped by her actions. But in actual fact he had been caged by his own. It was time he let that go. She may have started it, but he was going to end it. Mathilda had been right. He needed to move on.

"We could be great, Alejandro." Camila's voice was too close. She wrapped her arm around his shoulder and stared at their reflections in the mirror. "We could do this and so much more."

Alé's mouth was like sandpaper. His pulse beat erratically, a jarring discordant rhythm. He shook her off and stepped back. It was time to let go of his past. But in order to do that, he had to face it, properly, this time.

"Know this, Camila. And this is the only, and last time I will tell this to you. I will never, ever, so help me

God, not even if I was desperate, dance with you again. *Dale*? You and I were through when you left me in that hospital bed. Hell, we were through long before that. I'll never trust or respect you. But I will forgive you for what you did. Leave now. And stay away from me and my friends."

She lifted her chin, eyes narrowing. She always took rejection and criticism head on, swallowing it down like sour milk. Alé had once admired her for her strength and stoicism. He could finally see her for what she was - heartless.

"You and your friends?" The small smile played at the corner of her mouth. "Oh, that's right, your little blonde dolly. Yes, I noticed her in the video. Good, I suppose, for an amateur. But I guess that's what you all are now."

Alé's voice rang with pride. "Mathilda is twice the dancer you were. Twice than you'll ever be, Camila."

She tipped back her head and laughed. "Oh, Alejandro. You always were the soft one. Men are so easily blinded by a pretty face and a bit of talent. A pair of open legs doesn't hurt either."

Alé's muscles trembled with restraint.

Camila's smile turned cruel.

"Yes, I see now." She looked him over. "Too bad I didn't get to visit your dolly. She has a charming little store, I will say that for her. In a charming little town. And I'm sure you will both live a charming little life, making her fat with your babies."

It was then he realised the woman he spotted at the fair, was in fact, Camila. That she had been watching them all along.

Alé's hands flexed. He shoved them in his pockets.

"Don't you dare go near her again. You hear me?" His mind raced. What had she said? Was Mathilda okay?

She shrugged a careless shoulder. "Too bad she was on holiday when I paid a visit. I could have taught her so much. I couldn't care less for her or your sordid little domestic life."

"Holiday?" Alé's mind whirled.

Canny as a cat, Camila goaded him. "Didn't you know? Did she go away and leave you? Poor Alé." She mocked. "Never could keep a woman happy."

Mathilda never took holidays. It was one thing that both admired and frustrated him. Was it Betty or George?

It felt wrong not to know. Odd that there would be no more contact between them. Unnatural. To think he would never know how she is, never dance with her or hold her. She probably hated him.

One day, she would move on and find someone else who was mature enough to give her the love she deserved. But the very thought...it simmered in his gut. That some other man would be the one to hold her, to cook for her, to watch her as she ran the bookstore.

He wanted to be that man. It was his deepest desire to be the one to share that with her. To see her joy. To give her pleasure. To eventually start a family.

In that moment Alé accepted that was all he cared about. A life with Mathilda was all he wanted.

His palms clenched. He had her as his woman. She had given herself generously and ardently.

Now she was gone. On holiday? It didn't make sense.

It wasn't like Mathilda. He knew, because he knew her. The strong, sweet, capable woman, with a heart bigger than the ocean. He knew her. Better than himself.

Something wasn't right. He turned to leave. Camila followed.

"Alé! Don't you walk away from me."

He raced — too fast — down the narrow staircase. He ignored Camila as she raved. Locking up, he ran to his car, shutting out the past and the woman who never really mattered.

Alé drove towards Riversdale. Something inside him warned that he was running out of time.

Mathilda was everything good, kind and compassionate in his life. She glowed in comparison to Camila in every way possible.

Alé drove a little faster. It was stupid of him to have said those things to her. It was stupid of him to have believed it - to have kept her at arm's length. For what? Fear? Convincing himself every woman would leave him like Camila had? He shook his head. What a fool he had been.

He merged on to the motorway and cursed. Traffic was bad. He drove off the next exit and weaved in and out of back streets. Alé looked at the time, hands shaking. If he was lucky, she would still be at work.

Would she? When once he knew her schedule like the basic eight, now he was uncertain. Maybe Camila had been telling the truth. Maybe Mathilda had taken a holiday.

Alé shook his head. No, that didn't make sense. She wasn't impulsive. Well, not really. She had grown more confident, without a doubt. It was appealing as hell.

But would she really just leave? He didn't know

anymore. He massaged his chest, trying to ease the pressure. If he stopped now, he would panic. Alé couldn't afford to panic. He knew firsthand how heartache could change a person. He prayed that she would forgive him, to let him explain.

Alé drove out on to the main road; cars whizzed past him in a sea of colour against the inky night. He was close to The Book Nook now. Certain she would never want to see him again, Alé breathed deep. His body trembled. What would he say to her?

Bright lights flashed — a phantom from long ago burned his eyes like acid. It blinded his vision, yet he clung to Mathilda's face, to the present like a man drowning. Past and present clashed.

Images of the accident reared its ugly head. Twisted, burning metal. Mathilda's gentle touch. The fire in his broken bones. Her soft, sweet laugh. The numb, heavy sensation below his waist. Vanilla and apples.

Alé's mind was caught in limbo. He didn't react to the oncoming flash of lights until it was too late.

The sickening sound of brakes skidding along the pavement only stopped on impact. Metal ploughed into metal.

Alé's last thought, before his world turned black, was of Mathilda.

George exclaimed, "Jesus Mary and Joseph! Betty, did you see that?"

The cars had collided with such force, Betty's heart thumped.

George pulled over to the side of the road and raced out of the car to the wreckage. She called out behind him, certain she recognised the red car. Betty convinced herself there were hundreds like it, afraid to think that it belonged to someone they knew. Someone they loved.

She approached the twisted metal. The steam from the little red car had her heart galloping like a wild horse.

"Betty, call the ambulance!"

She dialled in a daze, then watched in horror at George's attempt to prise open the door. He smashed the window with his elbow, ignoring the blood and chaos.

People started to gather around them. She steadied her voice when the woman on the line asked for details.

"Christ almighty, Betty." George's voice was thick with panic. "It's Alé!"

Betty clung to the woman's soothing voice, her own turning wild.

His name reverberated around her head. Betty glanced in the car and froze. The lifeless form was slumped over the steering wheel. Blood stained the windscreen.

George's voice pitched. It sounded distorted, as if coming from a great distance. "It's Alé! Betty, it's him...there's no pulse. Dear God, no! He's...he's..."

"Dead."

When the luxury car drove past the scene of the accident, Camila ordered the driver to stop. Car idling on the opposite side of the road, she unwound her window, taking in the carnage before them.

She should have felt pleasure. She waited for the quick bolt of satisfaction to strike through her veins, but all she felt was disappointment. Bitter disappointment.

Tears stung at her eyes. She blinked them away. Emotions were useless.

For the first time in her life, she felt some semblance of regret. It was an odd sensation.

The broken, lifeless body that lay on the pavement had meant something to her once.

As she watched people swarm around him, busy as ants, she knew that Alejandro had taken her dreams with her. Yet again.

She couldn't dance with a dead man.

Swallowing back her self-pity, she sat back against the leather seat.

It was over. For him.

It wasn't too late for her. Not if she could help it. When the lick of anger simmered low in her gut, she relaxed.

Camila Morales had learned to look after number one long ago. She was still beautiful, still talented. She didn't need *him* to succeed. She hadn't then, she wouldn't now.

Clearing her throat, she ordered the driver to take her back to her hotel.

Bold, red nails punched in the number on her phone. She looked ahead of her. To her future.

When the familiar, melodious voice answered, Camila plastered a smile on her, softened her voice.

"Alberto, *mijo*." She began.

She would never look back again.

CHAPTER FORTY-THREE

George wasn't a man who easily cried at funerals. But the sombre music that penetrated the crisp winter air, accompanied by the muffled cries around him, had his eyes stinging.

He knew he should focus on the poor bastard who would no longer walk this earth, but all he could think about was Tilly.

She would have wanted to be here today.

The back of his neck prickled; guilt never sat well with him. Knowing his girl, she'd jump on the first plane out of Argentina to get back home. And she needed some space before receiving more bad news. She needed to heal.

Being here wouldn't change anything. In fact, it would only make it worse. He was dead. Tears wouldn't bring him back. She had left in a fragile state. Dealing with another loss would only be a set-back.

The turnout was larger than he expected, given the circumstances, and how quickly the funeral had been put together. Betty's eyes were damp, he squeezed her hand, hating to see her upset.

Dex was inconsolable, sobbing softly into an oversized hanky. His new partner stood beside him, the puppy danced at their heels, oblivious to the occasion.

Eventually, Dex composed himself. It took a few attempts for him to speak.

"I want to thank everyone for coming today. It means a lot to us to have you here. Teddy wasn't just a dog — he was my best friend. I'm grateful that his passing was quick and painless, given that he suffered for so long."

The poor ol' dog had slipped away peacefully after another failed treatment at the vet. It had been a difficult decision, but instead of giving him another day of suffering, when his organs were failing him, Dex allowed Teddy to die in dignity.

George cleared his throat, blinking back tears. He was getting soft in his old age.

"I'm convinced he's in a better place. So today is a celebration of Teddy's life. He may not be here, but he'll always be in our hearts."

As people began to offer their condolences, George let his mind drift to the events of the past week. Alé's accident had been a hell of a shock. If they hadn't been there at the time — if he didn't know CPR — Alé wouldn't have pulled through. By the time the paramedics arrived at the scene, it would have been too late.

George shivered. He only hoped Alé would make a quick recovery. He had been disoriented when they had visited. Asking after Mathilda. Mumbling about holidays and keeping her safe. They put it down to his concussion and watched over him as he slept.

First Alé's accident. Then Teddy's death. He hoped wherever Tilda was that she was safe. He couldn't bear to hear more bad news.

And she didn't need to hear about what had happened either. She'd find out eventually.

Despite what happened between him and Tilda, George was convinced they belonged together.

In the meantime, they would check up on Alé. Be there with him so the poor kid didn't have to wake up alone. They would make sure he was alright for Tilda's sake.

They were family after all.

Alé awoke to bright lights. A familiar yet foreign smell stung his nostrils. It was a smell associated with death. His eyes fluttered open and he winced at the pain in his chest. It was a sterile smell and it made him want to vomit.

Panic gripped his hands and feet. It weighed down his chest. He used all his force to open his eyes again. The ache in his chest began to burn. It hurt to breathe. The sounds and smells were enough to make him wish he were buried six feet under.

Alé's vision wavered and shimmered, he caught sight of a familiar face before his body went slack.

Darkness surrounded him like a thinly veiled ghost.

When Alé woke the following evening, he was slightly more aware of his surroundings, not to mention the pain in his body. He knew he was in the hospital; the bed, the drip, the dull room and murmuring sounds were all familiar.

He tried to sit up and hissed in pain, clutching at his side. He had felt worse before, but experience told him that his ribs were broken, or at the very least, bruised. The sharp pain in his chest was constant. Breathing in air was akin to inhaling fire.

Alé rubbed his face and winced again. His hands brushed against the gauzy material at his head. It seemed he was lucky to be alive. Thankfully. For a second, he was transported back to the accident. He muttered a curse and closed his eyes. That was what got him in to this mess in the first place. He had been distracted. Caught up in the past, worrying about Mathilda...and then...he could remember the flash of headlights — a white car that came out of nowhere.

Then George had arrived. He had saved him.

Alé welcomed the tears.

He had acted like an idiot. He had discarded Mathilda's love and his chances of telling her how much he cared. Because of it, he was alone. Again.

Why had it taken him so long to figure it out? The ache in his chest spread, until it became a warm glow. The fear of being hurt again was a pathetic reason now that he could admit the truth. He hurt someone he loved dearly. Someone who offered her love as a gift.

It took Camila and his own reckless behaviour for him to finally accept the past for what it was - events in time he could never change.

He needed to see Mathilda. He needed to explain,

beg, grovel, plead, do whatever the hell it took to make it right.

He lay his head back against the pillow.

Alé could only hope and pray that Mathilda would forgive him. He didn't think he could ever forgive himself.

It seemed all he ever did was sleep. Alé tensed when the curtain was pulled aside half an hour later. A man in a white coat came in and Alé smiled as best as his face would allow.

"Dr Matheson."

"Alejandro. Glad you recognised me. How are you feeling?"

"Been better."

"You've two visitors here, keen to see you. If that's alright?"

Alé's heart leapt. He tried to pull himself up. The pain lanced through his side. It was nothing in comparison to the hope he felt at Mathilda walking through the door.

Dr. Matheson stepped aside as Betty and George entered.

His disappointment was short lived.

Alé's voice was thick with emotion. "Thank you, George, so much, for saving me. I —" he cleared his throat. "I wouldn't have been surprised if you'd left me there after the way I've treated Mathilda, but I wanted you to know that I'm grateful."

George squeezed his shoulder. "We all make mistakes,

son. Lord knows, I've made a ton." He glanced at Betty, nodding her approval. "Even though I'd rather wring your neck for the hurt you've caused our Tilly, I'd have done the same again any day."

"Mathilda means the world to me. I was scared and an idiot." Alé struggled to form the words. His mind was foggy with fatigue. "What I want to say is, I can't live without her, I want her in my life and I want to prove to her how much she means to me — how much..."

Betty moved forward and kissed him lightly on the head. "We know, Alejandro. We know. Don't try to speak any more." She patted his arm. "You need your rest. We can talk more when you wake up."

An odd lightness circled around him. He knew he didn't deserve absolution, but he succumbed in relief. As he drifted off to sleep, he wondered where Mathilda was and if she was okay. Did she know what had happened? Did she even care?

Alé woke gradually to find Betty sitting by his side, knitting. It wasn't the first time. Betty and George had taken turns keeping him company. He could only hope that it meant they were beginning to forgive him for all the pain he had caused.

Now he needed to convince them to help win her back.

He tried to kick off the sheet, struggling to get up.

"Woah there, sleepy head." Betty arranged his pillows before stroking back his hair.

He had dreamed of Mathilda. When she was happy. Before he had hurt her.

"Do you want anything to eat, Alé?" Betty asked. "I can get them to bring you a sandwich."

Alé shook his head.

All he wanted was to rewind time. He itched to move and run again. To dance and hold Mathilda in his arms, to tell her how he felt in the simplest of ways. It had been too long since he had touched her. Made love to her.

Love.

The sensation felt good inside him. Like a bright light that would never dim. There were no shadows anymore. No doubts. He was more than certain of his feelings for her.

Betty cleared her throat. "Something troubling you m'dear? Do you want me to get a nurse?"

"No... nothing external. But I wanted to ask... does Mathilda know? About the accident?"

Betty put down her needles. Then shook her head.

"I'm so sorry. I was going to speak to her about it when I called last night. That would have been morning her time, I suppose. It's all a muddle to me. But you know our girl. She would've dropped everything to be here if she knew. I think she just needs the time to grieve properly."

Alé shook his head. "You have nothing to apologise for, Betty. I'm the one at fault in all of this. Not her. I shouldn't be surprised that she wants nothing to do with me. I wouldn't expect anything else."

Betty's words struck him. "What do you mean it was morning her time?"

Betty's eyes rounded, her mouth forming an O. "Did I?" She feigned ignorance, twiddling her needles. "I must have it confused."

"She's actually left the country? Despite her fear of flying, she's gone and left?"

Betty's look confirmed his suspicions.

The answer came to him before he could blink. He knew exactly where she was, and he had to get to her. Now. Betty shouted and tried to steady him.

He continued to struggle as if his life depended on it. But he was trapped by his own body. He managed to swing his legs off the bed when George came in with cups of coffee. He handed them to Betty and pinned Alé back.

"Easy, buddy. Easy, now. You're gonna bust ya stitches bouncing around like that."

Alé thrashed and struggled. "I have. To. Get. To. Her." It wasn't until he lay limp and exhausted, sweat perspiring at his brow, that George let go.

"Jesus, kid. Relax. You ain't good to anyone half dead. Trust me, I speak from experience." George's mouth went grim. "Now what's this all about?"

"I know," Alé bit out. He shifted against the pillows. "I know Mathilda is in Buenos Aires."

George's head whipped to Betty's. "You told!"

Betty raised her hands in defence. "I didn't tell...it, sort of slipped out and Alejandro figured out the rest."

"Is she okay? Please tell me that at least."

Betty pressed her lips together.

"Please. Betty." Alé winced and lowered his arm. His ribs were bruised, and still tender. "I need to make things right."

It pained him that he couldn't run to her. He wanted to be fit enough to fight for her and bring her back home.

"Betty, I love her. Let me bring our girl home."

It took him the better part of a week to get back on his feet. Whilst he was eager to fly out to Mathilda, he was impeded by Betty and George, and the wise advice of Dr. Matheson. So it wasn't until the end of the following week that Alé reassured them that he was fine and booked the next flight to Buenos Aires.

Betty wouldn't tell him where she was staying but he hoped he would cross paths with her at one of the *milongas*. Betty had given him that much.

He was nervous, uncertain how she would feel about seeing him. It had been too long since he last spoke to her or heard her voice - other than in his dreams.

Alé's injuries had begun to heal enough for him to move with only a moderate amount of stiffness.

With hope in his heart, and determination in his eye, Alé boarded the flight back to the one place he vowed never again to visit.

CHAPTER FORTY-FOUR

*T*ilda disassociated and stepped back into a *giro*, a box-step move around the rotund man who held her slightly too close for comfort. He was a maestro according to the few people she met. One who liked dancing with only accomplished dancers. She should be happy he had asked her, but her heart was filled with sorrow.

The faces dancing in small tight circles around her became a blur. She wanted to lose herself in tango, like she had so many times back home. Her eyes filled. *His* face flashed before her eyes. She closed them, shut out the phantom images, then opened them again as the maestro led her backwards.

She knew her feet were turned out perfectly, she could see some of the women sitting on the outskirts of the floor watching and smiling. She followed his lead, but it was cold. Mechanical. It brought her no joy.

His face flashed before her again. She turned away.

The music increased in pace and the maestro guided

her around the floor. She glimpsed *him* again. Leaning against the back wall amongst the crowd, his white shirt a beacon in the *milonga*. Her stomach jittered in nervous anticipation.

It had happened every now and then since she arrived. Thinking that a dark Argentine head was Alé's, freezing when she saw a tanned cheek and dark lashes, hoping, despite herself, that it would be him. It was a stupid move coming to his country. There were 'Alé' clones everywhere she turned.

She knew it wasn't him. He was back in Australia. In his dance studio, moving on with his life. As was she.

Tilda saw nothing but an empty space where the clone had been. Relief and disappointment flooded her senses. She didn't want to feel anything.

Tilda settled her head against the stocky man's bald, sweaty one. She had hoped for the other ladies' sake that he had brought with him a handkerchief. Perhaps even a change of shirt. His hand settled firmly on her back. Tilda desperately wanted to feel a connection.

She closed her eyes remembering the first time Alé bought her a pair of *Commes*. She had been so flattered that he had thought of her. Deep down inside she had wondered if it meant anything special. But she now knew it was all a lie. It was clear from the very beginning, when he had kissed her and told her it was a mistake.

When he told her they weren't friends.

When he rejected her love.

Tilda bit her lip at all the stupidly obvious signs.

The music pierced the air and stung her eyes. She blinked, the sheer mortification of being found crying in a man's arms on the dance floor was too embarrassing.

She would not allow herself to fall apart. The loss of him was a familiar ache in her chest, but she had to stay strong. Where better to be than in a *milonga*, dancing the tango; just another expression of heartache.

She wanted to block out the music, the sounds of the mournful singer, crying out in despair. Isn't that what many tango songs were about? The pain of love. She was a fool to once think it romantic.

By the last song in the *tanda*, Tilda was restless.

She wanted to leave. She didn't think she could hold herself upright, with this man's crushing embrace, his breath warm and shirt damp under her hand. Tilda wanted to be anywhere but here. In fact, she wanted to be with the one man whom she knew she couldn't ever have a relationship with. She was stupid to believe that she could. And now she was suffering for it.

The last bar of the song closed, and Tilda breathed a sigh of relief.

She extricated herself from the man, who gallantly tucked her hand in his arm and led her back to her seat. It took Tilda every ounce of strength not to run off the floor and race to her apartment in Palermo. Instead, she sat down and nodded her thanks to him, smiling carefully as a stream of words flew from his mouth. Her face tightened from the effort.

When the opening sounds of the next *tanda* began, Tilda took care to avoid eye contact. Ladies nodded and moved to men of all different shapes and shades. Tilda lowered her head. She found her shoe bag under the chair and checked the cheap phone she had bought in the city. Three AM. More than time for her to call it quits.

Tilda crossed her legs, shifted aside her blue skirt, and

reached down to unbuckle the strap of her shoe. Her fingers were like jelly. She glanced around at the couples dancing, distracting her mind, whilst her left hand fumbled with the buckle.

The dancers parted as a tall figure weaved through the crowd. Tilda froze. Her breath stopped short. She blinked.

"You're not going home so early are you, Mathilda? At least without a dance first?" Alé asked, standing before her. "Pugliese's *Remembranza* - fitting, *no*?"

Tilda breathed in tentatively, uncertain of everything. Especially the man standing before her. Was it real? Had she had some psychotic breakdown? As seconds melted away, the music penetrated her mind, reminding her of all she had lost. The song spoke of love turned sour; the singer pleaded for love to return again.

Alé bent to fix the strap of her shoe, the gesture squeezing the air out of her lungs; she drank in his face, noted the dark smudges under his eyes, the tightness in his compressed mouth. She gripped her hands together, against the desire to run it through his thick sable hair.

His movements were stiff. Her heart pummelled. Tilda opened her mouth to question him, but no words came out. He was asking her to dance. After everything he said to her. After all this time.

Tilda was caught between past and present. It was surreal. She was mute. But now all too aware of the lyrics. Jorge Maciel mourned, '*que triste es recordar*', how sad it is to remember. '*Nuestra pasion se marchito*'...yet their passion had not withered.

Her desire for Alé had been insatiable. It had bloomed and budded repeatedly, until they had both become half-mad with its intoxicating scent. They couldn't get enough of each other. Physically. Not emotionally.

Alé's hand rested on her ankle. The jolt of electricity travelled up her calf, past her knee, to hover just at the apex of her hip.

He drew her up from the chair, her feet unsteady and led her to the dance floor. Just at the edge, he turned to face her, singing softly along in Spanish. Tilda stopped. A cast iron weight chained the heels of her blue tango shoes to the floor. Maciel begged, Alé echoed.

Tilda's throat constricted. The violins soared. She let go of his hand. She would go no further. If she danced with Alé now, like this, she would break in to a million pieces all over again. It had taken her nearly two months to get to this stage. She couldn't go back.

"Mathilda?"

She shook her head.

'*A nuestro amor*' — to our love. The words sliced through her as efficiently as a sword. How dare he sing those words back to her? How dare he mock her love? Like some arrogant *milonguero*. He was no better than the men in suits, trawling the tango hall, bartering foreign women for sex. What was wrong with her? Where was her spine? Her pride? Her self-worth?

Those words held no meaning. Alé didn't love her. Wouldn't love her. Wasn't capable of it.

Tilda sucked in air, and finally managed to speak. "I can't, Alejandro. I can't dance with you. Not now. Not ever again."

Tilda fled.

Her lungs burned. A fire raged in her chest. Maciel's voice taunted up the staircase, '*nuestro querer*'...

Streams of the late night *milongueros* flooded down to the milonga, slowing her escape.

Her vision blurred. She needed air.

Tilda didn't stop, even when she reached the road. The crunch of gravel and concrete beneath her new shoes paled in comparison to the crushing ache in her chest. She didn't care. She didn't care what happened so long as she stayed away from Alé.

"Mathilda!"

She raced ahead. A cab waited, idling along the street. She jumped in one of the few that had a driver behind the wheel and rattled off her address to him. She ignored his complaint at the short distance and sat back against her seat. With no self-control, she turned in time to see Alé reach the pavement, arms waving.

Tilda focused on the road ahead.

She wouldn't look back.

CHAPTER FORTY-FIVE

*T*ilda had slept fitfully at best. Seeing Alé in Argentina, in a crowded *milonga* had proven she still wasn't over him. The tears on her pillow and the hollow feeling in her chest were sage reminders of what she had lost. Of what was real. She was ashamed to think she had almost danced with him.

Even though her heart was heavy, she forced herself out of bed. She had wallowed for too long after seeing him again and she needed to take control.

She had signed up for a shared private lesson with Daniel Rodriguez — just one of the many adept tango teachers that taught at the dance school. She would be sharing him with four other women, but she didn't care. It kept the cost of the 'private' down, so that she could make her money go the distance. Not that she was doing too badly. She'd pay George and Betty back for their generous loan. She wouldn't have been able to afford the tickets on such short notice had it not been for them.

Dex kept her regularly updated as per her request,

not that she had anything to worry about there. On paper, her life appeared to be going well. The store was doing better than they expected, George had his health back, and she was moving on with her life.

She couldn't have lasted one more day in Riversdale. Her relationship with Alé, performing on stage and teaching tango had shifted how she viewed the world. Her old life had morphed into something far more exciting. She was no longer the same person, struggling to live up to her grandmother's memory.

Tilda had come to accept that there was more to life than living in the past. Alé — for all his faults — had opened her eyes to the world. She knew who she was and what she wanted in life. And whilst the thought of dancing tango with a stranger only made her think of Alé, it was what she needed to move on.

Even the plane trip had been worth it. She had hyperventilated twice but managed to survive without taking any of the sleeping pills her doctor recommended. The lovely man with a lilting Irish accent going to visit his best friend helped too.

When she arrived, the anonymity of not knowing anyone had been freeing. She danced with her heart on her sleeve, the pain and torment radiating off her in miserable waves. But she had gotten through the worst of it.

Her daily Spanish lessons with a local ex-pat had her coming a long way in understanding the beautiful language. She found herself pouring over tango lyrics with fervour. The tango community was a city of broken hearts. Many had offered her advice. Some, more than that. The very thought of which made her stomach roll.

Whilst Tilda preferred to catch the *subte* in to town, she needed fresh air. Walking to her lesson would give her time to clear her head.

The fact that Alé was now in Buenos Aires made her feel unbelievably self-conscious. As if he would jump out of the next street corner. She walked past Tomas, the resident beggar. His rags of torn, brown cloth were bundled close around him, his little sign in Spanish against his legs begged for loose change. Tilda wadded up a handful of pesos and stuffed it in his cap. It should cover his lunch and dinner costs for a few days.

As Tilda strolled through the suburbs, she recalled the colourful houses of La Boca, the heart of old-world tango. She had been mesmerised by the charm of the buildings, even if she was confronted by the poverty on the fringes of the tourist strip. Tilda was compelled to buy a tango ornament there, regardless of its price. It was a memento from her trip abroad. Her new-found sense of self.

She weaved around aggressive traffic, stepping quickly across the road. There were so many angles of Buenos Aires; the tattered, dilapidated streets, in contrast to the leafy pristine homes, it collided to form a cultural wonderland. It wrapped around her like a colourful scarf.

Tilda heard the trickle of tango music from an opened upstairs window. She sighed, indulging in the idea of living another life. She quickened her pace. She had — on too many occasions — given in to her fantasies of life in Buenos Aires, with a handsome Argentinian. Fantasies she admitted that had involved a tawny-eyed man. Shame painted her cheek.

But what of Alé? What did it mean that he flew

halfway across the world, to see her in a *milonga*? Tilda tilted her chin. She was no longer interested in a relationship with Alé, so it didn't matter.

Tilda crossed to the large, white-washed building. Battered stairs guided her way up the labyrinth of hallways and hideouts. The trickle of tango music, of instructors giving lessons filtered out the corridor. Tilda approached the woman at the desk, who, with a sly smile told her she was to go to the door around the corner. Room 14.

Frowning, Tilda knocked and waited. Then walked in. Tango music was playing, but the space was empty.

Sitting down, Tilda began to tie the laces of her practice flats. She had bought a proper pair on one of her many shoe shopping trips. They were made from the softest leather and were a balm to her aching feet. She checked the time again, not quite used to the lackadaisical attitude many Argentine tango teachers had when it came to punctuality. looked at her watch again. She was still getting used to Argentinian time. It seemed to operate at least ten minutes slower than the actual time.

Perhaps the woman at the desk had been mistaken.

Tilda stood at the window and waited. Holding on to the barre and staring out at the busy street below, she swung her leg like a pendulum and warmed up with a few *ochos*. When the door opened, she turned. Then swore. She should have known better.

Alé stood before her, effortlessly handsome in a simple blue t-shirt and black jeans.

Her mouth formed a thin line. "You've got to be kidding me."

"Hello to you too, Mathilda."

Tilda huffed, and braced herself against the barre as he walked towards her. "You're a quick one. I could barely keep up with you the other week."

"That was kind of the point."

"I need to speak to you."

"So you followed me to my private lesson?"

"No... not followed. I merely asked around. I have some very useful contacts, even still, in this city."

"Well, I have a lesson that's about to start, so unless you want to embarrass yourself, you'd better leave."

Alé's slow grin made her scowl.

"What's so bloody funny?"

"Welcome to class," Alé said, opening his arms and dropping them to his side.

Tilda's frown deepened. "What?"

"I'll be your teacher today."

"Like hell you will!"

Alé shrugged. "Daniel agreed that I could take one of his students today. Your private lesson with him will be tomorrow. He was happy enough to take the others elsewhere so that I could arrange this meeting. Today - it's you and me."

"Oh, how convenient for you. Throwing your weight around. If you think I'm staying, you're deluded. I have a lesson to attend."

Tilda picked up her stuff.

"You'd be a few hours early. He's changed the time."

"When is it?"

Alé simply grinned.

"How dare you!" Tilda paced, fuming. "You think you can just waltz back into my life and mess about with it, like it means nothing? As if the way you behaved back home was some big joke."

"Mathilda, it's -"

"No! That's so typical, Alé. And careless. You just steamroll over how I'm feeling with no bloody regard."

"Mathilda, that's not true."

"Oh really?"

"Yes, I wanted to speak to you."

"What if what you want doesn't matter anymore?" Tilda's eyes were hot. She crossed her arms over her heaving chest. "I told you I didn't want to speak to you, yet you went ahead and forced us to meet. Does what I want matter?" Tilda sat down to take off her shoes, shoving them in her bag.

Alé bent down before her and grunted at the effort. Her eyes narrowed assessing him. He was bent at an odd angle, his left side a little more anchored to the ground than it should have been. She could see the gleaming scar, red and angry against his forehead. "What happened?"

Alé gritted his teeth and stood, his right arm instinctively shooting out towards his left rib.

"I said, what happened?"

"It's nothing."

"Nothing?" Tilda stared at him in disbelief.

"It's not important."

"See, Alé?" Tilda's hands were balled into fists. "This is why we never could work. Because you can't seem to understand a relationship means you don't get to pick and choose what bits to tell the other person. A relationship means being open and honest. It's messy. But clearly, you're not wanting to get your hands dirty."

"Please, Mathilda — I'm trying to tell you that I'm sorry! I'm trying to explain my past."

Her head jerked up in assent. "Fine. You say you're an open book, Alé. Wonderful. I'm all ears."

She would hear him out even though he didn't deserve it. Then she'd leave. Even if it killed her.

Alé turned to face her. "I came here for a few reasons. The first was mostly to grovel at your feet and apologise. I know I hurt you. I know I said terrible things. But I didn't trust myself enough to trust you." Alé stood, pacing in front of her.

"Go on." Her arms were crossed.

"I didn't deserve your love back then. I kept myself hidden, a part of myself protected because I didn't want what happened in the past to happen again."

"That's no excuse, Alé. I was scared too. I put my heart on the line for you. I loved you. And you rejected it, not even kindly."

"I know. And I'm sorry, a thousand times I am. Mathilda, *por favor*, I wish I never spoke those words to you. I wish I could take them back and change them. But I can't. I can only offer you my apology." Alé trembled. "I was afraid because of what happened with Camila - my ex-partner."

Mathilda sat, stoic. She wasn't making it easy on him, and fair enough. He would have been surprised had she acted any other way.

She frowned at him. Then understanding began to dawn on her face. "That was the woman you mentioned. Camila."

"She had been doing a tour in Australia with her new partner. They were in Adelaide that same week. It brought back a lot of the bitterness I didn't know I still carried."

She nodded for him to continue.

"I know I told you about the accident, when I was younger. But at the time, Camila and I were rehearsing for the *Mundial de Tango* championship. I was teaching dance to little kids to make ends meet, working odd jobs to save money.

"That night, Camila and I had an argument. I got in the car, angry. It was dark, wet." He stopped pacing and sat back down. "I was distracted. Once Camila heard the doctors' diagnosis, she left me. She found out I was paralysed and fled. The *Mundial* meant more to her than I ever did. And that hurt. I was alone. And angry."

"Didn't you say you had family? Were they there?"

"Yes, my family helped me a lot. But I was young. I thought I loved Camila and we would conquer the world together. And the woman I thought I loved decided I wasn't good enough. It nearly killed me. She found a new partner, rehearsed and within six months competed. She never looked back since, and I never truly forgave her until recently."

Mathilda squeezed his hand.

Alé continued. "So after I avoided her in Adelaide, she came to the studio. She'd been watching us for a while it seems. Camila wanted to offer me a place as her dance partner again. I laughed in her face and told her where to go.

"But I hadn't realised until that moment that I had become everything that I hated about her. I was cold and unfeeling. I hid a part of myself from you out of fear. I had been stubborn in thinking I was right to do so. I was selfish. I hate that about myself.

"I made a vow long ago I'd never be vulnerable to a woman again. I couldn't forgive myself for trusting so blindly for believing that someone could love me. Not just my talent. Me." Alé's voice wavered. "I was fighting with myself, not you. I'm ashamed of blaming you, hurting you. I am truly sorry for that."

He looked at the woman who held his happiness in her hands. He finally understood what she must have felt all those months before.

"I appreciate you telling me this, Alé. I do. And I accept your apology...but what Camila offered you wasn't love. It hurts that you would think I could do that."

"I don't think that. I never did. But I couldn't risk being vulnerable again. I'm sorry. I am. I can see that now, Mathilda. Back then, I couldn't. I needed to let go of my past, but instead of dealing with it, I ran. And made even greater mistakes in hurting you. I realise it's not how you treat those you love."

"You're right. It's not." She stood now. "Thank you for your honesty, Alé. I just think we're better off leaving this all in the past."

Ale stumbled to his feet.

"We both need different things. Want different things. This trip has given me perspective on that and made me accept it. I wish you well, I do. I'm grateful that you wanted to make things right. But I'd appreciate it if you didn't contact me again."

Without a backwards glance, Mathilda picked up her bag and walked to the door.

Disbelief grounded Alé in place. She couldn't leave. He couldn't be too late. She had accepted his apology, calmly as if they were no more to each other than distant acquaintances. It was all too civilised. Too polite.

It scared the hell out of him. He was losing her all over again. His body trembled at the ever-real threat.

Alé called out to her. But she was gone for good this time.

CHAPTER FORTY-SIX

*I*t had taken all of Tilda's strength to put one foot in front of the other. To finally leave Alé. She had blown off a day of lessons, fearing that he would be waiting at the studio again.

Annoyance at her own cowardice was almost as sharp as her frustration at him. It was so typical of Alé to tango back into her life thinking he could apologise, and all would be forgiven. Sure, there was a big part of her that would never be able to resist him. The fact that she had wanted to jump into his arms scared her beyond belief.

When it came to Alejandro Garcia, Tilda had no buffer. No protective shield. Yesterday had proven that all-too well.

Tilda walked to the pantry and bit into another *Alfajore*. The sweet biscuits were the balm she needed right now. She'd give herself one more day of wallowing, then it was time to go home.

Buenos Aires just wasn't big enough for the two of them.

. . .

"*Hola?*" Tilda rushed to the phone, slightly out of breath. She had taken a trip out to La Boca for what she knew would be the last time before heading off.

"Tilda! Thank Christ. Where have you been? We've been worried sick!" George's voice, despite the static, boomed out of the speaker.

"George?" Her heart kicked. Something had happened. "What's wrong?"

"What's wrong? We've been trying to contact you and nothing. Are you alright?"

Tilda's shoulders hunched over. She had a few missed calls from an unknown number, but she hadn't trusted herself to pick it up, or listen to the voicemail on her mobile. Knowing Alé, she was certain he had somehow charmed one of the women at the studio for her number.

Typical.

Yet here she was making decisions again based on her fear of confronting Alé. It was just another reason why she needed to keep her distance.

"Sorry. Yes, I'm fine. Just been a rough few days." She leaned against the wall, rubbing at her eyes. It was time she high tailed it out of here.

"That's not what we heard. We've been worried sick. Alé was frantic on the phone, saying he lost you and needing to see you. I take it things didn't go so well?"

Tilda froze. Alé?

"Tilda? You there? What happened? We thought you and Alé would have patched it up by now. Betty is mighty sorry she let it slip, but after his near-death experience, she couldn't refuse the poor boy. I know what it's like to come back to life afraid of losing the one...Tilly?"

She shook. The icy fingers of dread had crept up her spine. Her senses were on high alert. Everything George said had become magnified in her ear, yet the message was lost in the fog of confusion.

"Near-death?"

"The boy is strong as an ox. I don't mean to bring it up again. No doubt Alé told you —"

"I want to hear it from you, George. What happened?"

Thirty minutes later, with assurances to George that she wasn't blaming them, and that all would be well, she hung up. They had caved in again and given Alé her address. Pacing the floor, Tilda replayed their conversation and waited.

There was no doubt in her mind that Alé would come.

CHAPTER FORTY-SEVEN

The knock on her door thirty minutes later made her jump.

She had eventually stopped shaking after her conversation with George to make herself some tea, but she couldn't settle.

All she could think about was Alé, so close to death. The thought of losing him, the man she still loved — despite her better judgment — left her hollow.

Tilda swung open the door. It took every shred of her control not to give way to the desire to shake him.

His jaw was shadowed with a few days' growth, the bruises on his face appeared stark, now that she knew their origin.

Tilda looked him over properly; the angry red marks on his hands, the way he carried himself signalled his pain. He was a man in need of bed rest. He seemed different. Not quite as proud as the man she left back in Melbourne.

Tilda stepped aside to let him in.

Following Alé through to the sitting area, Tilda knew she was at a precipice, that she would fall, either way.

It was about time she took that final leap.

Alé was beyond terrified. He didn't think it was possible, but when she had walked out of the studio and taken his heart with her, he nearly lost his mind.

After hounding Betty and George, he managed to get her address and knew that if he didn't tell her his feelings that he would be a broken man forever.

"I'm sorry. I called Betty and George and begged them for your address. Don't be angry with them. They knew I wanted to make things right between us."

Alé paced in front of her, his hands tugging at the ends of his hair. "But I screwed everything up and I know you don't have to listen, but you need to know the truth."

"I'm listening."

He stopped to stare at her. So calm, so distant. Perhaps he was too late.

Honesty was required. From here on in. She had been right to question him the other day. But she was wrong about how he felt. He knew he had much to learn.

"I should have told you the other day — when you asked about my bruises — I shouldn't have brushed it aside. But I've been hiding for so long, putting up a wall for too many years, that it's going to take some time for me to learn how to open up. You've shown me that it's worth the risk."

"I know."

"No, you don't understand. I had a car accident in Riversdale. I was on my way to see you, after Camila left. Yes, it was bad. If George and Betty weren't there, I could have died." Alé winced. "My heart stopped and —"

"George performed CPR. *I know*."

Alé tugged at his hair. "*Perdon?*"

"I spoke to George today. He told me everything."

Alé's stomach churned.

"I can't believe you tried to brush this off. Especially as you nearly died."

He moved towards her, but she stood, pacing.

"I'm sorry."

"Do you know what that felt like hearing it from someone else? To know that you didn't tell me? We're repeating the same cycle over and over. I'm sick of it! I'm so angry at you for not trusting in us. That means being vulnerable."

"I know. I screwed up. That's why I had to come here to tell you — to make you understand that it's going to take some time for me to be the type of man you deserve. But I don't want anyone else in this world beside me, but you."

"Well that's all well and good Alé, but like I said, this won't ever work because you can't give me what I need." She stood at the window, her back to him.

"Tilda — *per favor*, that wasn't the only thing I came here to talk to you about."

She turned.

"You've never call me Tilda before."

A warm sensation spread in his chest.

Alé walked up to her. Unable to stop himself he took

her hands in his. "That's because I knew it was reserved for people who were close to you, for people who loved you." Her eyes shot to his. "Don't you see, Tilda? I love you. I couldn't accept it because I was so blinded by the past. Blinded by my own fears. But you mean more to me than my past ever did. And it's time I proved it to you."

Her eyes misted. "Alé..."

"I kept pushing aside the feeling, hoping I was wrong. I knew — finally after the accident — after losing you like a fool, that I was completely in love with you.

"Tilda, I love you. I want you in my life. By my side. I want you as my partner, and friend. I want you as my wife and mother of my children. I want every part of you. All you can give.

"I flew back, to a land I swore never to see again, not to just apologise, but to hopefully make you mine. And I'll do it a thousand times over until you believe I'm the man for you. That is, if you're willing to accept me." His voice wavered. "I know I'm not perfect. But I promise I'll spend my life showing you how much I respect and trust you. Trust us. I'm committed to getting help to be a better man. I know now I need it. Give me a second chance, Mathilda. Say you'll love me back. Say it's not too late."

Tilda's axis tilted. Her world spun. She barely registered the tears on her cheeks, or the smile on her face. Her heart tripped, tumbled and fell. Harder than it had the first time. She knew who he was now. Loved every shadow, every flaw.

She had stepped off that cliff with carefree abandonment.

It meant more now that love was returned. Those arms she had grown to know so well held her tight. It was what she dreamed of hearing and she couldn't quite believe it was real.

"Alé." She half laughed, half sobbed. "The thought that I could have lost you, that you nearly died scared me more than anything. I can't say I haven't been angry at you. I can't say that a part of me still isn't. But to hear you say those words to me, to hear you feel the same way —"

"The same way? So... you still love me?"

She swatted his arm. "Still love? Oh, Alé, you fool! I've never stopped."

Alé brushed the tears from her cheek.

"I'm sorry, Tilda. For not telling you I loved you sooner. For hurting you. For everything."

His mouth was warm and firm, his tongue masterful. His kisses spoke of more than just their passion. It was a promise. Tilda felt it in her heart. Knew it in his touch.

"Mathilda, I swear to you, I'll make you the happiest woman in the world. I know I'm not an easy man, but I'm committed to you, to doing whatever it takes to making you happy. I vow I'll give you my heart. My trust. Everything I am."

Tilda looked up the man who had given her the greatest gift of all. "I love you, Alé. I promise to do the same, even though you might drive me crazy."

"You know I will."

His mouth devoured hers once more. His arms

brought her close to his chest. They began to sway to music only the two of them could hear.

Tilda raised her left arm instead of her right. "I've been learning to lead since I came to Buenos Aires," she said, boldly. "It's difficult, but I'm trying."

Alé assumed the position of the follower, placing his right hand in hers. "Then lead me, Tilda. Direct us wherever you choose, and I'll follow."

CHAPTER FORTY-EIGHT

Tilda opened the protesting gate and climbed the familiar steps to the studio. The violins stretched and sighed, calling like a Siren's song. She was besotted. Entranced. Enthralled. And that was just with the music. She brushed aside the strands of her honey-blonde hair that had been caught up in the wind. Winter proved to be a bitter one this year, but her heart was light as a summer's breeze.

Spring was around the corner. The very thought had her fingers and toes tingling in anticipation. With numb hands, she began to unbutton her coat, and smiled at the various beginners who were warming up.

A tremor of nervous excitement raced through her body - she had so many ideas of how to guide the new batch of winter beginners. She couldn't wait to start.

Tilda slipped off her jacket with one hand, balancing her phone and shoe bag in the other. In haste, she mis-stepped; the combination of her damp shoes and the newly waxed floors had her careening forward. She called out helplessly, and her phone skidded across the smooth surface. Tilda braced herself for impact when her axis suddenly shifted. Her body jolted in awareness as a pair of well-sculpted arms wrapped around her waist. She stood flush against an equally well-sculpted chest.

"We have to stop meeting like this," Alé murmured in her ear. "What was it this time?"

"My phone."

Alé planted a kiss on her nose before retrieving it. A few people waved at Tilda and asked if she was okay. She nodded and moved aside to the privacy of the back room, Alé's hand in hers.

"*Mi corazon*, no injuries?"

Tilda shook her head and leaned into the kiss. She purred contentedly when his hands skimmed her waist. Alé trailed kisses down her neck, lingering at the curve of her shoulder.

"You're well, my heart?"

"*Si,* Alejandro." She smiled. "I'm perfect."

"Yes, you are." He playfully pinched her butt.

Tilda batted his hand away. "Don't get any ideas. We have a class to teach."

Alé shrugged. "I still have the mattress upstairs."

Tilda rolled her eyes. "You know it's never that quick with you."

His eyes glinted like fireball whiskey. "I do recall a certain event at a bookstore one time."

Tilda's own blue eyes teased. "Oh really?"

"*Si, señorita.* But, now that you mention it, we may have taken a little longer. In fact." He continued, stroking her breasts. "I know I was distracted by a few things."

Tilda arched against him, then pressed her palms flat against his chest. She inched back. "Ah huh. Just a few? We'll have to test out that theory sometime, won't we?"

Alé's laugh was wicked and full of promise.

"Some other time." She clarified, biting his lip.

Alé groaned. His touch spoke of his love, while his eyes burned with need.

"I'm holding you to that, Tilda."

"Oh, I'll make sure of it," she murmured, shooing him away.

"*Te amo*," he called back before stealing a cheeky peck on her lips.

On steadier legs she followed him out, speaking to a few students who were warming up. Finding a space on the bench, she slipped on her new pair of golden *Commes*. There was an audible sigh. An older woman sat opposite her and cooed.

"Are they *Comme Il Faut*?" she asked, her round face alight with rapture.

Tilda nodded. "Yes, I got them in Buenos Aires."

The woman sighed again. "I'd love to go there."

"I'd definitely recommend the trip. We're going to offer a travelling tour of Buenos Aires soon, if you're keen. It's the best way to get immersed in the music and the culture. I'm running it alongside a possible literary tour of the history of tango in Argentina."

The lady's brown eyes lit up. "I'd *love* that."

"If you're on our mailing list, then you'll get all the info about the trip."

The lady nodded and joined the other students.

"We want to thank you all for coming to our beginners' winter series," Alé began once everyone crowded around. "We know you could all be inside with a whiskey or a wine, but instead you chose to experience the thrill of Argentine tango. Trust me, you will warm up quick."

"For many of you, before today, tango was just a concept in your mind, a series of romantic moves from the movies. Tonight, we want to introduce you to a dance that has captured our bodies and hearts. A dance that is personal to us both."

"Forget all that you know about tango," Alé grinned, "the rose in the teeth, the side split dresses, the movies, because tango is more than just a cliché."

"We hope that you've signed up to our mailing list. Imelda would have arranged this along with your payment, but if you slipped through a bit late, then please do so now. For the rest of you, let's get started."

Alé moved to their newly purchased sound system, mounted on the far wall. The beginning of Di Sarli's *Bahia Blanca* trickled across the open floor. The sharp, arresting violins had everyone on alert, the slowly sexual *bandoneon* begged for their attention.

"This is a traditional tango," Alé began. "All you need to know about tango is in the music, in your posture and in your walk. If you can walk. You can dance.

"There's a 'basic eight' steps we'll teach you, but today we focus on the walk. When you're comfortable with establishing a connection — the embrace or *abrazo* — then, we will show you how to play with movement."

Alé herded them to the side and took Tilda's hand. The canary-yellow gem glinted on her finger.

"My fiancée and I will show you what a simple walk looks like."

"Then we'll add some embellishments to show you

what's possible with time and a lot of practice." Tilda wiggled her eyebrows.

The music called, urging them to respond. Alé opened his arms, inviting her in. A bolt of electricity ran down her spine. It was always this way with Alé. Tonight, was no different.

His arm wound its way across her back, her left hand settled on his shoulder, and once more the stone on her finger danced in the light. Tilda rested her head against his jaw and breathed him in.

Both sighed into the embrace. It spoke of so much more than a physical connection. A match had been lit, and their world shone.

Alé's feet shifted, marking the beat, left, right, left, and his chest rose, indicating his intention.

Tilda responded, her right foot extending, moving playfully in an *adorno* that brushed the floor.

Alé walked with her, varying his stride, playing with the rhythm. He led her in the basic eight, adding flourishes for the benefit of the beginners, an enticement of what was to come.

Tilda closed her eyes.

All she felt was his embrace. All she heard was the music. All she knew was tango.

'Want to find out what happens next to Alejandro and Tilda? Click here to read Sex and the Stage, book 2 in A Sweet, Sexy, Scandalous Series

ACKNOWLEDGMENTS

This book would never have seen the light of day – let alone a BETA reader's eyes – if it hadn't been for the BRI in Team Brida. I'd like to thank my husband, Brian for his unwavering support at all times through this journey. I know that your confidence has given me the strength to persevere when the process became overwhelming.

Thank you for being my voice of reason, supplier of chocolate and all-round funny guy. An even bigger thank you for being the best partner and daddy to our kidlets. Adria, my darling girl, I hope one day you read this (when you're MUCH, MUCH older) and know that dreams really do come true; it's up to you to take that first step. 'Keep pressing play,' kiddo. To my fur-baby, Hugo, thanks for keeping my butt in the chair so I could finish the book!

Next, to my family – a massive thank you for all the love and excitement about my work. To mum and dad, for letting me lock myself in my room on the weekends when I was little and read, read, read. To my sister and brother for encouraging me to try new things. And to my Irish mammy and daddy – for all your love, interest and support in this journey. There are too many other people to list but know that your kindness and questions have helped keep the fire going when it looked like rain.

A huge thank you to Ally Blake. Your insight and passion for my work has been phenomenal. I've really valued your mentorship and am so very grateful for all your guidance and edits. You're amazing!

To Lisa Ireland and Vanessa Carnevale. It was at your retreat that I first had the courage to see myself as a writer. I'll never forget that moment, and I thank you both for all your warmth, encouragement and support over the years.

To Jeen, thanks for being my first ever BETA reader – and I'm referring to the 'ravishing' story in Year 8 English...it's where it all began, really. Your friendship means the world to me, and I look forward to many more milestones together, bestie.

A big thanks to my tribe – the funny, whacky, wonderfully inappropriate gang of the Romance Writers Meetup. I couldn't have asked for a more varied, encouraging, talented group of women to call my friends. You're the best cheer squad a writer could have, and I look forward to many more retreats together.

To my BETA readers, thank you for taking a chance on my work. Your honesty and feedback has helped in so many ways. I still get a thrill to think I have BETA readers, so thank you for taking the time to read my book!! It means the world to me.

Finally, to my readers. Whoever you are, wherever you may be, I hope that this novel gives you a chance to escape from reality, even if for a chapter or two.

ALSO BY IDA BRADY

Alpha Male Series

To Tango with Love

***

Teacher Chronicles Series

Before You Were Mine

When You Were Mine

If You Were Mine

***

A Sweet, Sexy, Scandalous Series

Sweet Spot

Sex and the Stage

Secrets and Scandals

***

The Gamer's Girlfriend Series

Virtue

Voyeur

Vixen

SUBSCRIBE FOR ALL THE NEWS!

If you want exclusive access to giveaways, sales, and new release alerts first, then subscribe to my monthly newsletter, With You in Romance.

ABOUT THE AUTHOR

Ida Brady writes contemporary romance novels that promise humour, heartbreak and a happily ever after. With all the sexy bits! A lover of chocolate (milk or dark) and thunderstorms (the bigger the better), she's usually dreaming about her next cast of characters or what she's going to eat for her next meal. When she isn't trying to tame her intractable curls, she's running after her kids, usually with a book in hand.

Ida used to live in Melbourne, but has shifted to the other side of the world to live in the Emerald Isle with her Irish husband, two daughters, one very big cat and their out-of-control collection of books. She sometimes daydreams about having a huge library in her apartment but will settle for stacking novels in the kitchen drawers instead. In her past life, she taught VCE Literature and English to a gaggle of teenagers. While she misses their enthusiasm, she sure as hell doesn't miss marking papers. You might find her dancing the sexy Argentine tango in her spare time, which isn't very often these days. She loves travelling with her family, observing strangers at café's, and getting lost in a good story.

Want to hear more?

Sign up to my Newsletter, With You in Romance for giveaways and prizes! http://www.idabrady.com

Follow me on <u>Instagram</u>, Tiktok, Facebook! and or leave a review on Goodreads.

www.ingramcontent.com/pod-product-compliance
Lightning Source LLC
Chambersburg PA
CBHW030341120726
47901CB00007B/1872